Tempting Skies

BOOK THREE
BEYOND THE WOOD SERIES

Tempting Skies

BOOK THREE
BEYOND THE WOOD SERIES

MICHAEL J. ROUECHE

Vesta House Publishing

Copyright

Tempting Skies

ISBN-10: 0-9976980-0-4
ISBN-13: 978-0-9976980-0-8
LCCN: 2016911021

Cover design by Nick Zelinger, NZ Graphics
www.nzgraphics.com

Vesta House Publishing
1893 Mapleview Dr., Ste. B
Bountiful, UT, 84010
www.vestahousepublishing.com

More light and light,
more dark and dark our woes!

Romeo and Juliet
Act 3, Scene 5
William Shakespeare

Prologue

Washington, D.C.

July 3, 1904

To the Honorable Judge George Washington Nelson

Dear Judge,

I hope this letter finds you much improved in health, and that it and the accompanying package are well received. We were heartsick that you were unable to travel for mother's funeral, as we would have been comforted by your presence. We pray you will recover quickly and visit soon.

I am going through mother's papers. It has proven to be a Herculean task due to my refusal to accept that my dear, sweet mother is gone. Surely, she, thanks be to our Lord, has departed for fairer realms, but I still find myself pausing every few minutes to grieve our separation and crave a joyful reunion in a far better world. The enclosed manuscript was one of the first documents I found as I searched her papers. William and I believe it is best sent to you. You will know better than the two of us what should be done with it.

William should have been the one to sort her possessions, and I encouraged him to do it; but poor William's colossal heart is in shards. He holds up as long as nothing reminds him of mother, but the sight of an object she once cherished or the mere mention of her name brings tears. The flicker of some shared memory makes his aged eyes overflow with human brine. Right to the sudden end, mother was such a force and fire in our lives that we are left wondering what to do in the wake she left behind. William wonders why he survived her and curses himself for still being here. He wanders from one room to the next, as if he hopes to find her.

Thus, the mournful task of organizing her papers has fallen to me.

I believe you will find the manuscript remarkable. Mother kept an extensive record of our lives and of many who have crossed our paths since we came to Washington City. From that diary, she created a third-person, brief narrative of the more important parts of all our lives during that great war of liberation. Her diary is filled with mundane, everyday experiences; but she has eliminated them in this document to refashion our stories into one flowing narrative. Among her papers, I found dozens of letters she must have called upon for facts and stories that are not in her diary. I suspect she also depended on her remarkable recollection of conversations and events for much of the story. Perhaps her fertile imagination and good judgment helped fill in gaps of time and details. None of us suspected the manuscript's existence, and I do not know when she would have written it. This leaves me all the more saddened thinking there were hidden depths to her I never knew which are now lost to all of us. Oh, how I loved her and now miss her.

You will chuckle when you observe how she has painted our lives with a romantic gloss. That sheen has worked for William's and my benefit as mother recreated me without a stutter and vastly improved William's grammar. Since we were her favorites, it can be no surprise that she did not hold us up to ridicule for our shortfalls. As I am sure you often heard even early on, she harped mercilessly on poor William about his grammar and pronunciation. He worked hard to get better, and he did. But some of his speech patterns were too deeply ingrained. He never could unlearn everything slavery had imprinted on him.

I look forward to hearing that you will travel here shortly and welcome your guidance on mother's manuscript.

With great love, admiration, and gratitude,

Adam William Richman

Editor's Note: This letter, Mrs. Richman's manuscript and the two letters that appear as appendices in this edition were discovered August 28, 2012, among various items in the attic of the antebellum Nelson Mansion near Lexington, Kentucky, as the structure was being prepared for demolition. The mansion dated to the early 1820s and was built as the manor house of a large plantation. George Washington Nelson, son of its builder and owner of the property at the time of the Civil War, broke the plantation into smaller plots after slave emancipation in Kentucky. He retained the house and adjacent property and distributed the remainder to African-American families who before the war had been slaves on the property. Nelson died in July of 1904, and there is no proof the manuscript arrived prior to his death. Nelson left no heirs, but gave direction that the house and remaining property be put up for auction at his death, with proceeds of the sale going to the National American Woman Suffrage Association.

Based on interest generated by the manuscript's discovery, there is currently a campaign to save and restore the mansion.

Chapter 1

"**S**urrender! Surrender!" timidly yelled the red-haired, young, stationary and flat-footed Rebel soldier.

Dark-haired, blue-eyed, soldier-thin, twenty-two-year-old Hank Gragg barely heard the order in the surrounding clatter. He knew what the boy demanded, yet the Southerner's visible indecision invigorated the Virginia-born Union private; and he rushed the Secesh at redoubled speed.

Muskets bellowed around him. Men groaned in early pain or screeched gritty battle cries. Others ran, eyes full of confusion: some toward something, some away. A few soldiers wilted suddenly to the ground as more sprang from unseen fountains. The shock of noise, disorientation and a threatening Confederate should have cowed him to obedience, but Hank's mind had turned unexpectedly inward. He perceived nothing of his physical surroundings as he plunged forward. Vividly he could see petite Betsy with her blonde hair pulled back in a bun; her green-eyes fastened on him as she pledged him in soft, pleading tones to survive. A vision of his coming child followed with its innocent, infantile gurgling beckoning him onward.

The visions dissolved as quickly as they arose, and their departure jolted him back to the disconcertingly real, hesitating, baby-faced Rebel. Hank kept up the charge, putting his life and future into adversarial hands. The boy stepped toward him; rifle primed and aimed. Hank shifted his own musket till he carried it as a cudgel.

"Surrender!" the young voice screamed with found determination. The newly committed eyes locked on Hank as the boy's hand squeezed the trigger.

He'd waited too long. He should have jabbed with the bayonet. Hank capitalized on the mistake, diving ground-ward as the lad's finger tightened. At the sound of the mus-ket shot, he somersaulted, rising to swing his own gun barrel toward the foe's upraised rifle. His strike lofted the startled enemy's musket skyward.

Hank shifted his rifle midstride, grabbing the stock at the lock, as he lopped toward what he craved—the Union line. In the retreat, waves of concussion battered him as he slowed to duck under narrow branches, dart around thin-trunked scrubby trees, and crawl through thick underbrush that sliced his skin and poked his eyes. With watering gaze, he glimpsed other blue-coated soldiers scrambling beside him.

Sweat flowed from his face, stinging the fresh abrasions. His clothes, heavy with wetness, clung to him, chafing arms, chest and thighs. He sucked in air, unable to get enough. His heart pounded and legs ached. His rifle suddenly weighed him down. He could run no faster. Glancing backward, he tripped, sprawling—gun grasped tightly—into the decayed leaves padding the ground. He lay panting in rapid staccato, but strong hands grabbed each of his arm pits and lugged him forward.

"You're almost there, friend. A few paces more," whined a high pitched voice.

Two unrecognized Yankees dragged him roughshod a dozen steps, dropping him unceremoniously and without comment to the ground behind a dug-in line of soldiers awaiting the enemy onslaught.

Hank heard a shout, "Here they come! Hold fire till they're on us! Ready! Aim!" He turned and rose to his knees, still panting uncontrollably, and joined the dug-in brigade, quickly biting a cartridge, and stuffing the load into his Springfield with throbbing hands. Fellow Iron Brigade lads in flight flowed through the porous Union line.

The enemy was close, and an authoritative, unfamiliar voice cried, "Fire!" The soldiers, Hank kneeling with them, shot in unison. There wasn't time to await the volley's effect. The soldiers anxiously reloaded, firing at will, as Confederate balls passed in the air or thudded into nearby trees, ground and Union bodies. Quickly the syncopated flashes of fire, light, smoke and balls stunned the foe, then stunted the Southern charge.

Hank reloaded, aimed at the closest Rebel. It was the same butternut so recently threatening him, and Hank's mind hung on the thought as he fired and the youth crumpled. Poor chap, he mused, as eyes, fingers, hands and powder-stained teeth did their work without direction. His breath had finally slowed to rapid, shallow gasps; and as he readied to trigger the loaded weapon, it slackened more. His hands and arms steadied, and his rifle belched another ball.

Men fell beside him, but the line didn't budge; and he felt an unbidden admiration for these stalwart defenders. The fighting abruptly became more distant as the Confederates began an orderly retreat. Fire-tinged exchanges diminished, and some Union boys put down their rifles to tend the wounded.

Hank turned from the front, bent low and moved down a hill, tracing the steps of his retreating regiment. As battle sounds receded, he rose to full height, still encumbered by his sweat-soaked uniform and trotted to catch his regimental brothers.

Chapter 2

Tall, bearded, uniformed Thomas Rathbone, his left hand against Betsy Gragg's back, gently pressed her toward the boarding house where she lived, north of the Avenue. She sobbed uncontrollably. Worried by her troubled aspect, he moved her quickly through Avenue crowds of bustling pedestrians and loiterers and half-lifted, half-pulled her up the wooden stairs to the stoop of the Federalist-style boarding house. Letting go only briefly to open the door, he pushed her through, followed closely behind and quickly shut the door, fearful someone had followed.

By the time he closed the door, Betsy was no longer weeping. As the tide of despair receded, numbness and stoicism followed, leaving undried tears lingering on her high cheekbones as the only physical mark of the trauma.

Betsy's landlady, Mrs. Brown, a stout, middle-aged, gray-haired matron wearing a worn black dress, her hair in a bun at the back of her head, entered the hall. Already concerned for Betsy and suspicious of Thomas after his earlier report that Mrs. Gragg was in danger, she stepped forward to relieve Thomas with a sharp look.

"Come. This way to the parlor," she commanded curtly. "Thank you, sir, I can manage."

Thomas removed his hand from Betsy's back as Mrs. Brown wrapped her arm compassionately around her boarder's shoulders and steered her to a comfortable chair near a front window. Thomas followed into the parlor.

"Sit here, my dear," the landlady said kindly.

Feeling Betsy's stiffness, she gently pushed her boarder into the seat. Betsy's eyes pierced the opposite wall as she fell rigidly into a chair.

"My dear, what's happened? What's the matter?" the matron inquired earnestly.

Betsy didn't reply, and Thomas answered methodically, "I think she met the man . . . the one who threatens her. He did something—I don't know what—to frighten her. I think it's the same man—a Southerner—who came to our house yesterday claiming to be her husband. She'd told us her husband was a Union soldier, so I doubt it was her husband. Whoever it was, he has stunned her. She was running and sobbing when I found her near that repulsive canal. She hasn't spoken since."

"Merciful Heaven."

"Can I leave her to your care?"

Mrs. Brown hesitated before responding, "Yes . . . certainly. Although when I let the room, Mrs. Gragg assured me she lived a quiet life. She also told me her husband was a Union soldier and that she expected few visitors. She did mention a friend . . . a family."

"My family befriended her. I left my card earlier."

"I didn't notice," she answered disingenuously. "Known her long?"

"A few days. She stayed with us, but we know little of her." He whispered aside, "She is with child."

Mrs. Brown glanced at Betsy, remembering her own excitability during her three pregnancies. Perhaps that was it. She was suffering the curse of all women. Had her plight conjured illusions of danger and an enemy? Or was this man himself the embodied devil come to torment Betsy? She inadvertently shivered at the thought and immediately rejected the inane notion. Stepping between Betsy and Thomas, with her back to Betsy, she probed with riveted, dark eyes and in a voice Thomas could barely hear, "What of the man who frightened her?"

"What do you mean?"

"If she stays here, will she be safe?" She paused, adding tentatively, "Will he follow her?"

Thomas didn't answer, and she revealed the kernel of her fear, "Are we safe?"

He shrugged.

Mrs. Brown eyed him, dread in her expression. "What do I do?"

Thomas measured her carefully, replying firmly, "Look after her. Keep your home peaceful, a refuge, till she regains her wits. Maybe she can answer our questions. I'll write my wife a note and have her take Mrs. Gragg out for a constitutional this afternoon. Maybe she—and our young children—can reclaim her. She's extremely fond of them . . . and they of her."

"Is that safe?"

"I don't know," Thomas answered with slight impatience in his voice. "I know no more than you."

Offended by what she took as a supercilious attitude and still half alarmed that it was this very man she needed to protect Betsy from, Mrs. Brown answered brusquely, "We'll care for her. Thank you."

Rathbone didn't seem to notice her tone and changed the subject, "I must go to the office. I'm late and have much to do."

He approached Betsy, bent till he looked directly into her eyes, and gently took her hand. She seemed not to see him. He spoke reassuringly, "You're safe here. I'll ask Mary to look in on you later."

Betsy shifted in her seat. Abruptly focusing her eyes suspiciously on Thomas, she spoke forcefully, startling Mrs. Brown and Thomas, "As long as she doesn't spy on me . . . for him."

"Spy? Mary? For whom?" Thomas asked gently.

"Am I to believe you don't know? Are you another Miss Morrow—all deception and fraud?"

"I'm not acquainted with a Miss Morrow."

When Thomas got to his office, he sent his family a brief message prompting Mary, slowed by her own pregnancy, to visit Betsy with the children in the early afternoon. The boys, excited to see Betsy, were disappointed by her listlessness. She sat in the same chair in which Thomas had left her earlier. When Mrs. Brown escorted the family in, she announced with artificial animation, "Ah, look who visits, Mrs. Gragg: Mrs. Rathbone and her brood. It's a beautiful day for a stroll. It will do you good."

Betsy didn't respond, glowering at the wall across from her.

Mrs. Brown approached, touching her shoulder softly, and leaned close to her ear whispering lovingly, "It will be all right, dear. They've come to take you out."

Betsy didn't move.

"Let me try," offered Mary, dressed in a small hat, white gloves and a loose red dress—worn to disguise the closeness of her coming confinement—that contrasted with the black mourning dress Mrs. Brown wore. The red caught Betsy's eye. She peeked at it; then returned her gaze to the wall.

Crouching awkwardly in her expectant state, Mary put her arm around her friend. "Betsy, love, we've come to take you for a walk. It's a lovely day. You can help with the children while I shop a bit. They've prattled all morning about seeing you."

As if on cue, the boys approached Betsy, cuddling her.

Betsy ignored them.

"Aunt Betsy," one of them said eagerly. "Come with us. You can hold my hand." He took one of Betsy's hands in both of his and pulled at it. Betsy's eyes slowly dropped to the tiny hands. She laughed and spontaneously lowered her head to kiss one.

Smiling, Betsy turned to the child as she pulled him close. Hugging him, she closed her eyes. Relief released her visible tension, and she whispered to no one in particular,

"Innocence. Oh, sweet, sweet innocence. You're not his; not you, and life is still beautiful."

She rocked back and forth slowly with the child, but the boy quickly became uncomfortable, squirming and turning to squint at his mother.

Mary crouched uncomfortably again at Betsy's side, hugging her new friend gently. "Life is a wondrous blessing. Let us go into the day the Lord has made. Come."

She arose unsteadily, struggling to raise Betsy with her. Betsy released the child from her smothering hug but immediately re-grasped the little boy's hand. Suddenly she pulled from Mary's hug, stooped by the boy and tenderly kissed his cheek.

Betsy looked up at Mary. "I think I can do this . . . with you. Thank you for remembering me; for not abandoning me."

Mary smiled compassionately as her eyes moistened. She didn't respond.

Looking at the boy, Betsy said cheerfully, "You promised I could hold your hand."

The boy giggled as Mary led the three children and Betsy from the house for an afternoon adventure among the market stalls.

Chapter 3

May 1864, the Wilderness, Virginia

"**H**ealth and fair greeting, Hank Gragg," a tall, chipper, English-accented, Union soldier in his mid-thirties called as Hank neared the 19th Indiana Infantry's battle flag.

"Fair greeting to you, Rivenshaw," Hank responded, entertained as always by his dark-haired, foreign friend, but feeling much less exuberant than their exchanged greetings.

"'Perish the man whose mind is backward now.' Eh, Gragg?"

Hank smiled mockingly. "Yes, perish him and us, as that's precisely where we've landed—backward."

"Momentarily, my fine friend, momentarily; and just physically at that. Yet are our minds forward, and 'all things are ready, if our minds be so.' Our bodies must shortly follow. Why, Gragg, 'you and I alone, without more help, could fight this royal battle.' They will send us forward shortly, and we shall go 'once more unto the breach . . . once more; or close the wall up with our' dead."

Hank scoffed, "We ran like scared rabbits. That's all we're capable of now, along with building those walls with friends' lifeless bodies."

A corporal nearby interjected, "We ain't what we were. Look 'round. Few remain. Fewer still after each battle. So who can point their finger at us? They'll send us back in—those left and accounted for—because they have to. Who else do they have to send? Like the Almighty, Grant asks, 'Whom shall I send? And who will go for us?' We, like the fools we've become, answer, 'Here am I. Send me.' You've no one else."

Hank responded wearily, "If he asks me, I would say, 'Lord, not me. Not this time. Send the other tens of thousands . . . all those shiny bounty boys. Send your hosts, but don't call on me . . . not again.'"

All three men stood still, tired and thoughtful.

Hank broke the silence, "They'll prove no more valiant than us, no less likely to run when the choice is desperate survival . . . and we'll be scattered in their midst . . . not wanting to be there, but not wanting to be too far from the action either. I do crave though the day that this will be a memory . . . a distant one, and we'll have lasting, fraternal peace."

Rivenshaw lowered his brow and broadcast in heroic voice, "We'll have no bit of that. Our mortal enemies will shrink before our eyes—if not today, on the morrow."

Hank couldn't resist a grin. "Shrink? They seem to get bigger and bigger . . . and there are more of them every time we fight."

Bolstered by Rivenshaw's enthusiasm, Corporal Smith, a dark haired boy of twenty-three, waded in, "Regardless of how many there are, we'll beat them back. Grant, in one fell swoop, will clear away Lee's army . . . and send the hobbling dregs to Mexico."

Rivenshaw shook his head mockingly, "Do all colonists insist on warring with Mexico at every opportunity?"

Smith responded earnestly, "I'm trying to say Grant will drive the traitors who survive to Mexico . . . or some other country. Doesn't have to be Mexico. They can take over Brazil; change its name to Confederate States of South America."

Hank chuckled at the odd corporal. "You miss the point of the Rebellion. They would change the name to Americano and claim to be liberty's true heirs. They'd start another war just to prove they were the real Americans. And you seem sure Grant can stop them. They said that about Hooker, Burnside. Remember Pope and McClellan? They were sure bets, yet we lost with all of them and are left knee-deep in a debt of blood—an unpayable loss to the dead. And we still have Meade who folded with a winning hand after Gettysburg. Are you sure Grant's different?"

The corporal answered, "Grant won at Vicksburg, didn't he? We'll beat them."

"Or die in the effort," Hank responded cynically. "We'll fight each other to the death. In the end, it will be the three of us left fighting the last three of them. We'll batter each other to submission, then death; and the states will simply evaporate."

Clearly discomforted by the conversation's tone, Rivenshaw straightened his back, raised his rifle to his shoulder and looked past his two momentarily bothersome companions. In a deep voice that blended majestically with the din of the nearby battle, he proclaimed, "'Knocks go and come; God's vassals drop and die; and sword and shield, in bloody field, doth win immortal fame.'"

Hank shot a quick smirk and tart reply at the Englishman, "Immortal fame?"

Officers were organizing the remnants of the regiment, and Hank got in line, ready to march due south, still pondering Rivenshaw's most recently cribbed words.

Chapter 4

William, tall, broad-shouldered, with dark eyes and complexion and short cut hair, stood expressionless, eyes focused trance-like on the ground, listening to the auctioneer whose hat-covered head was visible above the crowd of men bunched around him. The throng totally obstructed William's view of the "unfit for public service" horses being auctioned by the government.

"This mare's been worked hard. Won't deny that. But she's got years of work left in her. Will someone, one of you fine gentlemen in front, advance on forty dollars? If she were in her prime, she'd be worth at least two hundred. She's a little worn, but she's got much more than forty dollars work left in her. Forty dollars. Thank you, sir. That's nothing for her. Will someone advance to forty-two? They tell me she's the best horseflesh we'll see this morning. A real treasure, that one. Oh, the sinews, those flanks. You can use her in the garden. She can carry you to town. Forty-two! That's it. Will someone advance on forty-two?"

William raised his head to scrutinize the auctioneer. Sweat glistened on the man's face under his broad-brimmed hat. He stood on an elevated deal box, his big hand raised, ready if no one offered a higher bid to bring down his gavel to announce a sale made.

"No one will advance?"

No one raised the bid, the mallet came down hard on a large box resting on its end in front of the auctioneer, and the animal went to the winning bidder.

William's eyes stirred from disinterest and stared keenly at the auctioneer as he readied to take bids for the next animal.

The man smiled briefly and began his pitch. "I must be honest, gentlemen. This isn't the best we're selling today."

Sniggering agreement snaked through the gathering, and a disheveled man with mud-stained hands concurred in a slurred, stumbling shout, "Not even real horseflesh! Army cooks couldn't even make something of that!"

Laughter rippled again as a brief, slight smile loosened the auctioneer's visage. "We've got to sell them all . . . and none for dinner. What we have here is a gelding. A few gave him scant inspection earlier. I won't misrepresent him. Don't know how much longer he'll last. You can work him in the yard. Remember, gentlemen, this is for the army . . . for our Union. How about a twenty-dollar offer? Will anyone start us at twenty?"

"How about one dollar?" someone called out.

Knowing nods and audible assent pulsed through the crowd.

"Is that a bid, sir?" The auctioneer could see bids and money fading and reemphasized the army's dire need. "Can't one of you help us with this war? Give us a good bid. We need money to whip those Rebs. Someone start us out—I'll take the gentleman's suggestion—a dollar. He's a gem at that price."

"For the government!" the same man retorted.

A well-dressed man signaled a bid.

"Thank you, sir. Who will advance it? Ah, very good. We have a two-dollar bid. This is more like it, gentlemen. He's got work left in him, even if the army can't use him. Will someone bid two-fifty? Advance on two dollars? Gentlemen? At fifteen dollars, he's a gift. Are you going to let someone else take him for two dollars, when he's worth ten times that amount . . . and President Lincoln needs the money?"

"Maybe if I ate horseflesh," the disheveled, inebriated man called out, amidst a wave of embarrassed snickers.

"You have if you've been in the army," another bystander answered.

"Sell him to the president!" someone else offered.

Someone signaled.

"Wonderful! We have a patriot. Two dollars, fifty cents. Advance on two-fifty? Three dollars?" The auctioneer stared at the man who had begun the bidding, but the gentleman remained motionless.

"Five dollars," William cried out, still standing casually behind the crowd.

"There. Are you going to let him take that horse? He wants this horse so there must be something you're not seeing. I saw him give the gelding a real good look. He sees something you're missing . . . some hidden prize in this beast. Will anyone advance on five dollars? Six dollars? Very good, sir! Six! Seven?"

William signaled seven.

"Seven dollars, from the back there. Seven. Anyone bid seven-fifty? Seven-fifty, thank you sir. Eight?"

William shifted nervously and signaled eight.

"Eight dollars, from the back. Eight dollars. Nine? Thank you, sir. Nine dollars. Anyone advance us to ten? He's got far more work in him than just ten dollars. The boy in the back can see that."

William lowered his head, seeming to study the dirt at his feet.

"Won't anyone help crush this rebellion with a mere ten dollars? Ah, ten, from Mr. Bond, the man who started us off. Thank you. A noble gesture." Without hesitating, the auctioneer barked, "Advance on ten? Ten-fifty? Surely he's worth that. Perfect for light errands in town. He's more than he looks. Hitch him to the wagon. Is ten dollars all you'll bid for this prize? Eleven dollars?" He waited. "Ten-fifty?" He paused again. "Ten twenty-five? No one? Ten-twelve? Last call." The auctioneer brought his mallet down authoritatively. "Sold to Mr. Bond. Sir, you have purchased this fine specimen for ten dollars. Congratulations." He nodded to the well-dressed man before beginning to describe the next horse, asking for an opening bid of twenty dollars, which was quickly offered.

William, his expression still controlled, hurried from the corral. He distracted himself thinking about the round top of the nearby Naval Observatory. He knew its name, but not its purpose. He would ask Victoria when he got home. He had miles to go and kept up his quick pace, trying not to surrender to disappointment. He had wanted the horse to pull a cab. He needed it to support his family. The gelding had been the perfect blend of inexpensive and underestimated. Such a combination was the balance William sought.

"Was this the horse you bid on?"

William turned his head, startled to find a carriage close alongside. It's pace matched his, as its distinguished passenger, sitting in the backseat under a soft, black roof, considered William agreeably. The driver ignored William, focusing beyond the horse that pulled the vehicle. Tied to the back of the carriage was the gelding.

The passenger refined his question, "Is this the horse you're interested in?"

William was irritated. He'd stretched to offer his final bid for the horse, anticipating other coming expenses. The man was shaming him. William suspected he had purchased the horse merely to block William's bids. He knew others had bid to keep the horse from him as well . . . or to make him pay more. He wanted to ignore the man but resisted the instinct, responding civilly, "Yes, that's the one."

William's interrogator adjusted his black top hat as he noted, "I saw you examine him at the auction. You were careful, exacting. You think he's more valuable than he seems?"

William had given the horse a thorough check up, opening his mouth to check his teeth, patting him down, looking for blemishes and assessing his musculature. The horse was starving and suffering from saddle sores. He wasn't made to ride. He was bred to pull, and William was sure he was better than his condemned status. Approaching the horse and handling him as much as he could convinced William the horse might be the hidden pearl he sought. It would take a while to get him in shape, but the disregarded horse had promise. "Did look at him," William responded coldly.

Amused, the man observed, "Yes, you most certainly did. You wanted him. Why would you want him?"

"I had plans," William offered grudgingly but honestly.

"Plans?"

"Plans."

Softening his tone, Mr. Bond inquired, "What were they, if I may ask respectfully?"

"What would be the use, sir? You got the horse . . . what you wanted. Sir, I don't mean to be discourteous, but . . ."

"I don't want him," the man responded bluntly. "Never did. I started the bidding to get it going."

A flash of anger crossed William's face, and he looked back at the horse. "Thought so."

"Later I bid because I didn't think you could buy him. Others were bidding to make you pay more. I could see that. You felt it."

Unable to disguise his bitterness, William added harshly, "You included."

"I want to sell him to you."

"To me? How much? Twenty dollars?"

"I have no interest in him . . . but I do have an interest in you."

"Me?" William's tone softened in surprise, and he looked directly at the man's deep-set gray eyes.

"Yes. You're familiar with horses. I have a livery stable and came this morning looking for someone who knew about horses, to keep my horses healthy, scheduled; someone who might want a job. Are you looking for work?"

"Thank you, sir. I'm not interested. I'm going to drive a hack," William offered proudly.

"Ah. That's why you wanted the horse. I see. That means you'll have to buy a carriage, the tack, ten dollars to the government for the license. That's a lot more money than a few dollars for the horse. What was your highest bid? Seven? Eight dollars? A carriage will be more than a hundred. That's a lot of money if you could only spend seven on the horse. It would be better to work for . . ."

"Eight dollars. I bid eight dollars. I know how much it's going to cost. That's why I bid eight. I've got to be careful how much I spend. But I've got the money for a carriage. I've got the money."

The heavy-set, cultivated man was visibly surprised by the power and content of William's last answer. It took him a moment to recover. "Good. Good for you. You're a planner, too. I like that. Couldn't you use more money? Everyone wants more money. I certainly do. It's going to be a while before this horse can pull anything. Let me be frank. Business is good. We have more work than we can handle, but it's hard to get good horses . . . and harder to find people to keep them healthy. If you could work with the horses."

William thought momentarily. "A hostler?"

"Not as a groom," the man responded dismissively. "I can hire and train a dozen grooms. They're cheap. I need someone who knows about horses; someone who can care for all the horses in the stable—work with the veterinarian, maybe more if you work out. Help choose horses. You could drive a carriage on your own time, I suppose."

"Why do this? You don't know what I can do," William tendered skeptically.

"I've seen enough," Bond enthused. "I saw you sort through the horses rapidly, hastily choosing the one that caught your eye. I watched as you gave him a close look. I could see what concerned you by how your inspection slowed at times. You know horses. Now that I know what you were planning, I am that much more encouraged."

"My earnings: What would they be?"

"Good. You're at least willing to talk about it. Climb up with Erasmus. Let him take the reins, Erasmus. While you drive, we can discuss the particulars. If you're not interested, we can at least give you a ride wherever you're going. Where are you going?"

William was curious. He climbed into the seat by Erasmus, a young man with a complexion darker than William's and hair covered by a bolo. As he handed William the reins, Erasmus turned his head and nodded respectfully toward him.

From the back seat, the gentleman asked, "Your name, what is it?"

William kept his eyes forward as he responded, "William."

"William what?"

"William Richman."

"My name is Richard Bond, and I have a large livery stable at Ninth and D." He chuckled. "Do you know about horse medicine?"

"What I needed to keep them healthy for Marse Richman."

"A slave?" Bond asked tentatively.

"Not now."

"You're in Washington, so of course you're free," he offered reflectively. "Where are you from?"

"Virginia. Winchester. Am I going in the right direction?"

"Where are you going? I'll take you there."

"Freedman's Village in Virginia."

"Up on Robert E. Lee's land. He deserves it," he observed irritably. "New here then?"

"Just arrived."

"Already set on being a hack?"

"Seemed a good thing," William concluded dispassionately.

"As I said, I bought that horse to sell it to you."

"I can't pay you ten dollars."

"Maybe we can work something out. You pay me the . . . how much did you bid?"

"Eight dollars."

"Pay me eight dollars, and I'll let you work off the other two. You can keep your horse at my stable while you get him back to health. I'll feed him, no cost, as long as you work for me." Mr. Bond was clearly crafting his terms as they visited. "You can work at the stable and drive your hack on the side. Have you figured where you'll get a carriage? That will cost a lot more than a ten-dollar horse."

"I'm looking for something that will cost a hundred twenty-five. Maybe a little more. Do you think I can find something for that?"

"A buggy."

"A buggy won't do; not for a hack."

"The Evening Star—same issue I saw this sale in—said William Wall was selling all his carriages. He wants to retire, although I can't imagine why he'd do it with all the business around. There's much money to be made with the town bustling as it is. Still, he's giving it up. His auction's end of the month. Maybe you can find something there."

"Read about it, too. Hoping there'd be something I could get. Do you think that's what I should do?"

"You can read?" Bond hesitated, adding, "I do believe you'll figure something out. Before I send you home, let me take you to the stables. I'll stay there, and Erasmus can take you as far as Long Bridge. That will be close for you, and he won't get caught in bridge traffic."

Without prompting, William revealed, "They've been trying to get me to work on government projects, ever since we moved to the Village. If I could tell them I have a job, wages, and maybe describe the stables, they'd leave me alone."

"Do they make you pay rent?"

"Yes."

"Good. You should be paying rent, not living off the government. Now you're free, you have to pay your way."

"Yes, sir," William agreed humbly.

"I understand Freedman's Village is a stopping off place. How long will they let you stay?"

"Doesn't seem everyone's moving on. Some stay, but we don't want to. Want to move to the Island real quick. Maybe

buy . . . or build a little place, with an area for a stable behind."

"To keep your horse and carriage?"

"Yes."

"That's closer to my stable. That's good. It should only
take a few minutes to walk across Long Bridge, but with the
constant army wagons and men, backups and waits can be
hours long. Best be on this side. You probably have a question you haven't asked."

William kept his eyes on the road as he thought briefly.
"No, don't think so."

"Aren't you wondering why I chose you?"

"You said you could see I knew about horses."

"That's part of it, but I liked your demeanor while bidding. You're not going to cause me trouble; won't pretend
you're equal. You're going to cooperate. That's what I'm
looking for. If you use your horse sense and keep out of trouble, you can have a job for as long as I own the stable. First
sign you're causing trouble, you and your ten-dollar horse
will be out. William, I'm delighted to have you with us."

Chapter 5

May 1864, the Wilderness, Virginia

The day dragged. Hank was drenched from the heat, and having eaten nothing was exhausted from his morning clash with the butternuts. Orders moved them forward, and he shambled in a ragged formation along a narrow path through tangled woods in the silence of fatigue. Remaining energy focused on matching the pace of the two shuffling legs just ahead of him.

It was springtime, and the beauty of the dogwoods with their four-petaled, white blossoms adorning his passage remained unseen in his mental languor. As his stomach moaned at its unrelenting emptiness, he grabbed a handful of coffee beans from his pant pocket and forced them into his mouth, hoping they'd rouse him and stanch his hunger. He contemptuously dismissed a brief thought that reminded him he should be grateful to still be alive. He marched alongside the balding Rivenshaw, but neither said anything. The white arboreal flowers began to dim to brown as the sun set.

Hank's anxiety heightened as the rising clamor proclaimed battle ahead. This was no retreat. The dogwoods had disappeared. Where was the army going in the dark? He could barely keep his eyes open, although his feet kept scuffling along. The soldier ahead of him fell out and crumpled to the ground, but Hank marched on with the line of soldiers. How much farther could they go in the dark? He was nearly at the point of collapse, and his eyelids drooped, his head flopped and jerked involuntarily, waking him from a second's doze.

He was in his bed—their bed—and Betsy lay next to him, her arms wrapped around him as they cuddled in January's

chill. His head lurched again, and he was aware of the oppressive humidity as they trudged in near total darkness.

His head slid to the side as his eyes closed, twitching
back at the sound of orders. What orders? Sleep? They must
have ordered him to sleep. Yes, sleep. He fell out at the edge
of the road, flopping to the ground, rifle at his side, still
wearing haversack, hat, cartridge box and percussion pouch.
He had survived—barely—the day. Would he tomorrow? He
was too tired to care.

Naomi, his murdered dear friend, rose before him. She
was at her farm, cooking him supper, telling him about a
Confederate widow, when a knock came at the door. Betsy,
the widow, burst through without awaiting response. She ran
to Hank, but it was no longer Betsy. It was a man, and he
pointed a rifle at Hank, then turned and shot Naomi.

The dreamed sound of the gun awoke him. Aching from
his cartridge box that poked at him, he wondered how long
he'd been asleep. Men stirred around him.

Chapter 6

June 1864, Richmond, Virginia

She sat in her favorite summer dressing gown, brushing long blonde hair that cascaded in waves to below the middle of her back and looked admiringly at the image in the mirror. The lady was lonely and mildly blue as she always was after a performance. Faint traces of theatrical makeup still colored her pale skin, and periodically she'd put down the brush and wipe at the remaining powder with a stained cloth that rested on her nightstand. It was well after midnight, and she started at a gentle knock at the door of her sumptuous and large bedroom. As an actress, she was well acquainted with late hours, but not with such unexpected, early morning disturbances.

Rising quickly, she pulled her light, red robe tightly around her and stepped to the door. It wasn't locked, but she turned the knob slowly, warily opening the door an inch. It was the landlady's servant girl. She exhaled and opened the door wider.

"What is it? It's late," she whispered. "I'm about to retire."

"You have a caller, a gentleman," the yawning girl announced. The slave, who slept on the boarding house front hall floor in case of late visitors—and there were many—had clearly been awakened suddenly. The cunning matron of the house approved of the late evening visits for she reasoned her ladies would be better able to pay their room and board if they earned extra money. She knew what the neighbors thought about her and her tenants—most of whom presented themselves as actresses—but she didn't care. Life in Richmond was difficult and getting harder each week. Her boarding house had once been a home for proper young women from wealthy families, but the war had changed her fortunes.

"Visitor? This late? Tell them I'm asleep. No, wait. Wait. Who is it?" She never entertained gentlemen in her room, but she wanted to know whom she turned away.

The tall, stocky, deep-voiced, dark-skinned girl answered, yawning again, as she extended her hand. "His card."

Anna Whitehead took the carte de visite. Her eyes rested on the photograph of a man identified as Daniel Jefferson. The left corner of her mouth curled in a knowing smile, recognizing him as her friend Oskar Dante.

"Charlotte, tell Mr."—she peeked at the card—"Mr. Jefferson I'll welcome him shortly. When you've told him, come and help me dress."

The slave was visibly dismayed and responded, "Yes, Ma'am," but waited as if hoping Anna would change her mind.

When she saw the slave's hesitation, Anna smiled affectionately and said softly, "Go on. It'll be fine. It's not that."

The girl disappeared down the dark hall, carrying a dim candle with her.

Anna turned from the door, carefully hung her nightgown in her wardrobe and adroitly added a petticoat unassisted. Charlotte returned quickly and tightened her corset and helped with the final layers. Anna left her hair down, unpinned. She glanced around the room for stray items out of place and reordered a few.

"Charlotte, I'm ready. Bring up Mr. . . . ." She scrunched her nose trying to remember his name.

"Jefferson, Ma'am. I could pin your hair."

"Do you think I should?"

"Yes, Ma'am." Without Anna's direction, Charlotte glided to the nightstand, picked up the brush and a pin and began ordering Anna's hair, parting it down the middle, loosely braiding the back and pinning it up.

When Charlotte was finished, Anna walked to the mirror, looked at her reflection admiringly. "I'm ready. Invite him up. Then go back to bed."

"Are you sure, Ma'am? So late?"

"It'll be fine. Don't worry. He's an old friend. Probably needs urgent help, else he wouldn't come so late. Else he wouldn't come at all."

Charlotte nodded, picked up her nearly exhausted candle and disappeared down the hall.

Moments later, she returned escorting a young, flowing-haired blond man. His inch-long full beard covered most of his face, but a few, faint scars visibly marred his skin above the beard.

"Mr. Jefferson, it is an honor and pleasure to see you." Anna grinned. "You look well." She stood facing him and didn't think to invite him to sit down.

He smiled, but didn't respond, glancing meaningfully at Charlotte who still stood in the doorway.

Anna said gently, "Charlotte, that will be all."

The servant hesitated and looked at her questioningly, seeming to hope for different instructions. When none came, she slowly, quietly closed the door.

The room's sole gas light hung above the nightstand and mirror, spreading eerie, feeble shadows around the spacious room.

Daniel Jefferson appraised the room admiringly. "You don't share your room?"

"A queer greeting after such a long, silent absence."

"Yes." His face relaxed. "It's a splendid room at a time of crowding."

She smiled. "This room, I assure you, is not for let. Daniel—it is Daniel, isn't it?—I've been fortunate. I'm making headway on the stage. Tell me how you're doing? How did you fare on your trip to the odious capital of our enemies? Why a different name? Why 'Daniel Jefferson'?"

"You're a smart wench. Can't you guess? Jefferson. Virginia. Patriot. I thought it would smooth the way as easily as money turns a congressman."

"What way?" She looked at him slightly confused. "Never mind. How was Washington?"

"A wonderful time," he proclaimed enthusiastically.

"Did you see her?" she asked, her face revealing a glint of betrayal and hurt.

He saw it, smiled and prodded, "Jealous?"

His engaging smile and stately presence enchanted her as it always did. She blinked and shook her head, adopting a firm expression. "Of course not . . . just concerned. I worry I hurt her . . . by not being honest."

"Hurt her? What poppycock. I've told you it was a misunderstanding. I never harmed her. I loved her . . . or thought I did. In helping me, you helped her. She escaped, didn't she? That was thanks to me . . . and your help." He stopped and looked comfortingly at her. "I don't love her. Never really did. You mustn't worry about something that's not . . . that was never true. My heart is elsewhere as it should be, attached to someone far more worthy of my admiration." He paused. "But I do feel Christian charity for the woman. The Yankee private—the one she knew before this war; the one I told you about—he conspired with that sheriff to turn her from me. They told her lies about murder . . . that I murdered someone. It's unfathomable cruelty . . . and inexcusable—what they did." He shook his head disbelievingly. "But she's not to blame. It was always the others, and they told her they wanted to arrest me for murder. A murder I didn't do. I could never harm anyone, no matter the sordid condition of their soul. I—I swear to God—I could never betray a lady. You've seen me abused. Have you seen me strike back in anger? Strike back at all? Hurt anyone?"

"I've heard you say terrible things about the dog," she responded, smiling nervously, hoping to calm him down.

"Of course. Look what he did to me. He's made me Frankenstein's monster. Shouldn't I hate the dog?"

"He was trying to protect Mrs. Hender . . . Mrs. Gragg. Surely you can understand that. He thought you were going to hurt her."

"He thought? How do you know a dog thinks? As if the thing were human." His tone was darker.

"Those men deserve your ire, not the dog. It's amazingly big. If I had been in your shoes, I would never have gotten near it. Besides you're as handsome as ever."

Relaxing at her compliment, he smiled. "If life allowed second chances, I wouldn't get near the dog. But don't worry about him. I'll do nothing to an innocent creature, but I don't like the beast. As you say, it was loyal to Mrs. Henderson. I value that: loyalty. A wonderful trait."

"I never really thought you'd do anything to the dog, not with the warmth of your heart."

He looked kindly at Anna, softly explaining, "My desire has always been to help the so-called Mrs. Gragg, if that's her real name. I still believe she is Mrs. Henderson. I can't believe she married that pestiferous Yankee soldier. He is beneath her. I sometimes wonder if he forced himself on her as part of a Yankee plot to deflower the South and disgrace her . . . to force her to marry him, to spy for him."

Uncomfortable with the thought, Anna turned the conversation. "Tell me about your visit with her."

"Lovely Betsy? She is lovely, isn't she?" He watched Anna carefully.

Undisguised hurt seeped from Anna's eyes.

"Our time together wasn't really a visit; more a happy stroll. Delightful in every way. We promenaded leisurely, arm-in-arm along the city's lovely canal. I felt fashionable, and you can imagine how emotional she was when I explained everything I'd done for her. She couldn't control her gratitude . . . her emotions, her tears."

Jefferson smirked as he remembered walking with Betsy Gragg along Washington's fetid canal. He had arranged, unbeknownst to Betsy, to help her escape from Castle Thunder Prison in Richmond where she had been held for murder and for betraying the Confederacy with a Yankee private, whom she had loved before the war. She had killed and betrayed no one but had jilted Jefferson under the name he had used at the time—his favorite name—Lucius Walthrope. She was already paying for her rejection of him. He had enabled her escape with Anna's innocent help only to keep the freed inmate in his power. Once the money he had stolen from Betsy had delivered her safely to the Northern Capital, he had left her without resources, friends or plans—left her, a desperate pauper, to her own devices.

He had awaited Betsy in the city, and after she'd arrived had forced her to walk with him along the canal. His smile widened as he thought of their short minutes together. He had stolen upon her, but she was too frightened to resist him as he had pinned her arm in his and threatened her with his free and hidden hand that aimed a pistol at her side.

He had toyed with her to demoralize her, hoping to strike terror in her heart, making sure that when he let her go, he would be in her mind constantly. He was certain that no minute of any day would ever again pass for Betsy without her expecting him to materialize from nothing to violate her, cut her throat or—still more exciting—cut the throats of those she loved. As he had once scarred her face with a slap of his ring-bearing hand when she rejected him and accused him of murder, he now sought to scar her mind. He had branded her outside and in as his possession. If he couldn't have her love and money, especially the money, he would own her as surely as if she were an imported African wench.

He focused on Anna warmly and added cheerfully, "As we parted, she couldn't stop crying. How grateful she was when she realized she had so long ago falsely accused me, yet I in a generosity she could barely comprehend had freed her. She cursed herself for ever suspecting me. She tried to kneel at my feet to worship me."

"Do you still love her?" Anna demanded harshly in spite of his denials.

"Love? What is love?" He laughed. "Of course not. Never did. I've told you that. I do pity her. She lost her husband, refused marriage to me because of damnable lies, and may have been forced into an unworthy marriage—compelled by a Yankee, like the entire South. That soldier of hers will die in the war and her Staunton friends have already cut her because of the treason charges. She is really and always will be alone. I couldn't leave her in that prison. It was simple Christian charity. And you helped in your small way. She couldn't stop praising you."

He remembered Betsy's face when he revealed to her that Anna, posing as a Miss Morrow, had been employed to deceive her. Anna had never sensed the evil of Jefferson's intention, and he planned she never would.

"It's good you don't love her as you can't have her anyway. Not now that she's married a Yankee."

Anger sparked his eyes and mouth, "I can have what I want." But quickly he softened his tone. "Yankee? If I wanted her, she would leave him. I need merely ask. He's nothing, and as I told you, I don't think he married her at all. Just soiled her. Abandoned her as a camp strumpet. That's what Northern soldiers do to Southern ladies. I can't help but pity her . . . and you should, too."

"Nonsense," she said playfully. "She married him and not you."

Thoughtfully he mused, "Perhaps, but if she did marry him, it was born of lies and coercion. After what they did to her, I wouldn't want her. Not defiled. She was never the virtuous lady she portrayed. Nothing like that. I'm sure of it now. I fear she was evil and has deceived us both."

"What do you want now?" she asked in a hopeful voice, ignoring the inexplicable shift in his opinion of Betsy.

Smiling again, he reached out and touched her cheek. "You. I've always wanted you . . . since that first day, even before I saw you on stage."

"Should I believe you?" she said coyly.

"Everyone should believe me. I don't lie. You must know
. . . . When I saw her, I grasped perhaps for the first time
how much I love you. How much I need you. I'd believed
there was something special in her, but as I promenaded
with her, I realized her brightest light was a deep shadow to
your sun-like brilliance."

"You love me?"

"I said it, didn't I?" He lowered his hand from her cheek,
took her in his arms, lifted her from the floor and forcefully
kissed her lips.

Her eyes gleamed and closed, and she returned his embrace, whispering happily, "I had hoped for that."

"Did you? Was it not plain?"

"You gave no clue. I thought I was merely a hireling
playing Miss Morrow."

"It was never that. When I met you that first time, it was
love at first sight, as they say. Then I saw you on stage. It
was as if the stage lights all focused their glory on you. You
shined brighter than everything around you. I was your prisoner from the beginning."

Hesitant to mention her prison performance, she nonetheless blurted, "When I visited Castle Thunder, I heard terrible things about you, frightening things. I never believed
them. No one could see you as I did. They'd all been deceived by that horrible sheriff. If Betsy had known you, she
would never have chosen the Gragg boy. I'm selfishly glad he
deceived her, as unchristian as that sounds." She stopped
talking, smiled and squeezed him tighter. "You love me."

He hugged her harder, then put her gently to the
ground, stepped back, and keeping his eyes on her face,
said, "Anna, I think I must go about in disguise as long as
that private is out there, so I bought these spectacles. What
do you think?" He pulled out metal-framed eyeglasses with
small rectangular lenses and rested them on his nose and
ears. "The spectacle glass is just clear glass. Are they ade-
quate? Will anyone recognize me?"

Anna studied him critically. "No, they're not nearly enough. I'd recognize you at a hundred yards." She thought briefly. "As long as you're blond, people might know you . . . or wonder. No, we must dye your hair and put a little stage makeup on your scars to soften them a bit. Eye glasses, black hair and beard, no scars: No one would recognize you then."

"Can you tell me how to do it? I've never had to wear a disguise. I've always lived my life open for all to see; walking proudly, prominently at noon day."

"I won't tell you," she whispered as she got closer and lovingly took the glasses off his face. "I'll do it for you." She ran a hand over his forehead, cheek and beard, finally cupping his chin lovingly. "I've kept the chemicals I used once to darken my hair for a role. I've got them somewhere." She moved to a chest under a window that overlooked an alley. She opened it and rummaged through its contents. "Here they are: gallic acid and acetic acid and a tincture of sesqui-chloride of iron."

She continued her soliloquy, "If I do it with your hair dry it will come out brown. We want it black, so I'll have to wet your hair." She placed the materials under the mirror and walked to a basin that rested by a water pitcher. She re-trieved both, turned to Jefferson and said lovingly, "Kindly remove your jacket and shirt."

She took his hand and led him to the seat in front of the mirror and nodded at him to sit. He removed his clothes and sat as she retrieved the basin and a pitcher. She poured a bit of water in the basin and took a comb from her dressing ta-ble. Dipping the comb in the water, she carefully and caress-ingly dragged it repeatedly through his hair and beard until his entire head dripped with water.

Discarding the residual water out of the window, she quickly returned to carefully measure out the portions. "Ready. Take one last look at Oskar Dante. When I'm done, you will be Daniel Jefferson—a tall, dark and exquisitely handsome man."

Jefferson observed, "I'll need a new carte de visite."

She dipped her comb in the mixture and gingerly transferred it to his hair, combing it in thoroughly. She repeated the process. "Tell me more about Washington. Did you see anyone else?"

He smiled. "I did."

"Tell me," she said excitedly.

"I saw that conspiring Staunton sheriff."

"He was there?"

"He'd gone to Washington to arrest Betsy; to convey her back to Castle Thunder. He was merciless. Couldn't he see she'd suffered enough?"

"Did he find her? You must have hidden her. Or did you dissuade him?"

"I did dissuade him in a way, but it was a mammoth effort. I called him out right away, proved I knew Betsy innocent and accused him of conspiring against her. He didn't want to let her go. He was vindictive. He wanted her hanged. It was like she had done something devilish and evil to him, yet we know her to be a simple, innocent child. As he raved, I feared I was in the presence of a panther—stealthy, patient, powerful, destructive. I knew he would be avenged on her, though he never clarified what he sought revenge for. We argued. It was terrible. Nothing could stop him from his demonic errand. I challenged him, and his braggadocio evaporated when I unsheathed my knife to strike him for cowardice—speaking of a virtuous lady in such a way."

Anna listened intently as she combed the color into his hair.

"He attempted to run, but I pursued him, convinced he would spread his poisonous calumny if I let him escape. I couldn't bear that Mrs. Henderson should be maligned. I was sure it would end in her poverty and desperation . . . her hanging. Through long city blocks he ran with me close behind. He wound through crowds thinking I could do him no harm with so many witnesses, but I pushed him farther—to the suburbs. When I caught him, the foul creature prostrated himself on the dusty road and beseeched me not to kill him. He swore he'd never again utter the holy name of Mrs. Henderson or approach her saintly person. But his Faust-like soul glimmered through. The devil would never release her in peace. 'Don't kill me; don't kill me,' he trolled, but I detected deceit in his eyes. I could not let him hurt her again. I would not let this fiend from the underworld recapture . . . and murder her."

"What desperate thing could you do?" She stopped combing and looked wide-eyed at her newly declared lover.

"The worst a man can."

"He's dead?"

"I did it for her, as you would have compelled me to do if you'd witnessed his malevolence. It was you I thought of as I fell upon him and slashed his throat." He breathed heavily.

"Dead," she said reflectively, trying to understand and deal with the news.

"I'm mortified to have done it. Ashamed."

"You had to do it—for Betsy, pitiful Betsy." Gripping tightly the dripping comb, she stood erect. "You did what was right."

He looked at her gratefully. "If you truly believe that, I'm comforted."

"Be comforted." She remembered the sheriff and his unwillingness to help Betsy. When she and the sheriff had visited Castle Thunder's commandant in her effort to get Betsy released, he had been obsessed with arresting Jefferson, who called himself at the time Oskar Dante. But it was undoubtedly a ruse. He must have wanted her kept in prison; or fouler yet, he was waiting like a big cat, for Betsy to be liberated from the Castle, for his chance to pounce and slay her. Her thoughts suddenly returned to the present. "Oh, dear, we've got to finish this before your hair dries."

With no additional conversation, Anna completed her task, dried, oiled and combed his hair. When she was finished, she stepped back and directed Jefferson to look in the mirror. "Mr. Dante, may I present my dear love, Mr. Daniel Jefferson."

She stepped between him and the mirror and gently placed the spectacles on his nose, softly placing their temple arms over his ears.

Jefferson shifted his head to alertly inspect his new aspect in the mirror. "Remarkable. It's not me, but for the scars and the eyes. A masterpiece."

"A work of art, I suppose." She laughed. "Let me look closer. I'll work on the scars, but I can't do anything about the eyes, not from the outside. Only you can disguise those—not shape or color, but the expression, the power—you have to transform them."

He stared at the mirror, trying to change the intensity of his gaze. He worked to make his eyes look sad, weak. "There. What do you think?"

"I don't like it, but it's different, less noticeable than usual—much weaker. You'd be still harder to recognize. Do you think you can look like that all the time?"

"A lot's at stake. For your happiness, I can do anything."

"My happiness?"

"Of course, isn't that why I've really come? Look, the sun is rising."

"Have you been here so long?"

"It's almost time to get married."

"Married?"

"You said you loved me, and I've confessed my passion for you. Shouldn't we be united as husband and wife?"

Chapter 7

May 1864, the Wilderness, Virginia

It was still dark. Hank roused himself, downed a tasteless breakfast and filled his cartridge box. By the time he finished, the regiment was forming. In spite of his sleep, he was still too drowsy to chat, and for the most part the other soldiers kept their own fatigued silent vigils.

His dreams had unsettled him, especially as he remembered Naomi dying. He was anxious, remembering he had a wife and a coming child awaiting him in Washington City, should he survive this battle and the next and the next. He recalled his visit to Indiana during the winter furlough and thought that might be a fine place to settle. Leave the army. Slip away during the night or after some confused skirmish. There were so many disorganized units after each battle, he could disappear unsuspected for days. All he wanted was his wife and child, both in his arms, and he wanted to have both arms when he held them. What would it be like to have a son? A daughter? Betsy—she was a stealthy few days away. He could find her and whisk her from the capital before anyone realized he had deserted.

Maybe Indiana wouldn't be a good place to go; too many veterans from the 19th returning there. No, they'd have to go where no one knew them. Utah Territory? Yes, Utah. He didn't know any Mormons. They'd never suspect he was a deserter, but they might want Betsy for one of their wives. To flee with Betsy just so the Mormons could steal her wouldn't do. No, not Utah Territory. Maybe California.

As the sun rose, he focused for the first time on the unit's forward movement. Beside him stepped Rivenshaw. Hank glanced at him and found he was smiling to himself, lost in some pleasant thought.

"What are you thinking, Rivenshaw? Your smile's as wide as the gates of hell. It must be good, and I need to hear something good this morning."

"I'll impart to you my deepest and most moving thoughts."

"Just distract me."

"From what?"

"From where we are . . . what we're doing. From what we're missing."

"Missing? I thought you had nothing to miss. I thought the two of us were a sworn pair—no family and no place or care claiming us, nothing but this bush-strewn battlefield. Do not turn cowardly, young Gragg. Don't let some new desire weaken your resolve and our fellowship. Have you not heard that 'cowards die many times before their deaths; the valiant never taste of death but once. Of all the wonders that I yet have heard, it seems to me most strange that men should fear; seeing that death, a necessary end, will come when it will come.'"

"It may come when it comes, Rivenshaw, but pray that it be decades before it sneaks in on me as an old, wrinkled, gray, little man with fawning children and grandchildren at my feet, and my dear wife expiring at the same blessed moment."

"Gragg, you present a different self-portrait than you painted yesterday. I am betrayed. Have you hidden the truth from your friend? What explains the alteration? The battle yesterday? Was your courage breached, torn down in that melodious metallic hail of Rebel balls? Did you come too close to the end and suddenly treasure the light of this brief, 'brief candle'? Oh, Gragg, my fair youth, do not place your hopes in this fading world. 'Life's but a walking shadow, a poor player that struts and frets his hour upon the stage and then is heard no more: it is a tale told by an idiot, full of sound and fury, signifying nothing.' Do not suddenly crave a family or anything more than we can carry in our knapsacks and pockets. Stand with me, united as a bulwark, with no one and nothing claiming our affections. 'Wherefore do you droop? Why look you sad? Be great in act, as you have been in thought; let not the world see fear and sad distrust govern the motion of a kingly eye: Be stirring as the time; be fire with fire; threaten the threatener, and outface the brow of bragging horror.'"

Hank smiled distractedly. "A letter's turned me cowardly."

"A letter? Something and someone does await and prays the gods your safe return."

"Rivenshaw, I believe she prays to one God."

"You are a literal lad. Don't deter my inquiry. What did this missive say? Who was it from? Why does it now color you yellow? Has one of the camp strumpets slipped you a note proclaiming herself the mother of your coming child? Does a grass widow feign you are her child's father? Is that the 'lady' you see dying beside you, while her dozen children—each with different hair color, height, breadth and complexion—gather around during your decaying last minutes to claim you as their paternal forebearer?"

Hank chuckled. "I haven't told you this. Haven't told anyone."

"Say it loud enough, my boy, and the regiment will hear," Rivenshaw shouted.

Hank lowered his voice, "I'm married."

Rivenshaw whispered, "To the hussy? Good. She won't long be a grass widow."

"There's no hussy."

"I'm pleased no trollop has caught your fancy."

"I am married to my great love."

"Romantic indeed—a great love. Where did you find this great love . . . on the battlefield? Do not let it threaten our lonely brotherhood."

"I secretly married her during the furlough—she's from a Southern family."

"Married. From the South. Unfathomable. Shameful. And is her family so chagrined by a Union match that they refuse you membership in the clan?"

Hank laughed.

"You have waited too long to reveal this happiness to me."

"There's more."

"More?"

"We're to have a baby."

"A bairn."

"Bairn? Yes."

"A coward's wife and a child. Great news for you; but what of their honor? How can they raise their heads when their father and husband is nothing more than a . . . ?"

Rivenshaw didn't finish and Hank didn't respond as a shout ordered battle lines. They were to push against the Confederates ahead.

Rivenshaw said softly, "Here we go."

The Union men formed and screamed as the line surged forward, across the Plank Road, toward a remarkably close enemy.

Chapter 8

May 1864, Washington City, District of Columbia

A servant girl informed Mrs. Brown of a tall, finely dressed man awaiting Betsy in the parlor; or at least from his description, Sally thought he had come to visit Betsy. Sally handed the gentleman's card to Mrs. Brown, explaining it was a Mr. Henderson and that he had happy business to conduct with Betsy whom he called Mrs. Henderson.

Previously instructed by her employer that no visitor be announced and no message taken directly to the troubled boarder, the servant had taken the message and card to Mrs. Brown, not Betsy. The stout Mrs. Brown was determined to screen Betsy's visitors and messages, and she effusively praised Sally for bringing her the card.

She scrutinized the card which bore the name Thaddeus Henderson. She thought of Betsy. No previous boarder had been like her. Mrs. Brown had long ago realized, before the war, that even with faith in Jesus, life seemed unfair. Evil in its many forms and disguises and hardships shaded every life. She herself had lost her three sons at Bull Run . . . in the same battle. Three years later, she still wore mourning black and would rise earlier than was her practice in past years so she could pray, petitioning the Lord for relief from the loneliness weighing on her, a many-years widow. Some days were better than others. Certainly the empathy she felt from neighbors and long-time acquaintances consoled her, and she tried to return the support as many of them had since lost sons in the Union cause.

But Betsy brought a new, purer testament to life's injustices. It seemed to Mrs. Brown that each day since Betsy had stepped through the boarding house door that odd discouragements had descended on the distraught lady. Mrs. Brown felt agony for her and had already begun to consider the tortured woman as her own daughter—someone to nurture and protect, especially protect. Unfortunately her adopted maternal feelings meant any sorrow, fear or anxiety crushing Betsy weighed heavily on her as well. As she looked at the card, she wondered what catastrophe this new visitor brought.

Clutching it, she walked briskly to the parlor where Sally waited anxiously in the doorway. Mrs. Brown passed her and approached the gentleman. He rose immediately, hat in hand.

"Mr. Henderson, is that right?"

"Yes, Ma'am. Thaddeus Henderson from Staunton, Virginia," the man replied in a warm, Virginia accent. "You know that from my card which I see you carry in your hand. Discourteous as it must seem, I do remind you I gave it to your girl for my wife."

"You want to visit Mrs. Gragg?"

"I'm not here to see a Mrs. Gragg, Ma'am." His voice was elegant as was his manner. "I want to see my wife, Elizabeth Henderson."

"Ah. Sir, that gets us to the point. You are here by mistake. No Mrs. Henderson resides in my boarding house. I've never lodged a Mrs. Henderson." She paused briefly. "I shall keep your card, and should we hear of one, we will tell her of your visit." She smiled at him politely, relieved it was a confusion of identity and that no further turmoil need roil Betsy's life. "I do hope you find your wife. Sally will show you out." She nodded to him, but he didn't move.

"Ma'am, I spoke to a Mrs. Rathbone where my wife resided previously. She assured me several days ago that Betsy . . . Mrs. Henderson, my lawful wife, my hope and joy, was at her house briefly and that she now resides in the comfort of your establishment." He stood still, smiling congenially.

Mrs. Brown was anxious. Mention of Mrs. Rathbone muddled her thoughts and disconcerted her.

He spoke quickly. "There may be some confusion because my dear Betsy may have thought me killed in battle. I was sorely wounded, but I have recovered my health fully and have come to claim my dear wife . . . take her home. Though why she would go by another name, I cannot fathom."

Looking into the stranger's face, Mrs. Brown wondered what his visit and claims would mean. Why would Betsy use a name not her own? Was she hiding from this man? He seemed a gentleman. What was she to do? She couldn't keep a wife from her husband. If Betsy was Mrs. Henderson, she'd deceived Mrs. Brown. She'd said she was married to a Henry Gragg, a Union man at the front in Virginia. If Betsy had lied about that, how else had the woman misled her? A rising suspicion of betrayal caused her to shudder involuntarily. But betrayal and deceit or loyalty and integrity didn't matter. If she was his wife, it was Betsy's responsibility to go with him. If not, Mrs. Brown would protect her informal ward. She said abruptly, "Please excuse me," turned and left the parlor. She rapidly climbed the stairs, stopping at Betsy's door. She breathed deeply before knocking. When there was no answer, she slowly cracked the door, peering into the room. She could see Betsy sitting in a chair looking directly at her. She pushed the door open wider.

"Mrs. Gragg, there's a man downstairs asking to see you."

"Mr. Rathbone?" she queried harshly.

"No, a Mr. Henderson."

Without hesitation, Betsy responded gruffly, "I don't know a Mr. Henderson."

Allayed, Mrs. Brown breathed deeply. "I'm glad to hear that. Relieved. He said something about you being his wife and that you thought him dead. I'll send him . . . ." She stopped when she saw Betsy's eyes widen in horror. "My dear, do you know him?"

Betsy didn't answer, but stoically turned her head and stared blankly at the wall.

Mrs. Brown closed her eyes. What had she done? Was Betsy going to sink again in an emotionless morass? She stepped farther into the room and closed the door behind her.

Neither woman spoke until the silence agitated Mrs. Brown and she probed, "What do you want me to tell him?"

Betsy turned her steely gaze to her landlady for an uncomfortably long time. Mrs. Brown was already moving back toward the door, unsure of what she would say to the man when Betsy finally blurted out defiantly, "Tell him nothing. He's an imposter. I'm sure of it, and I will come to see him for myself. Mrs. Brown, my first husband, Mr. Henderson, was killed at Second Manassas. I can think of no greater travesty at this point in my life than to find that he—a good man—is still alive. It would be my doom. But it cannot be him. I heard it from an eyewitness that Thaddeus died. What monster would pretend to be him?" She sighed audibly. "Let us not put off confirming the truth merely for fear of descending doom. Let's go immediately and find this imposter out."

"You remarried?"

"Yes. I married Henry Gragg."

"How long ago?"

"Four months." She smiled sadly as she rose. "Mrs. Brown, you must think me the most peculiar person you've met. I'm beginning to think that myself. I once lived an uneventful, contented—if not happy—life. In January it was briefly happy for the first time in many years, but there's been no happiness for months. I can't predict what will happen when I go downstairs, but I have every intention of surviving the moment. He can't be Thaddeus, and it won't be. Where has he been all this time? It's not him. I spent months in Castle Thunder in Richmond as an inmate because they claimed I spied for the North . . . because I married the man I loved, who happened to be a Yankee. The man who frightened me so at the canal once tried to woo me for evil purposes, stole from me, murdered a man, and is dedicated to haunting and destroying me. Maybe killing me. This man . . . the man downstairs is surely an imposter, though why he plays this game I cannot guess. It's probably the Satan from the canal or one of his devils." She shut her eyes and said softly, "I hope he's an imposter." She reopened them and asked, "Will you stay with me as I meet him?"

Mrs. Brown, stuttered, trying to regain her composure after the shocking revelations, but finally whispered, "Arm in arm."

"Then I can do it."

Betsy held out her arm, and Mrs. Brown took it. Betsy smiled resignedly at her, and they descended the stairs. They walked boldly toward the parlor. The man was standing, hat still in hand, with his back to them; looking out the window onto the street below. Betsy couldn't see his face, but his stature and back of his head were so like Thaddeus's. Mrs. Brown felt Betsy's grip on her arm slacken, and glanced questioningly at the young woman, fearing her determination was weakening with her grip.

Betsy stared at the man as her worst suspicions solidi-fied. Could it be him? What would it mean? Was she not mar-ried to Hank? Was she this man's wife? And the child? Did she carry the child of a man not her husband? Had she cuck-olded her husband unknowingly? She stopped.

She couldn't do it, yet she had to. She had to confront him. A thought arose. She turned and whispered to Mrs. Brown, reversed her course and scurried up the stairs with her landlady a pace behind. Betsy stopped outside her door. Mrs. Brown, without acknowledging her, passed and knocked on a different bedroom door. Invited in, she slipped into the room for several minutes. When she reappeared, another boarder—blonde like Betsy—followed her. The wom-an glanced questioningly at Betsy.

Betsy mouthed, "Thank you," as she passed.

Mrs. Brown descended and approached the parlor, fol-lowed quickly down the stairs by the second boarder. With-out hesitation, they entered the room. Betsy crept down the stairs and peeked surreptitiously into the room as the women approached the gentleman.

He turned as they neared, but Betsy couldn't see his face from her vantage. She strained to hear to his voice and the conversation.

"Mr. Henderson," Mrs. Brown began enthusiastically, "I present Mrs. Henry Gragg."

He looked at Mrs. Brown first, beginning, "Regardless of what you call her, I recognize my own . . . ." Catching sight of Betsy's substitute stopped him. He searched the woman's face closely.

Betsy was too far from the room to determine if the voice was Thaddeus's, but his hesitation frightened her. If he knew the woman with Mrs. Brown was not Betsy . . . the unimaginable would crush her life. Was he truly Thaddeus come back to life . . . most tragically for her? How could it be him? Two years ago, she would have prayed for such a moment. Ten months ago, she could have survived it. Now it lingered above her slender neck like a finely honed guillotine blade. The confidence she'd felt minutes earlier cooled, and she fought panic.

Mrs. Brown offered, "Why don't we sit down, and I can have coffee brought for us."

The man, out of Betsy's sight, didn't respond. Betsy couldn't wait idly while her destiny was decided. She walked to the kitchen where she helped the servant prepare and arrange coffee and cakes for the guest. Sally was about to take the food to the parlor when Betsy grabbed her wrist firmly and stopped her. The girl looked at her questioningly.

"Your apron. Let me put it on," Betsy directed, without explanation.

Sally, without comment and understanding Betsy's intent, pulled it off and helped Betsy tie it. Betsy picked up the tray with trembling hands, inhaled deeply, smiled and nodded to Sally and carried the refreshments toward the parlor.

When she entered, the man was still standing though the two women had settled on a sofa. He was looking confusedly at Betsy's substitute.

"I can't believe . . . it's you," he said haltingly.

Mrs. Brown intervened mischievously, "Has she changed so much?"

"Yes, I suppose that's it. Maybe it's me. I've been ill for a long time. She's not what I'd imagined."

"Imagined, sir, not remembered? Why would you have to imagine what your wife looks like?"

He laughed, throwing his head back. He turned to Mrs. Brown grinning. "Ma'am, I have in the past year been given up for dead a dozen times. Every nurse, male and female, in the Confederacy has, at one point or another tended to my needs and my life. It's so dream-like to be here." Tears beaded at the bottom of his eyes. "She's like a dream, and I never imagined it . . . this way. It's not solid. It's like a wispy fog that you swing your hand through and feel nothing but coldness."

Betsy interrupted, placing the tray on a side table near him.

"May I pour you coffee, sir?" she said as she stood at his shoulder with a pot positioned to pour into a cup and saucer.

He ignored her.

"Some cakes, sir," Betsy said in a servile voice, still baffled by what she was seeing and hearing.

"No, none for me," he answered, still staring at the other woman.

"Mr. Henderson," Mrs. Brown broke in, "I don't believe you are married to this woman. I don't think you've ever seen her."

"Of course, I have . . . and we are married. It's . . ."

"Have you seen this man before?" she asked Betsy's substitute.

"I have not."

"Don't say that. I've changed. I have. When a man nears death, it leaves him marked. Please acknowledge me . . . at least that. I acknowledge you . . . although my memory of you is . . . different, surely because of my illness. My memory suffers."

Mrs. Brown added, "I don't believe you'd recognize your wife if she stood beside you."

He looked at Mrs. Brown with squinted eyes and scrunched nose, trying to understand what she suggested. "I'm in the same room with her," he responded hesitantly. "I am embarrassed not to be able to say I recognize her; ashamed of it really. I have been through so much. I can't help it. Surely, Mrs. Brown, you can appreciate that."

"Mr. Henderson, who are you? Why do you pretend to be someone you're not?" Betsy interjected calmly.

The man, clearly offended, turned on Betsy angrily, and said, "Mrs. Brown, do you allow your servants to speak uninvited to guests?" His eyes instantly brightened and his tone sweetened as he scrutinized her face. "Ah, Betsy, there you are. You test me." He laughed briefly and spoke slowly. "Clever. You test me with this pale imitation. I should have known you would be clever . . . careful. I should have expected it." He waved his hand dismissively at the second woman. "I have been sick and hurt for so long. It's left me"—the nascent tears grew in his eyes—"always doubting memories. I knew it wasn't right, but I couldn't be sure . . . not quite." Sadness crossed his face. "I cannot doubt what I see before me now. The beauty of my beloved and my oh-how-much missed wife. Did I pass the test, your trial of loyalty? I've been true in my tribulation and suffering. I have prayed you would be true in your ease and comfort . . . the comfort my money bought you. Oh, tell me you have been faithful. That you have remembered me each day."

"You're not my husband. I've never see you. There are some similarities." She turned to her landlady. "I grant him that, Mrs. Brown. But that does not make him Thaddeus Henderson. He is not Thaddeus."

"Betsy, suffering has altered me." His voice broke. "Am I not the same height, the same hair—now sprinkled too early with a bit of gray. Have I not the same eyes you have so often gazed in and dreamed upon? My face has changed a bit. It's older, paler; indubitably. The long illness has done that. You will come to recognize it . . . to love it again. In it you will find your faithful Thaddeus. Come . . . let us leave these women to their duties. Let us leave for home and the life of comfort and peace we've always craved."

"Get out. You're an impostor. Why are you doing this?" Betsy screamed.

"I recognized you right away, did I not?" He turned to look at Mrs. Brown. "Isn't that proof enough for you, Mrs. Brown. You knew I was uncomfortable with the woman you deceitfully presented to me. Mrs. Brown, Betsy has been under such strain since my death . . . or my near and supposed death. We've both been parted so long. It's no wonder she can't . . . doesn't recognize me in the remains of her own despair when she sees me in my weakened, diminished state. Though if she was honest with herself, she would acknowledge me." He smiled knowingly. "Betsy, you have not changed a bit. You are so young, lovely . . . a salve for my wearied eyes, battered body and my worn heart."

He approached Betsy extending his hand lovingly toward her, gentle compassion in his expression, but she moved from him.

He reproached her. "Come, you're my wife. You must obey me. Thank you, Mrs. Brown, for reuniting us."

Mrs. Brown watched them both questioningly, beginning to wonder about Betsy's sanity.

"Betsy, you will come with me immediately. I don't want to embarrass you, but I have noticed you have not been faithful to me. I overlook it because you did it ignorantly; oh, but my leniency must have righteous limits. You must come with me. Your obedience is my right as your lawful lord before God."

Betsy stopped retreating and asked, "What did you call me?"

Mrs. Brown saw worry dart across the man's face.

"Betsy. It's your name."

"When did you start calling me Betsy?"

"I don't remember. Some time, maybe in my constant dreams of you, dreams that have kept me alive, anticipating this sweet reunion. Do you prefer I call you Elizabeth until you've recovered from the shock of my survival; until we're intimately reacquainted? I will. I'll call you whatever you want. Forgive me that in my dreams I thought of you less formally, more intimately as Betsy. I will call you anything you like."

"If you were Thaddeus, you'd know you never called me Betsy, and after we were married, you never called me Elizabeth." In a mocking tone, she added, "You hated the name Betsy."

His face reddened. "I was injured! I can't be expected to remember everything that happened between us so many years ago . . . before I was ill. I've forgotten much."

"I haven't," Betsy said placidly. "Show us your wounds. Let us see your thigh."

"Elizabeth, let us have decorum. Come with me as you must. I'll show you my scarred leg and use that intimate appellation you want me to disrespectfully banter in public. To show off my wounds to strangers is pandering. I refuse it as Coriolanus refused. Must I parade them before Northern commoners to gain acclaim and recognition? My scars are remnants of a sacred sacrifice . . . my sacrifice for the nation. Your hesitation frightens me. It makes me suspicious. Have you knowingly been unfaithful to me? Is that why you refuse my husbandly claim?"

Betsy spoke softly, turning her head to her landlady, "Mrs. Brown, I cannot imagine who this man is or his intent, but I have never seen him. He shares a few traits with my first husband. His face, his voice and the brute force of his commands, however, reveal him a most rank imposter. He doesn't even know the name Thaddeus used exclusively for me. His ignorance of the wound that killed my husband betrays him the more. My husband, Thaddeus Henderson, died of a wound to his stomach and chest, not his legs . . . not his thigh."

Mrs. Brown stepped between the two of them, eying the visitor suspiciously, almost angrily. "That's testimony enough for me. Sir, you will leave immediately, or I'll send for the authorities."

"Not without my wife."

"May I remind you that you have acknowledged being a Confederate soldier? You're either in Washington as spy or deserter, and I believe the army will arrest you either way. They would hardly be concerned about a woman who had been held in a Southern prison as a Confederate traitor. They would be most interested in a scoundrel like you." She turned toward the parlor door where Sally watched, thoroughly engaged in the drama. "Sally, go for the authorities."

The imposter didn't wait for the girl's response. He looked threateningly from Mrs. Brown to Betsy and back to Mrs. Brown. "Do you think you can do this? This will not end here."

Betsy looked at him sincerely, "Why would you do this to me? Who put you up to this?"

He didn't acknowledge her or the comment, but turned toward the door and left the room and house, descending onto the street.

The four women moved to the window and watched as the man entered a waiting cab. Betsy was disappointed she couldn't see his expression, hoping it might have illuminated his intentions.

When he was out of sight, Mrs. Brown turned to Betsy, took her hand gently. "It's done. He won't be back. We've caught him at his game, although why he thought he could get away with it, I'll never fathom."

The second lodger added, "He did pay you a wonderful compliment. I wish someone would say I hadn't aged in years."

Betsy looked at her, stunned with an unexpected realization. She inadvertently reached up to her face and touched her scar. Betsy looked at her and said, "He recognized me by the scar. You didn't have the scar. He had been told to look for a scar." She glanced back out the window as the carriage disappeared. "I don't want to go through anything like that again, but this outcome is better than the alternative. If it had been Thaddeus, my life would have been ruined."

Mrs. Brown asked, "Do you have any idea why he came?"

"He—at someone else's bidding—was sent to frighten me."

"He wouldn't have taken you?"

"Oh, he would have taken me . . . if we'd wavered. If we'd not been so resolute, he would have taken me."

"For what purpose?"

"I shudder to think."

"He won't come back."

"I wish I could be sure, Mrs. Brown. After all I've been through, I could easily imagine him coming back or waiting for me somewhere or even following me. It's enough to drive a woman insane." She shivered, but steadied herself as the reality of what she'd said settled on her. There was no doubt about who had sent him. This imposter was the latest Miss Morrow, acting out Walthrope's evil haunting of her.

Chapter 9

May 1864, the Wilderness, Virginia

As the men of the Indiana 19th crossed the road, cannons rumbled in the distance and artillery shells exploded among them. Hank consciously slowed his breath as he pushed on, trying to ignore the rumbling din. When a commanding voice thundered, "The Rebs are firing too high! Ignore the racket!" he glanced questioningly toward Colonel Williams, the regimental commander who had shouted the encouragement. At that moment a solid shell smashed the colonel's chest.

The sight stunned Hank. The colonel was gone, leaving Hank feeling unexpectedly mortal and vulnerable. Thoughts of Betsy and their child overwhelmed him. He had to live to see their baby, yet he exercised little influence over shells and balls and soldiers. An exploding shell could erase all trace of him from the earth. He could exist one moment and be obliterated the next. He could be a charging soldier confident—like the colonel—no shell or ball could harm him at the precise moment when a ball crushed his body. What calculus did God use to determine who would stand where a shell fell? Did he move Williams to that exact spot knowing the moment of impact approached? Why Williams? If Williams, why not Private Gragg? The bearded Williams had five young children. If a colonel could be snuffed out, why not a private? What special claim did Hank Gragg have to life?

The earth trembled as artillery thundered an encircling barrage. Hank was disoriented: Concussion of the guns, whistling of balls through the air, pounding of the ground by solid shot, the scattered yet constant yelling of the men came together in a fierce roar. Hank imagined his child, but pushed away the image. He looked at the men of the 19th, now far ahead of him. They were plunging with seeming abandon into the woods ahead, yet he knew each felt the same fear that paralyzed him. Why couldn't he move forward? He steadied his shaking legs, peered sternly after the regiment and compressed his lips. He saw tall Rivenshaw looking at a distance like a toy soldier, and the sight brought resolve.

He began trotting forward, moving to the front for Rivenshaw; for the others: they needed him, and he was one of them. His trot became a wide, rapid gait, and he forgot himself. He held his musket in one hand as he ran to catch his fellows. Hank could see the regiment's progress slow, then stop, in the face of an angry Confederate countercharge. Men staggered backward or fell to the ground. Hank didn't slow. He could still see Rivenshaw holding his ground with Secesh mere yards away. The pressure on the 19th was enormous. They couldn't possibly hold without Union reserves to bolster the charge. The Southern forces pressed the advantage as more Rebs streamed in from behind. Row upon row of Confederates poured balls into the 19th. Rivenshaw and the rest of the front line were wavering, wilting. Hank had nearly caught up to them when the regiment began to dissolve. Rivenshaw turned backward, terror on his visage, blind to Hank's arrival.

Hank shouted encouragement.

Rivenshaw didn't hear it, but broke into a mad dash as did all the men of the 19th. There was no caution, no calculation, no protective retreat; merely a madding dash to the rear. Every soldier fled as if he were alone, unthinking, an animal in flight. As the wave of panicked men abandoned Hank, his anxiety burst like a boil—his own fear, no longer suppressed, squirted out. His head raced, his face burned, his stomach churned. His hands gripped his musket so tightly they ached. He joined the brigade in its helter-skelter, hysterical run.

Hank's scramble to the rear accelerated instinctively with each step and without thought. The Confederates halted their charge at a fortified line far behind the Union run, but Hank didn't notice.

"Skedaddle! I know what that means now. As I ran, all I could think of was skedaddling. You colonists do have a few good words—remarkably few, mind you." Rivenshaw could barely get the words out between sucks of breath.

Disgust twisted Hank's expression. "Skedaddle. I think the Iron Brigade ran . . . really ran from the enemy for the first time. I don't ever remember running like that, not from a fight, not without a fight."

"'The better part of valor is discretion; in the which better part I have saved my life' and so have you. I am no veteran—not like you—but I begin to wonder if it gets harder to fight as time goes on."

Hank glanced thoughtfully at Rivenshaw. "It's getting harder for me. I almost couldn't make myself charge today and was delighted to retreat."

"Perhaps that will save you, young Gragg."

"How then can I help save the nation and our friends?"

"That, my lad, I cannot foresee, but I think you'll survive to see your child."

"What of you? Do you have family to return to?"

"'Feed yourselves with questioning; that reason wonder may diminish, how thus we met, and these things finish.'"

"What?"

"Obfuscation, my boy. Obfuscation. It's better to ask no questions, and far better to answer none."

Chapter 10

Well after dark, Victoria Richman heard a soft knock at the door. She was there in the swift, anxious movement of her worn, blue skirt. She was a tall, strong but lean woman of light brown skin and dark eyes. Her face was enticing, with its elegant nose and full lips. She cracked the door, pushing her full weight against it. It took her eyes a few seconds to dilate to the blackness of the night, but when they did, she grinned and jerked the door open wide.

She whispered, "Where have you been? I've been frenzied for hours, worried something had happened—that the army picked you up or someone kidnapped you back to slavery."

He beamed, grateful to have someone worry about him. He put his arms around her and held her firmly against his chest, deeply breathing in her scent. He squeezed her tighter, enjoying the physical contact. They were still new lovers. If he could have had his way, he would forget horses, stables, hacks and everything else to spend every moment near her. He gently lifted her and stepped into their ground-floor, one-room dwelling, one of the four apartments in the story-and-a-half-tall structure. Still holding her, he gently kicked the door closed as he lowered his face to kiss her lips. She kissed him back. This was happiness he could never have imagined a few months earlier. His hand rose to the back of her head and pulled her head to his shoulder, where she willingly rested it.

She spoke in a barely audible tone, "I'm glad you're home."

He spoke excitedly, too loudly, "I have a horse and a job."

She smiled and pulled her head back from him so she could see his face. Still in an undertone, she responded, "You bought one of the horses at the auction."

"In a way."

"A way?"

"I'll tell you later, but you ignored my other news—the job."

"I heard it. I didn't know you wanted a job."

"I have a job, a perfect job," he proclaimed eagerly.

"I'm glad about the horse, but don't put on airs because you've got a job. Anyone can get a job now. And be quiet. Adam's asleep."

"Yes, probably true, but I have a job in a livery stable, a big one. It will be my first real job. I'll be paid for it—my own money."

"Will you share it with us?" she whispered impishly.

He laughed softly, finally lowering his voice, "If you're good to me."

"You wouldn't want me to promise that."

"You may go hungry."

"Not as long as I can eat you," she said, tickling him, cornering him by the door, biting him gently on his arm. She paused mid-bite, pulled away to look at him, and spoke more thoughtfully, "You didn't think it possible that you'd get a horse."

"No, and I almost didn't. I was outbid."

"You haven't stolen it? Can I see it? Where have you stabled it?"

"Not so many questions at once. The horse isn't here. Left it at the stable, the one I'll be working at beginning tomorrow morning." He paused for effect. "I still can't believe it. A horse. I own a horse."

"I've told you since we got here that you can do anything you want. After such a memorable day, you must know it now for yourself."

"Still doubt it," he responded honestly. "Spent ten dollars on the horse."

"That's more than you said we could afford."

"Like I said, I didn't win the bid. Not really. Was outbid by the owner of the livery, but he could see I understood horses. He gave me work. Said he would sell the horse to me for the eight dollars I bid, and I could work off the other two. I know it's your money. I wasn't going to spend more than I promised."

"Promised? It's our money."

"It's what you saved for so long back in Kentucky."

"Some the Judge gave us—both of us—when we were leaving to help us get started. More importantly, there's no longer mine or yours, only ours, in the Lord. 'Therefore shall a man leave his father and his mother, and shall cleave unto his wife: and they shall be one flesh.'"

"Like that bit about 'one flesh,'" he responded, eyes faintly shimmering in the room's lone candle, as he tickled her, forcing her to retreat to escape his advance.

She tried to divert the assault by turning the conversation. "Ten dollars. Someone told me today you can't get much horse for eight dollars. I was afraid you'd come home disappointed. Thought maybe that's why you didn't come home. He is alive, isn't he? He's not dead, is he? I hadn't thought of that. Is that why you didn't ride him home?" She laughed softly.

"Didn't get on his back today because he would've collapsed under my weight."

Her diversion had worked. He had stopped tickling her, and she was disappointed. "A Rosinante. Can you get him healthy?"

"Going to take a while, but he's got potential. Lots of years left. The man, Mr. Bond, from the livery stable, said he could tell I know about horses. So he hired me. I can get him healthy."

"The horse or Mr. Bond?" she asked smartly.

He smiled but ignored her question. "Still have to get that carriage, so the horse can rest for now. Mr. Bond will keep him at the livery stable till I can get a carriage . . . as long as I work for him."

"Mr. Bond sounds like a Christian gentleman."

"Don't know. Didn't talk religion." He looked at the floor and added, "Did say he hired me because he could tell I wasn't trouble."

Victoria's tone and expression changed simultaneously. "Ah. Good boy. Here boy. No talking boy." He could sense her anger.

"No one wants someone who makes trouble."

"He's not saying that. He's saying you won't demand much, maybe not even what you deserve. He wants a freedman to be his slave. That's what he's saying. You're free, but don't expect to use that freedom. Do what I tell you. Don't think. I'll tell you what to think, what to say, what to wear, what to eat. He's no better than a slave owner. It's no better than slavery. He doesn't see a man. He turns his head and gazes right past your humanity. You're lumped with his possessions, his animals—something he can keep in his stables. I'm surprised he let you come home . . . let you out of his sight. Does he have an overseer . . . or maybe a slave driver, or does he do his own whippings? He's going to keep you with that broken-down horse at the stable; both his animals."

"Victoria," he protested in a whisper, clearly crushed by her ire.

"I'm sorry." She paused and softened her tone, "I'm tired of them seeing, yet not seeing us. We've become like the word of God. 'Because they seeing see not; and hearing they hear not, neither do they understand.' When will this be past? When will they recognize we're just like them? We are them. We're all part of the human race. 'No man is an island . . . Every man is . . . part of the main.' When will they remember the command, 'All things whatsoever ye would that men should do to you, do ye even so to them'?" Her voice was no longer a whisper. "If they get sick, they pass it on to you. If you get sick, you share it with them. They can pretend we're neatly separated; but there is no them, no us."

"Isn't there something about not judging in the Bible?"

She looked at him and waited to answer until she had calmed herself further. "You are a good man, William Richman. He's right. You won't make trouble, and he'll find you faithful and hardworking." She grinned and whispered, "It's best he hired you, William, and not me."

"You're too smart for horse work."

"That's not what I'm thinking."

"I know, but you are, and you don't need to worry about white men anymore. What can they do to you now?"

She stiffened. Her eyes nearly glowed in the dark. "Why do you say that?"

"Because I love you, and I don't want you to worry. I don't want you to be ashamed or worry or be sad about it . . . about anything. You've given yourself to me, and most important, you have Adam. Don't grieve more about evil all those years ago."

She looked at him silently, sternly.

"I hope I haven't angered you. I just said it so . . . ."

She was furious he had alluded to it. She hadn't decided if she would ever tell him about it, and for him to bring it up at all . . . and with Adam in the room.

"Don't be angry . . . not with me. I'm trying my best," he pled. "Got us a horse. Got a job. Going to get a carriage. I want you and Adam to be happy. Don't be angry with me. Please. Don't be angry."

His words had no impact on her, but she'd never detected such nervousness in his voice before, and it tempered her anger. In reality he had hoisted a smothering burden from her chest. She would never have to explain what that man . . . . Adam's unworthy father—undeserving of the title or the thought—had done to her. William already knew, and he told her it didn't matter. The shame and anger she'd always felt rushed out of her like breath. It hung in the air around her with no place to go and dissipated. She looked at William.

With his love, she would never again breathe it in. How did he know? He must have guessed it when he had rescued her from the monster's attempt to attack her a second time. She remembered how she had kicked the beast's body as it lay unconscious from William's blow to the back of its head. William must have deduced the source of her anger as she vented her hatred on the unconscious, stuttering man. "William," she whispered, barely audible. "You can never imagine the pain of what happened, and how much it hurts every time it skulks uninvited into my mind. To be thrown to the ground, held tight, threatened, a knife at my throat, to be used, not as a human being, but as . . . as . . . . It was horrible, and it has been every day since. If I could blot out the memory by cutting off a hand, I'd do it. How could anyone do that to another? If I could return to that moment, I would let him cut my throat before . . . ."

"If you had, you wouldn't be with me, and I can't survive without you. We wouldn't have Adam."

"Adam," she whispered hauntingly. "He's the one thing that gives me the strength to endure the memories. I don't associate him with it. He's too precious, too innocent to be linked to such filth. I do know but for that I . . . we would not have him. You can never conceive of the horror . . . the humiliation. You would think nothing they have left can humiliate us, after all we've been through. But it's not true. Shakespeare wrote a play about a Jew who was hated and persecuted, and in a lovely soliloquy, he says what I felt . . . what I feel. 'I am a Jew. Hath not a Jew eyes? Hath not a Jew hands, organs, dimensions, senses, affections, passions? Fed with the same food, hurt with the same weapons, subject to the same diseases, healed by the same means, warmed and cooled by the same winter and summer, as a Christian is? If you prick us, do we not bleed? If you tickle us, do we not laugh? If you poison us, do we not die?'"

Both were silent for a long time before William offered, "But you're not a Jew."

Victoria laughed.

"Shush. You'll wake Adam," William whispered urgently. His eyes glistened mockingly.

"I don't care. I want him to know what a loving, wonderful imbecile I've married."

"I think he already knows the imbecile part."

She wrapped her arms around him, pushing her cheek against his. She never wanted to let him go and asked, "Did you walk home?"

"Not the whole way. Mr. Bond had his driver Erasmus take me to Long Bridge, so I just had to get across, and the wait wasn't bad."

"I take back what I said about him. He's a kind, Christian gentleman, and I like that name, Erasmus. Let's name our next son that."

"I want a daughter."

"Let's not quibble, but get working on getting me fat."

"With pleasure, Mrs. Richman." He forced her gently back across the small room, but suddenly stopped. "What of your day?"

She was disappointed but grateful he thought to ask. "Adam and I spent most of it at the Village school with the children. There are so many of them. Some of the children are learning quickly. After supper, since you weren't home yet, and I wasn't ready to worry that you had been sold down the river, we went to help at the night school for the adults. Adam loves helping them read; lets him show off; lets them see his stuttering doesn't mean he's stupid. They make such a fuss over him because he reads."

"He still asleep?"

"I think so. He wanted to wait for you. I let him for a while, but when he fell asleep at the table, I sent him to bed. You start tomorrow?"

"Have to be there by six."

"How far is it?"

"About four miles, so I'll leave about four. At that early hour, I hope the bridge won't be too busy. I must be early on my first day."

"To check on your new steed?"

"Steed? He will never be a steed. He's a Percheron . . . made to pull." William laughed, thinking about the exhausted, malnourished horse. He's a gelding, and he'll be a wonderful workhorse. You could use a saddle on him, but he's made to pull . . . but not yet."

"That's exactly what you need."

"He is."

"Have you named him?"

"Haven't. What do you think? What should I call him?"

"I can't answer that until I've met him, but if he serves us well, Judge would be a good name."

"Judge? Homesick?" He didn't wait for an answer. "Come to the stable. It's on the corner of Ninth and D streets."

"I would like to visit, but I'll wait a week or two, till you've settled in. Besides we're busy at the school. I missed you today," she whispered in his ear, pulling him toward her, hugging him.

Chapter 11

The disorganized flight of the 19th Indiana from the field was a memory. The regiment had been in a defensive position overnight and throughout the subsequent day, staring across at similarly defensed and weary Confederates. After twenty-four hours, new orders directed the unit, with the rest of the surviving Iron Brigade, to begin a post-sunset march along a narrow, tree-and-brush-enclosed path toward an unknown destination.

Hank found it hard to go forward. In spite of the day's rest, he was exhausted by the constant fear of an enemy assault; the battle sounds that had reverberated relentlessly across the hilly and forested landscape; the anticipation that at any moment he—with his comrades—might be ordered forward in another futile, ill-reasoned attack against a fortified foe.

From nearly the first slow step, his stomach churned as he breathed the acidic stench of animal and human decay. He could see little and navigated in silence following the dim form of the soldier in front of him. His eyes blinked long and slowly.

Momentarily, his footsteps veered to the edge of the road as his mind relinquished consciousness. His eyes rolled to the side, his grip on his rifle loosened, and the gun began sliding from his shoulder. In an instant flash of panic, his eyelids bolted upward and his hands grabbed for the rifle butt. Unfortunately he had wandered from the cleared road. He tripped, tumbling headlong across a large and stiffened body. The gun fell from his hands as his face buried itself in the rough hair of a swelling, dead horse.

He moaned and instinctively jumped up and back from the grizzly death beneath him. He swore at himself, the horse, the war, the Confederacy and Grant's nighttime march. He felt for his weapon as he lost himself in a loud, rhetorical diatribe, "Why in the dark? Why are we wandering in the dark, when we can't find our way to Richmond in bright sunshine? Will the dark hide the hideous truth that our generals cannot grasp what needs to be done? We're not moving toward Richmond, but back to Fredericksburg where our new, imperial general can plan another failed sally into the open jaws of an invincible foeman."

Laughter behind him brought him back to awareness of those marching by.

"Darkness has revealed your lunacy, my young hero. And if you continue to cry out in such fashion the enemy and provost guard will be upon you. So my brother and friend: Quiet."

"I'm looking for my rifle," Hank answered grumpily.

"Do it silently," answered the English-accented, jovial voice.

Hank kept feeling the ground and horse for his rifle. He could hear soldiers shuffling by him, but as he touched his gun, the movement stopped. Men grumbled at the sudden halt, but it gave Hank time to retrieve the rifle and slip alongside Rivenshaw back into the stalled formation.

Hank asked, "Will we retreat?"

"An actor I am, but no prophet. I perceive nothing but the current direction of my feet."

"What direction do they face?"

"Ahead."

"A new compass direction?"

"The surest, most accurate. If not by the way your toes point, you have to count on stars and sun and moon, and the earth's own magnetism, and they're ever shifting, hiding behind the clouds, blocked by the trees. Or they disappear at the horizon when you most need them. Never count on their constancy."

"Straight ahead doesn't capture anything meaningful."

"You are wrong, sirrah. Going straight ahead is the essence of progress—no diverging; no retreating."

"Your feet tell you all this?"

"Certainly."

"Smarter than all your other parts?"

"Doubtless. You know it is the navigation our cherished generals use. Whatever direction Grant's toes point in the morning when he slumps from bed, that's the direction he drives us."

"I do believe you have stumbled on a marvelous system, for it can never be wrong . . . until we march into the sea."

"Oh, how I'd love to see the seaside. Pull off my shoes, and walk through the cool, wet sand as gulls circle and cry overhead. I can feel the fresh airborne salt blowing softly against my cheek, the sand squeezing between my toes, the warm sun at my neck. Hank, can you hear the children giggling as they dart into the water, then retreat pursued by the playful waves? If only my feet would point me to the shore."

"I've never been to the sea."

"Never to the sea? We must go. When we've put all things aright, I'll return to my fair Britannia, and she will embrace me, and I to her will be wed and never again leave her shore. You will come as our guest and explore our cliffs and moors and beaches."

"Right now, I just want to visit Richmond."

"Then General Grant is your man."

"They said that about Burnside, McDowell, Pope, Hooker, Meade. Did I leave anyone out?"

"How would I know? During all your defeats, I enjoyed the warm sun of temperate England."

"England. Why did you leave . . . to come to this?"

"Probing?"

"I want to make sure I've not fallen in with a cutthroat."

"Cutthroat? If you have, I've experience enough to know the best time to sever the head is while a man sleeps. So this march saves you for a few hours. Why do we keep stopping? How far have we come since we last halted?"

"A hundred yards."

"As much as that? March. Stop. March. Stop. Perhaps your pessimism's foundation is a bulwark, and they have no idea where we go."

"If we can't get to Richmond, let us at least sleep and give us fresh air . . . far from the stench of the battle."

"We have become the stench, both the living and dead among us."

"What's the cheering?"

"Ask me no futile question, for I stand next to you with no better view of the darkness ahead or knowledge of the enthusiastic shouts."

"Someone's cheering."

"They must have their reasons."

"What did that man say?"

"What fellow?"

"Quiet, he's still talking."

Hank half-laughed and half-cheered. "We're turning south. We're going south. To Richmond!"

"Huzzah." Rivenshaw responded flatly. "I never doubted. It was you who questioned our new hero. Grant is not a man to turn tail, and I've heard it said he distains Fredericksburg. But overruling all, his toes are deformed and always point southward."

"We're moving."

"A few paces at least."

Chapter 12

June 1864, Staunton, Virginia

Caleb Moore, a former Confederate soldier and invalid caretaker of Betsy Gragg's Staunton farm and grain and woolen mills, sat at the desk writing furiously. Periodically he would pause, stare without seeing through an adjacent window, before returning to scribble on the paper. Finally the tall steward laid down his pen, ran his fingers through his dark hair and picked up the latest issue of the *Staunton Spectator* that sat at his elbow. He reread the article that had provoked his notes:

> *The enemy are again advancing up the Valley. As yet, we have been unable to learn their force. They will be met, and will probably be again thunder-struck as they were at New Market on the 15th instant. They have advanced as far as New Market. If some bird or traitor would communicate to them the position of Breckinridge and his command, and how soon he could swoop upon them, like an eagle upon its prey, they would consider "discretion the better part of valor," and go down the Valley faster than they came up.*

Ignoring the report's bluster and pretention, he focused on the news: Yankees were stealing up the Valley.

As a member of the home guard, he remembered with pride fighting on horseback with his unit during the North's last offensive. With the regular army and a corps of cadets from the Military Institute, they had valiantly repulsed and crushed the Yankees at New Market. He silently prayed for another miracle, but doubt permeated his mind: How many times could they stop such a rich and persistent enemy?

He felt burdened for the first time by the responsibility
that inadvertently had fallen to him of caring for Betsy's
businesses after she had been arrested earlier in the year for
murder and espionage. Reports were already spreading that
the enemy was destroying crops and more in the lower Valley. If the enemy made it to Staunton, they would surely destroy the town's railway station and Betsy's woolen factory,
crops and grain mills. Depending on their mood, they might
burn her home. The ideas he jotted were ways to protect his
stewardship should the ruthless invaders achieve the town.
Frowning, he reviewed the pages. No single idea was likely
to succeed. Would one or two work?

Caleb glanced again at the newspaper and scowled as he
noticed the advertisement he'd placed seeking wool:

> *Wool! Wool! We want wool badly, and will give in ex-
> change, either COTTON or WOOLEN GOODS or MONEY
> OF THE NEW ISSUE. Those who deliver first will be
> sure to get goods at the time of delivery. Henderson &
> Moore.*

If the Yankees should invade, he had wasted Betsy's
money on the notice. He snickered at his obsession with mi-
nutiae: If the marauders took Staunton, a few dollars spent
pleading in the newspaper would not register against the
destruction and loss they would inflict.

How long did he have to make his preparations? A
week? Two? Not long enough.

Days later, Caleb, in uniform, galloped onto the short path
to Betsy's house. His horse was lathered, and he was exhausted, sweating and anxious. Much to do, or all would be
lost. They were coming. Tomorrow. No later. The Confederate regulars and rapidly called home guard had been routed
this round. Many young boys, convalescents—Caleb included—and old men not rounded up by the Union force had

scrambled from the field. The barbarians were just north of Staunton. Stories of what they had done down the Valley to crops and houses had panicked Staunton residents, and many flooded the roads southward.

After supper, a weary, worried Caleb gathered factory, mill and farm employees and the remaining plantation slaves at the warehouse to buck up their courage and confirm readiness. After reviewing the preparations, he sent them home for a night's nervous sleep. He stayed behind, wandering the factory. Its idled machinery and empty storage and preparation areas seemed to grieve, as if they were human, falsely accused and awaiting execution at dawn. As he left the factory which had become a part of him, he locked—an important symbolic action in his mind—the front door and pulled himself up into his saddle. He gazed at the building for a long time, letting his mind ramble through a dozen sweet memories of his life in Staunton. Then he turned his horse and galloped toward the farmhouse. Dawn would come too quickly and much remained to hide.

Caleb, wearing his Hanger-made artificial leg, was restlessly pacing the library when one of the older factory employees arrived at Betsy's mansion to report the enemy would be upon them within the hour. Caleb thoughtfully regarded the bald, short and rail-thin worker as he considered their plight. He thanked the man, advised him to go home quickly to occupy his own place, voicing his suspicion the Yankees would be less likely to destroy a home still inhabited. Finally Caleb warned the faithful worker not to taunt the infidels.

As the man left the library, Caleb shouted for the cook. She came running, and he called, "Are you set?"

The dark-skinned, heavy, middle-aged woman with short hair parted down the middle stopped abruptly a few feet from him. Her intense eyes took his measure calmly from a heavily padded, smooth and rounded face. She was wearing a brightly colored dress with wide stripes of gold, red and orange. She answered calmly, "Yes."

"Good. Let's review what you'll say . . . what you'll do."

Her face creased slightly at the eyes as she almost smiled. "I watch the soldiers as they approach . . ."

"You should be on the porch even if they never stop."

"Yes," she said patiently. "Can I take someone with me?"

"If you want."

"I'll be calmer, I think. Mary said she'd do it. It might be more expected. One woman facing the soldiers doesn't seem natural. They wouldn't expect that, would they? Wouldn't we be too frightened to come out? Maybe with two, it will look like we're curious. We can hold hands if we get frightened. I think it will look better with two of us. Should I wear a cap?"

He smiled. "You will look fine. You will be perfect. May God be with you . . . and with all of us."

When the first Union column began passing the property, a cadre of Yankees wandered toward the house. The two women waited till the soldiers turned into the yard. Stepping from the porch, they strolled toward the road. The cook stood erect, proud, and the young housemaid cowered slightly behind her, holding her hand tightly.

An officer on horseback led the approaching men. The foot soldiers were laughing, talking and eyeing the two women as they approached.

The officer called to them, "You live here?"

"Yes, sir," the cook quickly responded.

"Slaves?"

"Yes, sir."

"Not now. I free you in the name of the United States."

"Yes, sir," she responded in an unimpressed tone.

"What white folk live here? Are they home?"

"No. Slaves are. Not the mistress."

"She have a husband?"

"In the Union army, 19th Indiana . . . with General Grant. Don't know exactly where since we can't get no letters through the lines."

"A Yankee. Don't that beat all?" The soldier hooted. "Where's your mistress?"

Several of the soldiers had slipped past the women, one making a bawdy comment as he winked at the shaking maid. The cook ignored them, but the maid moved anxiously against her back, tugging her sleeve, whispering in her ear.

The cook shook off her grip and glanced back with irritation at the small, young woman, answering, "Don't know, not exactly. She was a prisoner in Castle Thunder—that's a prison for Southern traitors in Richmond. We think she was exchanged. Arrested for passing secrets to the Yankees." She chuckled. "Neighbors can't abide her now 'cause she's with the Union. Suppose she always was."

"No other whites here?"

"We have one. A man who watches over the house while master's fighting for the Union. He's fighting right now to free us—the master."

"Do you have food?"

"Not much, but when we heard you were coming, I cooked up some soft bread, thinking you might be hungry. Hardtack ain't good for nothing. We don't have much, but it's hidden in the barn for when you got here. The Rebs took most of our food when they went north to fight you . . . when they found out who owned the house. They did miss some of it. I made thirty loaves for you. Will that help?"

"Where's this overseer?"

"He manages the place for money and a place to live, not 'cause he loves the North . . . not like us; not like the master . . . the mistress." She paused, looked back toward the house and blurted out, "He don't want to see us freed. No sir." She laughed sarcastically as she glanced at the soldiers who had passed them. "You think he'd stay? Ran—took his horse—a week ago when he heard you were in the Valley. He knew you'd free us."

"Where's this bread?"

"In the barn. Same place we hid food when the Rebs came through."

"Show me."

"Can you carry those loaves alone? You may need soldiers to help, not that they're heavy. My bread's light as air. Got a reputation for that around here. Everyone says so, and I cooked them special for you."

Without response he called to the men exploring the porch. The men were trying to peek into the house, but curtains and some shutters were closed. They turned, calling out that they couldn't see inside.

"Why the shutters closed?" the officer asked brusquely.

"Going to be another scorcher. We close them before the sun comes up—just like every day—to keep the house cooler. It's cooler than opening the windows . . . at least for a while. Come back later, we'll have them all open. Course, the kitchen, it's always hot, so I keep those windows open. If they want to see inside, they could try the kitchen."

"No, they just want to make sure there's nothing . . . no food or someone to shoot at us as we pass." He smiled at them. "Sounds like we needn't look. They might have been tempted to burn the house down, but if he's with the Indiana 7th."

"It's the 19th. You can go right in the kitchen and see the whole house, if you'd like. You can probably still smell the bread in the kitchen."

"Let's get the bread. You lead the way. Does the barn store hay? Anything useful for us in there? For the horses?"

"Those Rebs emptied it. Took the horses, all but the overseer's. He hid it from them, and we weren't about to tell those soldiers where he hid it. We ain't fond of the overseer, but he's not a real bad sort. At least he ain't fighting to keep us in chains, not like those Rebel soldiers. He treats us good, most of the time. Only whipped me a time or two for talking smart to him. I suppose I deserved it then. The army took all the hay, oats. Left us barely enough to live on—and that's all in the kitchen. You can look if you want, but please don't take all we have left. Doubt you would. Yankees aren't like those others."

The officer didn't respond, but followed the two women as they walked leisurely toward the large barn. The men who had tried to inspect the house trotted to catch up.

The cook opened the barn door and entered, followed by the maid who scampered in behind her.

The officer was spooked by the maid's nervous movements and stopped the men. He called out to the women, "Come back out here."

The cook came out, squinting in the sunlight.

The officer asked pointedly, "Where's the other one?"

The cook perceived he feared an ambush. "Don't pay her no heed. She's a nervous one. The overseer threatened us with what Yankee soldiers would do to us, and she's afraid you will. Then that soldier said something wicked to her. She's in the barn out of fear. I'll call her out. She'll come."

"Do it."

"Mary, you foolish girl, come out. These soldiers just want bread. That's all."

"Come out," the officer called to reinforce the matter.

Uncomfortable seconds passed until Mary peeked out of the barn.

The cook spoke curtly, "Come out you witless child. They think you're hiding someone. Come out, or you'll get us killed or worse." She turned her head calmly to the officer. "There's nothing but bread in the barn."

"Why hide the bread there? Why not in the house?" the officer asked, watching Mary suspiciously.

The cook started to answer, but the officer cut her short. "I want to hear it from the girl. Why isn't the bread in the house?"

Mary pointed at the cook. "Cook's idea."

"Oh?"

She glowered at the cook. "She said not to tell you. Said if you treated us nicely, she'd tell you where she hid the bread, but if you barged into the house or burned it down and the barn, you'd never get the bread. It was her idea. All hers. She said she liked the North. We all like the North since you're coming to free us, but she said she didn't know what kind of soldiers were coming. Maybe bad ones."

The officer smiled, "I guess we treated you nicely. Open up both those doors. Men!"

The cook stoically watched as the soldiers without explicit command lowered and loaded their rifles, attached the bayonets, and pointed them toward the barn doors as Mary pulled the doors open.

"You," the officer directed pointing to Mary, "stay right by me." He pulled his revolver from its holster and pointed it at Mary's head.

Terrified, Mary looked questioningly at the cook, who reassured her with a nod, "You'll be fine. He's a gentleman. I can tell. You're just making him nervous."

The soldiers stepped carefully into the barn.

"What do you see?" the officer asked.

"An empty barn, like the woman said. Except I do see a little hay all across back of the barn."

Cook laughed, "That hay's making it harder to see the false wall. It's the pittance the Rebs left. That's where we hid our food last time, and I put the bread in there this morning. You can have all the hay. We don't need it, but there's hardly any left. I'll show you the hidden door." She chuckled as if to herself. "The overseer was going to hide in there, so you wouldn't find him, but he was too scared and ran south toward Lexington. Think he feared we would tell you he was hiding. He's not like marse and mistress."

"How come your owners haven't freed you?"

"Never got the chance, I don't suppose. It ain't easy to do anything like that when they already think you're a traitor with a husband in the Union army."

"Why don't you come with us? You can cook for us. We need some home cooking."

"That would be good . . . get a taste for freedom. But who would take care of the place without me? I got a daughter lives on a farm nearby. Don't want to leave her. Course now overseer's gone, it'll be nice and quiet. Think I'll stay, even with freedom."

The officer holstered his pistol and walked his horse behind the cook into the barn as the men formed a short skirmish line to search for anything besides hay and bread. Within seconds they had scanned the loft and stalls and reached the back wall. Cook followed and brushed away the portion of the hay covering the concealed door. She opened it, chatting genially as she worked, "Maybe Mary wants to go with you. That's up to her. She's young." She whispered aside to the nearest soldier, "She can't cook a thing."

The officer called to him, "What did she say, Givens?"

The soldier responded flatly, "Girl can't cook."

A cat moved inside the barn and one soldier spun around and fired his musket at it with amazing accuracy, killing it before realizing what it was. The maid screamed, but no one else said anything. The cook, apparently completely unfazed by the gunshot, began pulling out loaves of bread she'd been making for several days and handing them to the nearest soldier.

Men's voices were heard outside and glass shattered.

The officer turned his horse and galloped into the sunlight. The cook fought her fear, trying to ignore the noise and kept jovially handing out the loaves till every soldier had shouldered his rifle and carried a full armful of bread. Mary ran after the officer, appearing frightened to be separated from him. The cook heard a second gunshot, and Mary shrieked again.

When the cook handed out the final loaves and one of the Yankees had peered in to make sure nothing remained, she closed the hidden opening, stepped across the hay and scooped it back against the door. She was shaking slightly, but steeled herself and walked as steadily as she could through the barn, following the bread-laden soldiers.

When her eyes had adjusted to daylight, the cook could see a group of soldiers walking toward the road. She looked carefully at the house and noticed several windows on the porch had been broken. The mounted officer stood his horse between the men and the house and watched the departing soldiers. Mary stood by his horse. The officer called several bread-toting soldiers to him, instructing them to deposit their loads and return to guard the house until the army had passed completely. The cook relaxed for the first time all day. Caleb's plan had worked exactly as he hoped it would. She doubted they had had as much success at the factory and the mills and briefly wondered what it would be like to follow the soldiers. She glanced at Mary who watched the soldiers with longing in her eyes.

Chapter 13

Hank was dozy in spite of the excitement engendered by Grant's push southward. His idle conversation with Rivenshaw had waned, and he tried to keep himself awake with lavish thoughts of food and sleep. But slumber fought to conquer his visions.

As night crept slough-like, they frequently stopped to allow artillery wagons and cavalry to pass. Chaos. Shouting. Anger. Discord. Darkness. Confusion. No one was in charge, and Hank overheard bits of arguments about which unit should go first and which must wait.

Again and again, they halted, waited, then proceeded slowly. His legs were as tired from the slow pace as from the late hour. He sweated constantly, adding the salty weight to his already soggy, chaffing clothes.

He castigated himself for reenlisting. Why hadn't he relinquished the war and the Union and accepted a quiet, separate peace in the arms of the woman he loved, the woman who carried his baby? Why had he come back? He could have stayed with her, deserted. Why had the South abandoned the Union? Why were there slaves? That was the problem . . . the core problem. Wasn't it? If there'd never been slaves, none of this would have happened. He silently cursed the first European who brought slaves to America. Whoever he was, he stained every citizen with the blood and suffering of all the slaves bought or birthed throughout the years. The avaricious man was dyed in the blood of every American who now fought because he had committed the original American sin.

Hank recalled William, a Richman slave he had befriended. Had it been just four months since the former slave had pulled Hank's neck from the vise-like hands of a mad renegade? What had become of William? Hank tried to remember what William was doing when the runaway had saved him, but he couldn't. He hadn't thought much about William that day as they had conversed. His mind had been focused on the shocking death of his friend Naomi and his hoped-for introduction to an unknown—he wrongly thought—Confederate widow.

A sharp cramp seized his stomach, and he inadvertently grimaced. Hunger. Food. His mind painted an exquisite banquet on his memory of Betsy's dining room table. He imagined the two of them together as he sat artfully carving mutton while she watched with pride. William was suddenly at the table, and Hank cut a piece of lamb for him. A servant passed it to William.

Hank's head listed to the side and woke him from his brief nap. They still marched. He imagined them vaguely as an army of Frankenstein-created monsters, set on revenge and murder. Created to save the Union, they had turned on their creators—the generals who had stitched together these hideous creatures. He saw Betsy's face clearly, smiling at him; baby in her arms. He was suddenly jostled by the soldier behind him, and Betsy and child were gone. Replacing them was the night, the buzzing of cicadas disturbed by the march, the hum of men talking in the distance, the muted rubbing of men's clothes and accoutrements and the constant clanking of bits of metal here and there.

How long would this night last? He was on a beach and Betsy spoke to him with a British accent. At last, he had seen the shore. His head bobbed up, and his eyes opened to nothing. Still impenetrable night. Heavy lids drooped over eyes. He sat at a fire with his brother John who wore a dapper Confederate cavalry uniform and regaled Hank with the logic of the Southern cause: They were oppressed long enough by the mechanics of the North, the Yankee Puritans. Virginians were not greasy mechanics, but cavaliers: beautiful, elegant, offering sacrifice on the altar of tyranny-less freedom.

He was with Betsy and Abraham Lincoln. The president in Hank's voice explained why the North needed to win. Betsy listened impatiently, her face growing increasingly red. She was angry, and Hank unable to watch, ducked his head in case she rebuked the chief executive. As he ducked, he caught himself nodding. The drone of the march was in his ears, accompanied with echoing percussion of artillery.

The guns seemed real, and Hank shook himself awake. The sun—the real one—was lighting the horizon. When would they be put into action? The march stopped inexplicably. The day was already hot. Hank's eyelids slid downward, transporting him to the Richman's stable in Winchester where a strikingly beautiful woman affectionately stroked William's face. Hank envied William's comfort.

He'd thought the battle ahead and the sunlight sifting through the trees would keep him awake, but he was so tired, his limbs so heavy. He was playing base ball among teams of men in gray and blue. As the striker, he launched a ball high into the air, far beyond the farthest shuttling-backward scout. An easy ace. But Hank couldn't muster the strength to leg it to first. He wanted to scream. His mouth opened, but nothing emerged. Everyone was roaring for him to run, but he couldn't, and the men on the field, the men in gray, retrieved the ball, tossing it casually to first. Out! They had beaten him. He felt an arm grab him as he stumbled and was instantly awake to the rising battle din.

Chapter 14

June 1864, Richmond, Virginia

"**W**hy not slower?" Anna queried when Daniel proposed immediate marriage. "Can't we make it a formal wedding, not like something we're ashamed of?"

He took her hand, pulled it to his lips and kissed it gently. He raised his head and gazed lovingly in her eyes. "We're at war. Lives are cut short every day. I don't want my life to end without holding you in my arms . . . as my lawful wife. I've dreamed it so long." His expression turned to disgust. "I had more than enough time to think about it when I was recovering from that dog's attack. Wasn't it Jesus who said, 'For this cause shall a man leave father and mother'? I don't want today to end without our being joined as one."

She stepped close, wrapped her arms around him, raised her head to his ear, kissed it and whispered, "Nor do I. How do we do it?"

He hesitated, thinking for a long moment. "I suppose we go to the city clerk and register. We can quickly look for a minister to marry us. I'm guessing, but I think we could get it done this morning. Or just use a justice of the peace . . . if you prefer. We don't need to do it in a church, if you don't want to. God will surely recognize it as if it were a sacrament in a church . . . with war constantly threatening us, with our sacrifices for his righteous cause."

She glanced happily at the quickly brightening window. "We won't have to wait long. The city offices open soon." She stood and commented reflectively, "This isn't exactly how I imagined this day, but these are unusual times. Minister or justice of the peace: Either can join us before God in these trying times."

"Let's do it at once," he said excitedly. "We must think of practicalities though." He looked somberly at her. "If we get married, we'll need somewhere to live immediately . . . today. Do you know of a place that would do?"

"Why not here? At least for a while. My room is plenty big."

"Would your landlady allow it? If she would . . . and if it's what you want, we could."

"It will be wonderful. She would be delighted to have one married couple under her roof. It would make her abode a bit more acceptable, and it surely needs that." She laughed, but remembering his visible scars she moved from him. "Let's mix a little oil and powder to cover your scars. Not much really shows, just that bit below your left eye."

She busily mixed oil with powdered makeup, walked to him, moved her head close till she was inches from his face. Taking a small cloth which she carefully dipped in the tinted oil, she lovingly patted the cloth on the scar.

Anna awoke slowly to the light already in the room and stretched her legs, yawning. She'd gone to bed late as usual, following a resoundingly successful play. Such adoration from the audience. She had grown to love it, nearly depend on it. It took hours for the applause to filter through her mind, leaving her awake each night long after she lay down. Each morning, she awoke to thoughts of the previous night's ovation, and the memory would leave her feeling empty and lost.

Daniel was already gone, as he had been every morning since their marriage. She wondered and worried about what he was doing and where he went. He was so charming, so loving, so caring when they were together, except when she questioned his activities. Then his face would darken, his eyes contract, his voice grow cold. He responded once to her inquiries about what he did when he was away from her. "I do what I do. We'll not talk of it again." Such threatening interaction taught her to accept the excitement of his presence and surrender hope of ever understanding him. She accepted his absences as payment for their blissful moments together and dreamed he acted in some vital, secret capacity for the government.

On the day of their union, he had revealed he was working on a business scheme that would give them money to live, even as the value of the Confederate dollar was collapsing. He had brushed aside her fears, promising to soon bring her a suitcase full of money, enough to live in luxury with her wages as the dollar slid toward oblivion. She was convinced Daniel could accomplish whatever he wanted. Hadn't he freed Betsy from notorious Castle Thunder? She still didn't know exactly how he'd done it. Her earnings from the theater paid their room and board, but she hoped his scheme would materialize with an accompanying large house and garden, elegant dresses and gowns, tables of cornucopian feasts and peace.

She heard the door handle jiggle and turn, and in walked her husband. She smiled at him.

"Still in bed? The day's wasting, and I've already dealt a mortal blow to your pecuniary worries . . . as I said I would."

She sat up quickly, eyes glimmering. "That suitcase full of money you promised?" she teased, but instantly worried he would feel badgered and grow irritable.

"Ah, you remember that promise. Good. On this special morning, I fulfill it . . . though you have ruined my surprise. Is not your husband the most wonderful man in the Confederacy?"

She glanced at a medium-sized case he had hidden behind him as he moved it toward her. Her eyes grew wide and childlike. "Is that it? You've done it," she cried, as she jumped from the bed to hug him.

He laughed and pushed her away. "I have, and it's only the beginning. I can't tell you what I'm doing, but it's for the government. We can't talk about it with so many Yankee spies among us, but the money will roll in now." He walked to the bed and laid the case down flat on it. He made a show of opening it with exaggerated slowness, glancing periodically at her as he did, with a smile on his face. That smile widened as he saw her stare in amazement at stacks of twenty-dollar bills crammed in the case. He jubilantly continued, "So what do you think of your husband?" Before she could answer, he added, "I should have discovered this years ago, but it will serve us now even so."

"For this week," she teased.

"And next, you'll have another case of money. You are a queen and shall have your royal due."

His eyes were bright, brighter than she'd ever seen them, and they made her want him more. She hugged him, longing to question him, but she didn't dare because of his increasing bouts of moodiness.

He put his hand on her arm. "One thing I ask. It's not important if you feel otherwise, but let's keep paying the room and board with your earnings from the theater . . . till we get enough saved to move to a better place."

"Why? What difference does it make now?" She was sorry she'd asked the question. Would he suddenly turn angry or sink into bitter silence?

Relieving her concern with a warm smile, he embraced her, "We don't want anyone to know our fortunes have turned. If you keep paying her with the money you get, she won't notice. If she sees you paying with new, crisp paper, she might ask questions."

"Can't we answer the questions?"

"Of course. But our rapacious landlady might raise our rent if she knows we've money." He smiled more broadly. "Anna, what was the biggest mistake the gold diggers in California made early on?"

"Daniel, I know nothing about prospectors," she answered, her face crunched up in curiosity.

"They told someone else about their discovery before extracting all the gold they could. Everyone started mining for gold. Imagine if the first men had kept it secret, how rich they might have been. Let's keep our discovery quiet as long as we can."

She looked at him thoughtfully. "Of necessity and preference, I agree."

"Good. We're settled: You pay the room, board. I'll pay all else."

"Have you discovered gold?" she pestered.

"No. No gold. As you can see, I've discovered paper—just ink and paper."

Hours earlier, before dawn, Daniel had ridden in a farm wagon with two men through Richmond. One rode in the back on a large, loose pile of hay. The second sat in the front with Daniel and drove the two-horse team. The wagon moved slowly and quietly down the street. Periodic gas lamps lit portions of the streets, but left dark shadows over much of the town. The driver, a tall, thin man with a dark complexion, round eyes and short, curly hair eased the horses to a stop as the wagon turned the corner and closed on Confederate sentries posted under a gaslight. The driver turned his head to Daniel silently seeking guidance.

"Go ahead." Daniel said confidently, "We've a pass. We're bringing hay to town to sell to the army. They're desperate for it. Go on. Relax. The both of you. Jitters will alarm the soldiers like it does a horse."

The driver flapped the reins without saying anything, and the horses jerked the wagon forward.

"Papers," shouted one of the sentries as they approached. "It's early to be out," he added conversationally as the wagon stopped.

"Coming from the farm," Daniel answered casually as he handed the sentry the pass.

The soldier examined the pass as carefully as he could in the gaslight beaming from atop the lamppost and gave it to a fellow soldier, who took it without comment and strained in the pale light to see the writing on the pass.

Daniel could feel the driver tensing and put his hand firmly on his shoulder.

The second soldier said quietly, "Looks fine to me."

The first soldier took the pass back, handed it to Daniel and directed, "Move on." He added jovially, "Next time, bring a bigger load. That's hardly worth your trouble."

"We do what we can. These are hard times."

The driver, Jake, commanded, "Move." He waved the reins, and the horses pulled forward.

The sentry called out as the wagon proceeded, "One thing worse than being a soldier is being a farmer. We both have to be up too early."

Daniel chuckled, turned and replied, "The burdens we share, soldier. The burdens we share."

After travelling several more blocks, Daniel signaled Jake to turn south toward the James River and soon thereafter had him stop in front of a warehouse. The second man—heavier than the first, with a slightly lighter complexion and wavy black hair—didn't move from his perch in the back of the wagon.

Daniel jumped to the road and approached the warehouse carefully. It was dark, and he pulled a key from a trouser pocket. The night was warm and muggy, and he grabbed a handkerchief from another pocket to wipe at the sweat beading beneath his beard. He put away the handkerchief and carefully put the key in the door's lock, turning it. The lock disengaged, and he smiled, pushing the door open quietly. The inside of the building was pitchy black, and Daniel pulled a Lucifer from his pocket and struck it. A candle sat on a desk nearby, and he moved to retrieve it, but the match failed. He dropped it to the ground, retrieved another and lit the candle. He heard noise outside the building and left the candle behind to peek warily out the door.

His two companions stood awaiting instructions. He softly cursed, directing it at the two men. He wished they were his slaves. He would beat them till they learned to be silent when he commanded. He was nervous. A pass could get them around town, but explaining what they were doing in this warehouse would be harder—they'd certainly be sent to Castle Thunder if discovered. He returned to the candle, took it and walked deeper into the building. He'd never seen the inside, and while the candle did little to illuminate the structure, it did enable him to reconnoiter through the spacious, heavily stocked room. He moved swiftly, holding the candle to promising voids among the piles of wooden boxes. He found several tall stacks toward the back of the warehouse set off several yards from the wall. This gap would serve. He returned briskly to the front door, placed the still-burning candle inside the door and beckoned his two companions who waited close to the building. They were as jumpy as he was, and he worried any sign of trouble would send the freedmen scurrying.

His companions could see him silhouetted by the weak candlelight emanating from inside the warehouse and approached.

He whispered urgently, "Get those four crates in the building. Then Jake, move the wagon so no one notices it. Walk back to get us. Willie, put the crates in the back of the warehouse. I'll show you where."

"Where should I put the wagon?"

Daniel responded impatiently, "I don't care, just not here—out of sight."

Jake said nothing, and Daniel watched as both men approached the wagon.

"Willie, clear back the hay so you can get the boxes," he called softly. "Not like that . . . not into the street. Keep it in the wagon. We can't leave evidence we were here."

Willie didn't respond, but more carefully pulled the hay back, revealing—if it had been daylight—four, unlabeled, heavy wooden boxes. He lifted one carefully, grunting as he hoisted and passed the full weight of the box to Jake who turned with it toward the warehouse.

"Inside the door," Daniel indicated and watched Jake comply. Jake returned to the wagon three more times, carefully stacking each box on top of the others.

As soon as all four rested on the floor, Jake leaped toward the wagon seat, but fell slightly short of the target in the dark. He felt the edge of the seat cut his arm and cried out in shock.

"Curse you," Daniel whispered under his breath as he peered from the door. He could see nothing and waited in the doorway until Jake had recovered from the fall and driven the horses forward.

Willie followed Daniel into the warehouse entrance, where Daniel directed him to heft one of the boxes. In flickering candlelight, Daniel led Willie to the void he'd found earlier. Willie made the trip three more times, until the four boxes lay neatly stacked against the wall.

Daniel was relieved. It was done within the time he had anonymously bribed the night watchman to abandon his post. No one knew who they were or what they'd done, and they probably wouldn't notice it till it was too late. He smiled smugly.

As they climbed to the wagon, Willie asked, "Why couldn't we deliver it during the day?"

Daniel was quick to answer, "I was doing a favor for a friend. He needed those boxes, but didn't want to take possession of them officially."

"Is he going to gouge someone?"

Daniel sighed. "Since we don't know what's in the boxes, I can't say. We've delivered what he asked. Those boxes and all that goes with them are his now."

Chapter 15

It was past dawn, and oppressive heat of the day already weighed on the soldiers. Hank's stomach groaned and rattled. He shuttled along, barely raising his feet high enough to clear bumps in his path. Conflict raged nigh, but still Hank's greatest battle was controlling his eyelids that teetered precariously between open and closed.

Faintly in one of Hank's brief dreams, he heard someone shout, "Battalions forward! Guide center! March!"

He woke to a new intensity in the men around him; reinforced by energizing marshaling music and Rivenshaw's refreshed voice. Silent for hours, the Englishman had begun a nervous chatter about anything that came to his mind involving war: "Those Southern savages meet us with 'fatal balls of murdering basilisks.' Hank, 'if we are marked to die, we are enough to do our country loss; and if to live'"—he raised his voice till it eclipsed the noise of the battle—"'the fewer men the greater share of honor. God's will!'"

Hank didn't respond, barely glancing at his friend whose face was still grimy black from battle days earlier. Under normal circumstances, Hank would have smiled, but there was no sport in him. He concentrated, funneling every ounce of remaining bodily energy to advancing into the enemy.

Rivenshaw prattled again to relieve his own nerves, starting too low for Hank to hear, but crescendoing to such a ferocity and volume that Hank's thoughts were driven from his head as the Englishman bellowed, "'For he today that sheds his blood with me shall be my brother.'"

Hank dipped into a ravine and climbed to the other side where he first glimpsed the enemy's line. In the distance, Secesh had stacked tree trunks length-wise upon each other, aligned along a slight ridge above the 19th. Soft puffs of smoke followed flashes of fire that danced in syncopated rhythm along the top of the barrier, each wisp rising to merge in a massive gray, malodorous cloud above the ridge.

"'Would I were in an alehouse in London!'" cried Rivenshaw.

Hollers erupted from the charging Union line. They stopped for one volley into the enemy, screamed in rage and stepped double-time toward the fortified ridge. Fire from the elevated, trunk-fortified position cut them down.

"'Blows, blood, and death!'" shouted Rivenshaw.

They ran forward with any strength they could muster; up the slope till they seized the top of the ridge with cries of jubilation that were straightway answered with a thundering, threatening Rebel yell and a countering enemy advance. Hank fired at the charging gray figures, but they kept coming. He scuttled backward, keeping up pressure in the front with carefully aimed defensive shots at the advancing Confederates.

At that moment, Hank heard Rivenshaw as his friend led the retreat across the increasingly blue-lumped field, "'O that a man might know the end of this day's business ere it come! But it sufficeth that the day will end, and then the end is known.' 'Come, ho! Away!'"

Chapter 16

*May 1864, Freedman's Village,
Arlington House Plantation, Virginia*

In the dark, William softly excused himself to retreat to the outhouse, trying not to disturb Adam who slept soundly on a thin mattress in the corner. A single candle on the kitchen table and the faint glow of a wood stove situated in the middle of the only interior wall dimly lit the room.

Victoria stood at the table, wrapping a large chunk of bread in cloth. She tucked a scrubbed carrot and a thick, square of cheese into a worn haversack and stacked the bread carefully on top. It was hardly enough food for a working man's dinner, but it was what she had, and it was better than the army rations most residents in the Village survived on. The rations had provided the full coffee aroma rising from a pot sitting on the stove and the cornbread and a hunk of soaked salt pork that fried in a long-handled cast iron pan.

As she waited for William who was commencing his first day working on his own behalf, she thought about her life. It wasn't what it was in Kentucky, and she hadn't anticipated such drastic change. In this troubled city, life was unpredictable, less routine, more exciting; and she was bewildered to discover she thrived on the chaos. She put the haversack aside and turned to the stove, watching the kettle and wondering about their future.

Was this their normal life? Victoria had long wondered where they would land, what they would do, how they would survive and maybe—someday—prosper. Was this it: a horse, maybe a carriage; William working as a hack or something at a livery stable; she as a teacher among freedmen and children? It sounded frighteningly mundane. How odd. She'd not imagined herself adventuresome, yet alone in the faint light, she yearned for something new.

Was it right to do what she'd done? William was no mistake. She smiled thinking of him; remembering his smell, his touch. But the question returned. Was it right to flee Kentucky? She'd had to run and remembered their awful flight: fighting with marauding Yankee deserters; her friend, sweet Robert, dying as he rescued Adam and her; the horses they'd taken from the wagon; the smoke and flames as they torched everything left behind, including Robert's human body and the less humane carcasses. In her mind, the coffee began to take on the repulsive sweet smell of the rapid, whiskey-stoked fire.

Shaking her head, she pushed away the memory and scent. The three of them, William, Adam and she, had ridden through the woods to Covington, where William had stolen an unattended boat and rowed them across to Cincinnati and the train to the Federal Capital. By the time the train reached Washington City, they were stiff, hot, dirty, smelly and generally miserable. Their consolation was that no matter how dirty and unkempt they felt or smelled every other passenger in the car was in a similar state. The benches in the cars for slaves and free blacks equaled unsurprisingly the hardness of any other wood bench; but because she'd never sat so long without respite, they left her bruised, tired and sore. The low seat backs added to her discomfort. Sleeping was a trial as the three of them had leaned upon each other and against the bench back, shifting as a coordinated unit. For more than a day, they had ridden in that car.

Adam bore the discomfort easily. He slept following the slightest yawn. When he was awake, he entertained himself, standing on the bench—in spite of his mother's reprimands—leaping to the floor, walking from one end of the cabin to the other watching and listening to the other passengers, gazing out the window with excitement at the rapidly changing scenery. If new passengers entered, he ran to them, greeting them as if he had an official company capacity to welcome all new riders.

Even as she remembered the discomfort, she knew this new mode of transportation had possibilities. From the far reaches of Cincinnati, they had crossed state after state, hill after hill, mountain after mountain, bridge after bridge. They had arrived at Relay House, eight miles south of Baltimore, in less time than it took them to get from the judge's Kentucky farm to Ohio. From Relay House, they had turned south, with stops at the Annapolis Junction and Bladensburg, finally arriving at a train depot in Washington City and a new life in the freedmen's capital of hope.

In the lassitude of the trip, Victoria and William had talked of Washington being a free land for them. With every mile passing, they talked of increasing distance from Kentucky, from slavery, from the sorrows of their past. All three were free; but more importantly, they were a family, moving by iron horse to a promised land, home of their great liberator President Abraham Lincoln. Pride and gratitude glimmered through their exhausted, frustrated expressions, as they suffered the final few miles in the overly stuffed car.

Reality in Washington City dimmed their hopes quickly. They had been sent to live in Freedman's Village and found it much like slavery. A "generous" Federal master bestowed on them a place to live and food to eat, but ordered them under constant military direction, control and guard. The family had been called as many demeaning names during their short stay in the Village as they had in all their years in Kentucky and Virginia. Still, all of this was different. They had each other; and as long as they were a free family, they could endure it.

A light touch on her shoulder roused her from her thoughts with a start.

"Didn't mean to startle you."

"I startled myself—thinking too much. Here's your dinner."

"You didn't give me that bread again? You need to keep that for Adam and you. Give me hardtack. I can suck on it all day. That'll keep me going."

"You'll take the bread."

"Yes, Ma'am." He lowered his head humbly and added, "I still don't understand why you stay with me. You would have a better life with a younger, stronger man."

She laughed softly. "Someone like Isaiah?" she said, referencing a slave on the judge's farm who had badgered her continually to marry him. She had found him simple, boring. Isaiah, in his efforts to marry her, had belittled William's age—too old for her, he'd said. Isaiah had disappeared shortly before they had fled Kentucky. She hadn't thought of him in weeks. "Is that who you're thinking of? Isaiah? I thought you loved Adam and me. I thought you wanted the best of everything for us. We have the best already. Sit down. Eat some cornbread and pork. The coffee will keep you awake on the way to town, so you don't fall off the bridge. Isaiah? If I'd wanted to marry him, I could have. He was always trying to propose. Isaiah? Never talk about him. Hump. He was too young for me."

William waited fifteen minutes at Long Bridge before he could show his pass. He breathed a sigh of relief at being cleared by the military guards even though he knew he was innocent and should have had nothing to fear from the soldiers. As he stepped onto the span, he was mildly frustrated to hear a boat approaching. They would raise the drawbridge section and delay him longer. He committed at that moment to move his family to the other side of the Potomac as soon as he could make arrangements.

Once the bridge resettled and traffic resumed he crossed quickly and hurried through the city streets to the livery stable. As it came into view, he smiled with warm satisfaction, reflecting that he had a job—real employment—not serving a white master or an ill-tempered, dishonest and unfair Union officer; paid employment and money he could spend as he pleased. What he worked for would be his. No one could take it from him. Freedom was a wonderful thing.

Entering the stable, he strode briskly to the small office where a young man sat chatting with Erasmus. The man glanced at William briefly without acknowledging him.

"You were right, Erasmus. He did come back," the man commented, loudly enough for William to hear.

Erasmus responded, also to be heard by William, "Probably to get that sickly horse of his. He paid ten dollars for it, and it's ready for the glue factory. The boss . . . he give him a big job 'cause he wanted a glue-factory horse."

"Now it's dead, he'll have to get it there quick . . . so he gets his sticky money."

"I reckon he can do it. Mr. Bond sure thinks he can do anything. He'll heft that horse carcass to his shoulders and carry it to the factory, if Mr. Bond knows anything about choosing stable hands." Erasmus laughed.

William didn't respond, bolting across the wooden floor toward the ramp to the second level where they kept the horses. He heard guffaws behind him, but gave no heed. His heart was pounding. Surely his horse hadn't died. He'd seen too much promise in him. Had he been wrong? If he had, Mr. Bond would instantly reassess his new hire. William would be on the street looking for work, because without horse and money to buy another, his dream of hacking would become the unpleasant reality of renting himself out to the government for menial work, like many other men at Freedman's Village. He thought he knew horses and had counted on that knowledge to give his family a future in this overwhelming new city. If he couldn't judge horseflesh, his hopes were dashed. He would have failed Victoria. She would have been better off in Kentucky—with Isaiah—under suspicion of murdering a white man, than to be anchored to an old failure.

Reaching his horse's stall, he didn't see Judge momentarily. He almost panicked, but the horse was there. As William opened the gate and approached him, the horse raised his head to look intelligently at his troubled, harried visitor. William consciously squelched the anger arising in his chest, reminding himself they were joshing and meant no harm; merely playing a prank on the new fellow. "You're no Judge, you're Lazarus, come back to life." A slow smile crossed his face as he added, "Yes, Lazarus, that must be your name."

Petting and patting the horse till he came to its head, William recounted to the animal the story of Jesus raising Lazarus from the dead, a story Victoria had recently rehearsed for him. He stroked the horse's head. "Lazarus, you're going to be a great one, aren't you? You're not dead or old. You're not broken down. You're like me—just never respected."

The horse responded, nuzzling William's shoulder.

"You're already looking better. Didn't the army feed you? What a strange government, not to care for its horses." William grabbed a nearby halter, fitted it on Lazarus and happily led the war-worn horse down the ramp to the first level, past the small office. He commented loudly to his tormenters, "You were right. Horse died, but left a new, healthier one named Lazarus."

The two young men heard him, but kept silent and dropped their eyes, not daring to look at William or his horse.

William and Lazarus walked out of the livery for a one square block constitutional. William laughed aloud as he saw the sun rising between two nearby buildings. This new life was suddenly better than anything before: Lazarus nursed to a new level of life and living; he, himself, raised to a new bliss with Victoria, Adam and a mighty "steed" named Lazarus. He looked up into the promising morning sky and guffawed at his own silliness. Life was suddenly wonderful. No shackles could ever again hold them back. It was all there for them to take. They were free.

When he returned, Mr. Bond stood at the entrance to the three-story brick stable. William shrunk briefly from the encounter, but forced his shoulders to square, ready for criticism from his new overseer.

"Good morning, William. Sun's barely up, and it's already hot. It's going to be a warm one."

"It feels good."

Mr. Bond smiled pleasantly. "How's your gelding?"

William grinned broadly. "Much better with one day's food. They must have been starving poor Lazarus."

"Lazarus? You've named him?"

"Thought it fit. Already back from almost being dead."

"I do believe he does look happier."

"Yes, sir. Happier and healthier already. He's a great horse."

"A great horse? I may have to change the purchase price."

"Raise the price?" William protested.

Bond chuckled, pulling a pipe out of his jacket, tapping it in his palm. "I'm giving you a ribbing, William. We had a deal, and I'll stick to it," he said, grinning, "even if he does end up being the best horse in the Union."

Gazing admiringly at the horse, William boasted, "He just might be. I'll put him back in the stall and get to work."

"Fine." Mr. Bond remained as he was, enjoying the morning light as William passed.

As William led Lazarus up the ramp, Erasmus sidled up to him. "I'm sorry, brother."

Too pleased with Lazarus's improvement to be bothered by the earlier jape, William responded cheerfully, "That's fine."

"It's young Robert. He gets carried away and doesn't like new folks."

"I'm fine, Erasmus. Truly am."

"He's jealous, not that he could do what you have to do."

William stopped, shifting his gaze to Erasmus, his eyes betraying increasing irritation. "Erasmus, you don't have to say that. Everything's all right. I don't have bad feelings toward you. You were just larking. It's . . . I'm fine."

Erasmus's shoulders relaxed. "I'm glad. I shouldn't have gone along. I should have stuck up for you."

"Doesn't matter. You got to stick up for Robert now." Wanting to end the conversation, William excused himself by commenting, "I got to get Lazarus back to his stall. Lots of work to do."

"William, I am your friend."

"Didn't doubt that. Hope you're Robert's friend, too."

"Oh, I am. I am."

"Good."

Chapter 17

May 1864, Laurel Hill, Virginia

How long had the constant battling raged? Hank tried to count the days but was too tired to concentrate as he once again marched in nearly comatose exhaustion from one more futile battle. How far could they push him? How many times had they charged that hill? He counted: One. Two. Three.

His count was disrupted by unwanted memories of men dying around him during the battle and their final screams. He shivered, remembering the cries of the wounded caught helplessly in a small, ragged cedar grove as it ignited into deadly flames. He cringed, hearing again in his mind their groans and shrieks, knowing they were his friends and that he didn't . . . couldn't do anything to save them. But even in the dreadful moment, he couldn't cover his ears and pretend it wasn't happening. It was real, happening to real human beings; men he had fought shoulder to shoulder with; men who had protected his flank; men he would have given his life for; men who would have given theirs for him. Yet he couldn't reach them to pull them from the blaze. He hated war. More than anything else he wanted to get away . . . alive. He wanted to think about something else, divert his mind, and he renewed his count: Four. Five. Six. Seven.

Had they really charged seven times? No. He'd forgotten one. Eight times. With no success. Useless. Futile. Precious life wasted. He had been and was still angry at the generals for ordering the charges. No troops had supported the attacks. They had been sent alone on an impossible task—to take a well-fortified enemy.

He craved the chance of firing down on the enemy from a heavily fortified hill as the enemy had done mercilessly upon them eight times. Lunacy. What qualified a man to be a general? Idiocy? Insanity? Both? He'd had modest hopes for Grant—hopes he would change things, not just multiply the numbers dying and disfigured.

Chapter 18

July 1864, Richmond, Virginia

Weeks after his nighttime task at the unguarded warehouse, Daniel sat at the table reading the newspaper. His wife was waking. She yawned, stretched her body its full length, and rolled over to look at him. He was smiling slyly, and she was curious of the cause. She didn't dare ask, but watched silently, trying to see what part of the paper he was reading.

Anna leisurely rose, wrapped herself in a gown, walked around behind him, and laid her hands lightly on his shoulders. She bent down to kiss the top of his head and noted the page he was perusing. She'd read it later after he'd gone out, which he did day and night. He ignored her touch and kiss, and she said softly, "Morning."

Impatiently folding the newspaper, Daniel placed it on the table and stood up. He turned toward her, pulled her close and kissed her. "Oh, how wonderful it is to be married," he said as he tightened his grip around her, kissing her again.

"You're hurting me."

He squeezed her more tightly. "It's my love. I can't contain it."

She wiggled against the pressure, but he had trapped her arms at her side.

He kissed her again. She pulled her head back.

"What's the matter, Love? In one of your moods today? They seem constant now. What's wrong with you? You hid this morose, rebellious side until you trapped me in this suffocating marriage." Knitting his brow, he looked at her sternly. "Never mind, I suppose it's just you." He emphasized "you" and, smiling, began to release her. But he stopped, again squeezing her in his tight grip. "One more kiss," he commanded and kissed her hard as she struggled to free herself.

He let her break from him, and she immediately turned away, wiping her face and lips in disgust.

He laughed. "You can't be satisfied with one kiss." He moved after her, and she spun around to face him.

"Enough!" she commanded with fury in her eyes.

"Enough? Oh, my dear, I'm your husband. Don't you dare tell me 'enough.' You can care for me, feed me, house me, but you can never order me. I think you know that now. You've learned that, haven't you? You must always show me, your husband, the deepest respect. You may command vast audiences when you're on stage, but here . . . everywhere and always, I command you."

Letting her emotions overcome her, Anna turned from him. "Am I so stupid I let you marry me . . . so you could stay in this room and use me as you want? You're evil." She regretted saying it the second it crossed her lips. She had tried to act content as his treatment had turned increasingly brutal, carefully disguising her rapidly growing fear and abhorrence—substituting a feigned total submission—in the hope she could slip away unexpectedly at some fortuitous future moment. After the play the previous evening, she'd decided to run; although she had no place to go, no elaborate plans. Now he would know what she was thinking, what she felt; making it harder to flee.

With her back to him, she realized fully for the first time in their month-long marriage that his relationship with Betsy was not as he portrayed it. The dog in the prison certainly had saved Betsy from some harm planned by Daniel. She hoped Betsy was safe, but doubted she was. Anna was reexamining everything Daniel had ever told her, conversation by conversation, line by line, lie by lie, manipulation by manipulation. Her horror and anxiety flourished as she completed a mental portrait of his depraved character.

"Yes," he responded softly.

She turned to find him regarding her affectionately.

"Yes?" she demanded.

"You are stupid." He smiled kindly. "All women are. Every one I've known. Stupid. Pawns to be moved on the board. Soulless creatures . . . or you wouldn't watch silently as horrible things happen around you. This whole war is your fault. All the women who stand silently and let men butcher others. Yet it's not in silence that you watch. No. You cheer them on. Huzzah. Send the brave, handsome boys to fight. An awful specie: women. I know you would willingly stand mute as a boy is beaten by his drunken father day in and day out. No, I'm wrong: You'd surely join in. They say Eve ate of the fruit, and you must be punished. God's gift to you is that you are fools, and he commands us men to mete out divine punishment—punishment that every one of you deserves . . . demands. That's what the law says, and the law is wise, and God expects it."

He was crazy. His rant was irrational, but it further angered her, and she verbally released her fury in palpable bitterness, "I know what you are."

Softly he answered, "A faithful husband." He grabbed her wrist and squeezed, pulling her toward him. "I'm honored you hold me in such great esteem, and I must agree."

"You're hurting me," she screamed.

"Ah, you've discovered my intention—yet only now. Yes. Stupid. A dolt." His voice was a cold tone she'd not heard before. "Now you comprehend I can and will hurt you because I must. You merit it so." He smiled wickedly. "We need no more misapprehensions, no more games of deceit . . . because you will do what you must, because you know what I would happily do if you don't."

He twisted her arm backwards, grimacing threateningly as he did it. She shrieked and tried to move her body in the same direction to undo the twisting.

"I've heard no answer to my question, unless that yelp was your submission to your lord. Was it that?"

"Yes," she said haltingly as the pain increased.

He let go. "I knew you'd understand. You're intelligent in spite of your sex." He walked to the window and looked at the city. "Here are the rules my dear wife—a faithful . . . a loving wife—will live by in your temptation to rebel against your lawful ruler and god."

He looked at her. "I own you as surely as if you were an African: your body and soul." He chuckled. "You are my slave. Don't think you can find protection in the law. I am your law. You will never question anything I do. I thought you knew that, but it does take time to train a dog. You will not ask where I go or when I'll return. You won't talk to anyone else about me, except to laud your loving husband and proclaim your delirious happiness. You'll worship me. You'll be grateful I let you talk to anyone at all. And I won't if you don't obey my every whim. If anyone asks, you'll explain the heavenly news that you are with my child. You'll say you're suffering from the condition; that you must stay in your room. And that's where you will stay, except to go to the theater, perform and bring the money you owe me. You will take your meals up here. If you don't agree, we can cut this conversation short . . . and your neck. You are to fear me. I am a vengeful, omnipotent god."

Motionlessly she stared at him as he looked out the window and raved, but when he turned to look at her, she dropped her eyes. What should she do? He had enslaved her. Escaping immediate death would hinge on convincing him she had given in to him completely and that she was a petrified dupe. She loathed him but dropped onto her knees at his feet, imagining it a stage act, and began to weep softly. Keeping her head humbly bowed, she elevated her crying progressively. She squeezed tears from her eyes until she felt the sorrow of submission and real tears followed. "Don't hurt me. You are my lord."

With her head still lowered, she felt his arms reach down and wrap lovingly around her. She didn't resist, focusing wholly on feeling the submission as if it were the deception of the stage.

"There's nothing to cry about. We've had a tiff. We've made up. All is ordered. Stand. I acquiesce: You may stand."

She looked at him and saw joviality in his eyes. What a strange creature she thought, to be able to turn off and on his feelings at will. Did he have feelings?

He put his hands to her face and raised it. "Oh, tears." He wiped them from her cheek gently with his thumbs and lowered his face to kiss both her cheeks gently, then kissed her lips passionately.

Masking her revulsion, she put up no verbal or physical resistance.

"That's why I married you," he said. "You're beautiful, but a stupe. You need a master." He kissed her hard on the lips and pulled her up and tight.

Every particle of her ached to push him away, scream and run, but she said nothing and endured the embrace and his brutal passion.

It was late afternoon when Daniel finally left. He smiled and touched her shoulder gently as he walked to the door. As he opened it, he turned and with an icy glare and an incongruous loving voice proclaimed, "My Love, I won't be home before you leave for the theater. I'll announce your pregnancy and fragile emotions to everyone in the house and that you don't want to leave our room except to go to the theater." He lowered his voice to a whisper, "Don't you think that will explain your rebellious screams?"

Suddenly his eyes danced. He grinned widely, stepped into the hall and closed the door. She heard him turn the lock on the outside.

The first happiness of the day heartened her. She would never see him again. Daniel was so sure he could stop her from fleeing, but escaping would be child's play. She didn't give into the anger, hate, disgust and humiliation she felt or focus on the physical pain from his most recent aggression. The last thread of influence he held over her had broken in his forced embrace. The doubt about Daniel or Oskar—or whatever his name was—which had stubbornly lingered in her mind was gone, and she cursed herself for her own inanity. She would wait patiently till it was time to go to the theater. Once out of the boarding house, she would run. Her empathy with Betsy was complete. She understood what he had been doing to Betsy, what he had in mind for her, and it shamed Anna that she had played a role in another woman's humiliation . . . and degradation. What had Daniel done to Betsy in Washington? Had he killed her? Was she held captive and used in some house in Washington as she herself was in Richmond? Had he done this to other women? Why?

She shook her head in frustration. She would escape his suffocating grip. She moved to the newspaper he'd been reading, hoping for a clue of his intentions. She would then make sure she stayed away from whatever it was he had in mind. The back page—he'd been reading the back page of the Dispatch when he'd smiled. It was somewhere on the last page.

She grabbed the paper and rustled it as she, with overwrought, shaking hands, unfolded it. She glanced above the fold of the back page. Someone was looking for three blacksmiths; others wanted governesses to teach English; someone wanted tallow and damaged candles. Rooms for rent. Property for sale. Was he setting up a second house for himself? A gentleman exempt from military service was looking for work. She doubted he would want to work. Someone was selling condemned horses and wagons. Would that have been of interest? She looked through the many notices on the page, finding no concrete hint of his aims.

Slipping into a chair and sitting up straight, Anna concentrated, determined to uncover the motive for his smile, sure it was somehow tainted with evil intent. At once she was distracted by a repellant article about white boys and girls sold as slaves in Russia:

The shocking purposes of this traffic in beautiful Circassians are familiar to the world. Russia has long been laboring to break it up, whilst Great Britain and France, which affect such horror of African slavery, back up Turkey in every collision with Russia, and went to war not long ago in defense of the most beastly slaveholding and infidel population that ever disgraced the globe. How profound must be the hypocrisy which can connive, for its own interests, at a traffic in white boys and girls for the most horrible purposes, and shudders at the enslavement of African savages, whom their own forefathers sold into slavery, and who had been Christianized and elevated in the scale of humanity by their masters.

She paused to think about the article, uncomfortable with thoughts of little white children being kidnapped into slavery by the Turks. She shivered. That hadn't given Daniel pleasure. He wouldn't have cared about slavery of white or colored children. She looked again. Another article addressed the futility of hoping for peace with Lincoln. That wasn't it. He didn't care about politics. She flipped to the front page. Maybe he'd seen what he liked on the first page and was still enjoying the thought when she'd observed him.

A general order for the reserve forces, war news, a man lost a pocket book, a soldier offered one hundred dollars for a lost horse, a free woman of color offered a reward for the papers which freed her—she'd lost them. Kentucky was complaining the Union government was taking slaves from the state to use as soldiers. Yankees felt no shame.

She systematically examined the paper from top to bottom, left to right till she got to the Local Matters column: presidential pardons, murder of a baby; a Richmond man retained at Castle Thunder because he tried to flee to the Yanks; a second man retained at the Castle for possessing hordes of counterfeit confederate bills. They'd been found in his Richmond warehouse. A "very bad white boy" who stole ten dollars in the First Market was "committed for want of security for his future good behavior." A slave who stole meat in the Second Market was sentenced to be whipped.

She stared blankly at the paper. What would have raised his smile? She didn't see anything and gave up.

What could she take in her flight? Only what she could fit under the dress she would wear to the theater. Anything else might alert someone she was fleeing, and she wanted to give him no hint. He wouldn't realize she was gone till the morning, and by that time she would be beyond his grasp. She chose a few items, putting them on the table, and looked around the room. Was she forgetting anything?

She looked under the bed and saw the suitcase Daniel had brought—full of money. She had forgotten it. She pulled it out and placed it on the bed. It was locked. She looked at the door nervously. Would he return early? If he found her trying to open the suitcase, he would beat her. She suspected he would find some reason to beat her anyway. She grabbed a knife and stabbed and cut at it, eventually prying off the lock and clasp. She opened it and found it not quite full. She smiled. There was still plenty to aid her escape. She took as many stacks as she thought she could secrete under her dress and in her makeup case. With this money—deflated as it was—she could get wherever she needed. She closed the suitcase, broken beyond securing, and slid it under the bed. She heard a knock at the door and called out nervously, "Who is it?"

"Charlotte, Ma'am."

"What do you want?" she answered impatiently.

"The Mister said I should help you get ready for the theater."

"I don't have the key to open the door. Mr. Jefferson forgot and took it with him. I wanted to be undisturbed. I'm not feeling sound today. I have no way to open the door."

"Mr. Jefferson . . . he left the key with me. He said you weren't well—in the family way—but you had to go to the theater. He wanted me to take good care of you . . . help you get dressed, like always."

As Charlotte spoke, Anna moved quickly to conceal the money and clear the table, then called out, "If you have the key, you can open the door."

She heard the key turn and the large, gentle young woman stepped quietly into the room.

Anna, slightly disheveled, greeted her warmly. "Thank you. You are prompt."

"You don't look well, Missus."

"I'll be fine. I've rested all day. This condition can make a woman feel odd."

"I ain't been with child."

"It makes you tired and sometimes sick and sad—so if I cry, ignore it. I cry . . . I scream about the silliest things."

"I ain't noticed, Ma'am. Do you feel sick?"

"A bit."

"With all that color you put on, you can hide it so no one will be able to tell. Ain't that so?"

"I'll try. The way I feel, I think I'll take the makeup to the theater tonight. Put it on at the last minute."

"Are you ready to dress?"

"I am."

Chapter 19

May 1864, Jericho Mills,
On the Far Side of the North Anna River, Virginia

Rivenshaw, face sweating and grimy, chuckled. "We had our own civil war."

"I've heard something of it. It did in the king."

"In true French fashion—before it was their fashion—he lost his capital."

"Did it make a difference?"

"Well . . . he could never speak again." Rivenshaw laughed, but when Hank didn't, he continued, "The church lost power and the king, he . . . or at least his son lost power."

Hank chuckled, "I think this war's going to give our president kingly powers. It's working opposite of yours, Rivenshaw."

"No, it worked that way for Cromwell, too. But do you know the most important lesson from the rebellion against Charles?"

"No."

"Civil wars must be avoided."

Hank smiled, "A lesson lost on us colonials?"

"Yes, and on me. I stand imprudently with you."

"Tell me why you came. You're probably a spy for Charles's ghost . . . looking for ways England can take back the colonies."

"I confess to being the personal emissary of Charles I."

Hank smiled, feeling relaxed for the first time in weeks. He'd spent his morning with the brigade watching the bulk of the corps wade across the North Anna River, and took delight in seeing General Warren's engineers completing a pontoon bridge just in time to keep the feet of the Iron Brigade dry as they strolled to the other bank.

With no enemy resistance as they crossed, the brigade quickly stacked arms on the far shore and leisurely began preparing dinner—hot, steamy coffee and ham. Hank was hungry, and the smell of the warming ham made him more so. He lay down on the ground for a minute while the meat warmed and looked at the hazy sky. He closed his eyes pleasurably and dozed briefly, smiling as he happily dreamed of meeting Betsy for the first time.

While he grinned, Rivenshaw put his foot unceremoniously on his midsection and rocked him back and forth.

Hank's smile faded to a grimace of irritation as he awoke. "Let me alone. I was with her . . ."

"We're forming."

"We haven't eaten."

"Do they care? Gulp some coffee. Grab the meat. We're moving."

Hank stretched, stood up and looked around. Annoyed with Rivenshaw for disturbing his dream, he glanced toward the river and noticed a few artillery pieces had already crossed to the near side of the river. He retrieved his bayonet to stab his ham and raised the meat with his left hand to nibble on it as he swung his rifle to his shoulder. He grabbed his cup of coffee, still too hot to drink. Waiting for the order to move out, Hank took larger and larger bites of the half-warmed meat.

The brigade advanced as a thin line across a wide field toward a wood. Rivenshaw chattered about the English Civil War, but the colonial wasn't listening, lost in savoring the salty ham. The coffee had cooled enough that he took a long drink as they walked casually. It wasn't so bad a day: hot, yes; but strangely relaxing.

Hank glimpsed a bright reflection in the darkness of the nearby woods and stared curiously at the shimmer as he took another long swill of his coffee.

He pulled the bayonet toward his mouth for another bite but dropped it and the coffee as the woods erupted with flashing light, smoke, the piercing Rebel yell and artillery fire. Instinctively, he swung his musket down and charged with the line toward the woods. By the time he consciously realized what was happening and that he had no bayonet, the Union line had begun to collapse in a wave as bullets tore the air around him. The man next to him faltered, turned and ran toward the river. In response, Hank likewise spun and sprinted. Blind to others rushing rearward, he was absorbed with reaching the safety of the far shore.

A glimpse of Union artillery crews readying the guns, lowering them to fire canisters full of balls to deter the advancing Rebels slowed Hank. At first he ignored them still thinking of the safety of the river. But when he glanced back at the fast-charging enemy, he realized the guns were at risk. They might be taken and turned on the brigade. He veered toward the cannons, reached them and spun to face the Confederates. He and others who had likewise turned to protect the guns peppered the Secesh with rifle fire as the canons began a torrent of double and triple canister fire, cutting down the advancing enemy mercilessly. Hank sweated profusely and his stomach ached from his undigested meat and the fear of being overrun, but the Confederate onslaught dissipated like a threatening wave rolling harmlessly onto the sand.

Chapter 20

The nurse glanced uneasily over her shoulder at Victoria who followed. Her grim expression assured Victoria she too was uncomfortable with the dilemma—a colored nurse in a ward of white soldiers, doctors and nurses. Victoria fought to expel her own doubts that were quickly weakening her resolve.

She had felt compelled to volunteer. She loved teaching freedmen and women to read, but she had been agitated by a ragged parade of suffering wounded that had passed in ambulances as she made her way weeks earlier to see William at the stable. The groans and grimaces of the wounded had stung her as the ambulances jarred along from the men's disembarkation on the Sixth Street Wharf toward hospitals scattered throughout the city. Stepping behind the last ambulance in the procession, she had marched for blocks behind it. She couldn't keep her eyes from the ambulance's two occupants, neither much older than Adam. They lay on their backs, and she strained to see their young, ashen and agonized faces. She was distraught picturing hundreds, thousands of them—all like Adam and these two boys; all fighting for her freedom—suffering. This war wasn't only about freeing subjugated men and women; it was horrible torment and death parceled out generously.

She awoke the next morning cognizant she could no longer sit a safe distance from the war, enjoying its fruit without alleviating the suffering of the pruned branches. Teaching the newly freed to read was safe—too safe and too far from the conflict. She had to get closer. Many in the school encouraged her to keep teaching, but she couldn't after seeing those two boys.

When she'd first queried the government, its functionaries told her they'd be delighted to place her as a nurse, with her experience. They'd put her with colored soldiers. She bristled at the thought and remonstrated emotionally and definitively that all soldiers had done her people a great service, and that she could not limit her affection and attention by any criteria. Would they limit her to nurse blond soldiers, or brown-eyed youths, or men measuring less than fifty-seven inches? This would not do. She would minister to any needy soldier regardless of his appearance or his attitude toward her. She would do it, regardless of what the government said.

Her demands surprisingly had been met, and a Washington hospital superintendent had approved her to work—not as cook, cleaner or laundress as many freed slaves did, or as a nurse among dark-skinned soldiers, but as a nurse for any soldier. At her assigned hospital that meant white soldiers, and she was about to meet them for the first time.

Rejection by the distressed soldiers, regardless of her resolve, worried her. She had spent long, sleepless night hours for a week thickening her skin for whatever wrath spewed from the wounded. She told herself she didn't care what poison driveled from the mouths of nurses and surgeons, but needed only the men's acceptance. Silently she committed herself to ignore even that rejection, to work tirelessly to care for the torn, the enfeebled, the ailing, the broken-hearted. As she followed Nurse Rogers, she smiled, remembering William's astonishment when she had explained what she sensed was her call from God. It had taken days and countless passionate late-night conversations to convince him.

As the women walked to the pavilion, Victoria was gratified to have cleared so many obstacles. Still the coming reality of soldiers frightened her, and she fretted that the first hateful look would propel her to full retreat and the safety of the freedmen's school. Sweat glistened suddenly on her forehead, and she licked her lips nervously and knit suddenly clammy hands.

Far from her thoughts was her young son whom she had assigned to William's care. With his position at the stable stabilizing, William had excitedly agreed to apprentice Adam in the business. With utmost confidence in her husband's love and paternal competence, she had easily relinquished all worry for Adam.

Terror of rejection had resurfaced moments earlier when she entered the presence of spinster Nurse Rogers. Rogers, a tall, gaunt, middle-aged woman with thinning gray hair, had a tiny chin, deep-set dark eyes, large nose, narrow face and thin lips. She wore a small white cap and a dark dress covered by a white apron—both of the latter sporting dark, blotchy stains.

Upon meeting in the hospital general offices, Rogers had greeted her cordially, "The new laundress? Your arrival is timely. We expect boys from the front. There will be much to clean."

As the woman spoke each word, Victoria's pulse raced. She realized it wasn't merely the soldiers she needed to accept her. She needed this nurse, the surgeons, the ward master—everyone—to approve of her. She softly groaned, realizing she couldn't do it unless they included her as one of their own. She hesitated to correct Nurse Rogers's assumption and let her finish speaking. Maybe it would be easier to say she was the laundress. She straightened, sighed and said firmly, "I'm not here to do laundry."

"No? Do we need something else? Perhaps you're not assigned to our hospital. Do you know which hospital you're to report to?"

"I'm the new nurse."

A shadow crossed Nurse Rogers's face. "Nurse? The new nurse? Mrs. Richman?"

"Yes. Victoria Richman. I was told you expected me." She extended her hand tentatively to Rogers.

"Yes." She hesitated. Victoria knew she wanted to finish her thought with, "I . . . just didn't expect you to be colored."

Rogers quickly recovered her wits and extended her hand, grasping Victoria's fragilely. "I had been told to expect an energetic woman with vast nursing knowledge. May I ask where that knowledge comes from?" Doubt wound palpably around the question.

Victoria smiled. "I've read a bit and did some nursing on a farm in Kentucky, to help out the owner."

"Your owner?"

"No, Ma'am. I was free, both me and my son."

"Your husband?" the matron asked suspiciously, her deep eyes narrowing to a squint.

Victoria controlled her anger and offered softly, "He wasn't from the farm either, but he did escape before emancipation."

"Emancipation Proclamation. Quite a document for your people. Have you read it?"

"Preliminary or final?"

Rogers looked expressionlessly at Victoria. "Yes, you are as they said." She paused, her features communicated concern. "I worry you won't be accepted, that the men won't let you . . . . For some of them, it's hard enough when they first arrive to have a woman washing them, wetting their wounds, bandaging their injuries."

"If they're in enough pain, they'll let me help," Victoria responded quickly, sounding far more certain than she felt. "We can, however, never determine how they'll react standing here. Let us put the proposition to them in the form of an active nurse doing her best to comfort, befriend and strengthen them."

"Have you seen surgeries?"

"A few. I helped the fellow who passed himself off as a surgeon at home. He wasn't good. His surgeries were poorly done, sometimes just butchery."

Rogers mustered a weak smile. "Nurse Richman, let us test this proposition of yours by taking you to the ward. Ready?"

Victoria breathed deeply, responding, "My readiness is not to be considered; only my duty."

Nurse Rogers smiled slightly and abruptly turned her back to Victoria, walking briskly from the office toward the hospital pavilions. Victoria followed, also wearing a dark dress, the front of which was covered by a clean, unstained white apron that Rogers had handed her without comment.

To orient her, the presiding nurse took her into several similar tall rooms, each with a row of beds on both sides, each bed perpendicular to the long walls. Windows also ran the full length of the room, each propped open to the muggy heat of the day and the indistinct repulsive scent of the nearby canal. Mosquito netting was gathered above each bed. Men lounged or rested on many of the beds; a few stood in small groups happily chattering; and still fewer sat in chairs—some chairs sporting wheels. The expressions of the men who glanced in their direction varied from sullen to curious to indifferent.

While Victoria appreciated the hospital tour, her thoughts tightened her stomach till it ached as she imagined armless and legless men driving her in fury from the ward. Miss Rogers was talking about something, but Victoria couldn't concentrate on her words and followed mutely. Fear was conquering her. It was hot, and she felt lightheaded. What would happen if she fainted during her first visit to her ward, even before being exposed to the wounds? Nurse Rogers took her toward another ward.

Victoria almost bumped into her guide as Rogers stopped, turned to smile at Victoria and announced, "Here's your ward."

Her words "your ward" soothed Victoria. Nurse Rogers already included her in ownership of the men she would serve. Suddenly she was not alone. She wanted to reach out and hug her fellow nurse, but refrained and smiled at the thought of such an inexplicable embrace.

Nurse Rogers took her smile as an answer, so she pushed boldly into the ward. A few heads turned to them, but their arrival went mostly unnoticed.

Midway down the long room, on the far side, a bed caught Victoria's attention. On it slept a young man on his back, and at his bedside sat a slightly older man with bandaged eyes. Compassion pulsed through her. What tragedy had left this man sightless? Why did he sit by this unconscious companion? As she glanced at the boy, she imagined Adam in his place. Without comment, she shuffled toward the bed.

"Sir, do you need help to go somewhere?" she clumsily asked of the man with the bandaged head, not exactly sure what to say, how to help or what to offer.

The man tilted his head sideways, surprising Victoria by speaking in an accent she'd never heard. "Where would I go? No, I'll await my young friend awakening. It will be soon." His head leaned forward toward the bed. "'Sleep dwell upon thine eyes, peace in thy breast.'" He moaned, "'Would I were sleep and peace, so sweet to rest!'" He righted his head and sat exactly as she had found him, as if she'd never spoken to him.

Victoria wondered about his accent and why this bedside vigil. Was this a younger brother, a nephew, a long-time friend?

"What happened to your friend?"

Nurse Rogers approached from behind in time to hear Victoria's question.

"Nurse Richman," she said respectfully and softly, "He's lost a leg and had a blow to the head. He's not been conscious since he arrived, and what's left of his leg is badly infected."

Victoria turned from Nurse Rogers and addressed the blinded man, "Did you fight together?"

"Side by side we fought and fell. But 'thou canst not speak of that thou dost not feel.' Had you been there, 'then mightst thou speak, then mightst thou tear thy hair, and fall upon the ground, as I do now, taking the measure of an un-made grave.'"

Victoria stared at the man, a dozen thoughts cluttering her mind. "Romeo and Juliet, Act III, Scene III."

The man's head moved as if to stare at Victoria. "Are you sure it's Scene III?"

"Yes."

"I would have sworn Scene II, but I do believe you are correct. You know the Bard, my dear lady?"

"Not personally."

He smiled appreciatively. "What brings you to our little, dark corner of the world? Are you but one more visitor of the thousands from the great expanse beyond that come to praise, to hail, to comfort the maimed, dying and fallen throngs? To make us feel whole, though we cannot walk, though we cannot hear, though we cannot see?"

She knew she should have been prepared for it, but Victoria was surprised by the hint of bitterness in his comment. "I'm your new nurse."

"New nurse? I haven't yet tired of the last. No matter. It's hard for me to tell one nurse from another, as you all look the same to me, and although the doctors don't say, I believe you will look the same for a long, slow, dark eternity. I am blind, you see. I'll see darkness till I die and darkness beyond if there be no creator."

"Has the surgeon told you that?"

"No, he's said only an elegant nothing. Isn't it the same? I've given my sight for a nation . . . not even my own. My head hurts, and my heart. 'When my heart, all mad with mis-ery, beats in this hollow prison of my flesh, then thus I thump it down.'"

"Where are you from?"

"England, of course. Can't you tell? And you didn't no-tice that quote."

"I've never heard an English accent. Titus Andronicus."

"Never heard an English accent? What has happened to our colonies, when an Englishman cannot be recognized for proper enunciation of our mother tongue? We should never have given you your freedom. You don't remember which act?"

"You, sir, did not give me my freedom. No, it was you who enslaved me. Freedom, my dear brother gave me. Act III, Scene II."

"Enslaved you? Me? Never. You are mistaken." He had risen to his feet. "Nonetheless the world is a wonderful place when nurses recognize the Bard. Have you been on stage?"

"Enslaved me, sir, you did. If you, the British, had not sold my people into slavery, I would have been born free. You above all here must know 'all the world's a stage.'"

"'And all the men and women merely players: They have their exits and their entrances; and one man in his time plays many parts.'" He dropped his head toward the bed and spoke with enthusiasm, "Wake up, dear boy. It's marvelous. I've met the love of my life, and you recline mutely." His voice became sorrowful as he spoke the last words. "'I have no way, and therefore want no eyes; I stumbled when I saw; full oft 'tis seen,'" he cried.

She moved and compassionately stroked his shoulder. "You do have a way, sir. You are surrounded by friends. Your cause is not lost, but waxes toward bright noonday. We will help you through this dark time." She paused, adding hesitantly, hopefully, "Lear, Act IV, Scene I."

"Yes, yes. Lear. Won't you please bless my sweet eyes? 'They Bleed.'"

"They do nothing of the sort. Your bandages are clean and dry. Same scene."

His enthusiasm rose. "A nurse sent by God. A nurse who acknowledges my Bard. She has been sent from God to remind me I am not forgotten in this backward wilderness."

Victoria smiled, wondering at the novelty of a Union soldier quoting Shakespeare in an English accent.

"Tell me your name. I must know it. Imagine a nurse that quotes Shakespeare in a Southern accent in the great Federal Capital."

"Nurse Victoria Richman."

"And named for the queen. England has her Queen Victoria, and we have our Nurse Victoria. I fear to say it, but I do believe we the more blessed. Quote me something from Shakespeare. Anything."

"I think we've quoted enough Shakespeare. Perhaps another day."

A soldier, whose arm had been amputated and bandaged below the elbow, approached the blind man, whispering in his ear. If the Englishman's eyes had been visible, they would have spoken wonder. As it was, his mouth opened in disbelief.

He turned his head theatrically toward the whisperer and said, "Is my great love a Moor? Of course she is. Why else does she accuse me of enslaving her? Oh, sir, you shall not play Iago in my ear. Never. Oh, with the eyes of my heart do I see her beauty and claim her mine, and no jealously will part us."

"Enough of this. I'm here to help, and I have a valiant and loving husband who has already claimed me. With him I'll stay."

"Then let me worship you from afar. Allow me that, my Nurse Victoria Richman."

"There'll be no worship . . . or mocking."

"Can we quote Shakespeare?"

She smiled, "To your 'heart's content.'"

"'Her sight did ravish; but her grace in speech, her words yclad with wisdom's majesty, makes me from wondering fall to weeping joy; such is the fullness of my heart's content.'"

After this introduction to the ward, no soldier ever again mentioned Victoria's race or disparaged her for the months she worked in the hospital, and Nurse Rogers, amazed and pleased at the introduction, happily lead her new nurse through the rest of the ward.

Chapter 21

June 1864, Near Petersburg, Virginia

Hank, with fellow skirmishers, moved ahead of the main Union line. He had climbed through the deepening Union trench and crossed toward the Confederate lines watching intently the enemy trenches from where the Rebels had fired down upon them the day before. He glanced along the line of skirmishers and wondered how many would survive as they felt for Confederate resistance. Dread infused him.

The Rebels held their fire, perhaps hoping to devastate the skirmishers as they reached the trench. When Union soldiers neared the trenches, surely a solid wall of gray would rise to pulverize the thin blue line. Hank studied the nearby trench intently, poised to charge ferociously the last few paces. He took each step carefully, bayoneted-rifle raised. No one fired. In mass and without orders, the skirmishers broke into a run, bayonets gleaming in the sun. They leaped the small man-made crest to assault the defenders, only to discover the trench empty. The Rebs had retreated in the night.

Hank dropped in, hearing for the first time the main line advancing rapidly behind them. Putting down his rifle, he rubbed his eyes and tender temples; then examined the random articles abandoned by the Southerners. Someone had dropped an image of a young woman, and a cup and scattered cooking pans littered the ground. He smiled to himself as he picked up a button that had fallen from a uniform, remembering the button he had inadvertently taken from Betsy's first husband at Bull Run as he had gasped his last breath. Without thinking, he dropped the new button to the ground.

How everything would have been different if he hadn't hurt Betsy all those years ago and run away in despair. Regardless he would still be separated from her by war. He'd probably have been a Confederate and just abandoned this trench. Entertaining thought: This trench might be the intersection of the life he might have had in Virginia and the life he meandered through when he left the Old Dominion.

His head throbbed. Gunfire echoed in the distance, yet the morning was quieter than the day before. Had the Confederate army disintegrated? Was the war won at last? Had the constant battles of six weeks finally broken Southern will? It had his. His sole pleasant memory of that time was diving into the Chickahominy River with clothes on, cooling off, cleaning a month's mud off his clothes, washing his hair, trying to drown the lice that plagued him. Weeks had passed since his bath; and the grease, mud and lice had returned.

The thought that the Confederate army evaporated enlivened him. Maybe he would have another river bath tonight. He laughed aloud at the thought of needing an entire river to get the built-up muck off. The laugh hurt his head, and he responded by lowering it, cradling it gently in his hands.

As the main line approached, he was ordered to the front of the trenches. Peering ahead, he realized another set of trenches hovered above them. Silently, with musket and bayonet raised, he stepped slowly, cautiously across the gap between the two sets of trenches. Again no rifle fire threatened the skirmishers. Had the Confederates really abandoned both positions, or did they wait as he had expected earlier till the skirmish line was an easier target. As the skirmishers neared the second trench, they scampered toward the trench works, still without resistance or enemy noise. In unison, the skirmish line climbed double-time to the top of the works to find them also abandoned, except for a young Rebel caught sleeping and abandoned on the ground, left behind when the enemy had sneaked from this second set of fortifications.

Hank shouted, "Surrender," as he jumped upon him, kicking the Confederate's rifle away. The subdued man, awoke abruptly, eyes brim with fear and pleaded for his life. Hank motioned him out of the trench on the Union side. He obeyed, glancing back at Hank, unsure of his captor's intent. The last Hank saw of him, a guard was escorting him rearward. Hank sighed and sat down, rubbing the sides and back of his aching head.

Chapter 22

July 1864, Richmond, Virginia

With Charlotte's help, Anna readied to go to the theater. When they had finished, she excused Charlotte, quickly hid the money in her petticoat and makeup case and made her way to the door.

The relief of coming escape warmed her as she walked to the stairs and down its tread to the front door. Instead of pausing to allow Charlotte to open the door as she usually did, she turned the doorknob and stepped into the fresher, but hotter, outside air. A rain shower had left the air heavy and oppressive.

Anna stopped beyond the threshold, looked back and nodded affectionately at Charlotte. Perhaps she hadn't been kind enough to this loyal servant. No matter. Charlotte, like Daniel, like all the house residents, would soon lodge as shadows in her memory. Anna pulled the door closed and descended the steps to the sidewalk. She was free. She could turn right or left or cross the street: Whatever she wanted. Which way would most quickly ensure escape? She smiled, savoring the decision and breathed in deeply the humidity. A carriage sat at the curb immediately in front of her, or she would have crossed the street. Instead she turned left—away from the theater.

"Ma'am," the carriage driver called to her.

She ignored him.

"Ma'am," he called as he moved the carriage along beside her.

She still ignored him. How dare he speak to her? A slave talking to her on the street. Abominable. Look what presumption the North had caused among the coloreds with its meddling with the rights of slave owners. The slaves would surely rise soon to slay their masters in their beds. She was glad she didn't own one.

"Ma'am," he called, sheepishly, clearly embarrassed she hadn't answered. "The mister told me to take you to the theater." He added nervously, "I ain't doing this on my own. He made me swear to do it, no matter what you said."

She stopped on the sidewalk, mortified to acknowledge this slave and angered by his words. She glanced around uneasily to see if anyone was in earshot.

"What mister?" she demanded harshly.

He looked down at the bit of street between them. "Mr. Jefferson, Ma'am: your lawful husband. He said you were sick and needed to be taken to the theater to be in a play. He made me swear . . . or he'd . . . ."

This was not her plan. No wonder Daniel hadn't worried she'd wander off. He had planned to post this freedman on the street to guard against her liberty; an unexpected lock on her prison cell. She spoke sharply. "The walk will do me good. Take your carriage away immediately . . . or . . . I will cry out."

"No, Ma'am," he pleaded. "Don't do that. He told me I had to take you. I can't go away. If he finds out you wouldn't ride, he'll beat us both. He told me to tell you that if you wouldn't ride, he'd beat you. He said it was his responsibility." His eyes still stared down at the strip of street visible between carriage and sidewalk. "He told me to say this to you and to smile mean-like if you refused. He raised his head to confront her, a threatening grin across his face, "Get in!"

How dare he? Both Daniel and this . . .

He snarled, "Get in. Now."

She looked away as she quickly analyzed her options. Would this man kill her on the street, acting on Jefferson's orders, if she didn't get in? No, but he would report everything to Daniel, and that might prevent her escape. She changed her demeanor and plan and approached the carriage, "How kind of Daniel to make sure I was comfortable. To the theater. Now."

"Yes, Ma'am." He responded, chuckling to himself.

"What's your name?" she asked pleasantly as he pulled into the street.

"Willie, Ma'am," he answered cheerfully.

"Willie, are you Mr. Jefferson's slave?"

"No, Ma'am. I'm a freedman," he announced proudly.

"You shouldn't be, Willie. You should be someone's slave, and you should be beaten twice a day."

He didn't respond or change his expression.

"Did you hear what I said to you, Willie?" She was angry. "Don't you dare answer, or I'll have you whipped for talking to a white woman. I wish I had a whip in my hand to do it myself."

He remained silent.

She quickly regretted speaking so cruelly. She might have offered to pay him to free her and keep quiet, but it was too late. They would not be friends.

Within minutes, he stopped in front of the theater. He waited momentarily before climbing down to open the carriage door. He did not look at her, nor did she acknowledge him. Anna stepped carefully out of the carriage, reaching back to retrieve her makeup box. As she walked toward the theater, she rapidly reviewed possible escapes. None seemed promising, but she had to try something. She remembered the broken lock on the case in her boarding room. Daniel would know her intent when he found it. If she didn't run tonight, he would kill her. She heard Willie close the carriage door and remount the driver's seat. He was undoubtedly posted till the play's end. One man would never be able to watch the back, side and front of the theater. She would announce to D'Orsey Ogden, the theater manager, that she was ill and walk out the back. She had a leading role in the play of the day—"Silver Lining; or, A Lining of the Heart"—but someone else could pick it up.

Her plan worked. Mr. Ogden was understanding and concerned and waved off the inconvenience. Others in the theater expressed hopes she would feel better quickly. She knew some, who envied her rapid theatrical ascension, were delighted she was ill; but she didn't care. She wasn't coming back. Freedom was more important than feigned life on stage. She walked to the back entrance, put her case down inside the door and stepped outside as if to breathe fresh air.

Immediately a black man in a wagon—not Willie—spoke to her. "Need your wagon, Ma'am?" He smiled as if they were long-time acquaintances.

She moderated her response, smiling back pleasantly, "I have a show to do. Just enjoying the fresh air."

"Fresh air, out here, Ma'am?"

She snubbed him by disregarding his comment and stood still, pretending to relax for a few minutes before re-treating to the theater. Back and front covered. How would she get out? He certainly would have someone watching the side as well. He was as crafty in ensuring her captivity as he was in liberating Betsy from Castle Thunder. She wondered what Betsy had done to Daniel to earn his abiding hatred. Or was it like her experience? He hated her because he used her.

"I thought you were ill," D'Orsey commented, as she rushed past him toward the front of the theater.

She nearly ignored him, but at the last second turned and answered, "I am sick, and it's made me so confused I've lost my way about the Richmond. I'll find my way out." She turned and dashed away.

He smiled equivocally, not sure if she was serious as she hurried on.

When she arrived at the door, she peeked out. Willie still waited, watching the door intently. Her puzzled look shifted to a smile as she whispered, "I'm in a house of disguise." Quickly she fled to the back of the theater.

She stopped by Ogden's office. He was seated at his desk concentrating on figures in a ledger. She waited and finally cleared her throat.

He raised his head, making a conscious effort to smile at his newest theatrical success. "Something tells me we're going to have an interesting conversation, you and I. You certainly don't look ill. You're as lovely as ever."

"I need your help."

"Help?"

"I need to leave the theater, but men are at each entrance to stop me."

"Why?"

"My husband . . ."

"You're married? Has he come to reclaim you . . . discovered you hiding in full sunshine? I say go with him . . . but that would leave me one actress short. You have my help. Come to think of it, I expect you won't come back anyway if he's found you."

She looked earnestly at him. "I would return if I could, but I think I'd be in grave danger."

He looked calmly at her. "A loving husband? What must I do? I have a small derringer I could use if I have to. How many men are there?"

"I don't know."

"Take my derringer. It may come in handy."

He pulled the pistol from a box in his desk, paused, pulled out a small bottle of powder and a ball and proceeded to load the gun.

Anna watched him silently and took the pistol quickly when he had finished loading it. "I hope never to use it."

"You have it as a remembrance of me."

"I want to borrow a brown wig, a dress and a hat to get out of the theater." She waited, but he didn't respond, and she added tentatively, "Would you escort me out and walk a block or two with me till I get past the men watching me?"

He laughed unexpectedly, "The actress to the end. I want to see these men myself when I take you out. We can stash the clothes at a friend's house a few blocks away. You can emerge as yourself a safe distance from the theater."

"Thank you. One more thing: He may have the play watched."

"We won't announce changes in roles till after Act II in case he's in the audience. Let him figure out on his own you've slipped his lasso. That might give you a few more minutes."

"That would be lovely."

"Hurry. Get dressed. I do have a performance tonight," he said, pulling out his pocket watch to check the time. He rose from his desk, having given himself completely to the coming adventure and relishing his role.

She walked quickly toward the wardrobe and was soon back, still carrying her case with no stage makeup applied, but in every other way altered. "I've swapped my hat for this one from your wardrobe."

"That's fine. It goes with the dress you're wearing and the one underneath. Are you hot?"

"Frightfully so."

"Come, Madam, please take my arm. Pistol at the ready?" He held his arm out to her, and she took it, nodding to him. They turned toward the front of the theater as he proclaimed, "You must leave by the front, with your head held high."

She suddenly seemed shorter, older, less elegant, more fragile, less conspicuous than when she had entered the theater. He smiled as he witnessed the transformation. At the entrance, she told him softly where Willie waited, but diverted her face and eyes.

"I see him. You could have screamed when he tried to grab you. A hundred men would have come running to happily hang him for molesting you."

"Perhaps," she said. "It would also have alerted my so-called husband, and I would have lost the advantage of time. These are precious minutes." In spite of speaking to the man to her right, she positioned her head away from the road, toward the theater.

Ogden walked initially on the street side, but as soon as they had passed Willie, he slipped to the building side, saying, "We must be proper for once in our lives, Anna."

They walked past dozens of people, some of whom greeted Ogden. He responded to each by doffing his hat, leaning his head forward in a small nod, eventually noting to Anna, "None of them seem to recognize you."

After walking four blocks, he eased her to the right, and they carefully crossed the street and railroad tracks.

"His house is on the next block."

She sighed.

Within several minutes, they stood at the door of a dilapidated house, from which a colored man greeted them in response to the knock.

"Is your master in?" asked Ogden as he led Anna toward the door. As the slave stepped back to give them space, they entered quickly; Ogden closing the door behind them.

"He is not, sir."

"We need to leave a few items in your parlor. I'm sure he'll agree to it. I'll collect them in the morning." Ogden nodded to Anna who immediately stepped into a small parlor and closed its door. Within minutes she emerged, having shed her costume attire. Her posture and clothes, but for the hat, were her own.

Ignoring the slave, she started toward the door unescorted. Ogden followed her rapidly, thanking the man and reminding him he would be back for the items the next day.

Back on the sidewalk, Anna formally thanked Ogden for his discretion and help. Unbidden, Ogden walked with her until he was able to hail a cab. He placed Anna in it without a word and smiled at her. She nodded to him with appreciation.

As the cab moved northward, Ogden retraced his steps to the theater, entertaining himself with thoughts of the best drama he'd seen in months. He wondered about Anna's husband, but with so many odd things constantly happening around the theater—especially with countless soldiers sneaking to town for shows—he easily dismissed his curiosity. He was sorry to see Anna leave, but he had other talented girls eager to take roles she would have played.

When he arrived at the theater, he noted the carriage had not moved; the driver still alertly watched the entrance. Ogden approached him and directed that he move his carriage as he would soon be blocking the way for the evening's performance.

"I'm waiting . . ."

"I don't care if you're waiting for Jefferson Davis. It will not do to have you blocking the way. Move that carriage, or I will call the authorities. Whose carriage is it, anyway?"

Willie didn't respond but grudgingly drove his team forward a few hundred feet and turned the carriage so he could maintain his vigil. Ogden laughed. He again wished he knew the story behind their charade but shrugged and entered the theater for the evening.

Chapter 23

Three parallel rows of abandoned Confederate trenches would have made a happy day for the Iron Brigade. But the Rebels hadn't given such a gift, and after the 19th skirmishers passed the second line of empty trenches and precariously crossed a damaged railroad bridge, they spied the third row of trench works a half mile away. The brigade grouped and formed behind a protective ridge, hidden from the clearly manned fortifications. Midafternoon they were ordered to attack the entrenched enemy, and the 19th ascended the ridge. As it reached the top, the Confederates opened fire.

Without delay General Cutler ordered the brigade to change direction: to march along the top of the ridge. The Sesech responded with enfilading fire that cut Union men down as the blue soldiers moved across the enemy's face.

Hank heard Rivenshaw reciting Shakespeare. He enunciated the words not as an actor to entertain, but as a frightened man offering prayer. The distraction helped Hank weather the precipitation of bullets, but his breath still came shallowly, rapidly, leaving his mouth dry. He watched as men fell along the ridge.

"'Cowards die many times before their deaths; the valiant never taste of death but once . . . .' May it not be now, dear Lord. Not today, Lord. Not me, today, dear Lord. 'Cowards die many times before their deaths; the valiant never taste of death but once. Of all the wonders that I yet have heard, it seems to me most strange that men should fear; seeing that death, a necessary end, will come when it will come.' Not today, Lord, let it not be today. See me to the end. Let me see the sunset. One last brilliant sunset, oh, God."

Hank licked his lips nervously. This was a new experience. Why didn't they drop behind the protection of the ridge? Lunacy again. Idiotic generals again. He could still hear Rivenshaw praying.

"'I am constant as the northern star, of whose true-fix'd and resting quality there is no fellow in the firmament. The skies are painted with unnumber'd sparks,—they are all fire, and every one doth shine; but there's but one in all doth hold his place: So in the world, 'tis furnish'd well with men, and men are flesh and blood, and apprehensive; yet in the number I do know but one that unassailable holds on his rank, unshak'd of motion: and that I am . . .'"

The orders came to turn and charge the enemy. Hank swung toward the Confederate line and heard Rivenshaw shouting, "'Et tu,' Cutler!"

The men screamed diabolically as they pressed forward double speed, but their shouts offered no talisman of protection. They fell and pressure from the Confederate guns shattered their formation. The charge collapsed. Hank worked backward to the illusionary safety of a slight ravine, but the balls targeting them didn't stop. The ravine shielded them only from the front, not the two sides. Confederates poured musket and artillery fire into the depression stuffed with prostrated men.

Chapter 24

Job Rivenshaw had become Victoria's living shadow. He followed her from bed to bed and stood behind her as she took dictation from soldiers for letters home, or as she sat at her desk in the middle of the ward writing to families of soldiers who had passed, or as she organized medicines for the men. He walked beside her, holding her arm for directional guidance as she emptied and cleaned immobile patients' chamber pots.

Victoria encouraged him to sit by his young comrade, "so you're at his side when he wakes. You can tell him what's happened. He'll need a friend. He'll need you when he realizes his leg's gone."

"You need me more," he would answer brightly.

Their conversation seldom probed deeper than testing their shared ability to memorize effortlessly. Victoria, often inconvenienced by Job's attention, never complained and was unconsciously flattered by his attention, amazement and constant compliments.

Victoria fully understood that the Englishman's attachment to her added to her status among patients in the ward and even with the surgeon. Thus in spite of the inconvenience of having this shadow, she accepted it as an unexpected help.

It was late in the evening. She should have been home hours earlier to get supper for William and Adam. The night watchers were already on, and she had finished her final rounds among her boys, checking they were as comfortable as possible. She had written letters for three different soldiers and cried at one bedside as its tenant faded. She doubted he would be there in the morning. Standing in the door of the ward on her way out, she cast a last, endearing look at Rivenshaw, who had given up his attachment to her for the day when she announced she was leaving. He sat with head tilted downward as if looking at his friend. She wondered about the boy. What attributes did he have to attract as odd a character as Job Rivenshaw?

As she studied Job, whose eyes were still protectively bandaged, he began to sob, his body twitching spasmodically. He had been with her most of the day with few complaints, except harping periodically about his blindness. Now something stirred his emotions. Was his young friend gasping a last breath?

She hesitated to return to the bedside. If she did, some soldier would ask her for food, though it wasn't mealtime, or another would request a drink. One would plead with her to scribble one more letter to his mother; another would want to share news of a wife or romance far away. She would probably not get home for the night if she walked back into the ward. Sadly she imagined William and Adam scrounging through their breadstuffs to find something to eat before retiring, just to get up the next morning long before sunrise, sad they hadn't been able to tell her about their adventures at the stable or hear about each soldier who occupied a bed in her ward.

A summer thunderstorm raged outside, and instead of cooling off the hot room, it made it stuffier as wafts of canal odors blew through the open windows. She watched Job for several minutes. Periodically he would raise his hand to his face, below the bandages, to wipe away the mingling tears and mucus. Why would this man whom she had never seen openly grieve be suddenly unable to control his feelings and weep inconsolably?

Unconsciously shrugging her shoulders, she walked toward Job, passing a night watcher who smiled at her, offering, "Not gone? The work never ends."

She nodded in response.

Victoria reached the bed before Job sensed her presence.

His head rose, and he asked suspiciously through his sobs, "Who is it?"

"It's me, Private Rivenshaw."

"Thought you'd gone."

"I was on my way, but I can't leave you weeping like that."

With his head raised, as if he could see her, he sniffed and wiped at his face with his jacket sleeve. His tears had drenched his bandages. Aching at his sorrow, she retrieved a nearby chair and sat next to him and wrapped an arm around him. He responded weeping anew and leaning his head on her shoulder.

When he had emotionally exhausted himself, he pulled his head from its resting place, sat straight in the chair, and turned as if he was looking away. "I wish you hadn't seen that."

"Why?" she asked.

"A man shouldn't do that, and a woman shouldn't see it."

"Not cry? Ludicrous. Didn't Edgar cry at seeing his blind father? Didn't Lear cry at his daughters' unfeeling cruelty?"

"Merely a play."

She leaned toward him and spoke barely above a whisper, so she wouldn't be overheard, "By all accounts, these plays seem the essence of your life. You quote line upon line, in context and out, day and day. They are not just plays to you . . . or to me. You do yourself an injustice. These plays peer into the souls of men; into hardship and misfortune; into vain ambition and failed aspirations. In the face of cruelty and failed hopes, men of stature . . . of great fortitude weep like young girls. My own husband, strong as an ox— I've seen him cry in disappointment and exhaustion, in pain and sorrow. Why should you be different? You have lost your eyes. They no longer see. So please let them do that other great service for which they were created. Let them wet your cheeks and release your deepest sorrows. Let your screams of regret fill this hall and reverberate from Washington to Jeff Davis himself, so he knows what treachery has birthed. You are blind, but you have not lost your way—you've found it. You have lost your eyes freeing my people, and in doing a great service to my country . . . and to the world. Do you think nations still holding slaves can see your sacrifice and not free their slaves? I don't know why you came over. I don't know what you left behind. But I know you've spent all you have to buy that which could not be bought with money—freedom for a people in slavery . . . to make sure those colonies you claim to revile take on a new freedom, impossible a hundred years ago. Cry, my fine gentleman and friend. Mourn freely for your friends, for yourself, for me, for all of us. You have cause."

He was taken aback by her directness. His mouth, held open in shock, was speechless.

She watched him closely. He was no longer crying. At least she'd stopped that, but that had never been her purpose. She could tell he was a good, decent man. Not religious, not open and frank, but a good man. She wanted to lift his burdens. She wanted his wounds, wherever they were, opened, cleaned, aired, cauterized and bandaged, so they could heal.

"I'm not what I profess," he finally said meekly.

"You're not English?"

He chuckled. "I am English. That part's true, but I am no great man of the theater."

She didn't answer him.

"Do I distress you? Can we still joust with Shakespeare?"

"I'm not distressed."

"You saw right through my façade from the beginning. Didn't you? You already knew."

"As hard as I stare, I see no façade. I see only a man with a remarkable knowledge of Shakespeare—a man I admire for that trait and others."

"Ah, but I held myself up as a great man of the stage."

"Did you? I don't remember."

"Don't you understand? I failed in London. I tried the stage, knew all the lines, but was as stiff on stage as a Confederate soldier three-days-dead on the field at Petersburg. They made that clear—oh, so clear—to everyone in London. The newspapers praised the show and disparaged my performance." He stopped speaking briefly and turned his head from her. "They never gave me a chance to improve. I think I could have."

"None of that makes a difference in our friendship. You have not been stiff in delivering your lines to me. They have moved me . . . and others. I've seen their tears, though you couldn't. You've made me think in new ways. No, the stage where you have touched an audience is better than any of London. You've inspired many when you toured other wards in the evenings. I've heard other nurses talking about it—your soliloquies and dialogue. No, you have found an appreciative audience . . . a real audience that doesn't just applaud but is made better by your performances. You have become a great man of the stage . . . a stage that matters so much more than the effete theater of a city far away and—to us—unimportant."

He ignored her comment, replying softly, "I was raised in a theatrical family, not like the Keans mind you, but my mother and father were successful."

"I don't recognize the name of Keans, for all the influence you suggest they have. They've never touched me—not at all. But you have."

"Charles Kean, the son of a great actor, is a favorite of the queen—the other Victoria."

"While we share a name, we do not share memory or opinion. So for this Victoria, Charles Kean remains unknown and Job Rivenshaw is the great actor of this troubled time."

"Think of the Booth family. Great tragedians. Alas, I mention them to show I failed. I couldn't suffer that failure, so I fled to America." He stopped and turned his head toward her. "You can see why you should abandon me to my blindness. Go home. Forget I ever trailed you like a puppy."

"I will eventually go home, but I have no intention of abandoning you. I do, however, Private Rivenshaw, recognize a melodrama when I see one expertly performed, and this is one infinitesimal step from that. Straighten that back of yours. Quit pitying yourself because your grandeur could not be contained by small London stages. You fought bravely on the grand stage of battle . . . and you with your love of Shakespeare . . . and a remarkably good memory have entertained us; helped us forget our sorrows for minutes and hours at a time."

"I . . . like you have a wondrous memory. I'm always amazed it doesn't come easily to others."

"What pendulum swings you from self-pity to arrogance? You play the melodrama once more."

He smiled. "You are my greatest critic."

"It's good I go home every evening then."

"To the contrary." He lowered his voice more, "When you are not here, the room is as boring as winter camp. I'm left one task: To grieve young Hank. I fear he dies and precedes me through that final door. I'd push him aside and go first if I could."

"He's like many others who chose to sacrifice everything to make the world a place where all can seek 'life, liberty and the pursuit of happiness.' If he passes that last door, he'll know the price he's paid when he awakens in that blessed place where God accepts and rewards the heroics of the heart. The price paid will be paltry."

"I wish I had your faith."

"What roles did you take up in England?"

"None noteworthy. I imagined playing Hamlet or Romeo or Henry V. Instead, I played a messenger, a watchman, an attendant."

"In London?"

"Yes, in London."

"On the stage?"

"Yes."

"Then you are a great man of the stage."

"Don't mock me."

"I've never been on stage in London. Not a handful of people in all this city have been on a London stage, but you have."

"Not as Macbeth."

"That only means no one feels their thumbs prick as you come near. You proved valiant in exertion to reach the stage, where expectations must have been high, considering your parentage. You proved valiant in real battle. You are no Macbeth, because you have a good cause, not ambition-fueled murder. You have battled for the good of others, not selfishly killed a king to be a king."

"You try to make me feel better."

"I speak the truth. 'These deeds must not be thought after these ways; so, it will make us mad.'"

He smiled drolly. "Thank you, my dear Mrs. Richman. You have raised my head and my spirit—not exactly I must say, however, as the playwright raised the spirit of Hamlet's father."

She smiled wryly. "Sir, wander to your own bed. 'Rest, rest, perturbed spirit!' You can do nothing for your young friend. Be with those still alert, and leave the surgeons and nurses to revive him."

"If you knew him, you wouldn't say that."

"Why not?"

"He's the best of us. He confided in me as we marched to our last battle that he has a wife here in Washington; a child on the way. It was an all-night march, and I think he forgot himself and told me something he'd never revealed; something he meant to keep secret. Yet she's not been to see him."

"She's lost track of him in all the confusion," she offered.

"Will you search her out?"

"For a few last moments with him?"

"A few moments she'll forever treasure and recount to her . . . their child year to year."

She looked at him kindly. "I'll do that. Tell me about her. Do you have an address?"

"Alas, no address. She is nearby. Her last name is Gragg. You already know that."

"Yes. So I'll be looking for a Mrs. Henry Gragg somewhere in Washington City?"

"Yes."

"An extraordinary task. How are your eyes?"

"They hurt. Have you talked to the surgeons? When will I see again?"

Victoria frowned. "Have they still not told you?"

"They have, but I don't want to believe them. I hope they quietly, behind my back, speak hope."

"Private Rivenshaw, I've redone your bandages enough to discern you'll never see, and I'm sorry it's so."

He shook his head. "I knew the answer."

"You're not blind, I'm sure of it."

"You just said . . ."

"You see far more than you reveal. Your physical eyes may be forever gone, but your soul, it sees and knows. I'll put a notice in the newspaper to find her."

"Would you?"

"Yes." She smiled to herself. "So tell me more about your young soldier friend, so I can convince his wife I have good intentions in searching for her."

Rivenshaw's head tilted thoughtfully. "Let's see. He's from Virginia—the Shenandoah Valley, I think. He moved west before the war, and ended up fighting for the North. He has a brother or two fighting for the Confederacy. I think his family still lives in Virginia, but the rest—besides the brothers—are quiet Unionists."

"Where's Mrs. Gragg from?"

He squeezed his lips together and shook his head. "He mentioned her just once. I've known him for six months or so; since I joined the 19th."

"How did you get to be such good friends . . . in so short a time?"

"War does that to friends and lovers. When you give yourself so completely and depend on others so much, it quickly opens you to intimate fellowship, not easily found I suspect, elsewhere. Truly I liked him from the beginning. He, like you, knew Shakespeare—but not like you. We could have conversations that meant a great deal to both of us. We participated in debates in the camp. We debated slavery, President Lincoln, the secession from Great Britain." Rivenshaw chuckled. "His weakness was he was obsessed with that base ball game. Barbarous. I offered to teach him cricket, but he wasn't interested. He'd met his love and gave her everything he had."

"Base ball? Cricket? I know nothing of either."

"I'll take you to a cricket match when I get out, if such civilized undertakings can be found in this backwater town."

"Not base ball?"

"Never." He hesitated. "He likes Abraham Lincoln. He likes former slaves, but doesn't think they should be able to vote—I do, but then I'm from England. He thinks Southern generals better than Union."

"I don't think any of that will help much with Mrs. Gragg, but I'll try my best. If she's in Washington, wouldn't the army have contacted her? Wouldn't she be with him?"

"He never told the army about her. I'm sure of that."

Chapter 25

June 1864, Near Petersburg, Virginia

In spite of the shallow depressions Union soldiers had scratched into the small hollow behind the ridge, Confederates peppered them with deadly musket fire from both flanks. Hank lay exhausted and still in the hole he'd scraped out with his bayonet. He was plagued with an uncommon lethargy—not just from lack of sleep, not enough food and too much marching and fighting. His eyes burned, his head throbbed, and he shivered feverishly. His thoughts were muddled, his perceptions slow. When he moved his head, it felt as if his brain followed reluctantly creating slight delusions.

His stomach revolted as he curled in his hole, and he retched violently. As his muscles cramped, his back arched involuntarily. Minié balls pounded the ground around him in instant response. He tried to prop himself up to look around. Everything wobbled. He could see Rivenshaw huddled in his own nearby hole seemingly unconscious of the bullets whizzing around his English head. Hank pulled himself higher and futilely attempted to load his rifle. He rolled on his back and propped himself on the edge of his depression. He raised his arms along his body, lifting his rifle to shoot. Something punched his leg. Looking down instinctively, he watched with detached curiosity as his pants reddened near his hip.

He'd been shot. The realization came slowly, and with it irritation. Sick and now shot. This never-ending fighting would kill them all. He tried to move his head to the side and dry heaved. His leg and foot were numb. As he lay there, a ball hit the ground near his head. He was tired of this war. He was leaving. They could court martial him if they wanted, but he was going home. In a minute, he'd rally his strength, get up and walk home. Home? Where was home? Remembering his wife and the coming child, he tried to move but collapsed. He was hot and panicked and struggled to tear off his gear and clothing—cartridge and cap boxes, blanket, haversack, canteen and jacket. He was sweating, then suddenly cold. Where had he laid his jacket? He could hear Rivenshaw calling him from somewhere, and in response, raised his arm in a wave.

Rivenshaw spotted him and dug with hand and bayonet a shallow trench toward Hank. The Virginian slowly lost consciousness listening to Ravenshaw as he cried, "'O piteous spectacle! O bloody times! Whilst lions war, and battle for their dens, poor harmless lambs abide their enmity. Weep, wretched man, I'll aid thee tear for tear; and let our hearts and eyes, like civil war, be blind with tears, and break overcharged with grief.'"

Rivenshaw reached his comrade and held his head. He was weeping as an artillery shell hit nearby. It knocked Rivenshaw backwards out of the hole and into a silent stupor. Everything was oddly dark—completely black. He groped for Hank and the protection of any depression. What had happened? He slid down into the hole he'd found. All was darkness as he lay helpless and blind, disoriented, frightened, head aching, listening to the Confederate fire and the horror of the suffering wounded.

Hours passed slowly. The moans grew louder. Rivenshaw covered his ears. Why could he still hear? He'd rather see and not hear. He wouldn't suffer so if he could see the violence and not hear the pitiful pleading cries. If he could see, he could watch over Gragg. If he couldn't hear, he wouldn't have to bear the clamor of constant artillery and marksmanship all aimed at the 19th, trapped on the forsaken field. He wondered if it was night. How would he tell? His eyes burned, but he couldn't bring himself to touch them.

He thought of his life in England. Maybe he should have stayed at home and become a carpenter. He could never appear on stage in America; not without sight. Even before his injury, it was unlikely. He could memorize and recite unlimited numbers of plays without effort or thought, but he couldn't deliver lines with passion—he could never capture the hatred, the love, or any emotion he would have needed to be a great actor, maybe because he'd never felt any of those emotions deeply. He delivered memorized monologues on stage in a monotonous monotone; and now blindness. This is how it ended: His last hope for the stage obliterated in a blast like so many other explosions. But this one made him feel.

"Please let this day end," he prayed aloud as the pain in his eyes became excruciating.

Chapter 26

It was late when Victoria arrived home, but neither Adam nor William had yet retired. She surmised they'd eaten as she could see food was set out on the table for her where they both sat. As soon as she entered, they rose in unison and began marching around the room as in a parade, Adam carrying two pans and crashing them together. They laughed, William throwing his hands up in the air to clap as Adam beat the pans in a steady, joyful cadence. She smiled, and the exhaustion she had felt as she opened the door melted away as their warm excitement infected her.

"Thank you for waiting up, but certainly my arrival doesn't deserve the welcome Solomon gave the Queen of Sheba."

"Mother, look at Dad. He's the new manager of the stable," Adam proudly proclaimed.

She, eyes glowing, turned to William. "Already? I knew they'd soon learn how wonderful you are."

Adam chanted jubilantly, "Already! Already! Already!"

The marching stopped, and she noticed William eyeing her expectantly. She rushed to him, wrapping her arms around him, delighting in his responding tight embrace.

She spoke softly in his ear, "You are a wonderful man. I've known it, and others are finding out. I'm proud of you."

William smiled. "Can't believe he asked me."

"How did he tell you . . . and what does everyone else say? I bet they're jealous and angry. Will it make it harder for you?"

Adam piped up, "They are jealous. I heard them talking, but they all said he was the right one, if it was going to be anyone, because of his gift with horses."

William finally spoke, "Maybe they'll make it hard for me, but I'll ignore it. Victoria, he chose me. Me."

"Because he saw how valuable you are. You said he seemed to recognize that right off, when you bought that horse of yours. How's Lazarus doing?"

"Fine. Fine. Better every week. I haven't had a chance to take him out because I've been so busy at the stable. I've let others use him, and he's docile, smart and getting strong."

"That sounds like me. Is that why you chose me?" She laughed.

"Smart and strong, yes, but you're not so docile."

Still smiling, she ignored his reply. "William, I'm proud of you."

William released the embrace as she said the last words, contentment in his eyes.

Adam directed, "Sit down, Mama. Eat some supper. You're late . . . again. Dad was getting worried. He has another surprise for you."

"Has he?"

William glanced impatiently at Adam. "We were going to wait to tell her."

"I couldn't. She comes home so late, walking the whole way. I can't wait to tell her."

"Best you go ahead then."

"Can I?" Adam's eyes grew wide. "Mama, we're moving. We've been building a house for you on the Island, much closer to the hospital. We've put up a little stable behind so we can keep a horse and carriage to take you to the hospital, so you don't have to walk anymore."

"Built a house? When?"

"At night. We'd leave the stable as early as we could and work on it. When it got late, we'd build a fire for light. You were getting home so late, we knew we'd get here first."

"Are you telling me I've been so busy and come home so late that I never noticed?"

"Doing good every day. Adam and I, we're fine working on the house—which ain't much of a house. It keeps us busy, but it's not finished."

"Where'd you get the wood? You haven't spent all our money . . . the money for your carriage on the house?"

"There's enough wood around. Army leaves it behind all the time. We found a little here, a little there. We've been building it as fast as we could."

"How did you buy the land?"

"Remember the carriage?"

"You spent carriage money on the house."

"The land. I don't need the carriage. Working at the livery stable is working out. Thought maybe I didn't want to be a Jehu. I thought we could make it without buying the carriage and still get a house."

"You didn't tell me." With her eyebrows raised, she added menacingly, "I told everyone I was to get a carriage and a driver. What will I tell them?"

William answered bashfully, "I . . . we wanted to surprise you."

"You did." She smiled widely. "I had no clue. When can we move to this mansion?"

William responded, clearly embarrassed, "No mansion. A shabby shack. A rough shell. We'll keep working till it's finished . . . till it is that mansion."

"When can we move in?"

William shrugged, "Anytime, I guess. It's not finished, but we could live in it while we finished it. Roof's on. Walls are up. It would make it easier for Adam and me. Closer for you."

Adam interjected, "Let's move tomorrow. We can get a wagon from the stable and move all our stuff. We can be in our new home tomorrow night. You won't have to walk so far, Mama."

William looked at Adam and said gently, "Time for you to go to bed."

"Now?" Adam whined.

Victoria winked affectionately at Adam, reinforcing the command, "You get up so early. You need sleep, especially if you're going to move us tomorrow."

Adam began to complain, "But, Mama . . . Tomorrow? We can really move tomorrow?"

"If you want. I can't help. I'll be at the hospital, but let's move. It would be nice not to cross that bridge, and another family could use this house. Heaven knows the town is drowning in refugees."

William responded enthusiastically, "Adam and I will take care of it, but how will you find your way home tomorrow?"

"I thought you were to pick me up in an elegant carriage."

"Probably not elegant," William answered sheepishly.

Victoria smiled. "Inelegant suffices," and added after a brief pause, "after all, I bring elegance with me."

William laughed, "Sure is right."

Victoria ate her supper after she coerced Adam to his bed where he slowly fell asleep, listening happily to his parents talk about the new house and their unexpected move.

The boy's breathing gradually grew deep and rhythmic. As elation from the day's news and next day's plans waned, William noticed Victoria's jaw draw tight, her eyes narrow and her mind wander.

"Something you want to tell me?" he asked.

"About what?"

"What you're thinking about."

She looked at him somberly, "I'm thinking of a young soldier I left tonight." Her eyes filled with tears that dribbled down her cheeks.

William shifted in his seat uneasily. "Been talking about all my work—and it's not important, not like yours—and you've got something sad you're thinking about . . . something important, more important than a little stable."

"Little, William Richman?" She smiled through her tears. "That's no little stable, and that's a great responsibility you have. People need horses and wagons to get around in this town so they can plan how to win this war. Everything you're doing is important, and now you're the manager of a livery stable."

"It's not fighting . . . and it's not caring for the men who have been fighting."

"Everyone helps as they can. I'm still getting glares from neighbors because I stopped teaching at the school. They think that's more important . . . helping our people learn to read. Everything's important, but everyone has their own roles. For me, I can't think of anything I'd rather be doing—teaching reading isn't as important . . . not for me . . . not since I saw those soldiers. Sitting by a soldier and hearing him tell me about his girl back home, or even cleaning up after a sick boy or taking out a filthy chamber pot: It makes me feel close to the war . . . the battlefield. Some of them tell me what it was like when they fought. They talk about seeing a friend fall or the kindness of an enemy who found them wounded and thirsty on the field and left them a canteen filled with life-saving water as they retreated south. I'm no man, and I'll never fight with the army." She hesitated. "William, some women have dressed up like men to fight."

"That's unnatural . . . madness. Don't want you doing that."

"Don't worry. I'll never do it. I wouldn't want to. So I'll never know what it's like for soldiers . . . what it's like to be in a battle." She smiled sadly at him. "When they recount how it was, I can hear the sounds, smell the smothering odors, imagine the carnage and death. One young man—his wife doesn't realize he's in the hospital . . . that he's been injured"—she had begun crying softly as she spoke—"told only one friend he was married. His wife is probably at home thinking all is well while he lies in the hospital dying a few blocks away. I promised his friend—he's the man I told you about, the fellow following me around, always bothering me, always quoting Shakespeare—I promised him I'd look for the boy's wife and tell her where he is and what's happened to him." She stopped crying and wiped at her wet cheeks and eyes with her hand.

"Write her a note."

"I can't. I don't know where she lives."

"What's his name?"

"Henry. In that hospital bed, he's dying . . . a young man who's given . . . What did the president call it at Gettysburg? His full devotion. He's dying while we talk of new houses and big jobs."

William shifted nervously.

She saw it and quickly added, "I didn't say that right. What I mean is we are living a normal life. Sure it's not an easy life, but it's life. Yet at this precise second a boy's earthly existence fades."

"If you want, I'll quit my job and join up. I'd do it in a second." His eyes gleamed earnestly.

"I know. You would have already, but for your concern for Adam and me." She regarded him lovingly. "Do you think I could bear to have you leave us? Not now we're together as a family. That's not what I was saying. I don't want you to join the army. I'm sad so many are suffering, and I'm seeing a few of them first hand. It's not some blood spilled hundreds of miles away, unseen and unknown . . . read about in the newspaper. It's blood in my parlor, as it were." She gazed at her dress below the white apron. She picked up the bottom of the dress and raised it so they could both see it in the faint gas light. "Their blood has dripped onto my clothes; some from men who will recover; some from now legless or arm-less men; some from boys whose hearts have stopped."

William didn't respond. It occurred to him she really just needed to talk about what she was feeling.

She let go of her hem and the dress swooshed to the floor. "You are so important to me, you and Adam. You are why I keep going to that hospital and endure a world that seems too cruel and too wicked—all because they made slaves of us."

She hugged him and kept talking, "I might never see

that young soldier again. He'll die tonight. Tomorrow the bed will be empty. The night watcher will have changed the bedding, and it will be as if he never existed. It will be as if our lives never crossed. I doubt I'll find his wife . . . if she exists. She'll never learn what became of him. Maybe later tomorrow, they'll bring in some other unfortunate brave soul to that bed; and it will be his for a time, till he vacates it. The procession goes on and on, and no one can stop the violence or hatred.

"If they could let go of the hatred . . . accept us as people like them. I fear they never will though, even after this war. They want dominion over us, not just over the cattle and the fish, but over the black man, too, because our skin is a shade darker than theirs. Hatred: It will never die, so there will be another war, maybe a bigger one." She breathed deeply. "Jesus never gave in to the hate. Is there no one else big enough to reject the hate? Can I, can you . . . in Christ Jesus give up the hate?" She smiled. "William, you have let me talk too long. Thank you. I love you, but I think we best get ready for bed. You've got to get up in a few hours."

"What about finding that boy's . . ."

"Hank."

"I thought it was Henry."

"Yes, but they call him Hank."

"How can you find his wife?"

"Take out a notice in the paper. That's what I planned, but I'm too tired to think about it. I'll come up with something specific tomorrow." She grinned. "How can I think about it tonight when I've discovered I'm married to a stable manager? Think of that. I'll be the envy of all the other nurses . . . or at least I would be if my skin were white."

"You're perfect as you are."

"I love you . . . young man." She smiled at him gently and touched his hand.

Chapter 27

Rivenshaw knew the sun was down when the rifles began to quiet and men around him began moving from their holes, moving quickly to somewhere. He called for help, but no one responded. He lay silent and listened for a long time. The groans of men around him had grown louder. He sat up, moaning as he did. He would wander back to the Union lines. Which way? "'I have no way, and therefore want no eyes; I stumbled when I saw,'" he said to no one in particular.

He climbed from his hole, feeling his way toward Hank, touching the ground with outstretched fingers until he found him limp on the ground. Rivenshaw pulled at his shoulders and crawled backwards until he had pulled Hank completely from the hole. He turned his head trying to determine by sound where to pull his friend.

"I 'must embrace the fate of that dark hour'; darker than night," he called out.

He heard men approaching and lay down still on the ground, worried they were Confederates and that they'd heard him. One came near and seemed to pause as if to consider him but passed without comment. He wondered what the man had been doing and where he was going. Was he a Union man from a skirmish line going forward in advance of a nighttime assault against Rebel trenches? Was he a Southern spy, slipping across the field to tell Northern secrets? Was he part of a Confederate skirmish line stopping to admire the death and destruction as it hurried on as the vanguard of a nighttime attack on the Union position? Rivenshaw inadvertently laughed aloud at the endless combinations of possibilities that materialized in his sightless ignorance. Blindness, he mused, trying to ignore the agony, had opened a creative door for him. But his reflections stopped when he heard voices nearby. He could barely discern their words, but caught enough to comprehend they searched for the wounded.

He called out softly, and he heard someone shuttle toward him.

The soldier recognized his voice. "Rivenshaw, what happened to you, friend? Something wrong—other than being English?"

"I'm blind."

"Blind?" The voice, which Rivenshaw couldn't place, paused before repeating, "Blind. Poor fellow. Stay with us. We'll get you across. Put your hand on my arm. Hold on. Don't let go. You can follow us back. But first we've got to help a few others."

"Here's one. Unconscious," Rivenshaw offered.

Rivenshaw felt the man move toward Hank. He heard the soldier struggling to manipulate Hank's body. The man leading him then began crawling and Rivenshaw followed on hands and knees, concentrating on clutching the man's sleeve.

Chapter 28

William expected to finish the inside walls of the second bedroom in their simple, two-story house when he and Adam arrived at home after a long day at the stable. Finding Victoria sobbing uncontrollably at the kitchen table, he didn't get the chance.

Her tears brought a grimace of guilt to his face for moving her from the relative comfort of their Freedman's Village home. Even when the new house was finished he feared it would never be fit for her. Shame enveloped him and sorrow that he couldn't give his family what they deserved. Maybe if he'd had more time and money, he could have made it comfortable and cozy, like the home she'd left in Kentucky.

Adam tarried outside putting away horse and carriage. The pair had gone to the hospital to pick up Victoria about the time they thought she'd be released, but she'd already left. Worried, William had urged Lazarus on wildly; adroitly maneuvering one of the stable's carriages between several shaken carriage drivers and pedestrians.

William pulled his hat from his head, holding it meekly in his hand and approached the table. She didn't look up. It was worse than he'd imagined. She hated the house. She hated him. She and Adam would abandon him and return to her brother in Kentucky. She was waiting there only to get Adam. What could he say? He slinked into a chair at the table, dropped his hat carelessly to the floor and timidly reached out to lightly touch her hand with the last of his hope.

Her sobs slowed, and she grabbed his hand tightly. Neither said anything for a long time.

Finally she murmured, "I can't do this anymore."

William's throat tightened as he waited silently for the announcement that she and Adam were leaving for the protection of her brother.

When he didn't respond, she offered, "One of the young men—I think I told you about him—I thought he'd die a week ago, but he didn't. You remember the one with the blind friend, Rivenshaw, who sits by him every day, unless he's following me around talking about Shakespeare. The boy died this morning."

William waited for the rest of the news.

"Hank was his name, and no wife came. I put that notice in the paper to find her. It ran, ironically, yesterday. He died alone and had been sick for so long. He died, and only one faithful friend cared. Rivenshaw is insensible. He didn't quote any Shakespeare today. He sat by his friend's body till they took him to the death house. They'll bury him soon, if not already. I don't know why his death has affected me so; maybe because I've grown fond of Rivenshaw. I think I've begun to think of the two of them as one person . . . or part of the same. It hurts to see Rivenshaw so lost."

"I understand," William uttered sadly.

"Understand what?" she asked softly.

"That you've had your fill. That you can't abide any of it any longer: the patients; the hospital; this roughed out, pathetic house; Washington City; being tied to an old man. Now Rivenshaw . . ."

"What?" She squeezed his hands and pulled them to her lips, kissing them gently. "There is no old man. It's hard to watch so much death and suffering, and I'm not sure I can go on at the hospital. My failure there has nothing to do with you. I love you and this beautiful, growing house and our son. I could never grow tired of you. I could never live without you being by me. The Lord has given you to me, and I will cherish and cleave to you till death. I can imagine nothing else, certainly nothing better. I can't survive this without you."

He looked at her, tears brimming in his eyes. "I thought when I came in you'd decided to go back to Kentucky and leave me miserable."

She snorted an impulsive laugh. "Going back to Kentucky would be misery. You and Adam are my home. I do miss the judge, but I write, and someday he'll respond or visit . . . and see our splendid mansion."

"You're crying just because that soldier died?"

She frowned. "Just? William Richman, that's cause enough." She smiled lovingly at him. "It's not only his death. It's the constant river of blood and loss. Maybe if they all died right away it wouldn't weigh so heavily, but they don't. They suffer. They are so dependent on us. They become like family. They call us 'mother.' Imagine that. I'm younger than some, yet they call me mother. I call them my boys, my sons. When one dies, it's tragic; but the tragedy never ends. They keep suffering and so many die. I'm being morose, but talking is already strengthening me for tomorrow." She let go of his hands. "I can endure it one more day . . . for them. It was particularly hard though today to see Job—that's his first name—suffering so for his friend. I left. I couldn't bear it longer. I didn't know the boy who died—not really. He was so sick. I never had a chance to talk to him, to tell him I loved him for his sacrifice. I only imagine the boy in bed twenty-eight was celebrated by hopeful parents years ago—parents who could never have seen what dire destiny awaited their son Henry Gragg."

William started at the name and stared vacantly at Victoria. Surely many Henry Graggs fought in the army. There couldn't be just one. Hank—his long, lost friend—was a Union soldier. He'd divulged that when they met unexpectedly in Virginia, back when William still wanted to join the army. William had saved Hank's life that day by killing a murderous rogue.

He began to speak slowly, "I once knew a boy named Hank Gragg . . . from Virginia."

She looked interested, but unconcerned. "This one's from Indiana, but Rivenshaw did mention Virginia. A dozen men named Hank Gragg must fight in the army."

"Last time I saw him, he said he was fighting with Indiana."

Grim-faced, Victoria picked up and nervously played with a fork that sat on the table and thought for a long time. "This Hank Gragg was from the 19th Indiana. Could that have been him?"

"How many Hank Graggs do you really think are in the Union army . . . in Indiana regiments?"

"Not the dozen."

"Could it be my friend?"

She shrugged. "You would have had to see him to decide."

"It couldn't be my friend. He can't die, not after his kindness to me."

"You were close?"

"I must have told you about him. He treated me kindly when most didn't. He used to teach me stuff. He was in love with Betsy Richman—the master's daughter—and we all loved him."

Victoria picked up William's hands to squeeze them.

"It couldn't have been him," he opined.

"I suppose not," she answered, still holding tightly to his hands.

Adam had entered the room minutes earlier and listened to the conversation. "Papa, you've told me all about him: how he rescued your old master, your old mistress hated him, and how that girl told him she wouldn't marry him."

Victoria studied him solemnly. "I hope it wasn't your friend, but if it was, maybe that would explain the deep sorrow I felt . . . feel. If I'd known, I would have told you, and you could have sat with him shoulder to shoulder with Rivenshaw in his last days."

"I want to see him. Make sure it's not him."

"It's too late. It happened this morning. They took him away. He's buried by now."

"I'll dig him up."

Perplexed, Victoria queried, "Why?"

William raised determined eyes to Victoria, "If he is my friend, I want him to have a funeral and be buried properly."

"He'll be embalmed. Probably already was. They'll hold a brief ceremony, then bury him. He'll be buried with others."

"If they embalm him, it will take time to bury him."

"They'll still do it quickly."

William sprang to his feet, saying, "We've got to get there before he's buried," as he dashed through the back door.

She immediately heard him hitching the horse to the carriage.

He'd left the door open, and she quietly followed him out, closing the door behind her.

"You can't go now."

"Both of us have to go."

"What about Adam?"

"He can stay here. He needs sleep. Are you ready?" William asked as he finished hitching Lazarus to the carriage.

"Must it be now?"

"You said they'll bury him. It may be too late if we wait another hour."

"They won't bury him in the dark. Wait till first light." She looked at his somber face, finally responding grudgingly, "I'll go. I'll tell Adam what we're doing."

"Hurry. I'll light the lanterns."

When she returned, he helped her into the carriage and mounted the driver's seat. He prompted Lazarus, and the horse jerked forward, pulling them past the small house into the alley, then onto the street where William let the horse run more rapidly. The two gas carriage lanterns illuminated their path indistinctly.

Chapter 29

July 1864, Richmond, Virginia

"**V**irginia Central Depot," Anna called to the cab driver once Ogden had assisted her into the carriage.

"Where you going?" the driver asked casually as the carriage started.

"Shenandoah Valley. Staunton," she answered calmly.

"You want to go there?"

"Yes."

The driver glanced back at her, questioningly. "Did they reopen the line?"

"I think . . . I hope. I assumed . . . . I didn't realize it was closed." She thought briefly. "If it isn't open to Staunton, I'll go as far as the line will take me."

"Need to get out of town?" he pressed suspiciously as he turned to take a careful look at her. "Haven't I seen you somewhere?"

Anna ignored his last questions, beginning to be irritated and wary of such a nosey driver.

He didn't notice. "The Yankees have been burning the Valley. Destroyed the railroad at Staunton—station and all. In Lexington, they turned families into the street and burned their homes. They burned the Military Institute, but you surely know all this. Burned out folks in Staunton, but Lexington got it worse. Yankees also are pretty close to the railroad up north where they're fighting General Lee."

Anna was alarmed by his report of the Valley. "I haven't paid attention lately to war news. They burned homes in Staunton?"

"Everything in their way." He growled, "I hate Yankees." More reflectively, he offered, "If they do get to Richmond . . . I can't think about it. If the army pulls out, I'm following.

Maybe I'll go first. Course, Early came in at Lynchburg and pushed the devils back down the Valley. I hear he's up in Maryland . . . old Jubal. Least, that's what I heard. Hope he captures Washington."

"Have they fixed the line?"

"The line?"

"The railroad to Staunton?"

"That's what I asked you," the hack replied impatiently. "I suppose they have. Haven't heard otherwise. Are you sure you want to go to the station . . . Staunton? Fighting might break out along the line anytime. It's getting hot. Ain't it?"

It took Anna a moment to realize he'd changed the subject to the weather. "Yes."

"The passenger and mail train doesn't leave till morning, six o'clock."

"I didn't know," she sputtered nervously, thinking of Jefferson finding her before the train could leave. "I'll spend the night at the depot."

"Family in the Valley?"

Anna didn't answer. Tired of the conversation and feeling a headache coming on, she sat back in the cab, trying to relax by closing her eyes. But she couldn't keep them closed and soon watched the street warily worrying Willie had discovered Ogden returning to the theater and realized she'd fled. She had to get out of Richmond, yet the train didn't leave till morning. Her nemesis had hours to track and recapture her. Her fingers tapped nervously on the seat beside her.

At that moment, Daniel walked a nearby street, following a man in a Confederate uniform, inching closer to him with each step. This was his last bit of business in Richmond before returning to Washington to entertain Betsy, with a brief detour to the Valley where he would call socially on Caleb Moore. Caleb, who had driven him from Betsy's house, was feeling safe and happy, and Daniel yearned to rough him up.

The one-legged soldier deserved at least that for living comfortably on money and in the mansion that should have been Daniel's. He'd scare Caleb after he attended to the man who walked leisurely before him. The Confederate ahead of him had mocked Daniel when Daniel had served as a Confederate messenger to Washington, but the hands on the clock had turned: It was time for Daniel to belittle him.

He hastened his pace, quickly closing the distance. His heart beat rapidly. His hands trembled with excitement.

His target strolled slowly, enduring the evening humidity as he made his way home for supper. Daniel wondered what waited on the man's table and amused himself contemplating calling on the man's wife shortly and inveigling an invitation for supper.

He was close. Feet away. Daniel put his hand out as he reached him and patted him congenially on the back several times, saying, "Why, an old friend."

The man turned his head smiling at the intimate greeting, but didn't recognize Daniel with his black hair, beard and glasses and only nodded formally, picking up his pace.

Daniel kept up with him. "Don't remember me? We met in your office months ago."

"I'm sorry, I don't."

"Why should you? I didn't have black hair then, and you laughed at me as Oskar Dante."

Fear flared in the man's eyes as recognition came, and he staggered as Daniel turned his hand and plunged a knife into his back.

"A man must be treated with dignity."

Daniel pulled the knife out and thrust it in a second time, as he gracefully grabbed the officer's flailing arm, guiding him stumbling into a nearby deserted alley.

"Dignity and respect: a gentleman's due."

The man's eyes revealed agony as Daniel shoved him to the ground.

"Dignity and respect."

Daniel smiled as his victim struggled to reach the knife buried in the small of his back. His energy was visibly waning.

"I'm gratified that you see me more clearly and discern your error." Daniel smiled compassionately. "Your silence signals agreement, and I forgive you." Placing his boot heal on the man's throat, he pushed down with nearly his full weight till the man no longer struggled.

Turning away, he glanced at his hand and jacket sleeve bloodied in the work. Inconvenient. He would have to go home, clean up and change.

He moved quickly toward the boarding house, damp jacket sleeve hidden in his pocket. Willie would have already taken Anna to the theater, so he could slip in and change without her seeing this bloody witness. He had hired Willie and others to watch her. They expected to report their efforts and to be paid the following afternoon; but unknown to anyone, Jefferson planned to leave Richmond early the next day. Once out of town, it wouldn't matter what Anna did or knew or how angry Willie and his fellows might be at being swindled. For Anna, he would kindly leave a little of the counterfeit money under the bed to help her get a new start and maybe a new husband—a legal one this time. He smiled. She had been fun and had deceived Betsy completely. Without him, Anna could reclaim her life, such as he left it.

Under different circumstances, he would have dropped by the theater and watched her one last time to celebrate their time together and his dominance over her. She was devoted to him, in spite of the anger he'd seen earlier. But he didn't dare appear too much in public, not after killing the Confederate. He would forgo the entertainment and catch the morning train to Staunton. Anna was now just a pleasant memory, a fun diversion that had kept him from other memories, memories that dragged him back to a past he wanted to forget: his father, a brute; his mother, as cruel. He hated her most. Everyone praised mothers as loving and gentle; but through her, he'd seen what women were.

He still bore physical scars his mother had inflicted. Women deceived men. They looked so soft, modest, kind. He'd seen those qualities in Betsy. Then she, like his mother, rose up a living nightmare, accusing him of murder to drive him from what should have been his home. He would burn that house in a day or two—if Yankees hadn't already taken the pleasure. He hoped they hadn't. He yearned to light the Lucifer.

When he arrived at the boarding house, Charlotte looked unsettled as she opened the door to him and quickly blurted out. "She ain't here. She went to the theater like you said."

"Good," he replied flatly, walking briskly past the slave and up several stairs, turning so she couldn't see the blood on his sleeves. "Open the door for me."

"It ain't locked," she called up.

"I want to freshen up. Bring water." He stepped into the room, and leaving the door open, sat in an upholstered chair, keeping his bloody hand in his pocket. He closed his eyes to rest them briefly.

Daniel woke to thoughts of Anna. Noticing Charlotte had already brought the water he'd demanded, he wondered how long he'd been asleep. It was dark outside. He must have slept for hours. No harm. She wasn't back yet. He yawned, stood up and lit the gas light on the wall.

He scrutinized the room and realized Anna had cleaned and straightened everything before heading to the theater. He smiled thinking of her. Why did he have to leave her? She was a convenience, and thus it would be inconvenient to abandon her.

Slipping into the same chair, he fell asleep again ruminating about how exhausting revenge was.

Waking to the abrupt feeling of falling, he jerked and opened his eyes. He was sure he'd again slept for hours, yet Anna hadn't returned from the theater. He'd always planned to leave without her knowing, but he began to worry. Something wasn't proceeding as planned.

He yawned, remembered the bloody evidence he was still wearing and tore off his jacket, shirt and pants. He pulled a suitcase from underneath the bed and put the bloodied clothes in it; then he washed his victim's smeared, dried blood from his hand. He went to the wardrobe, where he pulled out a laundered shirt, pants and tie. He walked to the mirror and put them on, quickly knotting and adjusting the tie. He admired his image momentarily. No one could have imagined his impoverished beginnings, not seeing him dressed so elegantly. He returned to the wardrobe and pulled out a jacket. He looked at the open suitcase. How could he keep the bloody clothes separated from the clean till he could dispose of the former? He remembered the case full of money under the bed.

He could put the bloody testimony in it and drop it from the train when no one watched. Bending agilely, he pulled out the case. The lock had been broken, and it fell open as he picked it up. Much of the counterfeit money was gone, and he watched as the remainder flittered to the floor.

What was Anna up to? If she'd planned to turn him in, she wouldn't have taken money. She was running—running from him. The thought calmed him, and he relieved his remaining stress with a long guffaw. As long as she let him get out of town, he didn't care what she did. He grinned at the thought of her being arrested for passing counterfeit bills and the irony of her fleeing as he was abandoning her. Life was full of irony—pleasant and unpleasant. She'd probably get away with passing the bills, and that would be fine. The real problem was the destroyed clasp and lock.

He thought through possible solutions as he gathered the remaining money from the floor and stacked it neatly upon the bed. He carefully stuffed the bloody shirt, pants and jacket in the medium-sized case Anna had damaged. How could he close it permanently? He didn't want it popping open at an inopportune time. Another irony: He was worried about getting caught with dried blood on his clothes while a few miles away men slaughtered one another, and no one cared. Their clothes dripped with uncoagulated blood. He would be hung if caught, yet they murdered to both nations' acclaim. Wasn't one life of the same value as another? Wasn't that America's growing claim? Why then was it murder when applied to one insignificant life and praised as valiant when applied to many? The answer came swiftly: more men profited from war. That was the difference: magnitude of butchery and distribution of the benefits. The North sought to subjugate a whole people; he wanted to subjugate a few. No matter. His was the better cause, even if labeled murder by the undiscerning.

As he reviewed such social injustice, he wiped flakes of dried blood from the larger case exterior and packed his clothes into it. Eventually, he tucked the smaller one under his arm, picked up his hat, adjusted it stylishly on his head, grabbed the larger suitcase and headed to a nearby bar to pass the hours before the train left.

At sunrise, Daniel hailed a cab and directed the driver to the Virginia Central Depot.

As the vehicle pulled from the curb, he sighed. He was on his way, distancing himself from his latest murder. He had so much to do, and he must hurry to do it. It was helpful the country was split, so he could wreak havoc in the South before escaping to deal a final blow to Betsy in the North. At the moment of her final disgrace and death, he would be a free man, with no lingering obligations.

Such contemplations should have excited and comforted him. Instead he was buffeted with his usual loneness and emptiness. What would he do after he finished? To distract himself from the pain, he thought about Anna running away. Why would she do that? He imagined her flying farther south, maybe to Atlanta. Atlanta boasted a theater or two, and she'd find them and rise there as she had in Richmond.

Their life together would have ended perfectly if she hadn't instigated that final fight. It was sad that their sham marriage ended in antagonism. Best of luck to her in Atlanta.

The carriage arrived as the train was preparing to leave. Daniel paid the driver with several counterfeit bills, hurriedly paid for a ticket with several more, lugged his large case to the luggage car and boarded the train as it pulled from the station. He found a seat quickly and settled for a day-long ride.

Anna dozed to the train's rhythmical movement, exhausted after a sleepless night at the depot. It would take eleven hours to get to Staunton. As she had paced the station during the night, she was sure the trip would seem unending, exhausting and unendurable, but remembering what she fled made it worth the discomfort. She could survive anything as long as she was away from him.

Jostled awake by a seat companion shifting periodically to find a more comfortable position, Anna would open her eyes fleetingly, begrudge her inability to slumber and fall back to sleep, lulled again by the monotonous, pounding tone of the train traveling the tracks.

Overhearing someone boast of Early's exploits in the Valley finally roused her permanently. Yawning she listened to gossip of the general's feats in the lower Valley, Maryland and at the doorstep of the Capital. She looked around the car at other travelers, many slumbering in the hot, late summer afternoon light. Soon she would be off this wood bench and find a supper. With her stash of money—she could afford it and much more. The thoughts of food made her stomach ache, and she was embarrassed by its frequent and audible gurgles.

In the next car, Daniel had slept soundly until the train was west of Gordonsville. When he awoke, he observed that most of his fellow travelers dozed or were busy visiting. He casually stood up, placed under his arm the broken case he'd kept with him, and walked to the back of the car. He was pleased it wasn't the last on the train. He opened its door, looked out at the rails passing beneath him and as inconspicuously as possible dropped the broken case onto the track. He smiled in relief as he heard it crunch under the iron wheel of the next car. The bloody evidence was gone. He wandered back to his seat and amused himself watching fellow passengers, grateful to admit he didn't recognize any of them.

Chapter 30

July 1864, Staunton, Virginia

When the train arrived at Staunton, other passengers piled off quickly. Daniel waited, observing the crowd, looking for anyone who might identify him. He was grateful Anna had re-dyed his hair and beard black. No one in town would detect his true identity thanks to her magic and the glasses he still wore. Yet the circumstances required caution.

When the other passengers finished collecting their luggage and abandoned the station, he made his way to the baggage car, handing his claim ticket to the baggage master. With case in hand, Daniel hailed a cab and made his way to a hotel where he learned rooms were tight, with multiple boarders in each. But with the leverage of a pile of currency pushed across the desk, Daniel learned the hotel had one small room where he could stay alone. As he was escorted up the stairs, he was already planning an early morning excursion.

A midnight clock chime stirred Lucius Walthrope. He opened his eyes, instantly alert, and swiftly scanned the darkened room, surprised at how rested he felt. Excitement surged as he thought of coming business.

Reflecting on the random vicissitudes of his life, Walthrope sat up. Each day seemed to hold some new twist, some unforeseen bombshell. Yesterday—or was it the day before?—he would never have suspected Anna capable of mustering the courage to flee from him. She had possessed a spunk he had never recognized. Betsy also had it and in that moment it made both more attractive, enticing, challenging. Perhaps he should have kept Anna a bit longer. Yes, he might have used her to lure Betsy and her grubby Yankee into a final trap. He had relished having an actress at his command, especially as she gained fame. He spoke aloud, "I wasted her."

He recalled his confrontation with Betsy's Union private after she'd rejected Walthrope. The insipid soldier had—Walthrope conveniently twisted the memory—tried to better him as he fled from Betsy. But Walthrope had beaten him nearly to death. He should have killed him as he was the font of Walthrope's problems. It reminded him of something he had learned long ago: Showing mercy to an enemy was never wise. Yes, he should have killed him then. He walked painfully through a memory of Betsy revealing she knew Walthrope had killed Stokes, the factory foreman. Walthrope had been a word away from marrying her and controlling her wealth, but at that final moment she'd jerked it from him. It didn't matter. He didn't have all her money and possessions, but his first revenge on her had come unanticipated and unbidden, making sure her money would slip through her fingers. Her lunatic cousin had betrayed Betsy to the government because she had learned that the love-smitten—and well-beaten—Union soldier had visited Betsy. The imbecilic cousin had convinced herself, which was easy to do in her fretful state, that the couple had hatched an elaborate Northern spying scheme.

As he sat on the bed, Walthrope made a gratifying decision: He would kill Caleb. Frightening the cripple wouldn't be enough. Killing him would make it that much harder for Betsy, if she survived the war, to reclaim her wealth. It would dissipate into a thousand hands before she could return. Fingers intertwined, he rubbed the heels of his hands together, remembering Caleb, pistol in hand, forcing him from Betsy's house on that black day. He stewed, angry that Caleb lived off Betsy's wealth.

Caleb certainly wouldn't expect him. With surprise, a disabled Confederate officer—a one-legged man—would be an easy conquest and quick murder.

He jumped from the bed, invigorated with thoughts of vengeance. Before doing the actual deed, he'd make sure Caleb knew who was executing him. The fright in Caleb's eyes is what he most anticipated. He would give him a few minutes to whimper and beg—a lovely thought. He grinned as he imagined carrying the news to Washington . . . to Betsy that Caleb had cowered and bowed to him in death as he had in life.

Walthrope had already taken care of the Confederate soldier in Richmond who mocked him when Walthrope wanted to set up a promising business in Washington. He had also framed his so-called friend Matthew with sham evidence of counterfeiting. Matthew deserved worse for turning his back on Walthrope in Richmond when he needed his aid. Only for old times' sake had he given Matthew a few more years of life.

Walthrope was nearly dressed—not carefully groomed as he usually demanded of himself—and felt euphoric. It was coming soon: the thrill of extinguishing one more life that had marred his. He regretted not bringing Anna. He could envision her putting on a marvelous performance to flirtingly coax Caleb from the protection of his house. A little promised romance—Anna could be so convincing. For a flash he doubted her: Had she been feigning love for him? No. She had been thrilled to have been possessed by such a man.

He made his way unobtrusively through the quiet lobby and walked to the nearest livery stable, one he had spotted earlier. He hired a horse, and shaking with excitement, awkwardly mounted. The hunt was on, and he loped through town toward Betsy's plantation.

Gas lights blazed within the house when he arrived. The house should have been dark. Was it an evening party? He walked his horse slowly to the back till he could see the light emanating from the library. The room's windows stood open to the breeze. He halted the horse and watched the windows. Lights also blazed in the kitchen. He found a tree, tied his horse to it and crept slowly toward the library windows, hugging the shadows.

He inched forward till he could see into the room. Someone was laughing, and he listened a long time. He recognized Caleb's voice, but a woman was with him. Her laughter drifted from the window. It was familiar. The gangly, awkward fiancée? What was her name? He couldn't remember. He watched as Caleb rose from an unseen chair, moved toward another chair and stood, smiling affectionately at his unmemorable fiancée who sat with her back to the window. It was the perfect moment. Walthrope could kill him in the cripple's moment of exultation.

He fingered the derringer in his jacket pocket. He'd have to get close to use it. He mentally measured the large window and planned his hurdle across the room. He'd have to be quick. Walthrope would put the gun to the lady's head faster than Caleb could react. When Caleb's honor drove him still closer to protect his love, Walthrope would kill him.

He pulled his hand from his jacket pocket, sure he could reach it quickly once in the room. He again plotted his run to the window, his hand-supported leap into the room, his perfect landing and sprint to the woman. He breathed deeply. He was ready.

At that moment, Caleb retreated across the room and sat down. Caleb would still have to come to rescue her. The couple no longer laughed, but jovial bits of conversation continued to waft toward Walthrope. Odd Caleb—anyone really—could marry such a strange creature.

Anna had been one of the first to descend from the train in Staunton. The mountain air was fresher, cooler than the oppressive Richmond air, but the evening was still muggy and warm. She had outlined exactly what she should do when she arrived, but as she disembarked she discarded her plans, grasping the reality that she didn't have the patience to delay her business to the next morning. What she intended frightened her, and she knew she had to act straightaway lest her courage dwindle.

In the back of her mind, she also worried Daniel would trace her when he discovered her flight. How much time would she have? Supper and repose would have to wait till she'd seen Caleb. She found a cab and asked the driver to take her to the Henderson plantation.

"I've been up to the farm . . . before the war. Most won't go up there now, but I'll take you."

He drove uncomfortably fast and the cab bounced and beat against the road, jostling Anna constantly. As the driver pulled to the front of the mansion, Anna was delighted to find the house intact, but dismayed by its rough and un-kempt appearance. She spilled out of the cab as fast as she could with her small case in hand, paid the driver handsome-ly and sent him off directly, believing she would be less likely to be turned from the house and from her purpose if she was stranded on the doorstep. She climbed the steps, noting two boarded up windows as she knocked at the door.

A distinguished, elderly man opened to her after a short delay and scrutinized her. "May I help you?" he asked in a formal voice and with perfect manners.

"Yes, I'm a friend of Elizabeth Henderson . . . Gragg"— she added the Gragg part anticipating it would create more interest with Caleb. "I'd like to see Mr. Moore."

The servant opened the door and let her pass into the hall, which was to Anna's bewilderment filled with barrels as if the home were a warehouse. She couldn't see the walls or what hung on them for the stacked barrels and was nearly distracted from her business at the thought of such inexpli-cable furniture filling a grand foyer.

The servant patiently awaited the return of her atten-tion. When she looked back at him, he said, "I will see if Mr. Moore is at home. Who shall I say calls?"

"Miss Whitehead: Anna Whitehead from Richmond. Here's my carte de visite."

He took the card gently from her, nodded and retreated toward the back of the house.

While she waited, she glanced up the stairs, oddly relieved that no barrels were stacked in the visible portions of the upper hall.

The old man returned quickly. "Miss Whitehead . . ."

She nervously interrupted, "Not at home? I understand."

He smiled at her and announced, "He's at supper, as he was not expecting a call this evening."

"I do apologize for not sending a note, but I just got to town. Perhaps tomorrow?"

He waited till she finished. "He asks if you've supped."

Her nose crinkled at the question. "I haven't. I just got off the train from Richmond."

"Would you care to join him in the dining room?"

"I'd be delighted." Her voice betrayed excitement.

"Please follow me."

The dark-complexioned, tall servant with thinning short, tight curly hair, walked in long, smooth, elegant strides ahead of Anna to a large dining room where a handsome young man sat alone at the far end of the table. The man's meticulous dress and the elegance of the room contrasted sharply with the disheveled entry, tired exterior and barrel-filled hall. His brown hair was long and matched his penetrating brown eyes. His face was angular and open, his immediate smile wide and welcoming. As he rose, Anna realized he was taller than she'd anticipated and more attractive. As she took his measure, he approached with a pronounced limp.

"Miss Whitehead, good evening."

The slave commented, "She's arrived from Richmond by train and has not yet supped."

"Excellent. You must eat with me. I would be honored."

"Thank you. That is most kind."

"John, another setting. We've enough food. No need to bring more."

"Miss Whitehead, please come sit with me at the table and tell me why you've come. Visitors don't call out here now . . . with the war. I understand you're a friend of Mrs. Gragg." He looked at her expectantly, but neither moved.

"I knew Mrs. Gragg in Richmond."

"Did she go by that name?"

"I believe I was her confidante on that point. They called her Mrs. Henderson. She said you knew."

"She told you about me, about the farm?" he asked skeptically.

"She did. I believe you and I visited her on the same day in Castle Thunder. I visited after you and found her uplifted by your visit—yours and your fiancée's."

He visibly relaxed in response to her comment. "It still horrifies me to think of her locked up like a thief," he admitted grimacing.

"It was an awful place: filthy, bad food . . . and she suffering the sorrow of our sex."

She glimpsed brief but definite shock in his face.

"Sorrow?"

She hesitated, but eventually plunged forward, convinced she had to communicate all she knew to persuade him. "She was married and in a woman's condition. No one knew it. But instead of getting plump, she was dwindling; thinner and thinner."

He looked at her inquisitively, "How did you meet her? I hesitate to ask, but were you an inmate as well? She did mention a woman in her cell . . . at the beginning."

"No, gratefully. I'd never been in a prison."

"She was convinced that one woman, early on, was put in her cell to trick her into confessing murder and treason." He looked at her sternly for the first time. "Is that how you found out about her coming baby . . . and her husband?"

She consciously matched his severe expression and spoke in a tone that emphasized that she was carefully couching her answer, "No, I did not spy for the government."

She hoped he would interrogate her more closely on the question, but he looked on silently without probing.

"I would have told you eventually," she blurted out.

"Told me?"

"I did deceive Betsy and was a spy of sorts, but not for the government."

"Yet you pose now at her door as friend? I received you as an intimate acquaintance of Mrs. Gragg, and you . . ."

"There is a man in Richmond who hates Betsy. I didn't discern his motives when I first met him. I thought he was trying to help her. I agreed to visit Betsy without her knowing he had sent me. I know the truth now by painful personal experience." Anna was clearly uncomfortable and embarrassed and dropped her eyes to the floor. "He was so convincing that I agreed to marry him . . . did marry him. I thought he loved me, but he merely trifled with me. He was doing something equally . . . maybe more cruel—I don't know what—to Betsy."

"The man's name," Caleb demanded coldly.

She raised her head but closed her eyes, "When he came back he called himself Daniel Jefferson, but when I was helping Betsy . . . or thought I was helping Betsy, he called himself Oskar Dante. I suspect neither was real, and I never knew what his real name was."

"Not Lucius Walthrope?"

"I've heard someone refer to that name. I'm sure it's the same man . . . if he was set on harming Betsy."

"How did you help him?"

"I'm an actress. I was new to Richmond. Now people might recognize me, but not then. With Betsy, I posed as a woman who wanted to help her escape prison because of her coming child."

"What were you really doing?"

"Helping her escape." She nodded her head. "That's what Oskar Dante wanted—to help her escape from Castle Thunder. He did it, and I helped."

"Why did he want that?"

"I don't know. I thought it was a benevolent act. I suspect it was a way to harm her somehow. Maybe as long as she was in Castle Thunder, he couldn't get at her. He tried, and paid for the effort when a dog attacked him. So he freed her . . . I don't know why. I just suspect he still wants to hurt her, so I came . . . to you, her friend, the only friend besides your fiancée she ever mentioned. You were the people I thought to turn to."

His eyes relaxed. "I don't know how Betsy is . . . or precisely where she is. We haven't been able to get messages to each other for a while, but why am I telling you anything? An actress. You could be acting now, duping me at Walthrope's bidding. You've already admitted to deceiving Betsy. Walthrope would surely attempt to deceive me given the opportunity. I half expect him to sneak in, with you as his dodge. But I can't believe he would dare come to Staunton. I assumed he'd hunt me down after I left the town . . . after the war."

"That's the other reason I came here. It's safe from him. He wouldn't dare . . . couldn't come here."

"So since he can't show his face in Staunton, he sends you as his weapon to injure me as you harmed Mrs. Gragg?" His eyes were on fire.

His fury humiliated her, and she lowered her head meekly. "Please don't turn me away, not yet. I have money. I'll take a room in town. I can leave without eating. I didn't come for that. You won't see me again. I'll do you no harm. Please believe me"—she raised her head, pleading in her eyes. "I came because there was no one else. I've failed if you won't listen to me."

"I can't risk trusting you, but you know that," he said sincerely. "You've told me more than I would have expected." John had set a place for Anna at the table while they conversed. "Our supper is waiting. I hope my questions—they were rude—haven't spoiled your appetite."

"I'm famished." She smiled nervously. "But you mustn't stop asking questions. Perhaps in society questions are not fashionable, but I want to tell you everything I know as quickly as I can. Time is short."

"Tell me between bites," Caleb offered warmly.

"It would give me strength to keep the story going."

"A simple supper for a story—a complete story—from a renowned Richmond actress is a one-sided business deal, benefiting me."

"Renowned? Not so. And there is no such thing anymore as a simple supper. This is a royal feast."

"Come, come. Eat." He led her to and helped her with her seat, just to the right of his own and sat down.

As soon as the meal was served, Caleb realized she was telling the truth about being famished. She ate with the urgency of starvation, and Caleb was entertained by her enthusiasm. He smiled.

She suddenly realized he was watching her and stopped eating, putting her fork and knife down on the plate.

"No, please keep eating. You're hungry. It's a pleasure to see you enjoy your food so."

"I'm sorry. I haven't eaten since dinner yesterday, and I had no appetite then. I was afraid for my life and planning my escape."

She expected him to show concern, but he ignored her last comments and said, "What did you pretend to be . . . with Mrs. Gragg?"

She thought for a moment, remembering the role she had played as straight-laced spinster Florence Morrow. Her back straightened, her eyes suddenly penetrated him. She shifted in her seat, stiffened her movements and spoke in a harsh, frank voice, "Miss Florence Morrow, a spinster, a do-gooder, there to comfort her. I chose Florence because of Florence Nightingale. With so many women taking up nursing, I thought it might help her think of me as her healer . . . or to at least trust me more."

Caleb watched the transformation with unexpected foreboding. If she was playing a role with him and lying about everything, he would never discern it. Seconds earlier, he had assumed she was at his mercy and within his control, but her brief role play convinced him control and mercy lay in her lap. He hoped she was as kind as she portrayed. He shifted apprehensively in his chair. "You must have been convincing."

"I was. I did my best, hoping she would trust me. If she did, I could help her escape from the gates of Hell. As I visited, I grew to love her . . . and hurt for her sitting among the literal and figurative rats. I wanted to help her. If further mishap now befalls her, I'm to blame. If he hasn't harmed her yet, I want to make sure he doesn't . . . that he can't."

Caleb smiled warmly. He was beginning to like her. If she was cheating him out of everything he owned—which wasn't much—he would still enjoy her company. She was enchanting. He was unexpectedly embarrassed and looked down at his plate to avoid her eyes. He began eating, leaving her to enjoy her meal.

After a few minutes he politely inquired, "In what plays have you performed?"

His query startled her, but she answered, "Many."

"Shakespeare?"

"Certainly."

"Much Ado About Nothing?"

"Yes."

"Were you Beatrice?"

"Yes."

He could see her deeply felt pleasure as she answered.

"You would be a good Beatrice."

"Is she your favorite Shakespeare female character?"

"No, I think that would be Isabella . . . from Measure for Measure."

The answer made her uncomfortable, but she hid the embarrassment by looking at her plate and taking a bite.

"You would be a good Isabella. Have you played Isabella?"

"Yes," she answered, keeping her head down and raising her fork from the plate to her mouth.

"I would have liked to have seen it. Would you do a bit of it for me?"

"I'd have to review it. It's been a while."

"Then we'll have to keep you a little longer so you can refresh it."

She was flattered, yet uncomfortable with the suggestion. Was he mocking her? Did he expect her to be the exact opposite of virtuous Isabella who refused to redeem her brother with payment of her chastity to a hypocritical blackmailer? Did he think Daniel had blackmailed her into giving up her virtue to save Betsy? Or did he think Daniel had sent her to . . . . Her face turned dark.

As if he understood exactly what she was thinking, he said abruptly, "Please excuse me, Miss Whitehead, I've been too forward. It was ungentlemanly. Sitting by you in this dire situation has made me less formal than I should have been. I apologize."

"It's fine," she answered humbly. "If circumstances were different—less urgent—I'd be honored to read a few lines."

He forced a smile. He was sorry to have trampled on the animated conversation, and he tried to revive it. "Have you played Romeo and Juliet?"

"Yes."

"Which part? Let me guess: the nurse."

She giggled.

"I was right. You played the nurse." He smiled. "It's too bad we have no theater to do justice to Shakespeare here in Staunton."

"Maybe they'll build one someday."

"Perhaps."

Her eating slowed, and she unexpectedly remembered visiting Betsy at Castle Thunder. She put down her fork and looked firmly at Caleb. "I remember one visit to Betsy. She'd been imprisoned a while. I think it was during the visit where I introduced the idea of escape. I came with a fresh loaf of bread. She was so skinny, especially for a woman . . . . I gave her the loaf, and she devoured it ravenously. Now you—and through you, Betsy—feed me in my desperation."

Caleb, somberly said, "Did you have as much joy watching her as I have in watching you."

She blushed, feeling oddly excited that such an honorable man spoke so personally to her. "I did, and I cherish the memory. Of all that's happened since, in spite of my innocent deceit and the unintended harm I brought, I still cherish that moment."

"Tell me your story from the beginning. Don't leave anything out. I suspect that's important."

She looked furtively at him. She could feel his growing trust, and she committed to be faithful to it. Her eyes teared up, and she quickly ran a hand across them to conceal her emotions.

Chapter 31

July 1864, Staunton, Virginia

With engaging stage-like exaggeration, Anna pushed her chair from the table to see Caleb better and began her story:

"When I first moved to Richmond, I tried to get on stage. I'd acted in smaller towns a few times and knew it's what I wanted. I won't explain the reasons—none are interesting.

"I wasn't getting anywhere in Richmond. I'd been turned away so many times, I was discouraged . . . really discouraged. Outside the New Richmond Theater, with my hopes at their lowest ebb after one last failure, a handsome and seemingly kind gentleman approached me and claimed he had heard I was a wonderful actress. He was trying to do a good deed for someone but couldn't do it himself. He wanted to do it secretly . . . as the Savior taught. He thought a woman—an actress could best help him. I was courteous, but suspicious and asked what he wanted me to do. He said he wanted me to pretend to be someone different and meet with a woman who was in unfortunate circumstances, not of her own making. If I agreed, I'd be able to help save the lady from her desperate plight. He added he would pay me for doing this kindness and assured me that, while I wouldn't be on a big stage, it would be a life-saving performance.

"Doing something good for someone sounded wonderful, and I should leave that as my reason for helping. The truth is I had exhausted the little money I'd brought with me to Richmond. That was the real reason I helped. One of my weaknesses is a love of money, but it wasn't that this time. It was never that. I was desperate for money to live . . . to eat. So I accepted his offer.

"He told me the errand was to help a woman held without cause in Castle Thunder. I was to befriend her, find out what she wanted, take her whatever she needed on following visits. Later I learned I was to help her escape. By that time I wanted to help because I knew she hadn't committed whatever murder she'd been accused of, and she hadn't spied with Mr. Gragg—only loved him. I fear, after feeling Daniel's violence, that if anyone committed a murder it was him or Mr. Dante or whatever you said his name was. I swear by the gods that I didn't suspect it at the time.

"The irony of this whole mess—and it is a mess—is that the next day, Mr. Ogden offered me a role in that evening's play. If I'd waited just one more day, Dante's offer would never have appealed to me, and I wouldn't have done it. My fortunes had changed, and I was on the stage in every play at the theater after that day.

"But it was too late. I'd promised to help this woman, and I kept that promise as best I could. At some point—and I thought for virtuous purposes—Dante went to see Betsy at the prison. Somehow while he was visiting with her, he was attacked by the prison's notorious black, mammoth-like dog, Nero. I saw him—the dog—not that day, but on another. He was huge and ferocious. His size alone terrifies . . . and his color. I didn't know anything about the attack at the time. Dante just disappeared. That was fine. He'd paid me some of what he'd promised. I was busy at the theater, learning new lines during the day, performing at night. If he no longer needed me, so much the better. I thought he'd found another way to help Betsy—that they'd agreed on some escape plan no longer requiring my help.

"Just when I was sure he didn't need my help anymore, I got a note hand delivered by a slave woman. Let me be particularly honest. Painfully so. Dante was handsome, charming, and seemed respectable. I had been totally deceived by him, and the note I received told me his account of a dog attacking him. He wrote he'd gone to the prison to comfort Betsy. It was all a lie. It said there'd been a terrible accident, that a mad dog had attacked him, that he was badly torn. He was in hiding because of his injuries and horrid appearance, but he still wanted to help Betsy. He wanted to get her to Washington City, so she could be free. He had proof she was neither traitor nor murderer.

"The note asked me to meet with the prison commandant to see if he would help get her released. Dante wrote I should also take to the meeting a corrupt sheriff from Staunton. The sheriff had actually committed the murder charged to Betsy. He was the traitor and would do anything to keep blame from his own shoulders, thus he had implicated Betsy early on. Dante had heard that the sheriff had shifted blame from Betsy to another innocent—Dante himself—and might now be willing to help free Betsy. He warned me the sheriff was conniving and convincing. Under no circumstances was I to trust him.

"I kept up my charade with Betsy and met with the commandant. The sheriff acted exactly as Dante had predicted, aiming the blame at Dante. He may have called him Walthrope. Maybe that's where I heard that name. But the meeting was for naught, as the sheriff and commandant were quick to agree Betsy was innocent and quicker to refuse to help her.

"Dante seemed to know what was going to happen or could explain everything that did. I believed him, and I was growing fonder of Betsy with each visit. I pitied her. The filth she lived in. I supposed at the time that the sheriff and commandant had convinced her Dante was trying to harm her. That he had committed the murder and was a traitor. That the dog had saved her. I recognize now that was reality, but I didn't know then. I was under Dante's spell, if I can call it that. I thought him a gentleman who was helping a friendless person and that I . . . I played a virtuous part.

"Once Betsy escaped, Dante assured me he was taking good care of her, that his friends in Washington helped Mrs. Gragg. He told me he was going to Washington to see her, and that's the last I saw of him for a while. I wish upon my life it had been the last time ever.

"One late night more than a month ago, he showed up at my door—literally—with no place to go. I thought—maybe more truthfully, I hoped he'd come to me because he . . . . He told me everything was fine with Betsy and admitted killing the sheriff who had followed Betsy to Washington for some devilish purpose.

"Please remember—it's important to me that you remember—that I believed . . . I really believed . . . everything he said. Everything. I didn't know what he was. Now that I know, I'm ashamed of what I've been a part of and mortified I didn't know. When he appeared, feigning love for me, he asked me to marry him. I did. Who wouldn't want to marry a man who was so kind to someone friendless and trapped? I'm humiliated to admit we were married . . . and more chagrinned . . . horrified that I lived with him as his wife . . . that he ever touched me.

"Soon I began to see he didn't tell the truth . . . ever. That he wasn't the gentleman he played. I began to fear for Betsy . . . for her safety. Yesterday it dawned on me I was in mortal danger, and if I was, Betsy was. I'd already been deeply hurt, abused and maltreated, but I didn't want to die; so I ran. If I'd stayed . . . it would have been worse than dying, to have him force . . . touch me again.

"I thought if I could get here, I would be safe and might get a message to Betsy—if she was still alive . . . I shudder at the thought she isn't.

"I came to you. I knew you cared for her house. She counted you and your fiancée—I'm sorry I don't remember her name—as faithful friends. So I came hoping you could help me. That you could at least warn her.

"If you'll help her, I'll move on. I won't bother you. Though I would like to stay in Staunton because he won't come here . . . even disguised as he is. That's one more thing I did. I dyed his hair and beard black, thinking him innocent and persecuted."

Caleb had listened intently without comment, encouragement or visible reaction. The story the woman told was so
consistent with Walthrope's character and so demeaning to
the teller he accepted it completely. Her visible pain panged
his heart as she admitted Walthrope had used her. He in-
wardly cringed as she spoke of him touching her and was
awed by her courageous flight from Walthrope. He wanted to
reach out and touch her hand to reassure her.

"Please say something. Anything," she pleaded when he
offered no response.

"I don't know what to say," he responded with resigna-
tion.

"You don't believe me." Her expression turned resolute.
"At least pass the warning on to Mrs. Gragg. I've done what I
could. Thank you for supper and for listening to my story.
You've been kind."

She rose to leave.

He watched her. She picked up her small case and
turned to the door.

Not rising to see her out, Caleb queried, "Where's your
luggage?"

She turned to face him, disheartened by his question.
"You didn't listen. I have no baggage. I escaped. I couldn't
take luggage. This small case is all I could muster. I use it to
take makeup powders to and from the theater. It was the one
thing I could carry without raising suspicion. I took money
from him. He had someone take me to the theater and watch
me so I couldn't escape. He must have suspected I would try,
after what he did to me yesterday." She began to cry softly.
"I escaped because Mr. Ogden, the theater manager, helped
me."

Caleb rose and walked to her. He reached out his hand
brusquely and said sharply, "Let me see your case."

Hurt by his tone and doubt, and feeling hopeless, she
surrendered it without complaint. Tears welled in her eyes.

She had felt something for him and thought there was reciprocity. Now that she'd disclosed the truth, he hated, despised and distrusted her. Why wouldn't he? She was fallen and had harmed Betsy. He surely suspected she had hatched this meeting as a plot in cahoots with Daniel.

Caleb took the case roughly, carried it to the table and opened it. When he saw the bills, he pulled one from the case and smiled. It was a common twenty-dollar bill. He pulled a similar one from his pocket and compared them carefully. She watched him curiously, moving closer to see what he was looking at.

He laughed. "It's not real." He picked up several more and glanced at them. "None of them."

"Counterfeit?" She stuttered, trying to comprehend what he was suggesting. How could it be forged? She remembered watching Daniel smile as he read the newspaper in their lodging. That was it: It was the story in the newspaper about boxes of counterfeit money found in a warehouse. He'd framed someone for counterfeiting. What did it mean? Why would he be pleased someone was arrested for possession of faked bills? Counterfeiting. That's what he meant by he could get more money any time.

She glanced at Caleb as he dropped the real bill on the table. He replaced the fake note she had brought in the case before approaching the fireplace, where he emptied the case. He crouched awkwardly to place the case on the floor, rose with a slight strain, reached onto the mantel and took down a long match. He smiled, lit it, let the fire catch and dropped it onto the money.

"Are you sure they're counterfeit?"

"Without a doubt. And it's not a good idea to have a case full of it should the railroad realize someone passed them bad notes."

"How can you tell they're fake?" she asked.

He'd lit a second match, but their conversation distracted him, and he burned his finger. He shook the flame out and scowled.

Without saying anything, he bent awkwardly, pulled an as-yet unburned bill from the fireplace and handed it to her. "Look carefully at this note. Look at the man's—I guess it's a sailor—at his face. See the shape between the twenty and the Roman numeral XX?"

While she scrutinized it, he limped to the table and picked up the real bill. He brought it to her. "Compare this."

She took the paper from him and held them side by side. "The sailor's hair. It's different. And that shape, whatever it is, is missing a little point on this one."

"There are probably other differences."

She continued examining the two notes while he lit another match. "Are you sure yours isn't the counterfeit?"

He dropped the third match onto the bills and watched the separate flame it spawned. "I hope it's not, or I've burned thousands of dollars. It's all worthless anyway . . . these days."

She chuckled. "He just started doing it, I think."

"Odd he would begin counterfeiting Confederate money when it's nearly worthless. He would have done better to counterfeit Union money. He always seems to make sloppy mistakes when . . . ."

She slid close to him as he watched the bills burn. She tossed the counterfeit bill she held onto the fire, and asked, still grasping the real note, "Do I get to keep this one?"

"An honest trade, don't you think? Stacks of worthless paper for one piece of worthless paper. I think I made out better on the exchange. At least I got a little heat out of mine."

"Something to be grateful for in July."

He laughed.

She was confused by his shifting demeanor. "May I have my empty case so I can leave?"

"Will you stay for breakfast?"

"We just finished supper."

"You've nowhere to go. I've burned your money. That twenty dollars won't feed and house you long. Where will you stay? Until you sort out what you'll do, stay as my guest . . . as Betsy's guest. It's what she—if she were here—would want."

She compressed her lips. "You're persuasive. The counterfeit notes changed everything, even though I still have some hidden."

"It's the possibility of getting caught with them that changed it," Caleb retorted smiling, grateful she smiled back. He liked her and hoped she was who she seemed to be, and it wasn't an act.

Chapter 32

July 1864, Staunton, Virginia

Lucius was suddenly anxious and had trouble rallying his nerve. On three he would charge the window, he committed. One, two, three. He took short steps toward the window, picking up speed quickly. He touched the outside of his jacket one last time to make sure the pistol was ready. All was as planned. He neared the window and reached his hands out to vault over the sill, but he misjudged the strength of his vault and the height of the large window. The back of his head caught the bottom edge of the raised window frame, and it exploded into a visceral anger as he stumbled to the floor. Instinctively he wanted to punch the fiancée, and he instantly rose and leaped the last few steps to her side.

Caleb jumped from his seat, shocked first by the noise, then by the black-haired stranger dashing forward. Anna, beginning to tire from a long evening of endearing, emotional, confessional conversation, was slower to respond and turned to the intruder only as he reached her chair.

Walthrope pulled the pistol from his jacket and pointed it at the woman's cheek, but Walthrope was confused. It wasn't her. Was the blow to his head serious? Was he hallucinating? It wasn't Caleb's ungainly lady at the end of his pistol. It was Anna's smooth, lovely face. Why was she in Betsy's house? His mind raced. An unending queue of questions perturbed him. Had Caleb sent her to Richmond months ago to plague him? Had she helped to free Betsy at Caleb's command, not his? Had she been mocking him all along? Had they as he waited outside the window been laughing about him? His wrath raged, and he grabbed her throat, shifting the gun to the other side of her head. Still no one spoke.

Walthrope looked across at Caleb who was frozen in front of his chair and weighed whom he'd rather kill. He detected undeniable alarm in Caleb's eyes as the failed soldier stared at Anna, then bewilderment as the cripple raised his eyes to stare at him.

Anna was perfectly still, gazing at Caleb. Walthrope couldn't see her eyes.

"Did I break up a lover's tryst? Anna, I thought you a better wife and of better taste than to betray me for a half man."

Caleb shivered, recognizing the familiar voice, recalling that Anna confessed to dyeing Walthrope's hair and beard. It was Walthrope. He tried to size up the situation. Had the demon followed this lovable creature in an agreed-upon plot? Or had he tracked her scent? Either way, he would stay as calm as he could till what he was witnessing became clear. "What do you want, Lucius?" he asked as if they met inconveniently on the street.

"I came to kill you."

Caleb snickered. "You're in the wrong place. Best move closer for a better shot. Aim at my head."

Walthrope stared down at Anna, still trying to see her expression, glancing periodically at Caleb.

"You're pointing the gun at the wrong head . . . if you've come to kill me."

Caleb could easily see both of them at once. Anna didn't move. Her eyes were riveted on him as if she hoped and expected him to save her. Was it a trap? Bitterness pulsed through him. He'd seen her completely immerse herself in another character earlier when she had taken on the mantel of Miss Morrow. Had the entire, delicious evening set this up? Was she merely playing the role of an Anna Whitehead? But she'd been so empathetic, so understanding, so attentive as he had revealed his most closely guarded fears and pains. Who was she really? He didn't move to help her.

"I'll kill her."

Caleb tried to maintain his composure. "You won't have a ball left or time to kill me. You have to choose who you most want dead," he said slowly moving farther from the pair.

"Stay where you are!"

"I don't think you'd wound me badly from that distance. To kill me, you'll have to come closer, or shoot your wife." He laughed unnaturally loudly. "She claims she's your spouse. Will you shoot your wife? Come here, Lucius, you old cheat!" He moved several more steps from them, keeping his eyes riveted on the scene, still attempting to make sense of what he was seeing.

Anna looked at Caleb, panic in her eyes. Regret had replaced the slight hope that had buoyed her moments earlier. She had been convinced Caleb trusted her. From their equally insecure emotional footing, they had formed an intimate friendship in the few hours they'd been together. She'd felt him an affectionate confident: She had been painfully open with him; and he had shared with her the loneliness of being a wounded soldier far from family and the psychological and physical suffering he'd experienced losing a leg. Now it was all changed. Was it possible Caleb had never believed her? Or had Daniel following her, showing up like this, smothered the embers they'd sparked? Under the circumstances, was there anything else Caleb could believe but that she'd lied to him; that she had conspired with this brute to harm Betsy and him? Her eyes moistened in frustration. It no longer mattered. She knew Daniel finding her with Caleb would stoke his anger to violence. Daniel wouldn't kill Caleb. He'd shoot her in frenzy. The thought surprisingly comforted her. She could understand why Caleb could no longer believe in her, but she would still die saving him. That would prove her integrity. What strange feelings—afflicted at the thought of Caleb harmed. Yes, yes. Move away, Caleb. Move to safety.

She took a short, desperate breath through her finger-constrained throat. He likely hadn't come for Caleb anyway. He'd followed her to see what she was doing—to bring her back to slavery. Now he knew she couldn't be trusted. By following her to a town where he was in danger, he was attesting he would never let her go. Death by pistol shot would be better than slavery. She would confuse Daniel long enough for Caleb to escape.

She strained to see Daniel's face and said hoarsely, "It's not going to work, dear. I thought by coming I would help you, but it's not to be. Not now. You came too early. I was about to stab him because you hated him. I didn't think you could come to Staunton, so I did. It was to be a great surprise; my gift to you. Alas you've spoiled it. He's alive, and we've missed our chance. You made too much noise. The slaves must have heard it. Let's escape before someone comes."

"Answer me: Did he send you to me in Richmond in the first place? I can see by his expression I've guessed your plot. I should shoot you and be done."

Caleb shrugged, encouraged by Walthrope's clear bewilderment. "I assure you, Lucius, until this very afternoon I'd never laid eyes on this lovely woman. She tells me she's a famous actress in Richmond, but I've never heard of her. If you didn't send her, she came on her own to kill me in revenge for what we—Betsy and I—did to you . . . with so much pleasure." Caleb glared defiantly at Walthrope and clamored, "I'm glad we did it. All this strumpet could do was talk about you—praise you—since she arrived, not by your real name of course. It became so tiresome. Your interruption is a relief. Of course, I never suspected it was you, till you stumbled through that window. You bumblehead. Are you bleeding? She's been here since supper when she came with a pathetic story, and you're all she talked about. Please do kill her . . . for me. I should have perceived what she was doing. She's disgusting. You'd never get to me anyway. Do I hear someone coming?"

"I have a second derringer in my pocket for you."

"You wouldn't have time to use it if you did. Kill her if you like. She deserves it for deceiving me . . . for slavishly dedicating herself to you. You sent her, and now you expect me to rush to her rescue, as if she's a medieval maiden in distress. You told her to inveigle her way into this house, to keep me awake till you showed up. You're no fisherman, Walthrope, and I'm not going to bite. Shoot the lovely actress . . . your beguiling wife. I doubt the stage will miss her much. I surely won't. By the time the bullet has passed through her lovely head, I'll be on you. And we can end our quarrel once and for all."

Walthrope imagined aligning the gun in such a way the bullet might pass through Anna's head and into Caleb's body to at least slow him down. But he couldn't get the angle as long as she was sitting down, and it probably wouldn't work even if he could. Maybe he shouldn't kill her. Maybe Caleb was right. Maybe she was loyal to him, to his charms. Maybe she had come to kill Caleb. Maybe she still did love him; understand him; appreciate what he'd done. He could accept such loyalty.

Still taunting him, Caleb moved toward the door. "It never works as you plan, does it Lucius? You fall shy of what you want, as you did in this very room . . . all those months ago. Do you remember?" Caleb chuckled. "Of course you do. Betsy told you she knew you murdered Stokes, and I drove you out. I drove you out," he cackled, "with a derringer, like the tiny thing you feigningly point at your trollop's head. Lucius, remember Hank Gragg? He was outside and pummeled you. He told me how easy it was to beat you . . . till you could barely stand. He laughed at you. I can't blame him for that. I bet you still remember the pain . . . the humiliation—prostrate before Betsy's love."

"Shut up!"

A knock at the door interrupted them. "Sir, you have a visitor," John called calmly from the hall.

Caleb answered curtly, "Go away, John. Tell whoever it is I'm not at home."

"It's the old sheriff, sir."

Caleb smiled, but shouted angrily, "I'm not in, John, to anyone, under any circumstances. I don't want to be disturbed and do not open that door . . . or I will beat you again."

After a brief hesitation, John answered proficiently, "Very good, sir. I'll tell him precisely that."

Caleb had watched Walthrope throughout the conversation and noticed his expression change as John mentioned Robert Sheriff, the former sheriff of Staunton.

"Lucius, I suggest you leave. Mr. Sheriff's retired, but he's still a bulldog; otherwise he wouldn't call so late. He often comes asking if I've heard anything of you. I sent for him after supper when I guessed she was your wife, come to kill me."

Anna remembered Daniel telling her he had killed the sheriff to protect Betsy. She sought to compound Walthrope's confusion. "Love, you told me you killed him. You said you killed him to protect Betsy. Don't believe that decrepit slave. He's trying to save his pathetic master."

Caleb glanced at her. He did like her. Very much. She was clever, quick and beautiful. He craved definitive verification she was who she had portrayed all evening and that she liked him. He wanted to rush Walthrope and rescue her but wasn't sure Walthrope would choose to shoot him and spare her.

Walthrope wanted out. This was too much; too confusing. He'd come back to finish Caleb. Robert Sheriff was a problem. He might shoot him in the back through the still-open window.

"Get up," he demanded, as he yanked Anna backwards, pulling over the chair, his arm—firmly around her neck—choking her as he pulled. She resisted his choking arm with both hers in a struggle to stop strangulation.

"Caleb, if you dare move, I'll kill her."

"Lucius, that's a tempting offer. She's your wife. Where'd you find her? A penny brothel? That's the only place women worthy of you reside."

"You still don't want to cause her death," he spat.

"I'm not going to move. Certainly not for her."

The couple had reached the window. Walthrope held her tightly as he clumsily climbed out the window.

"Don't come after us."

"Godspeed you both . . . to perdition," Caleb rejoined mockingly.

Anna, terror holding full sway on her face and squirming desperately trying to pull at Walthrope's choking hold, made little noises that came out as whimpers.

Caleb struggled to remain rational as every particle within him yearned to rush Walthrope. But he feared he would fail and cause Anna's death.

Once Walthrope was outside the window standing on the ground, he pulled Anna out after him as if she were an overstuffed bag.

Caleb involuntarily winced at the bruising she was taking. As soon as the dark swallowed the couple, he darted through the door to find John standing at the open front door.

"Where's Sheriff?"

"I told him you never beat me. He thanked me and went out the front door."

"John, I hope this whole day has not been an elaborate scheme to deceive someone . . . me, but I've got to try to save her regardless."

"Yes, sir."

"Get the carbine and my colt."

John returned quickly. Caleb loaded the carbine and tucked the colt in his pocket. He grabbed a handful of bullets for both and limbered out the door. Knowing he'd lost precious minutes, Caleb hoped Sheriff had already caught them.

He was uncomfortable with his own feelings for Anna and bothered by his rush to get involved. She was another man's wife. Yet he felt pulled to her as strongly as if she had been his own. Making his way to the stable, he swiftly saddled and bridled a horse despite an inner warning that

Walthrope had foreseen all this and waited to shoot him when he emerged from the stable; that Anna would be standing shoulder to shoulder with his nemesis, gleefully watching as he shot Caleb from his horse. He couldn't bear the image.

Chapter 33

July 1864, Washington City, District of Columbia

After Betsy's flight to Washington, her life descended to meager poverty. Pregnancy kept her from employment and lack of family reinforced her isolation. She longed for an answer to the letter she'd sent to Hank informing him of his coming child, but she'd never received one. Becoming despondent, she feared he had died without knowing. She took slight comfort in the disappearance of Walthrope and the man pretending to be Thaddeus, but that comfort was absorbed in fear that Walthrope was engaged in ever-growing, concealed machinations against her safety and happiness.

Keeping Betsy from full despair of her poverty was Mrs. Brown, an unexpected friend and ally. She allowed Betsy to stay and eat at her boarding home without payment, continually brushing aside Betsy's insistence that someday she would pay all she owed. Whenever Betsy raised the topic, Mrs. Brown replied she was not a woman to leave a pregnant lady—the wife of a Union soldier—on the street. When the baby came, she would help Betsy till Hank returned. She proclaimed Betsy's future straitened means or extravagant abundance didn't matter: She would never accept payment or reimbursement for what she was doing. It was her sacred duty, her blessed privilege, and no more.

Mrs. Brown had lost her sons at Second Bull Run. Being a sensitive woman, she shared the hovering potential loss shadowing Betsy. While she never admitted it, Mrs. Brown, who had migrated with her husband to the Federal City from Vermont, was also attached to Betsy because it was Southern men—probably Confederate agents—who had harried her guest. The distinguished Englishman Mr. Rathbone who checked in on Betsy frequently had assured Mrs. Brown her lodger's assailant at the canal was a Southerner. She'd seen for herself the Southern proclivities of the man feigning to be Mr. Henderson. Mrs. Brown was also offended by the unending Confederate rhetoric she heard from some Washington neighbors, and this added to her sympathy for Betsy's plight.

Betsy was careful never to mention to Mrs. Brown that she remained, in spite of all persecution, a Southern loyalist. The North had brought this war on when it tried to force its will on South Carolina, a sovereign state. Under orders of an imperial president, the North had marched troops across her beloved Virginia in its attempt to quell South Carolina's self-determination. If freedom was the charter of the nation founded in the blood of the Revolution, then South Carolina was entitled to her freedom, succession and rebellion, especially under a constitution contracted by the individual states. Lincoln had broken that contract. She hated slavery more each day and wanted it erased from the continent and world, but it should have been left to the individual states to determine. Hadn't Lincoln himself acknowledged that? But strong as her commitment to freedom and worthy rebellion was, she was vigilant in never manifesting support for the Confederacy to anyone around her, especially Mrs. Brown.

Always having desired a daughter, Mrs. Brown explained to Betsy that she finally felt she had found one in her lodger and that she was thrilled at the prospect of being a grandmother. Betsy wasn't sure she wanted a second mother, especially as she constantly fretted for the safety of her natural mother still presumably holed up in her home in war-torn Winchester. But in all, Betsy was profoundly appreciative of her landlady's kindness, attention and affection.

Mary Rathbone's gentle visits also buoyed Betsy. But Mary's increasingly full state tired her, and her trips necessarily became less frequent. Betsy understood Mary would soon need more help from Betsy, if she could give it, than Betsy needed from Mary.

While she fought it off with her full emotional and rational strength, Betsy would muck through grief and worry each night when she retired alone to her darkened bedroom. The list of causes of her private complaints seemed unending. If she wasn't grieving the feared death of Hank, she was frustrated she had lost her home and property. If she wasn't vexed her mother was sure to die in Winchester, she was filled with stunning fear Walthrope or the feigned Thaddeus would show up to murder her and her coming child. She especially feared Walthrope. She knew him to be sane; merely debauched by hatred and lust for revenge. She feared he would pop out of a parked carriage, emerge from some building, or climb down from an unnoticed but passing horse to enact his malevolence on her. After brooding for hours, instead of sleeping, she would horrify herself imagining she hadn't seen or heard from Walthrope because he was searching to find and kill Hank. Maybe he already had. That would explain no responding letter from her husband.

It was late one afternoon that she received a copy of the Washington Star from Mrs. Rathbone. Mary, panting from the long walk and with her brood trailing, handed the paper to her. She was visibly embarrassed, admitting, "Thomas saw a note to a Mrs. Henry Gragg last night and thought I should bring it as early as possible. I'm sorry it's taken so long."

"It's fine. Thank you. Thank you for bringing it." She took the paper with a shaking hand, looking at Mary affectionately, trying to suppress her budding excitement. "You'd better sit down. It won't be long. You look as though you're nearing your critical state."

"I feel it, too, and I'm frightened of it and grateful."

"Sit down. Don't faint on the carpet. One thing Mrs. Brown particularly dislikes and spends a great amount of time worrying and complaining about is women who faint on the parlor floor."

Mary nodded, not acknowledging Betsy's humor. She quickly chose a nearby chair, sitting down with an audible and long sigh. "Oh, that's better. My poor feet; my poor back. I can't walk around like this anymore. It's too much."

"How's Thomas?"

"Busy as always. Never stops going. Loves his work. They depend on him more and more every day, he claims. He's excited about the coming day. We both are."

Betsy's curiosity about the notice was growing, and it finally overcame her manners. "Mary, would you mind if I read the paper? I'm hoping . . . needing good news from some front."

Mary said sleepily, yawning, "Yes, please read it. I'll nap for a minute. Children, be good for your Aunt Betsy while I . . . ." She was asleep before she finished her thought.

Betsy winked at one of the boys and unfolded the paper, searching for the notice. She found it midway down the middle column.

Mrs. Henry Gragg, lately of Washington City. I regret to inform you that your husband, serving with the 19th Indiana, is ill. You may visit him at your earliest convenience. Come quickly.
Nurse Victoria Richman

The notice listed the address of the hospital, and Betsy in a stupor gazed several minutes at the paper with no visible emotion or comment. Mary snored. The children watched Betsy expectantly, but she ignored them in her daze and reread the note. Hank was alive. He was nearby, so close she could almost reach her arm out the window and touch him. He was ill; so ill the nurse had commanded her to come quickly. Odd the nurse was a Richman. Not the most common name. A relative? Likely, but unimportant. She had to get to Hank.

Balancing her shock and fear with her excitement, she called softly, "Mary. Mary."

Mary didn't respond, and Betsy spoke louder, "Mary." Without waiting to rouse her, she continued, "I've got to get to the hospital. We've found Hank." She called out, "Mrs. Brown, we've found Hank . . . in Washington."

She was leaving the room as Mary awoke. The children had cleared Betsy's way as she hasted to the door.

She called to Betsy, "Are you going to the hospital?"

With tears already on her face, Betsy confessed, "I must. He's alive."

"Do you want me to go with you?"

Betsy stopped and looked back at Mary who was struggling from her seat. She walked back and put her hand on her friend's shoulder, pushing her gently down into the chair. "Stay till you're rested. I can do this on my own. You look like you'll be delivered any minute. Thank you for bringing the note." She bent down and hugged her tightly, calling for Sally to bring refreshment to her friend and her children.

Betsy strode quickly to the door, where Mrs. Brown met her.

"Where are you going?"

"The hospital. I've found Hank."

Shock, then excitement, reverberated through her voice as she warned, "You can't go alone. You shouldn't go at all at this hour,"

"Then come with me."

Staring into her eyes, Mrs. Brown said tenderly, "Wait till I've served supper. Then we can go."

"I don't think I can wait."

"You can't go by yourself. It wouldn't be safe, and you need strength to go. After supper, I'll come. I long to meet your hero."

Supper was a tedious, unending affair for both Mrs. Brown and Betsy. They remained politely quiet through the repast, but several other boarders seemed unusually gregarious and talkative and the meal lasted far longer than usual. They chatted of the Union army sieging Petersburg, of fighting around Atlanta, of the likelihood of President Lincoln's reelection, of rumors of peace talks, of the destruction of the Shenandoah Valley. The talk would normally have interested both women and discouraged Betsy. Instead they barely heard the conversation, and Mrs. Brown in frustration finally directed Sally to clear the table, announcing she had urgent business to see to.

With the meal finished, the two women hastily excused themselves and in unplanned unison glided to the door. As they descended the stairs to the street, Mrs. Brown grabbed Betsy's hand and held it tight.

The sun was already setting as Mrs. Brown hailed a hack. Both women entered the closed carriage, and Mrs. Brown kept her grasp of Betsy's warm, gloved hand.

Like supper, the ride seemed unending and the silence suffocating. Betsy wanted to tell Mrs. Brown her entire life story and that she was worried Hank was dying, but she fretted that the news another "son" was beyond hope would undo her benefactor. Mrs. Brown was mute because she suspected something was wrong. In the hours since they'd discovered Hank's whereabouts, Betsy had exhibited nervousness, sadness, anxiety, but little excitement. She feared a second husband's death would soon acquaint Betsy with boundless emptiness.

As the carriage crossed the canal to the Island, Mrs. Brown looked toward the hospital complex, dreading the coming minutes. But regardless of what happened, she would remain at Betsy's side through the ordeal.

The carriage stopped in front of the hospital, and the women descended. For the first time since entering the vehicle, Mrs. Brown let go of Betsy's hand. She reached into her bag to retrieve fare for the driver as Betsy shifted nervously.

The two women strode toward the general office where Betsy stammered about Hank to a man leaving the hospital complex. Once he understood what she wanted, he disappeared into the office for several minutes, returning with information on Hank. The two women found the pavilion and asked for Henry Gragg.

A kindly, middle-aged night watcher greeted them, heard their quest and tactfully explained they had come too late. He had died earlier in the day and been moved to the dead house.

About to collapse in despair, Betsy overheard a patient call out pleasantly, "Ah, Nurse Richman, why are you here?"

Betsy looked toward the soldier and followed his gaze to the nurse. Betsy stepped toward the woman. With her back to Betsy, the lady was busy explaining something in soft, urgent tones to the broad-shouldered, colored man at her side and ignored the patient's greeting.

Within feet of the nurse, Betsy, closely followed by Mrs. Brown, called out, "Nurse Richman."

The nurse turned to face Betsy. "Yes?"

Betsy's overpowering grief was instantly snuffed, replaced with livid horror. This nurse—beautiful as she was—who had cared for Hank, who had watched as Hank had faded to the grave, who had placed the newspaper advertisement, who bore her family's name, was colored. Betsy stared at her.

"May I help you?"

Betsy didn't answer, but Mrs. Brown sensing Betsy's discomfort announced, "We're looking for Hank Gragg."

The dark-skinned man standing by the nurse whispered in astonishment, "Miss Betsy?"

Betsy's eyes moved hesitantly from Nurse Richman to the man. "William?"

William smiled warmly, "It's me. It's so good to see you." Quickly the joy in his face faded, and he looked sheepishly to the ground. "If only it weren't for this."

Ignoring William, Mrs. Brown interjected, "We're looking for Hank Gragg . . . of the 19th Indiana."

William answered, "We came looking for him. Came as soon as I heard . . . as soon as we figured out it was Hank."

"Why do you use that name?" Betsy blurted out as she glared at Victoria.

Victoria had already reckoned this unpleasant woman the daughter of one of William's masters who had for some dubious purpose attached herself to William's friend Hank

Gragg. Victoria quelled her emotions and replied politely, "From my husband."

"Who's your husband?" Betsy shot back. Betsy's father was gone, her mother crazy and likely to die at any time, her property out of her reach—probably forever—her husband suddenly dead. The only tangible link remaining to her family heritage was her name . . . and some bumptious freed slave, an African, had stolen it. Nothing was left her.

Victoria could feel her fury rising in correlation to her increasing humiliation. Her face burned, but she reacted meekly, touching William's arm gently, "William Richman."

"How dare you steal my name," Betsy decreed glowering at Victoria and shifting her gaze angrily to William.

Victoria turned from Betsy, glanced at William and began walking toward the door.

Betsy followed until they reached open ground between pavilions where she repeated her charge.

Victoria stopped and turned to Betsy and said softy, "I'm proud of my name, because it's the name my husband has taken. I'm ashamed of the people who enslaved him. He spoke so highly of you. Did you think to free him when you could have? Do you think of him as a human?"

William, stunned by Betsy's behavior, stepped in between the two women. "Please don't do this."

Mrs. Brown, confused by what she was witnessing and suddenly worried for Betsy's safety commanded William, "Get away from her, you . . . . Don't touch her."

William's eyes betrayed his misery.

Sternly, Victoria commanded, taking William by the hand and pulling him away from Betsy, "Let's look for Mr. Gragg elsewhere. We mustn't waste time where we're unwelcome."

"Don't go looking for my husband."

Victoria was struck by the sudden revelation of relation. "Your husband?" she asked with interest.

"Yes."

"I have cared for your husband for all these weeks. I posted the notice for you." She glowered at Betsy. "Yet you abuse me in this way because my husband chose to remember a family he thought loved him?"

Betsy was quickly becoming embarrassed at her own outburst and treatment of William and his wife, yet she lashed out again, "You have no right to look for my husband."

Victoria checked her ire: This woman whom William had so often described in glowing terms and her husband who had been kind to William were of no importance to her. They were—Betsy had so clearly reminded her—of a different world. Victoria smiled, nodded politely and turned to William. "I believe we can go home. Leave her to find her own husband's corpse. It's her right and privilege."

"I'll have none of this treatment of Mrs. Gragg," Mrs. Brown said, speaking forcefully to Victoria.

Victoria, realizing she was creating a social crisis, in what she took as the righteousness of her cause, backed down. "I'm sorry to have offended either of you. William. Please." She walked toward the carriage.

Tears ran openly, rapidly down William's cheeks as he watched the verbal wrestling and felt the lash of Mrs. Gragg's contempt. He followed Victoria to the carriage.

Betsy, horrified at what she had done and said, but too proud to apologize to a colored woman and a slave, watched them silently as the carriage pulled away. She turned to Mrs. Brown, aching from her mistake and misjudgment, and commented dryly, "I'm sorry you had to witness that."

"I understand completely," Mrs. Brown said haughtily. "They're given freedom, and they think themselves equal. It's hard to accept their arrogance. Do they really believe they're the same as us?"

Betsy didn't respond. Hearing Mrs. Brown parrot what she was feeling bloated her self-contempt, and she thought ashamedly of William's kindnesses when she was a girl. What had she done? She grimaced. Her only relief, surprisingly, came from knowing Hank was dead. He hadn't witnessed what she'd just done. He would never need to know how ugly she had become. Yet remembering his death unleashed torrents of angry buffeting waves. She wanted to melt into the earth, to cease to exist. Their child unborn would never be held in a father's arms. Her own brief, heavenly marriage was torn asunder in Confederate murder. Why, God? Why? Instantly she desired Walthrope to materialize with pistol aimed menacingly at her face. She wouldn't resist, not now. She'd run toward it to end her suffering . . . to end her. Hank dead. No one to share her sorrow. She craved another chance to meet William and his wife. They would have stood by her if she'd been kind. There was Mrs. Brown, but Mrs. Brown had joined in Betsy's hate. Was there even eternal hope left for her? What did it matter? Hank was dead. Hope was gone. Expectations dashed. Reason to live fled.

Would God forgive her sudden anger, her so quickly giving offense? It was her fault. Her husband was dead. That wasn't her fault. NO! It was God's fault. He had kept Hank from her. He had taken her husband—both of them. Where was his comfort for her? He sends a colored woman—a slave woman—to tell her. No, God was guilty . . . if there were a God. What had he done to give her happiness? If there were a God, he was spiteful and vengeful. What had she done to bring this? Nothing. She'd been faithful. Falsely accused. Imprisoned. Mocked. Carried here and there by others. Cheated by a lying man who stole her life and her possessions. Where were her friends? In good days, they had swarmed about her like gnats in a grassy field and held her in high esteem, but now they denied her.

She was like Job, but unlike that God-favored hero, the Deity had destroyed her new family, too. Her family had been wrenched from her grip. "Curse God and die," she said aloud suddenly, moaning pitifully and startling Mrs. Brown.

The ladies climbed in the waiting hack. As they rode home, Mrs. Brown thought for a long time without comment. When she finally spoke, she looked at Betsy and suggested softly, "We both have lost families, but let us not give up faith and hope in God. Remember, child, you carry a life, a new beginning."

How insensitive was this woman? Couldn't she see Betsy's woe? To talk about faith when God had stolen her husband; to talk about God when she had lost her land and home . . . her nation; to talk about hope when she had no idea how her mother fared; to talk about God when he had let that woman steal her name. That slave woman was like all her people—lazy, expecting everything without work. They'd steal food, anything; and now they'd stolen Betsy's heritage, her name, her nation. She had probably suffocated Hank. In the end they'd take her property. The sense of complete loss and ravaging hatred consumed her, but she didn't cry. She glared ahead silently, determinedly.

Mrs. Brown was frightened and took Betsy's hand, softly entreating, "My dear lady, don't be cross with me. I know from experience it hurts. It will for a long time. I wish I could say otherwise. You will still be here tomorrow and each succeeding day, and one morning you'll wake and realize you're happy again. Don't let this sting crush your hope in Jesus. Please don't be cross with me."

Betsy didn't say anything. How could she respond? Even her patron didn't understand. She was alone. Numbness poured into her soul. She was no longer angry and could feel no sorrow. There was no reason to feel. Hank was gone. Oblivion had arrived. She'd gone through this for what? One happy week with him. Not enough. If there had been a God, he would not have been as cruel as to kill Hank minutes before she found him. She'd heard that when you die, your life flashes through your mind. She was dying spiritually, and her life of worship—false worship, as she now recognized—flowed through her—every stern and loving sermon, every prayer vainly thought or spoken. Superstition. As real as witches in Salem, and no more substantial.

"Please Betsy, say something. Don't let it turn to bile in you."

Betsy, still staring at the back of the driver, asked matter-of-factly, "Where do they bury soldiers from the hospital?"

"I think Soldiers' Home."

"I'll go as soon as the sun rises. Perhaps they haven't buried him, and I can see him . . . touch his face once more."

"May I go?"

"You needn't my permission," Betsy responded coldly.

Chapter 34

July 1864, Washington City, District of Columbia

The two women left the house and walked without conversation to a nearby hack stand as soon as the sun was up.

The night had been warm and the day promised oppressive sun and heat. Both women wore dark hats and carried tasseled black parasols which would shade their heads, yet leave the heat little changed. They were already sweating, with only petticoats and hoops keeping the moisture off their morning dresses. Neither was happy. They climbed into a cab and set off on an hour-long, grim errand in nervous, quiet gloom. When they arrived at Soldiers' Home, they climbed from the carriage and approached the graves, still in silence.

A tall man with a dark beard and stovetop hat stood quietly at the cemetery's edge. He didn't move as the two women neared.

Mrs. Brown spoke softly to Betsy. "I was sure they buried the soldiers here."

The man turned slowly, smiling forlornly at the two women and spoke. "They've run out of ground. So many have died, they've no more space." He paused. "They're burying them at Arlington House, and they leave these to quietude."

The two women nodded in somber appreciation. He returned their nods, and they quickly retraced their steps to the cab. Neither commented on the man they had seen.

It took the women two more hours to arrive at the new cemetery grounds at Arlington House. Betsy spoke once during the long trip, saying in a whisper, "If I can just see him once more."

Mrs. Brown took it as a sign she was overcoming her shock and put her arm around her informal ward. Betsy responded leaning closer to Mrs. Brown in spite of the unbearable heat.

There was much activity in the graveyard which boasted simple, white markers along a few carefully laid out rows of graves and a small white caretaker's building. Dark-complexioned men dug new graves for a few boxed corpses queued for funerals and burial.

The two women descended from the carriage; Mrs. Brown first, and she extended her hand to help Betsy down. As soon as Betsy's second petite foot touched the earth, she let go of Mrs. Brown's gloved hand and walked anxiously toward a fair-haired man in the vicinity. Mrs. Brown hurried to catch her.

"Sir," she called to the man—a uniformed soldier—still a dozen feet from her. He didn't respond, and she repeated, "Sir!"

He indolently looked up from the paperwork he was inspecting and studied the two women.

"Yes, Ma'am," he answered pleasantly.

"I want to see my husband."

"To take him home for burial?"

The question took Betsy off guard, and she stuttered, "I . . . I want to see him." She looked across at the burying detail. "He has no home."

"His name?"

"Gragg. Henry Gragg. 19th Indiana."

His eyes opened in amazement. "Someone was here earlier to see him."

"Where are they?" Betsy asked anxiously.

"Gone. It was hours ago, just after I arrived."

"May I see him?"

The soldier's expression softened, "I'm sorry. They held a brief service and already buried him."

"Can you dig him up?" Betsy asked as if it were a routine, easy request.

Mrs. Brown, with a look of shock, glanced uneasily at Betsy.

Betsy, emotion rising in her breast, pleaded, "I want to see him one last time—one last time for me and our child."

"We can't do that without an official order. I'm sorry."

"Order from whom?"

"Someone with that authority."

"Who has more authority in a man's life than his wife?" Betsy inquired rhetorically.

"Someone in the government . . . the military," he responded in a respectful, but resigned voice.

"Did the person—the one who came earlier—did he see him before . . . ?"

The soldier looked deferentially at Betsy, glanced at Mrs. Brown and said politely, "I believe so. There were two of them: a man and woman. They asked the gravediggers where he was. I was at a distance, so I couldn't tell what they said. But it sounded like the pair argued when they found him. They never spoke to me. I suspect the woman wanted to take the body, but the man insisted they couldn't. At least that's what I gathered from the commotion. I didn't bother to ask anyone about it. Both seemed adamant, but after a while—I didn't watch for long—they were gone. They never spoke to me. Coloreds."

"Colored," Betsy repeated equivocally. "Can you show me his grave?"

"I will. You're Mrs. Gragg?"

"Yes."

"I'm sorry."

Betsy answered softly, "Thank you."

The soldier led the two women to the fresh grave where a slat of wood temporarily marked the head of the grave. He looked down at the mound of dirt, at the marker and finally at the cemetery map in his hand. "Yes, this is Henry Gragg of the 19th."

Betsy stared at the loosely piled dirt. Pain ballooned. This was his end? A pile of dirt to cover his body, a body that had fought against Virginia, a body that had given her this coming child. She began to cry softly, but quickly gave into body-contorting sobs. Mrs. Brown put her arms around her without a word, but Betsy broke free of her embrace and flung herself down onto the grave on all fours, instantly soiling dress and gloves. Mrs. Brown watched in horror, feeling helpless. The soldier looked away in embarrassment.

"No, Betsy, no. You can't. You mustn't," Mrs. Brown cried as Betsy began digging with her hands.

The soldier dropped his map and with Mrs. Brown gently pulled Betsy from the grave. Betsy fought them and broke clear to fling herself prostrate on the grave, shoving her face in the freshly dug dirt, knocking her hat from her head.

In a whisper she groaned, "Don't leave me, Hank. Not like this." She began digging again. "Scoot over. There's room for both. Don't leave me, not after all this. We can both be buried here . . . in Virginia. A few moments beside you and the deed will be done. We and our child can be together."

The soldier nodded to Mrs. Brown, and the two of them again gently reached down and pulled Betsy up, forcing her from the grave.

"Please, Betsy. Don't. He's gone. Let him go. Come home."

Betsy refused to turn from the grave, but the soldier and Mrs. Brown pushed her backwards, forcing her into the hack.

"I'll just come back. I will bury myself with him. I will no longer be separated."

"Quiet, quiet, my dear," Mrs. Brown said soothingly, as the soldier closed the door.

The gravediggers had stopped to watch as the pair struggled to control Betsy.

The soldier waved the hack driver on, and the carriage jerked forward quickly.

The trip across the river was delayed by a column of soldiers and ambulances at the bridge. When the hack crossed into Washington, the slow-paced ambulances and wounded soldiers clogging the streets reminded both women of the corpse they'd just left behind. Betsy stared at her muddy gloves, tore them off and hurled them into the street. She'd left her hat resting on Hank's grave. She looked at her milk-white hands with disgust. "You've failed me."

Tears dripped onto Mrs. Brown's cheeks.

Betsy thought of God, but only briefly. He had set His will against her, consigning her to a living hell. She would never again worship Him. She would build a tower to heaven, a tower of Babel, and replace Him.

Chapter 35

July 1864, Staunton, Virginia

As he emerged from the barn, Caleb guided the horse warily toward the back of the house. He was surprised to find John, gas lantern in hand, closely inspecting the ground.

"Can you tell anything?" Caleb queried urgently.

John looked up. "Grass is bent like he was dragging the lady." He lowered the lantern to show Caleb. "Grass is trampled. Maybe he kept his horse here. Maybe they fought here, and he dragged her up on the horse. Doesn't look like she went willingly."

"We need to find them . . . save her."

"If she wants to be saved," offered the honest servant. "Be hard for an old fellow like me to ride—especially if I wanted to ride fast—with a lady on the horse who fought me. May be the same for a younger fellow."

"You're saying he couldn't have taken her with him, not if he couldn't quiet her . . . not with Sheriff nearby. She did seem to be fighting him though, even with the gun to her head."

"I overheard—I'm sorry for that—that she was an actress. Mayhap an elaborate scheme of Mr. Walthrope's to catch you."

"I thought of that, John, but it doesn't seem right. I don't believe she conspired with him. Yes, yes, that might be what she wanted me to think. She is an actress . . . . What am I to do, John? I can't let him take her, if she was tricked by him like the rest of us."

"If she fought him and got away, going after him won't help her. He's an evil man."

"By the pricking of your thumbs?"

"Sir?"

"You recognize evil when you see it."

John didn't respond, but smiled, grateful for a hint of praise.

"Hand me the lantern," Caleb directed, as he climbed carefully from the horse. He took the lantern and handed John the reins and squatted, lowering the lantern so he could see the ground John had described more closely. From where he crouched he could see the marks in the long grass. Did Walthrope have a nervous horse that trampled the grass?

"I'm not sure I can tell anything from all of this." A smile spread his cheeks as he realized John hoped Anna had been sincere, in spite of his words of caution. He'd heard it in the servant's tone. Had they both been taken in? In reporting what he saw and surmised, perhaps John romanticized the evidence in the grass.

"Maybe you could look farther from the matted grass, where she would have run . . . if she'd gotten away," John softly suggested.

"You don't think he took her? Where's Sheriff?" Caleb asked rhetorically in exasperation.

The slave didn't answer, and Caleb followed his suggestion and walked around the matted grass in expanding circles to see if two matted paths led from the center. He saw grass slanted toward the house, and he followed it a few feet. It was headed directly toward the window.

John, who was watching him suggested, "That's the way Mr. Walthrope came to the house."

Caleb frowned. They were wasting precious time, while she was in danger. He made his way back to the matted grass and slowly, anxiously followed it step by step around its edges. He could see where the horse had come from earlier, where Walthrope had dragged Anna from the house and the direction Walthrope had ridden to escape. Caleb saw no other beaten grass, and if there were none, she'd gone willingly. Walthrope, informed Sheriff was nearby, would have fled as far from Staunton as fast as he could. With his strong instinct for survival, Walthrope would not have let Anna hold him back.

Was this an elaborate chess move to put him in revengeful check? Walthrope seemed to plan revenge as if it were a game of chess and he a chess master. Before the final checkmate, he proclaimed opponents in check, announcing they would soon lay down their kings. Is that what his library visit had been? Lucius Walthrope took a strange pride in proving himself in vengeance. Had he chosen revenge so many times that what was humane in him had died, leaving only the animal? If so, Anna would mean nothing to him, whether she'd gone with him lovingly or not.

He reached a bit of grass that leaned from the matted area and the house. Relief thrilled him like a revitalizing spring shower. She hadn't gone. She'd escaped. He followed the bent grass, in the dimness of the lamp's light, leaving John and the horse behind.

He suspected she'd go only far enough to escape Walthrope and hide. She would come out after daybreak when she felt safer. She wouldn't have to wait till then as he would find her and bring her safely home. He sighed happily. He and John had been right: She'd acted no dissembling role.

His artificial leg rubbed uncomfortably against his thigh. He wanted to adjust it, but he wanted more to find Anna, and even knowing the leg would eventually rub his stub raw, he kept searching. Farther from the house, he followed the beaten grass to the road. She'd circled back to the house on the road looking for help. Or had she, still frightened of Walthrope, gone south?

Seconds later a shot tore the nocturnal silence. It came from the house. Caleb dropped the lamp on the road, shattering and extinguishing it, and ran.

By the time he arrived, his eyes had dilated enough to make out objects. The house was dark, and he saw no activity there. He walked around the house and discovered light shimmering through the stable doors.

He hobbled to the doors and peeked in. A stable slave cradled John's head in his lap. Caleb, with breaking heart, threw the door open and scrambled to the wounded man. John's eyes were dim, his breathing rapid, shallow and labored. Caleb probed urgently, "What happened? Who did this?"

John struggled to reply, whispering raspingly, "I don't know." His breathing stopped.

The slave holding John's head began to wail.

Caleb unceremoniously pushed John's dead body over and found blood seeping from the back of his jacket. Caleb moaned.

Whoever had done this—Walthrope . . . or Anna—might be outside waiting to do the same to him or another slave. Why kill John?

He whispered to the man still mourning John, "Stay with him. I'll close the doors. Don't leave the stable till morning. Whoever shot him may be nearby."

As he spoke, his eyes began searching the inner stable. Whoever it was might be waiting for him here. He twitched involuntarily, slowly stood and readied his pistol. He pulled the doors of the stable closed and crept from stall to stall, searching each with the lantern that had been sitting on the ground by John's body. He reached the final stall in the back of the stable and held the lantern so its glow illuminated its corners. Nothing. If someone was still in the stable, he would hide behind the false wall or in the loft. The slave had stopped wailing and walked closely behind him. Caleb looked back at the man, irritated he had left John alone.

Quickly ruling out the concealed compartment, Caleb began climbing the ladder and reviewed the possibilities. If Walthrope had shot John, he might hide above. Anna wouldn't. She'd run if she'd done it. He cringed at the thought and the betrayal it would reveal. If she'd done it, without the motive of revenge, she was incomprehensively vicious. Why would she kill John? Whoever it was, he or she had sneaked up on him in the dark. Right behind him. Caleb kept searching. If Lucius was hiding in the loft, he was waiting to kill Caleb. He raised the lantern above his head, scrunched his face in anticipation of someone firing at the lantern. Nothing followed. He slowly stepped higher till his head was visible above the floor. He saw no one. He breathed slowly and climbed to the top, his heart beating rapidly. He was surprised to feel such fear. Caleb exhaled loudly. If someone intended him harm, he'd already be dead.

The questions returned. Had Anna stolen back to the house to kill John? Had Lucius circled back on horseback to kill the slave? He climbed down to John who still lay face down. He put the lantern down and respectfully turned the man's body back over, ordering the corpse's hands across his chest. He closed the servant's eyes and put his hands on top of John's. A most faithful friend and slave. Caleb had sent him with Betsy's mother when she insisted on returning to Winchester. In Winchester, he could have escaped to the North, especially after Betsy's mother died unexpectedly. He hadn't. He stayed till she was buried, then returned home. Caleb asked him why he returned. John smiled subtly, walked to a nearby window and looked over the farm, and said softly, "Freedom's coming. It's coming. Not much anyone can do to stop it. Not now. I want to be here when it comes. I didn't come back to be your slave or Mrs. Gragg's. I came home to be free here." As Caleb remembered his gentle answer and fine hopes, anger battled sorrow within him. Anger won, and he swore silently to avenge the slave's death.

He looked up at the servant who still seemingly anchored himself to the safety of Caleb's presence. "Stay here till morning. Whoever did this may plan more . . . but only for me. I don't want it to be you accidently. Stay . . . in the dark. No one else is here. You saw that. Take care of John till after sunup."

The slave nervously nodded, and Caleb made his way to the stable door. He carefully stepped into the dark and closed the barn doors as the servant inserted a plank of wood against the inside of the door. Caleb took two steps along the door and dropped silently to the ground. He lay motionless, watching and listening. The sound of a slight breeze rustling the leaves of nearby trees calmed him.

Once his eyes acclimated, he struggled to get up and slowly made his way to the back of the house. The lights in the library had been extinguished, but the windows remained open, as if nothing had happened. He climbed in, closed all the windows and carefully walked from the room. The kitchen was likewise dark, and he made his way through a hall of grain barrels saved from passing armies. He opened the kitchen door and was startled by the presence of the cook, the house maids and several field servants huddled on the floor in the dark.

The cook spoke, "John told us to stay here till he came to tell us everything was all right. We heard a shot."

Caleb looked at the cook without responding. He wondered when John had directed them here. Some had obviously been roused from their beds. He glanced at the windows and said softly, "Stay here together till morning. Get as comfortable as possible. Try to get a little sleep. Don't leave the kitchen . . . any of you . . . for any reason till sunup." He hesitated. "I've got to leave. Barricade the door when I'm gone. Don't let anyone in—even me—no matter what you think you hear or see."

"You're scaring me," the cook responded nervously.

"You'll be fine."

"What is this about?" the cook persisted. "Who fired the shot?"

"Remember the man that harmed your mistress—Walthrope. He's back. He's not going to harm you." The image of John's body passed through his mind. "No," he said in a more confident voice. "He's here to harm me. Stay here. You'll be fine. I suspect he fired the gun."

"Stay with us," the cook said, her voice wavering with fear.

"You'll be safe. He's not going to harm you."

"So you must stay with us. We can hide you so he won't find you."

Caleb was surprised and touched by her concern and smiled unabashedly. "I have to go, but thank you." He turned to walk out of the room, but stopped. "No matter what happens, know I have not forgotten how you saved this house, our food and my life."

He pushed through the door and heard the sound of the heavy kitchen table being shoved against the door behind him.

In the kitchen, it had occurred to Caleb that Walthrope—or Anna—whoever had shot John, thought he was shooting Caleb. John hadn't had a light with him. The other slave had brought that. So in the dark, John must have looked enough like Caleb to invite the fatal assault. In his hurry to escape, Walthrope may not have looked closely at his victim. That was the crucial question: Did Walthrope ever realize his error? If he did, he might be nearby awaiting a shot at his real target.

The weight of the colt in his pocket reassured him. He grabbed a lantern from the hall, lit it and walked through the entire house, except for the kitchen, searching possible hiding places. The tense moments reaped calm surety: No one but servants and he were in the house. He doused the lamp and walked from room to room, checking from each window for anything that moved on the lawn.

Hours passed during which Caleb continued walking from room to room in the dark. He knew his thigh was raw and bleeding, and he shifted and tightened his leg till it was more comfortable. The soreness signaled he'd waited too long and would have to use crutches for weeks until the rawness completely healed. He hated not using his leg.

He saw movement and heard noise outside and gimped to the front door. Someone was talking outside the door—a man and woman. One of them knocked, and immediately

Caleb tore the door open and pointed his pistol toward the head of the nearest one—the man.

"Caleb," Robert Sheriff said calmly. "It's me."

Caleb lowered his pistol and invited them in.

He closed and locked the door and exhaled a short breath. As he turned to his visitors, he realized Anna was the woman. She'd come in the door tentatively, silently.

Without waiting, Sheriff blustered, "I'm glad to see you. The snake did it again. I thought I had him. When I saw the horse galloping from the house, I was sure I had him. Alas, it was Miss Whitehead, an excellent rider, and it took me hours to catch her. Of course age slows a rider. That devil sent me on a wild goose chase while he set off on foot. I worried he'd stayed behind to kill you."

"Why is she with you?"

Sheriff breathed loudly, consternation on his face. After silently ordering his thoughts, he said, "Miss Whitehead was dragged from the house and ordered at knife point to get on the horse. She refused, and Walthrope made her an offer. Anna, you tell him what he said." Anna shook her head, but Sheriff pressed her. "Tell him."

She started haltingly, "He . . . whatever his name is or was . . . he threatened to cut my throat. My only chance to live was to get on the horse. I told him"—Caleb could feel embarrassment in her voice which seemed to get quieter as she spoke—"I wouldn't do it. He pressed his knife against my throat till it stung. His mind is quick, and he changed his demand. 'Get on the horse, or I will go back and shoot Caleb.'" Her voice was no more than a murmur. "I couldn't let him. You were innocent; kind to me. I couldn't let him hurt you. He told me to ride as fast and as far down the Valley as I could get. If I did that and didn't get caught till morning, he'd leave you alive and disappear . . . never bother us again. He said he'd watch from a safe place. If he saw me return too quickly, he would kill you." She paused, then quickly added, "I got on the horse and rode toward Harrisonburg. Got farther than I thought I would."

"My age, Ma'am. The darkness of night and age."

"And he left you alone," Anna concluded, smiling sheepishly at Caleb.

Caleb, confused about her, tried to read her expression in the shadows. He mumbled, "Thank you. I don't think Walthrope meant to keep his promise. He shot John, my . . . Betsy's . . . servant. I think he thought it was me getting a horse ready to go after him. It was John returning the horse to the stable."

"The kindly old boy," Anna said woefully.

"Yes."

The sheriff interjected, "He never keeps his word . . . unless it's what he wants anyway. As we rode back, Anna explained her role in freeing Betsy from Castle Thunder and placing her in that demon's hands."

"Will he try again?" Anna asked.

Caleb speculated, "I don't know if he stayed long enough to realize he'd killed John, not me."

Anna quickly observed, "He may come back after me because I betrayed him . . . or he thinks I betrayed him. But it was him. He betrayed me. If he comes back after me, he'll find you still alive."

"He won't return tonight with everyone looking and waiting for him. If he ever comes back, it will be months from now . . . when we've let down our guard."

The sheriff changed subjects. "I'm going home for a couple of hours. Can you put up Miss Whitehead for what remains of the night?"

Caleb was embarrassed at the suggestion. "Yes."

Sheriff opened the door and left without saying more, until he was mounting his horse. "I'll take your horse, too, Miss Whitehead. If we're wrong and he's still nearby, I don't want him to see his horse here. I think he hired it in town anyway."

Neither Caleb nor Anna responded, accepting Sheriff's judgment on the matter.

Caleb closed and relocked the door. "I'm embarrassed, but the servants are in the kitchen with instructions to stay until light. I hope I haven't inadvertently brought dishonor to your reputation."

"I'm not sure what my reputation is or should be. Whatever it may be, however, it will survive sleeping here tonight. I am so weary, I would like to retire."

"We'll put you in Betsy's room." He fumbled around until he found a lamp, lit it and led her silently up the stairs to the bedroom door. He handed her the lamp, saying, "Goodnight."

"Please check the room. Make sure he's not hiding inside."

"I already checked . . . but . . . ." He was uncomfortable at entering the bedchamber with her, but turned the knob and pushed open the door. He took the lamp from her. She closed the door behind them as he opened the wardrobes full of Betsy's clothes. He knelt at the bedside and bent lower, looking under the bed. He searched the water closet and the adjoining sitting room, finally proclaiming patiently, "You're safe." He handed the lamp back to Anna, smiling.

"Won't you need it?"

"I'll find my way without it, but please put it out quickly, as soon as you can, so no one knows anyone's in here."

"I'll be fine in the dark. Please take it."

"I think we're both better off in the dark."

"And together."

Caleb didn't answer; embarrassed by the suggestion even though he knew she spoke it only in fear. If only he could coax a servant out of the kitchen to sit with her.

"When I leave, close and lock this door. I'll sit outside till morning."

"You can't sleep like that." Compassion warmed the words.

"Slaves and soldiers do it all the time. If you hear anything or fear something, I'll be right outside."

He handed the key to Anna, passed out the door and heard her lock it. It sounded as if she had left the key in the lock. Immediately the light shining under the door went out. He felt along the hall until he came to a small, wooden chair and moved it to Anna's door, sat down and instantly fell into a sound sleep.

Chapter 36

July 1864, Staunton, Virginia

Caleb woke to the presence of a young slave girl staring at him. Still in the wooden chair in front of Anna's door, his back and neck were stiff and his leg throbbed and burned. He wondered how long he'd been asleep and what had happened while he dozed. He intended to catnap through the night so he could periodically check the house, but his body had failed him. The servant watched as he rubbed his eyes.

"Is it morning?" he asked dully.

"Sun's been up an hour."

He bolted from his chair. "An hour! Is everyone all right?"

"Haven't heard otherwise. We stayed—like you told us—in the kitchen. We came out together. Everything in the house was quiet."

"I slept too long. Has anyone been outside?"

"Don't know."

He looked at the girl. "Miss Anna, do you remember her?"

"No."

"The woman visiting yesterday."

"Ah, her."

"She's sleeping in this room. She's locked in for the same reason you stayed in the kitchen. Help her with anything she needs when she gets up." He still felt guilty for having Anna in the house without others around, and nervously added, "I sat here in case someone . . . Walthrope . . . tried to bother her. Take care of her needs."

"Yes."

"Have cook make up a breakfast for when Miss Anna gets up. I'm going to the stable."

Caleb limped gingerly down the stairs, out the door and across to the stable, where he found the doors flung open. The cooper was already putting the final touches on the lid of a simple pine casket and six field slaves stood across the room looking at John's body in the casket. Caleb gently pushed his way through them to look at the faithful Henderson family slave. If a slave ever deserved freedom, he thought, it was John. He instantly recoiled at the thought as he realized that if any one of them deserved freedom, they all merited it—each had a right to it. But what would you do with so many of them? Could they all be sent back to Africa? He shivered in spite of the heat and silently rested his hand on the slave's cold, stiff hand.

Memories of the day Betsy confronted Walthrope disturbed his reverence. Betsy had found in Walthrope an arm to depend on after the death of her husband. He had wooed and nearly won her. She had asked him to manage the woolens factory she inherited from her husband, and she thought him exceptional at the task. But Walthrope was not whom he pretended to be. In addition to manufacturing wool cloth for the Confederacy, he had used the building to hoard needed materiel, smuggle, and speculate in US currency. Payments from the profitable endeavor made their way unobserved to several Confederate officials to blunt probing questions. Betsy knew nothing of Walthrope's activities, but a slip of judgement by a conspirator—the factory foreman, a man named Stokes—angered Walthrope, and he had murdered the fellow. He thought himself safe from discovery because he assumed no witnesses, but he had been wrong. A woman—Stoke's unsavory mistress—hiding in fear, had witnessed Walthrope's violence and divulged it to Betsy.

Betsy, perhaps innocently infected by Walthrope's penchant for vengeance, had confronted the murderer. He denied everything, but the truth was obvious to Caleb and the three women in the room at the time. They had driven Walthrope from the house. As he left, he had directed his anger at John, slamming him against the wall—this John who rested so peacefully in the coffin.

John was the match for many white men Caleb had met. How odd, Caleb thought, that an inferior being could excel some of his betters. The reflection discomforted Caleb, bringing his thoughts back to the error, maybe the sin, of holding a whole race of Johns in slavery. He lifted his hand from his friend's. Struggling without success for words he quietly withdrew a few paces. He'd have to tell the house servants. He wondered what they would want to do about a funeral. Would they want a white preacher . . . or one of their own? Would they grieve? If they could grieve like white men, slavery was wrong. But it wasn't. It couldn't be. The scriptures told slaves to obey masters. It couldn't be wrong if it was in the holy writ of God. He wrung doubt from his mind.

Caleb had been busy managing Betsy's interests in her absence. Would she return? Could she? She'd been accused of killing Stokes and of being a traitor because her love—a Yankee—had come to see and marry her. He smiled remembering the naïve Yankee didn't know the identity of the woman he had come to meet. He thought he was visiting a Confederate widow, and she was. By what must have been extraordinary divine intervention, she was also the love of his young life. The Confederate government had viewed the acquaintance and clandestine visit in the worst possible light and sent her to Castle Thunder, the Richmond prison for traitors, deserters and escaped slaves. Betsy could never return to Staunton.

What would become of her remaining property: her slaves—these slaves—her land, her house, the shells of her destroyed mills and the burned-down factory? Caleb had saved prodigious amounts of grain by storing it in the house when the Yankee army had come destroying everything in their way. He had hidden the horses in a cellar they'd dug in a wheat field, and he personally had buried household silver and family treasures in a newly dug, feigned grave in the family graveyard to keep them from greedy enemy hands.

But after the war, what would happen to everything he'd salvaged?

Caleb loved Betsy. Betsy had saved him. He'd been injured at Gettysburg and left to die in a Winchester hospital. She, whom he had met once before the war, found him, took him home and nursed him to health. At the time, he thought he loved her romantically, but it was not to be, and his love matured into something different. She had encouraged his romance with her friend Marie Ann, now his former fiancée.

Marie Ann had long been infatuated with Caleb, so Betsy had brought her to Staunton to help nurse him, hoping to see them married. But eventually after the person who had brought them together had been arrested for treason and murder, Marie Ann abandoned her benefactor and fled Staunton. She could not endure the waxing social ostracism concentrated on her for supporting Betsy. She'd tried to entice Caleb to turn on his patron saint, but he wouldn't budge, and she soon abandoned him to join her family. As he remembered the parting, he acknowledged to himself for the first time that he had been relieved when she left. He'd formed the attachment when his social self-esteem—because of his lost leg—was at its lowest ebb. Oddly his self-confidence had since swelled as his social standing in the town had waned due to his adamant support of Betsy. He refused to think the worst of her and would not tolerate anyone else speaking evil of her in his presence.

Caleb had never really been attracted to Marie Ann and always found her physically awkward and mentally dull. He was glad she was gone, though he wished it hadn't required Betsy suffering the humiliation of arrest. Perhaps this history and an inner craving for approval and affection paved the path to his nearly spontaneous and inexplicable attraction to Anna and to his current confusion about the actress and slavery.

With a quiet sigh, he patted John's hand. Without comment to anyone around the box, he returned to the house. It was time to tell the house servants—although he supposed they knew—and to check on Anna. In spite of his grief and with suspicion of her still storming in his mind, he felt light when he imagined his guest.

As he walked to the house, he craned his neck constantly, looking for signs Walthrope still loitered. At the front door he met the maid he'd left to attend Anna. She looked at him disapprovingly.

"What's the matter?" he asked.

"She's in the dining room. She asked cook for breakfast and is eating. She refused to wait for you, and she's not wearing her own clothes. She's put on the mistress' skirt, blouse and jacket."

Caleb was as disturbed by the report as the maid was disapproving. He tried to understand Anna's rudeness. Perhaps she was frightened or trying to get away quickly to meet Walthrope and reveal that Caleb was still alive. He strode silently past the servant into the dining room.

Anna was already approaching the door to leave the room. He blocked her path, glancing at the table left cluttered with evidence of her meal. He couldn't help but note she looked particularly attractive in Betsy's clothes.

She spoke first, "I must leave, but I need your help."

Shocked by her assertiveness, he looked at her and stepped farther into the room, forcing her backwards. She didn't seem deterred or concerned by his advance.

"Where are you going?"

"You won't want me to tell you."

Caleb visualized her embracing Walthrope at a planned reunion and grew angry, but didn't respond.

"You'll try to dissuade me, and you mustn't."

"You owe me an explanation."

"I do, but can you trust me . . . and help me? I can't do it without you."

He ignored her plea for trust. "Why would I try to deter you? Please sit down, and you can explain it to me while I eat."

He softly grabbed her wrist and pulled her toward the table. She didn't resist, enjoying his touch. But she was disconcerted by his increased limp and slight grimaces.

"I didn't wait to eat because every minute delayed is lost, and one of those minutes might be crucial. Caleb, you don't know me. An evening is hardly enough—especially under these clouds—to trust someone; though I trust you completely. You must believe I want to set right past failings. Please let me go," she whined.

"A night's certainly not enough time to trust an actress." He knew from the fleeting pain in her eyes she'd felt the rebuke, and he suffered inexplicable remorse at the glint.

She watched him, hardly able to contain her attraction to him. How could she tell him how she felt? It wasn't her place, and if he saw her as an actress—a conspiring one—he would never see her as anything but a duplicitous wench, a despoiled woman, a woman sullied by a loathsome marriage to Daniel or Dante or Walthrope or whoever he really was. She couldn't let Caleb's opinion stop her from what she had to do. In that moment, his censure meant everything to her; yet it would mean nothing in the end for he could never love a woman like her. She had cherished every brief minute they'd spent together, laughing, talking, eyes caressing eyes, saying more than words. Walthrope had killed any hope she might hold for Caleb's love. She sat at the table, expecting him to sit. But he remained standing, towering above her; his lips compressed in a thin, stern line.

She took a deep breath. If only she could convince him there was some good in the woman who nearly cowered before his wilting gaze.

"Caleb, I didn't fathom what kind of man he was. I never suspected he tried to kill Betsy or that he would try to kill you."

"He's the one who scarred Betsy's face."

"How would I have discovered that, with him hiding his past? You have no reason to trust what I say, but I want you to hear it from my lips nonetheless. I have never lied to you. Not yesterday. Not last night. Not this morning."

He was still holding her wrist gently, and neither of them noticed.

"The day's still early," he said derisively. He saw hurt in her eyes, and it so distressed him that he determined never to cause it again. More kindly he said, "Go on."

She regarded him. What madness was this? Even in his anger, she adored him. He was defending what he thought was right. She might not—probably would not—see him after this conversation, whether he helped her or not, but she would take away an appreciation, a respect, an affection for him. Oh, if she hadn't been dishonored, they . . . . "Caleb, I've created the tragedy we live," she blurted out in frustration.

"I've come from seeing John's body laid out." He chuckled unexpectedly, bitterly. "They'd already made a coffin for him and arranged him respectfully in it. Walthrope and anyone who's working with him must be brought to justice for that, and for everything else they've done. John was a good slave, a good man."

His opinion of her was worse than she'd imagined. He actually supposed she had conspired in the gentle man's death. She was the one who should be angry: to be indirectly accused of doing something so horrendous. But she said meekly, "I'm so sorry. I thought he'd keep his word. I never suspected he'd renege and try to kill you, not after I led Mr. Sheriff from the farm. It was . . . it is my own continuing gullibility. Caleb, please listen to me. I've caused all this. I have to do what I can to restore what was lost, and I'm losing precious time."

"Where are you going?"

She hesitated, frowned and said, "I've got to get to Washington to find Betsy. He thinks he killed you. He got a man arrested for counterfeit bills in Richmond. I don't know who the man was or why, but he somehow organized the arrest. I've got to get to Washington to warn her . . . if she's still alive. But I can't tell with Daniel what's real and what's not. He told me he had killed Mr. Sheriff in Washington . . . to protect Betsy. He told me Sheriff pursued Betsy. Yet last night after you sent a message to Sheriff he showed up alive and chased Walthrope. I'm confused, but I've got to find Betsy to warn her before Walthrope gets there. He's got a head start. Please let me go." She imagined doubt in his eyes. "Even if you can't believe me and suspect I'm with him, letting me go won't hurt anything. It won't make things worse than I already have. In fact you'll be rid of me. Isn't that enough? Isn't that what you really want?"

"If you were in it with him, you might entrap Betsy," he challenged, wishing as soon as it left his lips that he'd kept silent.

"Do you think she would trust me . . . after what I've done? I suspect she thinks I did it knowingly with Daniel."

"If she won't trust you, why go?"

"I have to do something," she blurted out.

"Send a letter. I'll sign it. She still trusts me."

"Letter?" She laughed bitterly. "How do we get it to Washington? He'll kill her faster than you can post it."

"You must be a slow writer."

"Come with me. You can keep your eye on me, and I'll prove I will never again help Walthrope."

"I won't let you go."

"I would have sneaked out but you burned much of my money."

"Counterfeit. Money that would probably have gotten you arrested."

"Maybe, but I might have made it to Washington."

"You wouldn't have had money in Washington."

"I wouldn't anyway. It was Confederate."

Grimacing from his aching leg, he slid into the chair next to her still holding her wrist.

"You can't go. You can do nothing for Betsy. Sheriff will go after Walthrope. It's his obsession."

"He's done no good so far. He missed him last night. He's an old man. If he were equal to the task, he would have succeeded ages ago. He means well, but . . . Walthrope has escaped us all."

"If only Betsy had let me shoot him," Caleb uttered with regret.

"You had the chance?"

"When Betsy confronted him, but she wouldn't let me do it."

"It would have saved much heartache," Anna commented forlornly.

"I suppose, but there are always bad characters about. The circumstances change but some are always set on doing harm . . . and they find ways and words to justify it. It's natural in their eyes. I bet after the war the same people that led us into this catastrophe will be back in charge. Nothing changes. They manipulate us. When they get caught they slip into a corner until dark, and like mice sneak back into the center of the room when no one's watching."

"That's a morose view of life."

"I don't mean it to be. Life is like that. The bad ones survive. The ones on top—sometimes the same men—keep ending up on top. Mark my words: In ten . . . twenty years, it will be like this war was never fought. Power will be in the same hands. I won't let you leave. It will do no good. Walthrope might harm you. I can escort you back to Richmond if you need to leave . . . maybe to get back to the theater. Is that what you want?" he asked hopefully.

"I don't know what I want . . . beyond making everyone happy and safe. But I do know I must warn Betsy . . . somehow."

"I'll send a letter. It's the best we can do."

"I must do more."

Caleb looked at her. Why did he feel like this around her? "I don't want you to go."

"I can't go without your help. Without money, I'm really your prisoner."

"You aren't my prisoner."

"I'm trapped."

"Don't feel like that." He looked away from her and eventually toward the floor. "I have a confession to make."

She eyed him curiously.

He sat silently, eyes still downcast, not sure he could say the words. He finally raised his gaze and met hers. He smiled weakly and sputtered, glancing nervously back to the floor, "As foolish as it sounds, I've grown fond of you."

"Don't be daft, Caleb. I'm not what you think. I'm not worthy of consideration. Why would a man like you be fond of a woman like me? I've been used by Daniel, and what of your wife?" She craved Caleb's touch, wished he weren't already married.

"I'm not married," he said in surprise. "And no one's ever called me daft. It's invigorating."

"I thought you had a wife. You still haven't married her?"

"She wasn't daft enough to marry me," he said, snickering to himself.

"I can't stay."

He looked at her, trying not to reveal his disappointment. "I'll get money," he said grudgingly, still hoping she would choose to stay. "Maybe not as much as you brought in counterfeit bills—I couldn't afford that." He smiled tenderly. "I could give you enough to get wherever you wanted to go, and a little more to keep you while you're there. But please don't go. Daft as I am"—he shifted uncomfortably and dropped his eyes to the ground—"I am falling in love with you."

She tried to stop the tears, but she couldn't. "You can't love me. You don't even know me. You are a hero. I'm an actress, one who has deceived your friend, one who has been . . . ." She couldn't say more. She wanted him to love her. She had felt something in their time together. He wasn't married. Ah, to be his wife. But she was . . . . No matter what he said to her, he could never really want her.

"Anna, please. Don't go." He stood up and enigmatically stepped toward the doorway, leaving her confused. Halfway across the room, he stopped and returned quickly, putting his hand on her shoulder. She looked up and was moved to see his eyes water. He had stood firm against a town set on condemning Betsy. Maybe he was strong enough to forgive what she'd done. A warm happiness flowed through her, and without realizing it, she leaned her head onto the hand resting on her shoulder.

He pleaded, "Please stay."

"I can't. I have to warn Betsy. I owe her that. I helped snare her. I must help release her."

"Warn her some other way."

"You keep saying that, but none is sure."

"I don't want you to feel like my prisoner. I'll get the money. It's yours. Take it. You can leave, but please don't."

"If I promise to come back?"

"Will you . . . can you promise that?"

"I will."

"Still, don't go. Will you at least think about it?"

She stood up and reminded him ardently, "I'll lose precious time."

"Stay a while. I'll leave you to think. How will you get across the lines? Two armies camp between here and Washington." He turned away and walked toward the door, but stopped and retraced his steps again. He put both hands gently on her shoulders, leaned down and kissed her mouth.

She should have resisted, but she couldn't and closed her eyes, enjoying the full emotions that surged through her.

He broke off the kiss. "Please don't go," he added as he left the dining room.

She sat down and began to cry quietly. She wanted to call him back and tell him she wouldn't go anywhere without his permission, without his approval. She didn't want to leave his protection. She didn't want to leave his presence. She didn't want to live without him at her side, and she knew the kiss suggested he could accept her . . . even knowing.

Why should he love her? It was impossible. Yet, she loved him, and that was impossible, too. If he did love her, how could she leave him? Maybe sending a letter was enough.

Chapter 37

July 1864, Staunton, Virginia

Caleb descended the stairs after shaving and a bath. His leg was so raw from wearing his artificial leg awkwardly through the night that he left it off and used two crutches. He was dressed in full mourning clothes.

He clattered down the steps, sure Anna still waiting in the dining room would hear it plainly. She'd want to leave once she saw him on crutches. He knew that, but he wanted her to see the worst. He hoped she could accept a man with one leg. He made his way quickly to the dining room. She was gone. Panic seized him, and he hurdled into the hall, calling instinctively for John.

As the name came out of his mouth, he moaned audibly. Who should he call now? He called Anna.

The cook, seemingly in charge of the house, came from the kitchen, apron still on and eyes red from recent tears. She looked at him compassionately. "She's gone."

"When did she go? Where? Did she leave me a message?"

"As soon as you sent the money in, she left, walking toward town. She left no message."

Caleb shuffled to the front door and onto the front porch. He wanted to scream. She'd gone. He'd never suspected she would. His eyes scanned the path to the road. If she'd started out immediately after they last spoke, she'd already be in town. She was trying to get to Washington. From Staunton, she'd take the train or stage north. Before she could leave town, he would go to Staunton on horseback and convince her to come back.

He lowered himself down the stairs and hustled as quickly as he could across the lawn to the stable. He entered it abruptly, having forgotten that John lay in state. Caleb was trapped. He had to show respect to this old friend for the sake of the other slaves. He wanted to regardless. He wore his black suit in honor of the slain man. All of that was planned before she'd gone. Now these were wasted seconds, but he had to maintain the appearance of respect for the slaves milling around the casket. Field and house slaves mingled. They saw his attire, and he could tell it affected them. If he saddled a horse now, they'd suspect he hadn't come as a tribute and kindness to John. He would have to wait an appropriate while before scurrying to town on crutches. He knew he would wear himself out on one leg, but he had no choice. He had to convince her.

He remembered their kiss. He'd felt a warmth exchanged. She'd given as much as she had received. She liked him. He suppressed what he wanted most, and quietly, respectfully greeted each slave by name, expressing his sorrow at John's death. He thought he saw in each face a challenge to find John's killer.

As soon as he felt he could gracefully retreat, he left the stable, hobbled up the few stairs to the house front door and up the large staircase in the foyer. He shuffled quickly down the hall to his bedroom where he kept his store of rapidly devaluing Confederate bills. He had for many of his transactions resorted to bartering because the money had so little value, but he still kept a stash on hand. He'd sent half to Anna and now retrieved the other half.

Still in his formal mourning attire, he descended the stairs and began what would surely be a long, exhausting trip to Staunton. It was hot and the hilly road was dusty, but he pressed forward. Members of the Confederate cavalry galloped by without greeting, kicking up dust that choked him. A farmer passed him going to town with an empty wagon adding to the dust in the air. He knew the driver, but the man had stopped acknowledging him as the veteran had persisted in proclaiming Betsy's innocence. Much of the respect Caleb had gained in town because of his army service and injury had been lost in his ardent defense of a lady everyone else increasingly saw as a traitor.

Upon arriving at the main street, sweating, breathless and with a heavy layer of dust covering his hat and clothes, Caleb went to the Union-damaged hotel where the stage stopped on its way north. She would probably take the stage as the easiest first step in a perilous journey between two armies. He asked the old, stylishly dressed hotel clerk if he'd seen a woman matching Anna's description.

"Haven't seen any ladies this morning, Mr. Moore. The stage will be here shortly, if it's on schedule. Anyone hoping to catch it would already be here."

From a dark corner of the disheveled hotel office, Anna watched the clerk deny her visit in return for the money—Caleb's money—she had given him. She saw Caleb on crutches for the first time, and it took an immense effort not to run to him. She cried as she saw him turn away in visible anguish. He had followed her to bring her back. He really did love her, and she loved him. The feeling was intensifying with each passing hour. Her feelings were impossible, but real and undeniable. What was she doing?

She followed him discreetly as he left the lobby, quietly thanking the clerk as she passed. He responded with a quick nod and slight smirk. She stopped at the hotel door.

Caleb stood on the sidewalk, looking along the road, and she imagined him trying to guess where to find her. He turned toward the destroyed train depot and began swinging forward on his crutches. She followed him, angry first at herself for not giving up her futile trip to Washington and then for being so weak that she couldn't stop herself from following this man.

She trailed him to the station ruin, ready to duck out of sight should he turn her way. He stopped and looked in the rubble along the way. She wondered if he looked for her, stopped to rest or inspected the war damage.

After his slow, onerous trudge to the depot, he visually searched the area around the repaired train tracks, leaning heavily on his crutches.

Wiping rapidly falling tears from her cheeks, Anna sneaked back to the hotel and stood by the door waiting for the coach. Minutes later she saw Caleb pass within feet of her without glancing in the lobby. He drooped: His shoulders bent forward and his head was bowed, barely revealing his grim visage. It only then dawned on her that he hadn't ridden to town, but had walked the whole way alone . . . to find her. She couldn't let such devotion pass. She pushed the door open to follow him just as the stage pulled in front of the hotel. He was turning a corner to begin the trip home. She ignored the stage and headed to the corner.

When she was nearly there, the hotel clerk called her, "Your stage, Ma'am."

Anna stopped. He was just around the corner—a man who had shown her more kindness and love in twenty-four hours than all the other men she'd known in the uncounted days of her life.

"Your stage, Ma'am," the clerk repeated a little louder, as if she hadn't heard him the first time.

She remembered the warmth she'd felt as he'd held her wrist and in his kiss. Everything in her wanted to turn the corner and abandon Betsy to Walthrope's plots. Certainly Caleb was right: a letter would suffice.

But, no matter what she wanted most, she couldn't leave Betsy to Walthrope's cruelties. She remembered the monster's violence and brutality. Daniel would never be satisfied just to kill Betsy. He would humiliate her in every way he could imagine before murdering her. Every image of Betsy being harmed stung, yet she couldn't stop envisioning Caleb struggling home alone on his crutches because she wasn't there to help him. She imagined him in coming nights sitting in the library staring blankly at an unlit fireplace. She stood still, squeezing her eyes closed, her small hands curling to tight fists. She was fighting his attraction, dismissing his sacrifice; but her feelings were so powerful that she kept following him.

"Ma'am," the clerk had caught up to her. "Your stage is here."

Anna looked at him blankly at first, but forced a smile. "Yes, thank you. I hadn't seen it."

"Back this way."

She turned slowly, cringing as she passed each degree in the circling motion, and walked obediently to the stage. The clerk handed her in. Other people waited in the coach, but she took no notice. She sat down quietly, but suddenly rose and moved to the stage door still ajar.

One of the drivers, about to close the door, looked at her oddly. "Are you all right? Did you forget something?"

"I just wanted to ask when we're leaving."

"Immediately."

Her shoulders sank, and she sighed in frustration. She would never have another chance with Caleb if she left on this coach. Going to Washington would poison her hopes. Yet if she proved useful to Betsy, Caleb might in gratitude give her another chance and overlook her past. Maybe walking away now was her best hope of winning him forever. Life was too hard . . . and its choices left deep wounds.

Chapter 38

July 1864, Washington City, District of Columbia

Betsy and Mrs. Brown were mired in melancholia for three days after visiting the new graveyard at Arlington House. When Betsy refused to receive Mary, Mrs. Brown had taken the distraught visitor aside to explain the circumstances. Taking her meals in her room, Betsy spoke to no one. Mrs. Brown, struggling herself, still had a house to manage; and while she spoke less than usual, she endeavored to shroud her grief from other boarders.

It was late in the evening, after supper, that Sally opened the front door to a woman.

The visitor promptly announced, "I need to speak to Mrs. Gragg."

"I'm sorry," Sally answered contemptuously, "she's not at home. What's your business?"

"When will she return?" the woman queried, ignoring the servant's tone and question. She glanced briefly westward to gauge how soon it would be dark.

"I wasn't told," Sally retorted haughtily.

"I'll leave my card."

"Your card?" she asked with increased scorn. "Yes. Do leave your card."

Undeterred, "My name is Victoria Richman," the woman pronounced boldly. "Mrs. Gragg and I met under unfortunate circumstances, but I must speak with her . . . soon. It's important she come to see me tomorrow. I'll be at the hospital. She may not want to hear from or see me, but tell her I must speak to her, regardless of our personal feelings. Ask her to come."

Mrs. Brown, attracted by the unforgiveable tone of the servant's greeting, appeared half-hidden behind the girl and spoke to Victoria. "If you have something to tell Mrs. Gragg, you may tell me."

"I can't," Victoria answered haltingly. "I must tell her directly so there's no misunderstanding. There's already been too much. Will you ask her to come to the hospital tomorrow? If she's willing . . . comfortable, she could come to my home tonight."

"About her husband?" Mrs. Brown queried.

"Yes, but that's all I'll say. I must talk to her directly. Will you give her my message?"

Mrs. Brown stepped alongside the servant, answering, "Yes, but don't go. Let me make sure she's definitely out. She does come and go so often. If she's here, I'll announce you."

"Can she come in?" asked the servant disdainfully.

Mrs. Brown paused, frowned at the servant, and said as she turned her back on both of them, "Yes, of course, have her come in . . . if she'd like."

The servant looked questioningly at Victoria, leaving Victoria wanting to decline, but she smiled and accepted. Sally led her to the sitting room. Victoria glanced at the furnishings and décor, but her mind quickly revisited the discussion she and William had following their confrontation with Betsy:

William had been crushed by Betsy's incivility. He was silent as he helped Victoria climb into the carriage for the ride home. She had been livid. How dare that woman insult her in her hospital in front of her boys? She, as she waited for William to climb into his seat, reveled in Hank's death, especially because he had been taken before Betsy had seen his remains. If Betsy Gragg would not show her human courtesy and acknowledge her humanity, she would reciprocate. She took a deep breath, which ended in a quick, audible sigh. She would never again countenance the woman, so none of it mattered: not even her embarrassment at her public verbal flogging. She would survive it. The tie between the two families had been Hank, and he was gone. William would no longer hold sentimental attachment to a woman who had slighted them so callously, so openly. Her mind replayed the interchange. She had been right in every statement, while the other woman had been wrong in every word and gesture.

She watched William as he lit the carriage lamp, the light reflecting in tears moistening his face. She had been humiliated by the confrontation. But in that minute, she understood William had felt betrayed. A girl he loved from a family that had treated him decently—discounting its holding him in bondage at all—had become a woman who rejected his cherished familial connection. Victoria's heart broke for him. His sadness smothered Victoria's anger. How could she help him? She could go to Mrs. Gragg on hands and knees pleading forgiveness and acceptance for William as . . . as what? What would she accept him as, other than as chattel? Yet the uncomfortable impulse to reconcile the two badgered her as William turned the carriage homeward.

She spoke, "Are you all right?"

"Fine."

"Fine? William Richman, you're about as fine as when Adam found you nearly dead in those Kentucky woods. Shall we get a gun and shoot her?"

"Course not," he chuckled in spite of himself.

"It would feel nice."

"Wouldn't make me feel better."

"What would?"

He thought for a long while. "Wanted to be her friend. We ain't family, but I thought at least friends. But I was just property, not worth a surname."

"A surname." She laughed lovingly. "Last time we talked about it, you didn't know what that meant."

"Thought it was a name given to a gentleman . . . to a sir." He laughed at his own ignorance.

"You deserve . . . and did then . . . a surname. Your own family identity."

"Wish you'd talked me out of the name I chose."

"Would it have changed anything when we saw Mrs. Gragg? Don't you have a right to that name . . . to any name you choose?"

"It would have made a big difference tonight. She wouldn't have been mad at you. That hurt me."

"It hurt me, too," she acknowledged, remembering the poisoned sting of Mrs. Gragg's words.

"That's why it hurt me. I thought she was a friend, and she does that . . . to my wife. We're not family, but I thought friends. Hank was kind to me when I saw him after I es- caped. He's a friend, and I thought she was. I always think of the two of them together . . . as one."

"It wouldn't have made a difference tonight—which last name you'd chosen."

"She wouldn't have gotten mad."

"Maybe . . . but I think she was hurting, and if she hadn't had us to attack, she would have hurt the same way and found another way to show it."

"What do you mean?"

She thought briefly. "It's like this. She was sad to lose her husband, especially because he was gone before she could say goodbye. Think what it would be like if I died, and you didn't get to see me. It's the same. They are like us after all. She acted like she was angry at us, but she was really just hurt—not for anything we did or said. We happened to be in front of her, so she yelled and blamed us. We were a way for her to scream and yell out her pain. It was never about how she felt about you—I'm sure of that. I think it was the pain of Hank's death that came screeching out, and we were in range . . . so she put our names on it. Don't feel hurt. You helped her. You were a good friend. You allowed her to lash out instead of leaving her alone to suffer and stew in misery."

Victoria hadn't known what she was going to say when she started, but it sounded so convincing she began to be- lieve it herself. She'd said most of it to alleviate William's anguish, but it assuaged hers, too. Betsy Gragg didn't hate *her or that she was a freed slave who shared her last name. The outburst, the anger, the furor was an expression of grief . . . of frustration of being so close to being reunited with her husband and having that moment, that chance, snatched away.*

"She doesn't hate me?" William whispered.

"She doesn't hate you. She may be a little frightened of all the changes she's seeing . . . of your freedom and mine, but she doesn't hate you. She may not like me, but she doesn't hate you."

"Just hurting?"

"She's hurting."

"That makes it easier. Course, it wasn't nice what she said. It doesn't make me feel better to hear she hates you. It's the same as hating me."

"Maybe she doesn't hate me either. Maybe if she could, she'd go back and do something different."

William, admiration in his voice, reflected, "You knew all that while she was yelling at us? Is that how you stayed calm?"

"No, I didn't realize it until I was trying to convince you." She laughed. "I convinced myself. Odd as it is, I think it's true, and it makes me feel better, too."

Grim faced, Mrs. Brown entered the parlor and spoke quietly, "I don't want you giving Mrs. Gragg trouble."

Victoria's ire rose instantly, but she refused it dominance.

Mrs. Brown continued, "The good lady is full of woe thanks to you . . . and the loss of her husband. I don't want you pretending you're her equal or a friend."

Victoria smiled, reminding herself that she wasn't here to see this woman, and that she had to ignore whatever the lady said.

"She'll be down shortly," Mrs. Brown was saying. "I'm surprised she's coming at all, but I told her she ought and that you have come to beg her forgiveness . . . to tell her you won't steal her name. As soon as you do all that, leave immediately . . . by the back door."

"It's understood," Victoria answered cryptically,

Gazing at her quizzically and unsure of an appropriate response, Mrs. Brown said nothing.

Wanting to entertain herself as they waited, Victoria offered, "You have a becoming sitting room. Extremely comfortable, and the paintings are beautiful."

Pleased by the compliment in general, she was however uncomfortable receiving it from a colored woman. It implied an equality of sorts; and what would a freed slave know about art anyway. But she was proud of the room and the paintings, and she inadvertently mumbled, "Thank you. I do love the one of Rome, in particular."

"Have you been to Rome?"

"Oh, I've always wanted to visit Rome . . . and Paris and London. When my husband passed away, I had to open the boarding house. You can't leave a boarding house to go off to Europe."

"No, you must be tied down with care of your boarders. Maybe someday yet you'll travel."

In spite of her strongly bred attitude toward people like Victoria, Mrs. Brown relaxed in response to her guest's easy manners. "That would be lovely. Mrs. Richman, won't you please sit down?"

Victoria was amused by Mrs. Brown's abrupt change in manner and formal use of her name and by the slight grimace in the woman's expression as the title slipped out. She ignored the invitation to sit. "What would you most like to see in Rome?"

"The Coliseum. Since childhood, I've wanted to see it. Do you know what the Coliseum is?"

"Why the Coliseum?"

"It's so grand, and to think how old it is and what happened there."

"And in London?"

"That's easy: Queen Victoria."

"Paris?"

"Notre Dame and Versailles. I'd want to see where Benjamin Franklin lived." She suddenly stopped with consternation. "Have you heard of Notre Dame?"

"Yes, and Versailles."

"Benjamin Franklin?"

"Wasn't he the founding father who wanted to end slavery?"

"I don't know about that," Mrs. Brown responded nervously, "but he lived in France. The French adored him. He's a personal favorite of mine."

"He and his fur cap."

"You know about that, do you?" Mrs. Brown's surprise gleamed from her eyes.

"A little."

"Mrs. Richman, you surprise me. You are not like the other colored women I've met. I have found them wholly ignorant."

"Ah, Mrs. Brown, but I am. Exactly like the rest."

Discomforted, Mrs. Brown again encouraged Victoria to sit down.

Victoria accepted the invitation and moved to the least prominent chair in the room.

"Oh, not there. Please sit here, closer to me."

"If you feel I should."

"I insist."

Victoria stood and moved to the chair closest to Mrs. Brown. "You are so gracious."

Mrs. Brown smiled with deep satisfaction. "I do wonder what's keeping Mrs. Gragg so long."

"In her difficult circumstances, I imagine it takes time to receive guests."

"Yes. A most thoughtful observation."

Chapter 39

July 1864, Washington City, District of Columbia

Hank opened his eyes slowly and stared at a high pitched wood ceiling. Where was he? He tried to remember what he'd been doing when he fell asleep. He'd been in bed for days thinking little. He shifted slightly in the bed but the pain emanating from his leg stopped him. Was this never to end? He frowned in frustration. In Washington: He was in Washington City, his reward for an excruciating trip vaguely remembered—a dreadful and distant dream. Last time he'd been in the capital, he'd spent an afternoon at the city's Patent Office Sanitation Fair and had written glowing descriptions of it to Betsy. Betsy? She was in Washington. Had she visited? Betsy . . . and their child. Was the baby already born?

Abruptly he was reliving his final battle. He remembered charging the Secesh but his mind jumbled all other images, agony and sound into fleeting, untethered memories: The inside of an ambulance and a body writhing at each bounce. Something called a syringe and a liquid. A missing leg. Someone recounting a ball hit someone's hipbone. Bits of cloth from a wound. He overheard that, too. Fire erupting from a ridge. A lady fretting some soldier was feverish. Lying flat on the ground as bullets hit around him. A field hospital. A boisterous man claiming a ball had exited a leg. Injections. Whispering that marveled that a Rebel ball had been spent.

How high had the surgeons cut off his leg? High if it hit his hip. He reached down to search for a stump but surrendered the effort to foggy exhaustion.

He knew he was near a patient named Arthur, because everyone constantly talked of Arthur. Someone said Arthur was progressing. Arthur must have been important. He didn't know anyone named Arthur. Maybe Arthur didn't exist. Maybe they called all the patients Arthur, so the pain of each expired soldier wouldn't be so personal. That didn't make sense, but nothing made sense anymore. He personally couldn't muster the strength to care if Arthur survived.

There were brief moments when his mind began to clear, but they would inject that liquid into him again. He didn't like the foggy, liquid thoughts, but the pain would swiftly wane and sweet peace and sleep would follow.

Eventually, the procession of blurred faces and distorted voices stopped mentioning improvement. Worried looks. The liquid, the needles and sleep came more often. A grim surgeon ordered morphia. "Keep him comfortable." Infection. Serious. Doesn't look good. Arthur shared the prognosis.

Days and nights merged; sleep dominating both: sometimes peppered with vivid happy dreams, sometimes sprinkled with troubling, dark visions. One dream repeated: Betsy brought a baby to the hospital to visit. He would reach out to take the boy and awaken to the night groans of the ward or the day's commotion. It wouldn't matter if they were dreams if she would only stay—if he could only hold their baby. Maybe it wasn't a dream. Maybe they had come. Maybe next time she'd let him hold their infant.

In his mental fog, Hank remembered someone speak of recovery if they could get the infection under control. What was recovery without a leg? He was sure he visited lucidly with nurses from time to time but couldn't quite remember the conversations or clear faces. The exchanges he could recall were confusing. He spoke, but the surgeons and nurses looked at him in smeared movement and uncomfortable glances.

As he lay thinking, his frustration grew, and in unison, his arms rose—almost of themselves—and slapped down hard on the thin mattress.

The violent gesture startled a nearby nurse who was irrigating a neighbor's wounds. She stepped to his bed. "Is the pain that bad, dear boy? The morphine will help." As if in response, he began to feel sleepy and stopped caring for a while.

Betsy and the child visited him.

He was waking. How long had he been asleep this time? It looked like night. He remembered he was in Washington and Betsy was near. He'd never told the army he was married. If he could find the letter she'd sent, he could send someone to her. Oh, to have her sit by him day and night till he was bet-ter. He vaguely remembered other wives, mothers and sis-ters sitting by their boys, wailing in shared pain, laughing with joy, issuing sharp commands. Oh, if Betsy would come. Tears welled in his eyes.

How could he get a message to Betsy? Why didn't they stop giving him that morphine? It was the morphine. It did ease the hurt, but the haze, the drowsiness, he couldn't con-quer. He breathed shallowly and felt heavy pressure on his chest. Had he been injured again? He felt tired and dozed. When he again awoke, he felt slightly more alert than he had been. He was on his back. His hip ached. He stared at the white ceiling and cried softly.

A young woman in a dark dress and white apron was passing and heard him. She approached his bed.

"Are you still hurting? If you can hold on a little longer, you'll soon feel a bit better. The infection is lessening. We thought you were slipping away, but you fought back. You must have someone to live for. Girlfriend? Mother?" She asked hopefully.

"Wife and child."

She hadn't expected a response, as he'd said nothing coherent since arriving. Her eyes widened. "You're married? They've kept you on heavy doses of morphia—too much I think. But surgeons know best and so much more than the rest of us about everything: Don't they? You must be in great pain to be on such high doses. Are you in pain? I can give you another dose, if you need it."

"No. No more."

"You're still slurring your words a bit, but this is the first time you've made sense." She sat down on a chair by his bed. She picked up his hand and gently stroked it.

"Have letters come for me?"

"I don't think so. I'll check, though. Are you expecting letters from your wife?"

"Hoping."

"I'll check. Where is she?"

"Washington."

"Here?" she probed in astonishment.

"Yes."

"She could visit you. Do you want to send her a note?"

"I can't."

"If you tell me what to write, I'll post it for you."

"I don't know where she lives."

"But she's in Washington."

"We haven't been married long. The army doesn't know about her. She's just come to Washington, but I have memories or dreams that she visits. I thought they were real, but they're only dreams."

"Why don't you write to her old address? Maybe friends or family can forward the letter to her. It will be slower."

"I can't. Her address before she came to Washington City was in Virginia . . . Rebel-held territory."

"That makes it harder." She looked kindly at him. "You didn't tell the army about her because she was in the South. How did she get to Washington?"

"She didn't say. She wrote before we fought at the Wilderness."

"Did you keep the letter? It would have an address. They'd have it with your belongings, Arthur."

"Who's Arthur?"

The young nurse looked at him with a concerned expression. "Forgotten your name?"

"No."

"What is it? Tell me your name and a little about your-self."

"Hank Gragg . . . Henry Gragg. I grew up in the Shenan-doah Valley in a hamlet—Woodstock."

She listened intently. "How'd you end up in the Union Army?"

"I quarreled with the girl I loved and left Virginia."

"You came back to marry her."

Hank was tired, but the topic enlivened him, and he re-sponded, "After she married someone else and chose the wrong side in the war."

"A Rebel . . . and already married: impediments to a ro-mance." She stopped petting his hand long enough to adjust his pillow. "Is that more comfortable?" Without waiting for a response, the nurse added, "How did you marry her?" She laughed. "Maybe you should tell me your story . . . and hers."

Hank hesitated, but because he was still drowsy, he lacked his customary reticence. "I sneaked across the lines during a long furlough and married her."

The nurse smiled, slowly realizing this Arthur was no Ar-thur. "She was already married."

"Her husband died at Bull Run."

"So you could marry her."

"I didn't know she was married. We had a falling out. She was angry with me for pushing her to marry me against her mother's wishes. I left Virginia in anger."

"You went back to look for her?"

"I didn't. I was with her husband when he died on the field."

"A Confederate? Did he tell you he'd married your sweetheart?"

"No, he never knew. He gave me a letter to take to his wife in Virginia."

"It must have been strange to see her name on the enve-lope."

Talking about Betsy strengthened him and gave him rea-son to go on. This nurse could find her. She could bring her to the hospital. "I didn't realize it was her. He had a nickname for her and a new last name."

"Do you believe in the Fates? It seems they brought you together."

Hank looked at the nurse thoughtfully. "I believe it was a merciful God who has his hand in all our lives, enticing us to goodness. His mighty but unseen hand guided us."

"Why?"

"So we could marry."

"And have a child . . . a family."

Hank, still relaxed by the drug, ached to tell this nurse much more. "When we got a long furlough for reenlisting, I sneaked across the lines to deliver her husband's last letter."

"So you knew it was her?"

"No, not till we stood face to face."

"You married her in Virginia?"

"Yes. But I had to return to the army."

"She came north for you."

"She wrote before the summer battles began that she was in Washington carrying our child."

"The letter must have been lost. All the belongings we thought were yours belonged to Arthur Smith of Michigan. They told us you were Arthur when you arrived. They must have mixed you up. I wonder if I can find the man they think is you. He may have the address and your letter from . . . What's her name?"

"Betsy. Elizabeth Gragg."

"I'll ask about the real Mr. Smith. See if I can find him and that letter."

The middle-aged soldier in the bed adjacent to Hank called out to the nurse, "Mother."

She looked at Hank affectionately and promised, "I'll check tonight." She rose from the chair and turned to attend the older soldier.

"You're not looking for Mr. Smith. Look for Hank Gragg."

She glanced back at him. "I will. Hank Gragg."

Hank was exhausted but happy. She would find Betsy and bring her to him. He fell asleep, and Betsy came to his bedside with their baby in her arms. She extended the child to him, and he took the boy and cuddled him close for the first time.

Chapter 40

As the conversation between Victoria and Mrs. Brown waned, Betsy approached the room but hesitated at the door. Dressed in her best dress, her face freshly washed, her eyes red, she affixed a smile on her countenance.

Victoria stood as she entered the room. Mrs. Brown watched fretfully for any hint Betsy would explode in anger or implode in despair.

"Thank you for seeing me, Mrs. Gragg."

Betsy's tight smile trembled, "Thank you for coming."

"I have news . . . good news. Extraordinary news."

Betsy's smile melted into a sincere laugh, "I hope we can get beyond the description to hear the news."

Victoria smiled amiably. "I'm ready, but you must sit down. Please."

Betsy paused, keeping her eyes on Victoria, pondering what could make this woman, whom she had abused so thoroughly, dare approach her. She moved slowly to a nearby chair and asked hopefully, "Have they given approval to dig up his grave?" She settled in the chair and looked expectantly at Victoria. "Shouldn't you be seated, too?"

Victoria sat down. "I don't know where to start, so I'll blurt out the end." She looked meaningfully at Betsy. "Your husband's alive."

"This is no cruel trick you play because I was intolerable to you and William?" Betsy didn't move, but her face reddened in embarrassment.

"The other night is a long time ago. We all grieved, hurt. Things said then belong to that moment. This is no trick. Hank Gragg is alive and . . . not dying. This is no joke in poor taste, anger or hatred. We are connected, whether you and I want it or not. I hope you can accept that . . . embrace it as I am trying to."

Mrs. Brown whispered to no one, "Alive. Merciful God."

Betsy heard Mrs. Brown and turned to her. Her body was shaking, tears already beading in her eyes. "How can it be true? Alive. Mrs. Brown, you are right—a great and merciful God." She hesitated, her features contorted as she cried openly. "Yet I turned from him . . . betrayed him at the first hint of trial." She was barely able to speak. "How did this happen, dear Mrs. Richman?"

Victoria was taken aback by the respectful, intimate address and was unable to speak for a long while, looking kindly at Betsy, her own eyes watering. Betsy didn't rush her, and when Victoria controlled her emotions, she answered, "Two wounded, unconscious soldiers were collected from the battlefield at Petersburg. A third soldier, Job, had been blinded in the battle and thought he was with his dear, unconscious friend Hank. A few of Hank's personal possessions were collected on the field and, based on Job's word, attached to the wrong unconscious soldier. As Job traveled from hospital to hospital with the soldier, he affirmed repeatedly that this dying boy was Hank. Everyone assumed he was right. After all, Job had been with him on the battlefield. He knew him personally. But he was blind and never saw or talked to him. His blindness, I fear, led us all into a ditch.

"The real Hank was severely wounded and in terrible pain, and they gave him morphia for it—too much; enough to make him sleep all the time; enough to confuse him when he wasn't asleep. He was never able to tell anyone who he was. If he had, they wouldn't have believed him. They thought he was someone named Arthur Smith."

"Smith?"

"The other soldier, Smith, never gained consciousness— the one we all thought was Henry Gragg—and slowly faded away. In disastrous misfortune, I told you it was Hank. We— William and I—thought they were burying Hank at the cemetery in Arlington."

"You went to look for him?"

"Yes. My husband loves Hank, and I thought I'd been caring for him. I didn't connect the two of them until the night you and I met, the night I learned William's friend's name. We got to the cemetery as they buried him, and I was stunned . . . disbelieving when William assured me it was not Hank."

Betsy laughed bitterly, "You couldn't come and tell me: my anger, my rudeness ensured that."

"We had discovered a Mr. Smith was dead, but that's not the same as knowing Hank was still among us." She shifted her eyes slightly lower. "But, no, I wasn't ready to come to see you. What would have happened if I'd told you it wasn't him, and gave you hope . . . false hope . . . he was alive, and you found out later he wasn't? It would have been worse. I can't imagine how you would have felt . . . responded."

"He's alive," Betsy said, as she wiped at her cheeks with both her bare hands.

"Today a nurse from another pavilion came looking for Mr. Smith who was in the hospital under the name of Hank Gragg. She'd discovered the swapped identities and came looking for a letter you wrote him, so she could contact you. Hank has recovered enough and, at his insistence, they've cut back on his morphia. He's able to stay awake, remember and converse." She smiled. "I understand he's constantly asking for you. I told the nurse I would come immediately to you."

"How did you find me?"

"You dropped your card in the ward the other night. The ward master picked it up."

"I did?" She laughed, wiping again at her tears. "Can I go to him?"

"Yes. He's not dying."

Through choking tears, Betsy reflected, "Alive. Thanks be to a merciful God."

Mrs. Brown echoed, "A merciful God. The Lord giveth, and the Lord taketh away. The Lord taketh, and he bringeth back."

"Let me get my hat, gloves. Will you go with me?" Betsy asked Victoria meekly.

"If you'd like. William's outside waiting with a carriage."

Betsy stood up, approached Mrs. Brown, who also rose. Betsy hugged her tightly. "We've somewhere to go."

"You want me to come, too?" Mrs. Brown queried tentatively.

"Of course"—Betsy looked concerned—"if you can leave, if you don't have to stay."

"If the boarding house collapses while I'm gone, I'll rebuild it."

Both women retrieved hats, gloves and parasols and left the house with Victoria. William, in a bolo, had been sitting in the late-day sun waiting. He looked straight ahead as the door opened, unwilling to witness Victoria's crushed visage.

Betsy, excitement bubbling through her expression, was at his side before he dared move his head. "Mr. Richman, thank you for finding Hank for me . . . and for all you've done."

William glanced uncomfortably down at Betsy, smiled weakly and nodded his head.

"Forgive me, William, for being unkind. You are a Richman. I was wrong to claim otherwise. Why I said those horrid things, I'll never know."

William pivoted in his seat, a slight pride glimmering in his face, "Victoria said it was because you were hurting bad because Hank was dead . . . or we thought he was dead."

Betsy pondered briefly and responded hopefully, "She was right."

At that, William jumped down from the driver's seat and helped the three women into the carriage and urged the horse toward the hospital. When they reached it, William left the carriage unattended and entered with the three women. Everyone was excited and nervous, but no one spoke. Victoria led the company toward Hank's pavilion, entered ahead of the others and spoke briefly to the day nurse who directed her to Hank's bed. As she moved toward him, she caught his eye and smiled. Sitting with his back against the wall, Hank met her smile with a blank stare. The ward master intercepted them, politely asking their business.

Betsy couldn't contain herself, breaking into a wide smile, "I'm calling on my husband, Hank Gragg."

"Ah, you're the wife. We found you. Welcome. He's in bed sixteen, over . . ."

"I see him," she said, her eyes fastened on Hank, the smile still broad. Their eyes locked on each other, and she hurried to him. He was haggard, balding, rail thin and older, but she didn't notice. She wrapped her arms around him, and he limply returned the embrace. Betsy sat on his bed. Neither said anything but held on, fearing separation.

"I love you," he whispered finally.

She squeezed him harder. "I've missed you so. I thought you were dead."

"I wouldn't leave you, not when you carry our child. I wouldn't leave you like that."

She smiled through the tears. "You'd have a choice, would you?"

She let go of him, wiped at her cheeks, noticing for the first time how frail he looked, and hugged him again, more gently. "How are you, my hero?"

"With you. That's enough."

"Are you done with the war?"

"My hip is healing. I thought they'd taken off my leg. I don't know where I got that idea. If they'd taken the leg, I'd be done. If the hip heals and the butchery goes on, I might have to return. I'm praying for the one and pleading against the other."

"I can barely hold in everything I have to say . . . things I want to tell you, but I'm not alone."

She looked back at Victoria, Mrs. Brown and William who watched the reunion from midway down the pavilion. Betsy waved them over, turned and took one of Hank's hands tightly in her two hands. He kept his eyes on her the entire time, not noticing or caring who approached.

Betsy watched the women and William with satisfaction. She rose as they arrived but kept Hank's hand in hers. Hank turned to look at the visitors. Delight overwhelmed his expression as he recognized William. "William, how did you get here? Did you join the army?" Without hesitating, Hank turned to Betsy and said with more strength than she thought he had, "I don't think I told you our William saved my life when I was coming to see you in Virginia."

William, embarrassed, stammered, "You would have been fine. I helped a little."

Hank's laugh was cut short in pain and a groan, but he forced out, "A little? Betsy, a man . . . a murderer . . . had me on the ground, choking me. I was struggling but had given up ever escaping his grasp. William appeared from nowhere. I just saw his bare feet." He looked back briefly at William. "What happened to your shoes?" Without awaiting an answer, he turned to Betsy. "He tore the man off me."

"I killed him," William whispered sheepishly.

"You saved me."

"I told him not to worry about killing that man, when he told me what he'd done," Victoria said. "The man had already killed someone, hadn't he?"

Her comments caught Hank's attention, and he turned to her expectantly.

"Hank," Betsy said, "this is Victoria Richman, William's wife."

Hank turned questioningly to William who shrugged at him, then turned his gaze back to Victoria. "I am pleased to make your acquaintance. I saw you earlier in the ward. I didn't know who you were. Please forgive me for not rising, but Betsy is squeezing my hand so hard pain has incapacitated me."

The visitors laughed, and Betsy loosened her grip.

Hank continued, "I cherish the hope that next time, I'll be able to greet you properly."

"My fondest desire," Victoria replied formally.

Betsy interjected, "Victoria is a nurse in the hospital. She nursed the fellow everyone thought was you."

Hank said soberly, "I understand he died."

"Yes," Victoria responded gloomily.

"Then I'm glad I was in this ward." His eyes glistened mischievously.

Victoria glared in mock anger, "You were pampered too much in here. I would have had you out of bed mopping the floor."

"I am glad I wasn't in your care," Hank said with a mirthful look.

"She's also the person who found me," interjected Betsy.

"Thank you for that," Hank said somberly.

Betsy slowly laid down his hand on the bed, but he refused to relinquish hers, reaching and gripping them both tightly in his hands.

Betsy remembered Mrs. Brown who stood slightly behind Victoria, looking uncomfortable. "Ah, Mrs. Brown. Hank, this is Mrs. Brown. She's my landlady, a mother to me, a grandmother to our child. She has kept me whole when I had nothing."

Not understanding Betsy's meaning, Hank respectfully nodded to Mrs. Brown, "So many saviors in one day. I am . . . I don't have words to describe what I'm feeling. Mrs. Brown, thank you for what you've done for Betsy . . . for us."

"You've a lovely wife. Having her in my home is an honor."

Hank feigned a frown as he teased, "An honor to have a loyal Confederate in your home? Do you share her opinions?"

Mrs. Brown looked worried.

Betsy intervened, "Thank you, Mr. Gragg. You have certainly made me look a fool. And after I spent all those months in Castle Thunder as a Northern spy . . . because of you. I deserve a little sympathy."

Hank's smile disappeared. "Did you? Why were you in prison?" Hank demanded sternly.

"Because I entertained a Yankee soldier in my home, I was branded a spy. They were sure I'd given you voluminous Southern secrets."

"Why didn't you tell me?"

Betsy laughed briefly, "The secrets?"

"No, that you'd been arrested."

"I was sure if you knew you'd try to free me and end up in a prison camp or dead. As it was, I worried you'd see a copy of the Richmond Dispatch and read of the female traitor held in Castle Thunder."

Mrs. Brown said grimly, "I've heard terrible stories of that place."

Betsy quickly interjected, "Yes, but this gloom detracts from our reunion. Let's not dwell on it. We've all suffered things—lost things. Let's celebrate that I am free; that you, Hank, are alive and have both your legs; that Victoria and William married each other; and that you, Mrs. Brown, are our dear friend. Let's not think about prison or battles or the future. Let's take pleasure in being together."

Hank squeezed Betsy's hands and pulled them to his chest. Her eyes rested on him.

William drove Betsy home late and picked her up early the next day.

She could see from the pavilion doorway when she arrived that Hank was still asleep. Commotion rippled through the ward, but she paid no mind. Her sole focus was Hank, and she crept to his bedside, sat down and watched him, hoping to let him sleep.

He scowled in his slumber, and she shuddered in sympathy for whatever he was dreaming. She leaned toward him and touched his forehead. He was warm but not hot: another blessing from a most merciful God. He stirred, opened his eyes and groaned, but smiled as he realized it was Betsy. He reached to caress her face and gently brushed the scar Walthrope had given her. He wondered where Walthrope was, grateful he no longer threatened Betsy. His hand dropped slowly along her cheek, shoulder and arm till it came to her hand, which he raised. He closed his eyes and pressed his lips against her elegant fingers. His other hand reached out and touched her belly, lingering motionless. This was happiness. He could endure the pain if every morning he could open his eyes to find this fat angel at his side. Neither spoke for a long time but gazed keenly into each other's eyes.

He broke the mutual trance. "How long have you been here?"

"As soon as I sat down, I couldn't help but touch your face. I bothered you."

"You could never bother me, and you can touch my face anytime." He groaned.

"Your hip hurts?"

"A bit. Can you find the nurse? See if it's time for my morphine injection."

"Morphine. What does it feel like?"

"It depends on the dose they tell me. It made me sleep at the beginning for weeks on end. Now it stops the pain for a while. Call her," he pleaded pitifully.

Betsy sought the ward nurse, whom she brought back to Hank's bed.

"How are you today, Private Smith?"

Hank half smiled, half grimaced.

She pulled back the covers and sought a place on his non-injured side to inject the morphine. When she gave him the shot, she commented, "You'll soon feel better."

"Thank you," he said breathing heavily.

"It helps that much?" Betsy asked as the nurse took away her syringe and hypodermic needle.

"It does, and so fast. A miracle medicine, they tell me. You should try it some time," Hank interjected.

"For what?"

"Whatever ails you."

"Only you ail me, and you took the full dose."

His breathing was slowing down, and he responded meaninglessly, "We'll be all right."

She sat again. "I'm going to learn to do that."

"Why?"

"So she won't have to. I can nurse you."

"What about the baby?" he asked, putting his hand back on Betsy's belly.

"What of the baby?"

"You shouldn't even be here . . . not with all the illness."

"Our baby's fine, and I'll be fine. What else does the nurse do for you?"

"Typhus. There's typhus. Lots of other diseases. You can't get them, not with the baby coming."

She looked at him with thin set lips and stubbornly repeated, "What else does the nurse do for you?"

"Feeds me . . . or brings me my food."

"What else?"

"Cleans my wound. Puts on new, clean bandages."

"I can do all that."

"It's disgusting."

"I doubt it."

"I don't want you to faint."

"I'm of stern stuff."

"We're all becoming hard," Hank commented suddenly with a philosophical turn.

She put her hand on his forehead and slid closer to him. She leaned in till mere inches separated their faces. Hank had forgotten what it felt like to be so close to her. He looked into her emerald-green eyes. He never tired of them. She whispered, "We are going through hard times, but we must never let them harden us. If we become hard, we'll no longer feel. I don't want that. I love to feel. I love to feel your love and the passion I have for being with you."

He listened, still enjoying the closeness and vulnerability and openness of her eyes.

She paused, smiling tenderly. "When I woke yesterday I thought you were gone, that our child would never meet his father. I'd given up God. How could he have let it happen? But I found yesterday he hadn't. Mrs. Brown talked to me about faith at my lowest point and left me wondering if I was wrong. Maybe we have to love and accept what God has for us, hoping he has something greater, brighter, more wonderful in store for us in some future day. If you had died, I would have continued on. I would have loved you, your memory, and missed you so, but I don't have to. God made me face my greatest fear, made me feel it. Like Abraham's offering of Isaac, at the last minute he sent an angel to save me—angels named Brown and Richman. Let us solemnly promise each other to never let our hearts turn hard, to never doubt God regardless of what we yet pass through."

Hank pursed his lips as he listened.

"You may have to go away. Your hip may heal enough for them to put you back as cannon fodder. You may yet die. Or while you're gone, I may die giving birth to our child or of the influenza or typhus or any of a dozen other illnesses. Regardless of what happens, let us believe in the Lord and his goodness and hope for that brighter day. Let us keep our eye on the prize of being together, according to his grace."

Hank pulled his arm from her stomach and propped it behind his head.

She still held his eyes. "Will you promise me all of that? I promise it to you, and I do it with my greatest love."

"Betsy, you have always . . . since our reunion at Staunton . . . always been what has kept me going. You cannot imagine how my heart sang when I got your letter. Suddenly I had hope in spite of my stupidity and the paths we took away from each other. I read it over and over again and imagined we might make it through this together. God has joined us, and no man can part what God has joined. My heart is tender and soft, like a woman's, because of you. While my head . . . and yours may get so we no longer fear the sight and smells of blood and death, we can never let our feelings for each other die."

"Hank, it's not just our feelings for one another. It's the feelings of life: the amazement of seeing a deer in the forest, or stepping into a radiant October sun set in a blue sky and feeling a warm gratitude. It's the joy of hearing a child laugh. I don't want to lose any of it, and I don't want you to lose it. Promise me you won't, and that you'll make sure none of it disappears in me. When I was in Castle Thunder, I stopped caring for anything. Incarcerated, but innocent. They twisted everything, cornered me, starved me. Surrounded by vermin—human and other kinds—I saw no way out. My only friend was a dog, a sweet wonderful dog. Believe it or not, I think that dog gave me the strength to endure . . . though I almost didn't. I began to feel less and less, even after I escaped to Washington. Little was left in me, little that could feel anything. Everything died when I thought you were dead and covered in that fresh grave.

"I fell on the grave and tried to dig—not to get you out, but to join you, to die in your cold arms. When they pulled me away, the last of hope and love died. I didn't care about anyone or anything . . . even our child. I went through the motions of life mechanically. I was dead, as much as if you had been dead in Mr. Smith's grave. But a merciful God didn't require that of me. Suddenly the sky is blue, the clouds soft and white, the people around me full of love and life, a child begins to kick within, and my beloved husband lives . . . in my arms. I never want to die again, and I never want you to die like that. Physical death I can live with, but we must never let ourselves die in spirit. We've got to hold the faith that God will care for us, regardless of the misery and storms that batter our small vessels."

Hank felt her desperate hunger and whispered back, "I love you." He wrapped his hand around the back of her head and pulled her close. He didn't kiss her, but held her head to his chest, listening to the soft sobs that escaped from her. He stroked her hair, oblivious to the turmoil around them.

She didn't move her head for a long time, and when she did she was nearly overwhelmed seeing love glowing in his eyes. Everything would work out. She pulled her head from him, slightly embarrassed, abruptly remembering they weren't alone.

"I married the right woman: courageous, kind, loving, strong. You give me strength. I can endure this pain because I will be with you and our child, and we can laugh about all these memories, grateful they are but memories."

"Hank, I don't think we'll ever laugh about this." She smiled.

Chapter 41

July 1864, Washington City, District of Columbia

Both Betsy and Hank were emotionally drained from their tête-à-tête when Victoria entered the pavilion escorting a man Betsy didn't recognize. Hank grinned when he saw him.

Victoria spoke to the visitor as they approached, "Here he is, Private Rivenshaw."

"The real Hank Gragg? Alive?"

"Ask him directly. He can hear, talk and eat."

"Rivenshaw, you've come to visit me at last," Hank called out enthusiastically. "I've been wondering where you got to."

"Is it you . . . still alive?"

"Barely. What's happened to you, friend?"

"I've lost my sight. I'm blind. Hank, I'm blind." He shed sudden tears as he spoke the words, searching with his hand for someplace to sit. He crumpled into the chair Betsy had vacated to greet Victoria. "I'm blind."

Hank, embarrassed by Rivenshaw's emotions, offered feebly, "Surely it's temporary."

"No. Forever. I won't see light again. 'He that is strucken blind cannot forget the precious treasure of his eyesight lost.'"

"I suppose not," Hank, still discomfited, responded distractedly.

Rivenshaw's outburst ended as quickly as it started, and he called out, turning his head back and forth, "Nurse Richman, do you hear that? I quote the English-world's greatest playwright, and he stoops to supposition. Mrs. Richman, you must never leave me. Even Hank is no match for your greatness. He didn't recognize it. Hank, I can visit you but briefly for I am obligated to stay at the side of my dear Nurse. Mrs. Richman, tell Hank where the quote's from. Tell him."

Feeling acutely self-conscious, Victoria discouraged the topic, "Come, let's leave Hank and his wife to themselves and get back to our ward."

"His wife? Here? With us? Please introduce us, Nurse Richman. I must meet her. Is she lovely, Mrs. Richman? Is she beautiful? I bet she is."

Victoria took him by the arm, raised him from his chair and turned him toward Betsy. "Private Rivenshaw, it is my great pleasure to present Mrs. Hank Gragg. Mrs. Gragg, this is Private Rivenshaw."

Rivenshaw spoke in the direction Victoria had turned him, "It is the pinnacle of a man's life to make the acquaintance of the dear wife of such a friend. But please, kind Mrs. Gragg, you must treat me as you would any other person: You mustn't let my rank intimidate you." He reached out his hand as if to take hers, but it dangled awkwardly, until Victoria moved his hand toward Betsy. Betsy placed her fingers in his hand, and he gently raised them to his lips. "To experience such an honorific moment is a life-time aspiration." He lowered her hand, slowly, seemingly regretful to let it go.

"The honor is mine, good sir," Betsy responded.

"Come," Victoria encouraged. "Let's get you back to the ward before they miss you too much."

"Ah, Mrs. Richman, would they miss me so soon?" He began following her lead without saying more till he abruptly halted in the middle of the ward. He turned crisply and cried theatrically, "'And Crispin Crispian shall ne'er go by, from this day to the ending of the world, but we in it shall be remember'd; we few, we happy few, we band of brothers; for he to-day that sheds his blood with me shall be my brother; be he ne'er so vile, this day shall gentle his condition: And gentlemen in' New 'England now a-bed shall think themselves accursed they were not here, and hold their manhoods cheap whiles any speaks that fought with us upon Saint Crispin's day.'"

The soldiers, nurses, visitors and others in the ward responded with spontaneous applause, and Rivenshaw gracefully bowed, led by his long, elegant arm waving out and downward.

Victoria silently took his arm and led him from the ward.

"Do you think they liked my little performance," he whispered timidly.

"I proclaim it the most unforeseen occurrence of the day."

"Nurse Richman, I know you too well to let pass such subtle signs you chose to thoroughly ignore my query. Did they love it or not? I must know."

"Yes, indubitably." She stopped and turned to him. "Private, you proclaim your performances on London's stage stiff and passionless. Here passion erupts from you. I just witnessed—heard and saw—Henry in those fateful moments at Agincourt. There was no stage, for no stage could have held him . . . or you. He was on the broad battlefield of France. You have become the great actor from the London stage . . . the great actor of the Union Army."

Rivenshaw smiled, nodding his head. "Then I'm happy. I am happy in my blindness, for it has revealed life to me. Ah, Mrs. Richman, my audience loved my Henry V. Hank is alive and is married to a woman with gloved hands, and I am led by my wonderful Nurse Richman. What more could a man want? Nothing. I see that clearly now. Mother, you have become my eyes. You can never leave me, or I will be lost once and for all."

"Private Rivenshaw, I have a husband and son . . ."

"They can live with us."

Victoria laughed.

"Good. It's agreed. They will live with us, and we will be one happy family."

She watched his face, highly animated, droop sadly as he finished talking. She didn't want to think of him being alone, and said, "Yes, a happy family."

He tilted his head and walked silently as she guided him back to the ward.

Betsy spent every waking hour at Hank's bedside, but longed desperately to be alone with him. She was weary of the company that ever surrounded them. They were sweet boys, nearly to a man, and to see so many suffer wore on her. She thought about helping others in the ward, but something held her back. Was it Hank—that she wanted to be with him constantly? Was it fear of disease she might contract that could hurt her baby? Was it that almost all the patients were Union soldiers?

Early on Hank had tested her loyalty. Was she less a Rebel after her persecution and imprisonment by the Confederacy? He had hoped she was; that she had been won to the cause. He didn't ask her directly, but made disparaging remarks about the South. "The Rebels keep fighting—they are valiant soldiers. I've witnessed it, but I suspect . . . I've heard the South is bankrupt, financially and . . . morally. They're left fighting a desperate struggle just to retain a few remaining slaves."

Up to that point in the conversation, they had been discussing the miserable heat, the odors from the canal and the proliferating mosquitoes. He'd wanted to gauge her visceral reaction by making the comment unexpectedly. It worked. Instantly he saw her eyes narrow, her lips press tightly together and her face scrunch slightly.

She let his words drift briefly unanswered, smiled, lovingly put her hand to his forehead. "Feverish, hallucinations: I thought so." She put her mouth to his ear and whispered, "Anyone who expresses such revolting thoughts is desperately ill. So, let me, my love"—she kissed his ear gently—"help you see through your delirium. It was Lincoln who sent soldiers to invade the South, when all Southerners wanted was their property rights. He drove our mother nation from the Union.

"Because the North is coercive and has all the wealth, and is currently favored by time and luck, don't think God has abandoned the South. I think it a divine test of faithfulness. Will we stand firm and true to what the Divine has given us and be blessed? Or will we flinch when everything looks the darkest and lose heavenly approbation? You should ask directly: Are you still loyal to a noble state? Or have you collapsed into a simpering heap willing to do whatever King Lincoln tells you to do? Isn't that what you ask, my love?"

She gently kissed his ear and sat back in her chair, removing her hand that had previously rested affectionately on his. "But, let there be no doubt in your manipulative Yankee soul: I will not flinch. I am not easily deceived, Private Gragg. Private Gragg. Interesting you're still a private. All who survive these battles and who have at least the ability to breathe and feed themselves must get promoted in the Union army: advancement by attrition. You don't have to be good or smart or strong or brave. You just have to survive the day. I suspect that's how you get your generals. Private Gragg, why are you still a private? You've survived long enough to be a general. Although I do think you too capable to hold such a rank in the Union debacle. Do you know why you're still a private?"

Hank's eyes betrayed no embarrassment or hurt. "Your theories are always welcome to this humble private, though your political affiliations remain suspect."

She got closer to him, this time so as to not be overheard, "I don't think you really care about the Union, Private. I don't think you ever did. Not really. You have deluded yourself. I think you really wanted to be a Rebel, like your loving wife. You go through the motions of Yankeedom citizenship but merely take orders and never show initiative."

"I fought hard."

She responded softly still near his ear, "Most valiantly. I can't imagine anything else. Still you don't care for the war. Not really. If the South went its own way—if it won the war—

I think you would be delighted to see it go, as long as you could keep your incomparable wife."

Hank looked meaningfully at her and more seriously than she had expected. She had merely been tweaking his ear because he had tweaked her nose, but she saw she'd touched something deeper.

He smiled and with melancholy in his voice answered, "I am tired of war and wouldn't mind its disappearance. I worry Lincoln will lose the election; McClellan win and settle with the South. What a loss of life that will leave . . . for naught."

"No matter what happens in the end . . . look around this ward. Think what's happened to you. It is all waste; unnecessary."

"That's not your thesis though. You're hypothesis is that I am still, after a few battle-filled years, a private because I don't believe in the cause. Isn't that it?"

She saw he had something he wanted to say. "That's it."

"It's wrong, yet there's something to it. For a long time, it's been hard for me to soldier because of the South."

She wanted to interject a sarcastic comment about she and the Confederacy being right, but held her tongue.

"When I joined the army, I was lonely. I thought I'd lost you forever. I'd abandoned my family because I was humiliated when you rejected me. It was always my love for you that haunted me in my selfishness. I couldn't escape it. My only hope was in battle to be dispatched to a better sphere. The angels would let me in because I had sacrificed my life to maintain man's greatest political experiment, one promising freedom to all—from the beginning I wanted slavery to end. So wholeheartedly—no matter what happens—I believe in the Union cause. William, Victoria and all the other Africans enslaved deserve freedom in their sphere of capability. But I fought only to die, not for the cause. When I found the note Mr. Henderson sent his wife, it gave me some purpose beyond a lonely death in war, angels notwithstanding. I could align myself with both—the cause of the perpetual Union and my love for Virginia, and in a strange way my love for you—and find some semblance of peace in it all. I was ready to dedicate myself to rising in the hierarchy of the Union cause. I did when I came back from my first visit to deliver your husband's letter to you. You gave me, with your letters, a hope I'd lost. I wanted to be a corporal, a lieutenant, a captain, a colonel, a general to impress a widow in Staunton, but I didn't know yet it was you. Your slave John—Do you remember?—refused to help me find you."

"My servant John," she interposed seriously.

"A slave by any other name is still a slave." He pleaded, "Please let me finish."

She nodded, refusing to take offence at his point, still holding her face close to his.

"When we got the furlough, I came to see the widow Henderson. It was you—lost to me forever, or so I thought. The world changed in that moment. Everything was possible, everything sweet. You gave me new life, but a complicated one. A wife, my helpmeet and an enemy; a government that would destroy my wife's life; a carried rifle meant to harm what my wife believed in. I came back a most happy man because I had something concrete to live for—something real to look forward to beyond battlefields—and it weakened me. I had won you and lost my desire for a rapid death and survival of the Union. That first charge at the Wilderness, when I was nearly shot: Something happened inside. I fought on and hard, but my heart wasn't in it. I didn't want to die. Not anymore. I no longer cared for the Union . . . yet I was no Rebel. I wanted my family, only my family. I only wanted to survive to return to you."

She whispered, "I often felt the same about you: The South could win while I lost you. Or the South could lose, and I still could lose you. But you're not alone in wanting to survive to return home. Isn't that the sacrifice of every soldier? Isn't that what fighting for freedom is about? Isn't that the dilemma of every man who fights . . . the cost of each who dies?"

"Yes, but never on this scale of slaughter. How can anyone justify what happens on those fields? No matter what happens, all those lives will have been lost or affected forever. And the families? Destroyed and cursed as far as the mind can imagine in the future, far beyond our sight."

Her eyes sparkled, "So, you are confirming that you are a private because you love your Rebel wife."

He smiled. "I'm not sure that's what I said, but I have the feeling it best not to argue the details, especially as I do in the end love you, a most rebellious wife."

She got down close to his ear and whispered, "Only in the end?" She kissed him again.

Chapter 42

July 1864, Staunton, Virginia

Lucius Walthrope sat against a tree in the woods, a loud shout from Betsy's mansion. He fumed. It would have been easy, so easy, to deal with Caleb if Anna hadn't come to Staunton. She could have gone anywhere else, and it wouldn't have interfered with his plans. If she hadn't been in Betsy's house, he could have confronted Caleb in the way he'd planned. He would have made him kneel, cower, cringe and whimper in fear; before pulling back the pistol hammer and executing him for his crime—the heinous crime of keeping Betsy from him and for driving him away in ignominy. Instead he'd had to trick Anna into becoming a decoy. Under her cover he had stayed behind, lowering himself to the indignity of sneaking around like a criminal. Instead of humiliating Caleb, he'd had to sneak up behind and shoot him in the back in the dark. There could be no satisfaction in that.

It didn't matter. He was nearly done. He smiled. Anna's interference made no difference now. She was a fool to come, but he'd dealt the necessary death blow in spite of her. He chuckled to himself. Maybe he'd return to Anna in Richmond when he was finished in Washington. He liked being married to an actress. Whenever he watched her on stage, knowing he possessed and dominated her, he felt such power. Yes, he would return to his wife once he was done.

Before the joyous reunion, he would visit the dirty, muddy city on the Potomac. He smiled to himself. Betsy was probably at that moment thinking of him, remembering their times together; nervously awaiting their reunion. He was sure she woke every morning thinking of him, wondering if it would be her last day on earth. Would she be about ready to have her bastard child? It was time to confront her. He would now terminate his relationship with Betsy for good. It was her fault. She'd humiliated and shamed him. If she had just kept quiet about discovering he'd killed that useless factory man, Stokes, everything would have worked out for them. He'd be sitting in the house he'd just run from, and she'd be obediently kneeling at his feet. He would be rich. Rich. The word echoed in his imagination. It was the reward he deserved, not because of what he did or had ever done, but because of who he was. He was born superior to the riff-raff. She'd not been shrewd enough to see it. Her misfortune. Betsy had lost her chance to be possessed by such a marvelous man.

Instead she condescended to be the puppet of some insignificant Union soldier. She had greatness in her grasp but turned from it to trivialities. She was pathetic, to be pitied. Her death would be a kindness. She had made the mistake of resisting his will, of judging him wrongly. No woman would ever dominate him. They were his—always—to use as he knew best.

Anna's image returned. Her presence in the library had confused him. Why had she come to Staunton? Maybe she had come to help him, and he had mistaken her for a hindrance. It was too late to rectify the situation. He never expected to see her again, unless some night he went to the theater arm-in-arm with another exquisite lady, and saw her performing on stage. He relished the daydream, warming in the thought of knowing the starring actress . . . of humiliating her. No, he would return to her after his visit to Betsy. After all, he was married to Anna in a way. He hoped she would quickly return to Richmond. Let her fame flourish. Then she would be worth his time. He would return to claim his wife when his work was done. He imagined how happy she would be under his protection.

It annoyed him that he couldn't get Anna out of his mind when he needed to focus on Washington and Betsy. He had to put Anna away. Betsy was guilty and must be punished for her sins and rebellion. He was her God, her master; and she had failed him. He would smite her as God had smitten the earth in Noah's day. After the purge of her guilty blood, he would return to claim his true wife, Anna.

He rose stiffly from the ground and began walking north toward Washington. He couldn't return to Staunton to catch a coach. He'd wave it down along the way, sneak across the lines, and be in Washington before Anna could get to Richmond. It would be easy with the muddle of the armies struggling in the Valley.

Washington welcomed Lucius in its usual manner—without notice. While he had earlier hoped for recognition and praise in the Federal City, obscurity on this visit was his ally. Early the morning after he arrived, he made his way to the open market and beyond, walking up the Avenue toward Betsy's lodgings. He could feel his pulse increase; not from the exertion of walking, but in anticipation of seeing her. He always felt her influence as he neared her. The temperature was already on its way to a withering high, the way was dusty, and people crammed the sidewalks and street. He took energy from them as they passed or inadvertently jostled him. They didn't see him. He was as invisible as a wraith preparing a deadly apparition.

He was certain he could kill a woman on this busy way, and no one would notice the shadowy perpetrator. None could see him: strolling soldiers, marauding groups of roughs, busy women, distracted children, government officials and clerks. How many were murderers and cutthroats? This was his element. It was hard to tell what a man had in him when blended in such a throng.

He pressed on in the heat, nearing her house, his feet as light as his mood. Maybe he'd storm the house and confront her in the comfort and sanctuary of her home. Wouldn't that be the final irony? Afraid to walk the street because he had terrorized her, she would experience her final humiliation within the walls of her citadel. He would walk through the walls, appear before her, humiliate her, force her, kill her. A poetic end to an offense she could never otherwise recompense. Betsy's face flashed through his mind. No, it wasn't Betsy's. It was his mother's.

He was in front of the boarding house. Where could he stand inconspicuously? He had to make sure she still lived there. If she did, he would put in motion the "courtroom trial" and execution. A carriage pulled to the front of the house. A broad black driver remained in the seat and a young boy of lighter complexion jumped down from beside him and ran the stairs to the house. The door quickly opened, and Betsy emerged smiling, happy.

How could she be happy? How could she smile? But she was beautiful and seemed younger than the last time he'd seen her. He had a sudden urge to run to her and take her in his arms. But how could she be happy? He'd frightened her so badly earlier that fear should have gnawed her inner happiness, sanity and confidence until she knew only ruin and despair. In feelings of darkness, Betsy and he would have been partners, and he perhaps could have had compassion on her and loved her all the more because she could have understood him. She was smiling, happy, visiting with the little, black imp as if it were human. Where were her cautious, fleeting scans of every person passing nearby, expecting harm from each? This is not how he meant to leave her. Could it be she was not yet completely his?

The driver hadn't noticed her, busy watching something in another direction. She reached up and touched its hand. She spoke to it, still smiling, and the driver quickly dropped down to open the carriage door for her. As she climbed in, she reached down and took the little thing's hand, leading him into the carriage with her. They settled quickly, and she kept talking to both the little one and the big one. It was disgusting. He wanted to kill them. They had both touched her.

The carriage pulled away and joined the traffic on the Avenue. She hadn't glanced in his direction, completely immersed in happily talking to the animals. He was too far from them to hear their conversation and immediately began following the carriage.

He easily trailed it along the busy Avenue, past the market. Maybe she had moved and only worked as a servant at the boarding house. Yes, this was her new paramour, and he'd come to take her home after a night's work. Betsy shared a shanty on the Island with those two things. He knew lots of them lived there.

It was beginning to make sense. He had destroyed her happiness after all, and this new liaison was just an outward show of lunacy. Her cousin was mad. The entire family must have been prone to it. He suddenly felt light again. She'd abandoned the Union private for this animal. The dread he'd engendered in her had crazed her. His feet glided across the bridge. He had driven Betsy Henderson insane. She must have thought she was a black thing, too. The carriage was picking up speed as the traffic thinned, and he picked up his pace to keep up. If he could find out where they lived, he could set a trap for all three of them. It would be delicious.

The carriage turned at the hospital. He hurried to the corner and nearly overran it as the driver stopped the carriage. The little animal was already helping Betsy out. The boy saw him, but took no notice, and Walthrope slipped backwards around the corner, using the cover of the hospital pavilions.

He was frustrated. The scenario he'd imagined was not played as he'd directed. Visiting a hospital was not an act of trepidation, but an act of compassion, love. He thought he'd killed that in her. Had he failed?

He watched the carriage pull away as Betsy flowed toward one of the buildings. He followed as soon as he thought it safe and discretely approached the ward she had entered, stopping at the door. He watched as she moved through the room. She was visiting someone.

A man leaving the pavilion stopped in front of him, blocking his view of Betsy. "Are you looking for someone?" he asked Walthrope pleasantly.

"What? Oh . . . ah . . . I thought I saw a friend . . . go in."

"What's his name?"

To his consternation the man remained in front of him blocking his view of Betsy. "Ah, his name . . . It's not one of the patients," he said smiling broadly; "it's Mrs. . . ." He couldn't remember her real last name. "Mrs. . . ."

"Mrs. Gragg?"

"Yes. Mrs. Gragg."

"You can go in. She's visiting her husband. I'm sure she'd welcome you."

"How is Mr. Gragg?"

"Better. I think it's her presence that's done it. Go in. Greet them."

"I'd rather not bother them," he said slowly. "If I might take a moment to write a note, could you give it to them for me? So I don't interrupt them. That way they'll know I'm thinking of them."

"If you prefer. I'm leaving, but I have business in the office. I'll return shortly to take your note. That way we won't bother the nurse either, as she's already dispersing morning medicines."

"I don't have paper or pencil. May I bother you for them?"

"Come. We can get them in the office."

He followed the man and quickly wrote a note. He folded it and handed it to the night watcher saying, "By the way. What's wrong with Mr. Gragg?"

"Shot in the hip. Agonizing, I'm sure. It looked like we were losing him, but he's rallied."

"Good to hear it. I hope my note cheers them. Please tell Mrs. Gragg I'll call on her shortly. So exciting to think I've rediscovered friends." He grinned pleasantly.

"Are you sure you don't want to go in?"

"I don't want to surprise them . . . with him so weakened. I'll come another time—when he's better." He smiled. "Thank you for helping me rekindle an old friendship. If you'll excuse me, I have pressing matters I must see to."

"I'll deliver the note faithfully, sir, when I return to the ward."

"You won't take it immediately."

"Shortly."

"Then, good day."

Smiling, Walthrope left the hospital complex with its pavilions and temporary tents and strode rapidly from the facility.

A few minutes later, the night watcher delivered the note.

"A gentleman left this for you."

Betsy looked up at him from her bedside chair. "Gentleman?"

"Yes, he was pleased to hear your husband is doing better and glad to have discovered you. He hadn't seen either of you for a long while and was excited to refresh friendship. He didn't want to break in on you together . . . without warning."

Hank was asleep, and Betsy's face turned hard. "Give me the note," she demanded unintentionally harshly.

The change in her demeanor was dramatic and the man noted it. "I hope I've done nothing wrong. He was standing outside the door. He didn't want to come in; just left a note."

"The note," she persisted.

"Here . . . here it is."

He handed it to Betsy.

She unfolded it. The night watcher waited nervously for her reaction.

My fair and beloved Betsy,

It is with the greatest happiness that I discover that you sit at the side of your weak, invalid husband. I do hope you have not forgotten your old friend so quickly. I would so much like to help you both, and perhaps the best way for me to decide how I can help is to meet with you discreetly so as to not threaten your husband's recovery.

Please meet me tomorrow morning at eight o'clock at the entrance to the post office, Seventh and E streets. Till then, I leave you my best wishes that Mr. Gragg will remain healthy. I do hope you will act cautiously and confidentially for his recovery. Let us keep this between ourselves. To do otherwise is to put delicate, lowly Private Gragg in danger.

Till tomorrow, your loving and devoted friend,
Lucius Walthrope

"Are you all right, Mrs. Gragg?" the watcher stolidly asked as Betsy's face reddened in anger and her shaking hands shredded the note.

"The man is no friend. He mocks and frightens me."

The man looked confused. "Why would anyone frighten you?"

"It's a long . . . sad story, but all offense was on his side, all violence on his side, all evil on his side."

In an incredulous voice, the man offered, "I cannot imagine the gentleman would want to harm you . . ."

"That's how he does it. No one suspects him, certainly not of murder. He is too gentle, kind, helpful . . . till he isn't."

The watcher studied her with stupefied eyes. "I am sorry to have brought the note to you. I had no idea."

"There's nothing to be done, other than care for Hank." Determination erased her anger. "Nothing to be done." She looked at him, forced a smile, and said, "Nothing to worry about. Everything's fine. Thank you."

Chapter 43

Betsy was grateful Hank had slept through the conversation. She wouldn't tell him or anyone else that Walthrope was in Washington. She'd handle this herself. She had created the morass, and she had to dry it out. She asked William not to pick her up the next morning as she would walk to get the exercise needed in her condition. Her plan was to stake out the large post office early so she would see him first. It was her best chance to outwit him.

Early the next day, she visited the kitchen, seized a knife from its place and hid it in her small bag. She sneaked out the door and made her way swiftly to the quiet post office intersection.

He wouldn't dare approach the building till he saw her near it, so she strolled slowly scanning her surroundings for anyone loitering in the area. She had forty-five tense minutes to wait.

Nervous and sweating, she positioned herself in the shadow of the corner of a nearby building. Expecting him to be disguised, she scrutinized each person who passed, looking for anyone who might be him. A bell tolled the half hour. Thirty minutes, and the matter would be decided. Clutched tightly in her hand was the small bag. The street was awakening around her. Cabs, carriages, pedestrians and wagons appeared in larger numbers, making it harder to scrutinize everyone closely. He must have counted on that.

Why meet in such a public setting? Why not some isolated location where he could quickly dispatch her? She watched the post office. The clock struck eight. No appearance. Her agitation peaked. Uncounted, but painfully felt, minutes passed. Would he never come? Dread seized her.

Was this his way to sideline her so he could attack Hank unmolested? It was too late if he had. She breathed shallowly, rapidly. It wouldn't matter if she died. At least her fear would end. But Hank: If he'd killed him, the world would end. Without thinking, she stepped from the shadow and walked toward the post office.

"I wondered how long you'd wait," the familiar, harrowingly smooth voice called before she'd gone far. "I was losing patience with you."

She didn't turn, ignored him and kept walking toward the appointed meeting place, a more public setting. The entrance to the large, white, three-story federal style building—as he had proposed—would be better than turning and lunging at him when she couldn't determine exactly where he was.

His voice seemed to follow her. "Don't we have an odd friendship . . . a love really? Don't you think, my dear?" He was nearly yelling, and Betsy was embarrassed. "We meet in clandestine ways and in the most unexpected places . . . as if we have something to hide in our love."

He didn't seem to care if people passing heard. "Betsy, I've learned your husband's back from the front and wounded. Nothing serious, I hope. It's sad to see the cripples. Remember Caleb?"

She listened carefully, walking as fast as she could. Her hand slipped into her bag and clutched the knife handle. He followed still taunting her, "Yes, Caleb, a noble young man. The kind of man a woman could fall in love with. We both know he wasn't up to any task, Betsy, not really. He died last week, a bullet to his breast. An affair of honor found him wanting in that rare attribute of courage. Yes, poor, noble Caleb. Wasn't he your friend? Yes, he died . . . last week." The voice was getting closer. She was nearly at the building entrance.

Abruptly she turned. She didn't recognize the man nearest to her. He wore short cropped red hair partially covered by a hat, a full thick red beard, broad red eyebrows and thick spectacles. It wasn't him, yet it had to be him. No one else was close. The man passed her without a comment or glance. So, it wasn't him. How could he talk to her like that and not be there? Where was he? The red-haired man must have heard him. Was she going crazy? Was he a ghost? As she analyzed the possibilities, a scrubby boy approached.

"A man left this note for you," he said curtly, handing her a folded piece of paper without stopping.

She turned and called after him, "What man?"

The boy didn't answer or look back.

With her hands shaking in fury, Betsy clumsily unfolded it and read:

> *My ever lovely Betsy,*
>
> *I am sorry that we were unable to rendezvous this morning as you had so hoped, but I am sure you yet want to meet with me. Might I suggest we meet at rooms I have taken? Please come tonight, as soon as you have spent the day nursing your dying soldier, if he has not died already. Say goodbye to him at precisely seven o'clock, come to the intersection of South B and West Sixth streets. There you will receive directions to our much anticipated assignation. Please do not think your visit will compromise you as I am a married man. Our visit will be important in keeping your valorous husband alive, if he is. You should check on him quickly.*
>
> *Until tonight, I am forever faithfully yours,*
> *A loving admirer*

Crumpling the paper, she vowed she would not go. He was playing some fiendish instrument out of tempo and demanded she dance, but she would not play any part of his devilish quadrille. He could try to kill her if he dare. She no longer cared. She made her long way to the hospital, leaving her feet sore, legs exhausted, her body and spirit emotionally spent. She still carried the bag concealing the knife as she flopped in the chair by Hank who was very much alive.

"I was beginning to think you weren't coming today," he teased her.

"I needed a walk," she responded nonchalantly, trying to hide her fatigue and worry.

"William didn't bring you?"

"No. I told him I needed exercise. It really is a lot to ask of him to bring me every day. I really never did ask him. I asked to have someone pick me up, and he insisted he could get away from the livery stable long enough each day to do it. He insisted. Today, I needed a walk and told him so."

He looked at her thoughtfully. "Your walk has worn you out."

She flashed a smile at him. "Your child wears me out as much as his father does—much more than any leisurely stroll."

Something was wrong. He perceived nervousness but hesitated to probe.

The day sped for both of them, but just before seven o'clock she abruptly rose and said, "I better make my way back." She paused, looked sadly at him, leaned down and kissed his lips. "Goodbye, my love."

"William's not taking you home?"

"I told you: exercise. Walking's good for me."

"You walked this morning."

"I need more."

"I don't like it."

"I need exercise, and you need rest. You've been awake a long time today. Take advantage of the chance to sleep."

"I'm not worried about me."

She pulled on her gloves, touched her fingers to her lips and pressed them softly to his cheek. "Get some sleep. I'll be back before you wake. Soon we'll be together all the time, and you'll weary of me bothering you. You'll fondly remember these days and nights when you could sleep so freely."

He had taken hold of her hand. "Let me go. Will you detain me until I'm left to wander the dangerous streets in the dark?"

He unwillingly released his grip.

"What a wonderful family we make," she said dreamily, and before he could respond, she turned and paced quickly out of the ward.

Unsettled, he watched her go with no way or clear reason to stop her.

Chapter 44

July 1864, Washington City, District of Columbia

At twilight, Betsy located a small, single-story ramshackle dwelling at the address another boy on the street had given her minutes earlier. It was not the same boy who'd delivered Walthrope's previous note, which left her wondering how many people in Washington the demon employed. Frightened in the unfamiliar area at dusk, she summoned courage reminding herself Walthrope's torturous persecution had to be stopped to maintain her own sanity and Hank's life. She had to deal with Walthrope—kill him—to ensure he never bothered them again. Yet she anticipated failure and her own probable death haunted and at times paralyzed her thoughts.

The front door stood ajar, and light streaming from within drew her to cautiously peer in. A gas lantern flickered on the floor. Someone sat, back to her, as familiar voices conversed jovially. Across from the chair sat the man with the red beard who had passed her at the post office. From his vantage, he could easily see the door. He was hatless and wore no spectacles. Betsy stopped, hoping he hadn't noticed her.

"No reason to stand outside. Join us, my lovely Betsy," sang Walthrope's voice.

She sickened realizing the red head was Walthrope. He had been in her power, and she could have reached out hours ago to stab him as he'd passed or chased him down the street to plunge her knife in his back. It would have ended then. Frustration and anger drove her into the room toward him, her hand gripping the kitchen knife handle hidden in her bag. He would no longer haunt her. Wrenching the knife from the bag, Betsy lunged at the motionless, smiling fiend. But a strong arm grabbed her and held her back. In panic and rage at seeing her malefactor, she'd forgotten the unidentified head in the chair.

"That's not how we should do it, Mrs. Gragg," someone lectured calmly as he grasped her wrist and squeezed it till she dropped the knife. It fell to the floor, and a stout, quick leg kicked it away. Only then did she realize Walthrope was tied to a wooden chair with his hands secured behind him. Nonetheless, he guffawed merrily.

Fearing mortal danger, she wrestled and twisted to free her arm and turn on her unforeseen captor. It was the sheriff, the man who had arrested her as a traitor in Staunton. She grimaced, screeched in vexation, still trying to break his strong grip, but he spun her around, physically subduing her.

Walthrope's eyes twinkled as he watched the wrestling match between a pregnant woman and a stout, old man.

"Mrs. Gragg, I will let you go . . . if you calm down," Sheriff offered.

She tugged again. "Let go of me! Or . . . I'll . . ."

"I'm here to help. I've come for this miscreant. I'm not going to take you back. There's no reason to take you back."

"You had me arrested. Let me go."

Distracted by the clarity of her green eyes, he struggled to pull his thoughts together, finally explaining sincerely, "I never wanted you held. I argued your innocence at every point. I've sneaked into Washington only to take Walthrope back."

She screamed, and he released his grip in the off chance another cry would draw attention.

She ran to the still-open door panting, but stopped abruptly, eyeing the knife on the floor. She peeked at Sheriff, and before he could move, grabbed the knife and spun threateningly toward him.

Walthrope enthusiastically encouraged her. "Stab him. He arrested you, and—no matter what he says—he's come to take you and me back on trumped up charges. He told me there was a reward for us both, and he wants it all. Together we can stop him. Stab him. Cut me free. I've pretended to hate you for so long—I'm sorry I had to do it—just to draw this fiend into the open. He paid that woman in Staunton to say that I murdered old Stokes. Everything I've done since was to give me time to prove my innocence . . . and yours and to expose Sheriff. I've done it to protect you. Why do you think I wanted you to come tonight? So we could plot against this devil, but he beat you here. Stopping him is the only way to save you and your husband. He'll kill him, once he's done with us. This morning I worried he already had. Oh, Betsy, it was so hard to deceive you . . . to have you believe I meant you harm. Now you know the truth. This is our chance to be rid of him . . . at last. Then you can go back to your husband, and I to my devoted wife."

Sheriff listened without comment to Walthrope, watching Betsy's reaction carefully, weighing whether she believed the renegade. When Walthrope had finished, he began, "You are free . . ."

The redhead argued, "Don't listen to what he'll tell you. He twists the truth. Always has. If you walk out of here, he'll kill me; then follow you. He'll hunt you; kill you because you've escaped from him so often. He won't stand for it. He hates those superior to him, and you, dear Betsy, are superior to him in every way."

"Mrs. Gragg," Sheriff began patiently.

Walthrope's eyes glowed with rage, "Don't listen. He has the tongue of the devil. Stab him and run. Leave me, but at least save yourself . . . and your brave husband."

Betsy backed to the door still holding the knife. Looking from one man to the other, she began to say something but hesitated. Her hand rested on the latch. Her gaze rested finally on Sheriff. "Why were you always nearby when I was arrested or moved from jail to jail?"

"I tried to convince everyone your cousin was mad. I told them that in her hallucinations and the humiliation of being married to a good man whom she thought cowardly, she had accused you . . . to protect herself from her own fear of being called a traitor. It was her madness."

"Why did you arrest me?"

"I didn't." He spoke quietly. "I was with the soldiers, but it was the provost marshal's guard that arrested you. When the marshal questioned you—Do you remember?—he would leave the room to prove to me he was right in arresting you. Each time, I argued your innocence, and that inflamed him more. That's why he treated you so harshly . . . crudely. I'm sorry for that. It was because I so vehemently disagreed with him, and he was set on proving me wrong and you guilty. I can't determine if you're inclined to believe Walthrope's lies. If you are, ask this question: Has Walthrope ever told you the truth? He claims I killed your foreman. Why would I do that? I didn't even know the fellow. Consider if Walthrope had reason to kill him. When you came back from Winchester after saving Mr. Moore and your cousin's husband, you heard rumors your woolens factory was being used for nefarious smuggling, hoarding, speculating. Remember?" He didn't wait for her answer. "You asked your mill foremen about it."

"How do you know that?" Betsy asked suspiciously.

"I investigated a man's murder." His voice rose briefly, settling back to a patient, soft tone. "I asked a lot of questions . . . to you, too. Remember? Over weeks, I talked to your entire household and others. I soon knew exactly what had happened and easily pieced together the why."

"Why didn't you arrest him?"

"I would have if he'd still been in Staunton, but you had already chased him away. If you're weighing the evidence—and I'm sorry to bring it up—but you wear a small, endearing scar across your cheek. If he was feigning . . ."

Walthrope interrupted, "Don't listen to this conniving demon. It was an accident. I didn't mean to cut your beautiful face. Don't abandon me to this man. He'll kill me. Without me to help you, he'll come after you. He used me to bait and trap you. He was the one who just attacked you. I would never have touched you so. He intends to kill you. With that knife, you have the advantage. He's killed before and covered his tracks. Who would suspect a former sheriff? If he can kill us, no one will suspect he killed your foreman. We are the last two who know."

Betsy glared at the redheaded Walthrope for a long time, closed the door behind her and turned to Sheriff. "I should have called you in Staunton. All the pain after that moment would never have happened."

"Oh, Betsy, my lovely Betsy, I never thought he'd take you in, not like that. I thought you'd see through him."

"Sheriff, can you stop him from talking?"

Sheriff smiled as Betsy lowered the knife.

Walthrope began screaming, "Don't kill me! Don't kill me! Murder! Murderers!"

"Do you think that will bring help in this neighborhood? You've chosen a perfect block to hide from anyone who might testify against you . . . or rescue you," Sheriff said smiling. "Mrs. Gragg, for you, I will gag him to keep him quiet."

Sheriff pulled a soiled kerchief from his pocket and stuffed it in Walthrope's mouth, securing it with a second he wrapped around Walthrope's head. Betsy relaxed and laughed sardonically. "Sheriff, I was so scared of you. If I'd realized, I would have helped you . . . and made it easier for all of us."

"He's a master of chaos and confusion. The war gave him free movement. You undid him. He couldn't leave you alone. He couldn't forget you."

"What did I do to him?" With contempt on her face, she glowered at Sheriff's prisoner.

"Nothing. He convinced himself he was entitled to you and everything that was yours. Walthrope couldn't forget you. You became an obsession. He hated you but was drawn to you. In his eyes, you had betrayed him. You had beckoned and should have given him your love and all your money with its accompanying prestige, but you jerked it away at the last minute."

"Thoughts of it . . . of him turn my stomach." She turned from her foe. "What will you do with him?"

"It will be hard to smuggle him across the lines to Virginia because I would need his cooperation. I think I'd be discovered if I drugged him. On this side, I'm not in the good graces of officials in Washington. When I couldn't find him last time, I sneaked back across the lines without telling Union folk, although I'd promised to keep them informed. I didn't think I'd have to come back. Since I disappeared on them, I'm sure they think me a spy or would if they found me. So I can't really count on anyone in Washington. Regardless, Lucius Walthrope can't be freed without harm to us all. He killed one of your servants in Staunton, thinking it was Caleb. I also heard a Confederate official in Richmond who had crossed Walthrope had been killed. No one knows in Richmond who did it, but I suspect we do. What to do with Lucius Walthrope is what I was thinking through when you arrived."

"What servant?"

"What?"

"What servant did he kill? When?"

"He was a house servant. I think his name was John."

Shaking in anger, she turned toward Walthrope. "John." Her eyes were torches. "You should have let me kill him."

"You can do it if you'd like. I'll not stop you . . . not now. But I don't want to put that on you. You're innocent, and I would keep you that way. His blood on your hands might be justice in some ways . . . but not under the law. I don't want you to kill anyone, especially now you're in such a condition." He glanced meaningfully at her belly. "You must think of your family."

"I'm not innocent if John was killed because of me," she spat in fury.

Sheriff sensed her teetering toward violence and hastily changed the subject. "How's your husband? In our very frank conversation about what he's done, why and what he planned, Lucius mentioned your husband was wounded."

"He was, but he's recovering. I feared when I left him tonight I would never again see him."

"Why not . . . if he's recovering?"

"I just thought it."

Sheriff nodded understandingly. "You should return immediately to his side. You have a long life of happiness to look forward to now that Walthrope won't threaten you."

She looked at Robert Sheriff, breathed deeply and smiled. "I remember your first visit, how you loved my tea-cakes and ate them as if you'd not eaten for days. You were kind, but I was on guard and assumed the worst."

"I remember those wonderful cakes."

She ignored his comment. "My husband, Hank, had returned to the North to his Union regiment. I'd surreptitiously married him. Then you showed up asking questions."

"Perfectly bad timing."

She smiled, her features softening. "The worst. I hoped your interest was Lucius. But Hank's visit was so fresh, and I was so frightened of revealing anything. When I was arrested, I was convinced you'd done it."

"I hadn't."

"No, and you wouldn't have come so far to return me—someone so unimportant—to Castle Thunder."

The knife in her hand clattered to the floor. Walking toward him, she reached out her hand and said, "I have misjudged your intentions and integrity. I apologize."

He shook her gloved hand, but said nothing. She noticed him glance down at the knife.

"Goodbye. Will I see you again?" she offered.

He smiled warmly, "I think not. I'll return to Virginia . . . and to my dear, patient wife shortly."

"May God be with you . . . and thank you."

"Return to your husband and live a long and prosperous life, and may you have many more children," he mused, glancing again at her stomach.

She walked out, closing the door behind her. As she felt the latch engage, excitement, love and gratitude flowed through her. She glided to the hospital in the dark. She had to see Hank. Their trials were past.

As soon as Betsy shut the door, Walthrope tried to talk, but the handkerchief Sheriff had stuffed in his mouth muffled his words.

Sheriff, still watching the door affectionately, turned to his prisoner and observed, "A lovely lady." He noticed Walthrope trying to speak. "Oh, yes, I think we can take that out now."

He walked to Walthrope, gingerly pulled the kerchief out of his mouth and let it fall to the crude wood-plank floor.

"How'd I do?" Sheriff asked.

"I believed every word . . . and so did she. Did you have to gag me? You knew no one would come."

"You screamed. I had to do something, or it would have looked to Mrs. Gragg that I wasn't doing what I would naturally do."

"Are you going to untie me?"

"Have we an agreed price?"

"How much did you want?"

"I told you: five hundred in gold," Sheriff demanded. "With gold I can live well after the war."

"You've given up on the Confederacy."

"It's a matter of time. No one says it. Not yet. The papers are full of long-shot, promising news. Religious folk are calling on God to intervene to save his faithful people. But when I arrived in Washington and saw how it prospers even as Richmond decays, it became clear: Continuing the rebellion only serves up more dead men, more widows and fatherless children—a waste of humanity. I wonder why they keep fighting."

"Honor, Sheriff. Not something you have. I thought you had it . . . and integrity. I thought I was lost." He chuckled. "It's remarkable what a little money will buy . . . in these hard times. I pegged you as a man not to be influenced, yet we have struck a bargain. There is no such thing as honor,

Sheriff, not in you or me or anyone. Just weak sentimentality in many."

"When you're starving . . . when everyone's starving, things begin to look different. Honor isn't part of it."

"It looks the same to me."

"You've always seen so clearly."

"Untie me."

"Not till I have your word you will keep our bargain—that you won't try to escape or harm me. All I want is my money and to return to Staunton."

"You'll have it. Let's up it a little. I think it's been worth it . . . what you're doing. What you've done. I'll give you seven hundred and fifty dollars in gold. I'm generous to partners."

Sheriff licked his lips. "That would be fine. In real money. Imagine what it—not the faded Confederate type—will buy me in Staunton."

"We have a deal. Hurry, loose me so you can get your money and scamper homeward. Then I can finish my work."

Chapter 45

As Sheriff approached Walthrope to untie him, he asked casually, "Will you kill her?"

"Of course," the prisoner answered agreeably. "I'll visit one last time with her till she begs mercy at my feet. Mercy will be granted in my final judgement: a quick end. Think how she'll feel having been deceived by me, Miss Morrow . . . and now by you. So much betrayal in one life: Oh, it's glorious. I can't wait to tell her. She'll die in agony. I promise that. I'll wait till her husband's released and kill him first . . . before her eyes."

"Masterful revenge," Sheriff responded emotionlessly as he as kneeled to unknot the ropes binding Walthrope's legs.

"It will be sweet nectar."

"Then?"

"I'll return to Richmond and my wife."

"Wife?" Sheriff repeated casually as he loosed his hands.

"Yes, I married, in a manner of speaking, Anna White-head, a promising actress in Richmond. She's the woman who helped me kill Caleb . . . and escape from Staunton. Why did you say I killed the slave? That was an unexpected ad lib. I liked it. The news devastated Betsy. I think she was more upset then than this morning when I told her that her one-legged pawn had been murdered. Marvelous. Well done. At any rate, Anna loves me."

"Loves you."

"Completely. She's helped me with my revenge."

"Helped with your revenge."

Walthrope worked the loosened ropes from his hands, legs and body as he spoke. "Without her, I could never have controlled Betsy. She pretended to be her friend so I could capture her in Richmond. She is a marvelous actress . . . and beautiful when not parading as the straight-laced Miss Morrow."

"An actress. How would you ever tell if she was feigning love?"

"A sharp tongue you have, Sheriff; but we're partners, I'll not question it. Feigning love? Hardly. She helped me lure Caleb out so I could kill him."

"You didn't."

"Didn't what?"

"Kill him."

"I confronted him in the barn. He kneeled to me and begged me to shoot him for his sins, and I did. I saw him collapse."

"You shot the wrong man. It was too dark to see who you were shooting. You shot the house slave . . . in the back."

Walthrope gaped at Sheriff and cursed. "Who told you that lie? I confronted him and shot him in the face. Why are you irritating me now?"

"You shot the wrong man. Caleb told me."

"You couldn't have spoken to Caleb after I left."

Sheriff laughed. "He was definitely breathing."

Walthrope cursed again. "I'll go back to Staunton. I hadn't planned on that. With your help, it will be easy to finish Caleb. I had hoped Betsy's death to be the climax. I don't suppose it can be helped. I'll do it out of order."

"My help there will cost more."

"Avarice is a disease, Sheriff. Beware."

Sheriff laughed pleasantly, "I should heed the warning as you seem an expert on the subject. One other thing . . ."

"It's time to finish our arrangement. Let's stop this conversation, get your money and go our separate ways." Walthrope had risen from the chair and was walking toward the back of the house still rubbing his wrists chaffed by the ropes. "You tied them too tightly," he complained.

"I must warn you."

"Are you threatening me?" Walthrope stopped and glared back at Sheriff.

"No, I want my money. I'm not threatening you, but your Miss Whitehead."

"Yes, what about Anna?"

"I caught her after her ride to distract me."

"That was the plan. I needed time to kill Caleb and to get a head start."

"I had a long conversation with her."

"It seems you can't have a short one."

"I do believe she thinks you deceived her and seems to hold a disgusting attachment to Caleb."

Walthrope regarded Sheriff angrily. "Why tell me this?"

"You said you'd return to her. But can you trust her? She may reveal what you've done, and I don't want her anger at you to ricochet at me."

Walthrope shrugged his shoulders. "I'll go to Atlanta. I'll find another love of a lifetime."

"Sounds the safer plan, though I suspect most widows there will be penniless."

Walthrope shrugged. "Wait here. I'll get the money."

"I'll come with you."

"Stay here. It's harder than you might think to give up so much money. I need time, that's all . . . to settle it in my mind. Look, there's no way out." He opened the door wide and allowed Sheriff to look into the room. It was simply furnished with two crude chairs and a solid table in the middle of the room and no other visible exit. He repeated, "Stay here."

Sheriff laughed knowingly. "I'll help."

Walthrope eyed his partner crossly. "So be it. Bring a lantern." Climbing on one of the chairs, Walthrope proceeded to the table where he easily reached a trap door in the ceiling. He shoved it up and aside. "Since you're here, get up on the table with me. The box is heavy. I'll pass it to you." He raised both hands and reached as far as he could into the attic. "There it is."

Still on the floor, Sheriff heard the box scratch heavily across a wood surface in the attic.

"Since you insist on staying at my side, help me up here."

"I'll stay here." Sheriff placed the light on the table. "I'm afraid of heights," he offered drolly.

Walthrope scowled at him. The scraping had decreased and Walthrope's hands still adjusted the box above. "You're an untrusting partner, Sheriff. You offend me. We should trust each other."

Sheriff didn't respond, but looked down at the chair and stepped onto it.

"On the table," Walthrope persisted.

Sheriff raised one foot to the table top as Walthrope pulled the box again, scraping the attic floor more lightly. The retired sheriff raised his right hand as Walthrope's hands dropped from the attic bearing a large revolver.

It arced down toward Sheriff in a rapid motion, but only at the last second did Walthrope see the pistol Sheriff calmly aimed at him. Sheriff fired. Walthrope fell hard onto the edge of the table, shattering and snuffing out the lantern, and slowly slipped to the floor.

Walthrope gasped, forcing out the words, "No trust."

Sheriff climbed down from the chair carefully and gazed casually at Walthrope who grimaced with pleading eyes visible in the dim light drifting in from the front room. With raspy groans, he said something Sheriff couldn't understand.

Sheriff kicked the gun from Walthrope's loosened grasp, climbed onto the table and searched the small attic with his hands until he found a metal box. He pulled the heavy container to the edge of the trapdoor, hefted and lowered it to the table. He stepped down—leaving Walthrope breathing loudly but unevenly, unattended on the backroom floor—and carried the box to the other room. Lifting its lid, he found it half full of gold coins. "Payment as promised and quite a bit more," he mumbled.

He sat down in the front-room's upholstered chair to think and rest. After several minutes, he rose and stepped briskly toward the small backroom. It was quiet, and that spooked him. Was Walthrope better off than he had thought? Sheriff suddenly imagined his nemesis waiting, gun in hand. He leaned forward to peer into the room, watching to make sure Walthrope hadn't feigned injury. He could see a lump on the floor on the far side of the table. Momentarily, he was tempted to take the box and run from the house, but he knew he couldn't: He had to ensure Walthrope was dead. Warily slipping into the room, he examined his foe. He could no longer hear him breathing and reached down, pistol readied, to feel Walthrope's neck for a pulse. So long in pursuit of the devil, Sheriff still half expected Walthrope to suddenly wake to shoot him. He put his hand on the man's chest and pressed down as hard as he could. The body remained life-less—Walthrope was dead. Still uneasy, Sheriff studied the disguised face. It was definitely Walthrope.

As he confirmed the death, he heard the front door latch lift quietly. Had Betsy sent for the police? Was he caught? Would he never make it home? What would happen to his wife? Would the gold disappear into the hands of unscrupu-lous detectives? Or worse had some unknown Walthrope confederate entered?

He moved deliberately, quietly, with his pistol still in hand, from the body toward the door. His heart beat as fast as it had when he had awaited Walthrope's attempt to kill him.

Someone had entered the main room and was creeping toward the backroom doorway. He slid toward one of the dark corners, slowed his breathing and waited. A shadow fell briefly across the back wall. He raised the revolver and pointed it toward the doorway. The person, whoever it was, stood perfectly still, and Sheriff waited, motionless.

Minutes went by. Neither of them moved. How long could this go on? In spite of his ongoing internal conversa-tion about the necessity of waiting, his patience waned.

Crouched, he moved slowly along the wall toward the door. As he neared it, he rose to his full height, inadvertently brushing the wall. Still the person in the main room made no sound. He took one more step and grimaced as he heard a shard of broken lantern glass crunch under his foot. The breaking glass was answered instantly with sequential fire that erupted from the main room, sending three bullets toward Sheriff.

Sheriff fell to the ground. The gun was fired two more times in his general direction. He groaned, crumpled face down. He struggled to get up as a shadow again passed the door. A woman? Had Betsy come back to kill him and Walthrope? He could feel his mind slowing down. He was going into shock.

He whispered, "Help."

The woman's silhouette appeared at the door.

He called out loud enough for her to realize he was not Walthrope, "Help me."

The woman stepped into the room and whispered, "Who are you?"

"Robert Sheriff."

A gasp escaped the woman.

"I thought . . ."

"You're too late for that. Help me into the light."

"I don't want to hurt you . . . more."

"It's my arm. Hardly hurts. I'll be fine. Get me into that chair in the other room."

She bent, extending her arm toward his voice until she found him. He grasped her hand with his good arm. He was heavy, and she braced herself to withstand the pressure of his weight as he pulled. When he was standing, she put her arm around his protruding waist. He leaned on her, and they walked clumsily through the door, a tight fit with his girth, and toward the upholstered chair. He glanced down at the box of gold coins that sat open, but said nothing.

Anna sat opposite, noticing the loose ropes at the bottom of her chair. "What do we do?"

He smiled. "So it's you. You came after him. Unfortunately neither of us is where we should be."

"We're misplaced."

Sheriff stared at her without speaking.

"What must we do?" she repeated.

He ignored the question. "We meet in the most unusual places . . . the most unusual circumstances: Prison. A midnight horseback ride. A house where a man's been killed."

"Did you kill him?"

"Self-defense. He tried to kill me. I was hoping—more accurately, pretending to hope—that I could take him back to Virginia."

She laughed. "How would you do that?"

"I hadn't decided when the obliging fellow solved the dilemma. Even so, his death lies heavy on my soul." He sighed. "I should be happy. I can return to Staunton and live out a restful life."

"Mr. Sheriff, I don't see a quiet life for you."

"It will be peaceful with my wife."

"I pity the lady."

He laughed. "You should."

"What will we do? Should I take you to a doctor or hospital? You might end up in prison or a camp. I don't have money to bribe anyone. I can try and nurse you, but if Walthrope's lying on the floor in the next room, we can't stay here long. Eventually he'll stink. What have I done? I didn't mean to shoo . . ." She began to cry, her resolve undone, her shoulders trembling.

"You didn't do anything wrong. It could have been me dead, and you would have just shot Walthrope."

She didn't respond.

"If I weren't wounded, we could have escaped tonight, but I don't think I can go anywhere for a while. He will stink shortly, and neighbors—while they'll overlook many other things—won't like an offensive odor. We have to get rid of the body. Can you drag your husband's body out here?"

"Don't call him that," Anna paused. "I came because regardless of what happened to me, I had to stop him from hurting Betsy more."

"Commendable. Did Caleb follow?"

Her eyes betrayed fear. "Surely, he wouldn't. I doubt he could. He was getting around on crutches when I last saw him."

"I've given up predicting what people can or will do. I didn't think you would shoot me." He laughed. "Go on. Drag him in here."

She dragged the corpse through the door, leaving a trail of blood and bits of lantern glass across the floor.

"Take off his jacket. Be careful. It will have broken glass in it. Then tear off the cleaner of the two sleeves."

She struggled with the dead weight, pulling, shoving and tugging at the body till she wormed the jacket off.

"I'm getting blood on my dress."

"Yes."

In a quick jerk, she tore the sleeve from the shoulder.

"Take it off over his hand and bring it to me."

"A tourniquet?"

He breathed heavily. "Yes."

She wrapped the sleeve around Sheriff's upper arm, twisted it tight, and tied it as he groaned.

"Good," he whispered, "with luck that will stop or at least slow the bleeding. Help me up. I'll bring this rope. Drag him outside quietly."

She tugged Walthrope's leg, trying to pull his body across the floor and over the threshold as Sheriff disappeared out the door.

By the time she had wriggled the corpse to the edge of the small stoop, Sheriff appeared with a saddled horse. "We've got to get him in the saddle. Then you'll have to climb up behind him and tie yourself to him with this rope."

"It's not a good idea," Anna protested.

"It's better than two Southerners being found with a corpse. Ride to the river—not near the wharf. Keep far from the army and the dock."

"I don't know where the dock is . . . or the army, or the river."

He whispered, "You need to appear to ride with him . . . in a most unladylike way. That won't draw attention. What will draw attention is a woman riding with a corpse draped behind her saddle. If anyone stops you, claim he got in a fight, passed out drunk and you're taking him home to his wife." He chuckled.

"The blood?"

"That's from the fight. You'll think of exactly the right thing to say. You're the actress. Spontaneous, I hope. Ride with him to the river."

"Why can't we just leave him here?"

"If he's gone, we can stay here a few days till I get a lit-tle stronger. Go that way, past the Smithsonian Institution. You'll know it when you see it. It looks like a medieval castle. Ride toward it, get on the street that fronts it and keep going to the left . . . to the river. The road will end, but you keep going through the field. Don't turn to the left or you might end up at Long Bridge or the Seventh Street Dock or some other army-infested area. I think the army would be most interested in questioning your drunken companion and might ask about the blood splattered on both of you once they real-ize he's expired. If you're lucky, you'll end your ride in a qui-et, unobserved patch. Take him to the water. Untie him and let him . . . make sure he falls in the water. Ride back as fast as you can. Make sure you look back periodically so you'll recognize landmarks on the way back. If you make it, our biggest problem will have been solved. Then we can see to my arm, hide out for a few days, before returning to Staun-ton . . . or you can go wherever you want."

"He's dead. That's all I cared about. What happens to me now doesn't matter."

"Don't be so melodramatic. I need you to come back."

"Why?

"To get me help. I don't want to wander around Washington like this, and I do care about what happens to me . . . and what happens to you. I don't want either of us arrested or dead."

"But you want me to ride around town in a bloody dress with a dead man in the saddle?"

"Just come back. I'll need help and my horse."

She ignored his comment. "Let's get both of us up on that horse."

They struggled, she using her entire weight and he the diminished strength of his uninjured arm. When they had lifted and positioned Walthrope's remains in the saddle, the corpse slumped over the horse's neck. She climbed up behind him and wrapped a rope several times around the two of them at their arm pits. Sheriff handed her Walthrope's jacket, and she put it on the dead man as best she could to hide part of the rope and adjusted her own jacket to hide another portion. She tightened it till Walthrope's corpse rested clumsily against her. She tied off the rope at the side and Sheriff cut the excess dangling rope. Without comment, he stumbled back into the rough cabin.

Anna, disappointed he offered no last minute encouragement, pulled the reins, turning the horse toward the Smithsonian. She followed several streets, trying at first to memorize them. It had been hard to find the shanty in the light when she first scouted it. In the dark, coming from a different direction, it would be much more difficult. But riding behind a cadaver in an unfamiliar city and fearing arrest at any time, she couldn't concentrate on anything but dumping her passive cargo in the nearby river.

The streets were deserted until she came to a large intersection where a file of soldiers marched diagonally across it with several ambulances following, blocking the half-dead couple from crossing. She hurriedly turned the horse and detoured around several blocks hoping to beat the soldiers to the next crossroad. Arriving just as the column of soldiers

entered the intersection, she pressed the horse ahead of
them. Seeming to march in their sleep, none of the soldiers
raised their eyes as she passed within feet of the head of the
front of the column. Once beyond the juncture, she slowed
the animal to reorient herself using the building Sheriff had
mentioned.

Chapter 46

Sheriff had been dozing in the chair and awoke with a start. How long had he been asleep? The raw pain in his arm riveted his attention. He glanced down and found the sleeve below the tourniquet turned red; but little blood dripped onto the floor. How long had she been gone? He reached down with his good arm, glancing at the box—still open at his feet—and doused the lamp. Fortunately Anna hadn't noticed the box or cared. He closed the lid with his foot, scooped it up clumsily with his uninjured arm, rose slowly, stumbled slightly; then moved to the door. Surely she'd be back soon. He was dizzy and leaned against the door briefly before opening it. The coming sun already brightened the horizon. It was late. Had she been caught? If discovered and arrested, would she incriminate him? If she had, the authorities would come soon. He wanted out of Washington, but inconveniently she had his horse. He should have stayed home and let her come to Washington to shoot Walthrope. But if he had stayed in Staunton, he never would have had such an unfiltered conversation with Walthrope. Expecting that he would survive by killing a bribed former sheriff, Walthrope had detailed his relationships, actions and motives in dealing with Betsy and Anna.

Sheriff abandoned Walthrope's hideaway and passed into the street. Wincing at the pain in his arm, he scanned the road a last time perchance Anna was returning. It was possible—he grudgingly admitted—that she had abandoned him to save herself.

His arm was completely useless, and the wound needed to be cleaned and dressed. He had counted on Anna's help to do it when she returned. But he could wait no longer, fearing his escape was increasingly in jeopardy.

Dazed, Sheriff struggled to decide which way to go, eventually choosing the way he imagined in his stupor led toward Virginia. The heavy case rested uncomfortably under his good arm, and he struggled not to tilt it as he walked. The clatter of a shifting gold fortune would surely attract unwanted attention.

The sky was coloring, with physical features around him that were invisible minutes earlier quickly appearing as out-lines. Two faintly visible people approached, and he looked away, hoping they would ignore him.

As they neared, a man's voice called out pleasantly, "Morning."

Sheriff glanced grudgingly at the pair, nodded and re-sponded, "Morning."

They stopped as if to talk to him, but he walked by.

"Are you well?" the same man called after him.

"Well enough."

"Your arm, it's . . ."

"I'm fine."

"I recognize a man in trouble and know someone who might help."

"Why would you care?"

"Don't like to see people suffer, even if they've done something wrong."

"I've done nothing wrong."

"Course not."

"This person . . . the one who can help. Is he nearby?"

"A few blocks. It's early yet. I think she'll still be at home."

"Show me the way," Sheriff said brusquely.

Sheriff carefully considered for the first time the two men as they talked between themselves. Strong accents re-vealed that they were new to the city and freedom; probably recently escaped from the Deep South. They were young and dressed shabbily as laborers.

"Hurry. We don't have much time."

"Where you going?"

"To work . . . for the army."

"A woman?"

"I lived at Freedman's Village across the river in Virginia. Met her there. She was a teacher, helped me learn a little reading. She left the Village school to become a nurse . . . at the hospital."

His fellow laborer blurted out proudly, "She's the best nurse they have in the army."

Silently the three men fell in together and walked southward rapidly. Sheriff huffed as he struggled to keep up with their fast pace. They turned several corners, striding briskly until they stood in front of a small, attractive two-story house. The first floor was finished and the entire exterior was nicely painted, with the exception of the two small windows on the upper level.

One of the freedmen went to the door and knocked softly. When no one responded, he pounded louder. By the time he finished the second knock, one of the windows on the upper floor opened and a rich, deep voice called out softly, "Who is it, and what do you want?"

"A man's been hurt, and we thought Nurse Richman might help."

"How'd he get hurt?"

"I didn't ask. Should I?"

"No, no. We'll be down."

William shut the window.

The three men stood in the street. After several excruciatingly long minutes for Sheriff, the door opened and William peered out.

"Which one is hurt?"

"I am," Sheriff offered breathlessly, stepping toward the door. "I'm sorry to bother you, especially at an early hour, but they said you'd help."

"Come in."

One of Sheriff's guides proffered, "We've got to get to the bridge. They've got us working on it."

"Go on. We'll look to him."

The two men nodded appreciatively and disappeared quickly along the road.

William ignored their departure, scrutinizing the exhausted man he had invited into his home. "How'd you get that?"

"I would like to say . . ."

William, grumpy at being awakened, cut him off. "Just say how."

"I was shot."

"Shot?" His voice betrayed surprise. "By whom?"

"Does it matter?"

"Suppose it does."

"A man by the name of Lucius Walthrope."

"Strange name."

"He chose it. Not his real name."

The voice of a woman approaching from behind William observed, "When they've stolen your name, you have to choose one."

Sheriff saw a beautiful young woman, more than a decade younger than the man, step slightly behind him. Was she his daughter? A younger sister? He thought about her comment and understood she had mistaken his meaning.

"He wasn't a slave. He was a white man. Took different names for nefarious reasons." He was sorry he had used such a difficult word. "For bad reasons."

He saw the inkling of a smile on the woman's face as she said, "Come on back. We can look at your arm in the kitchen."

As he followed her, Sheriff glanced at the top of the stairs where a young boy sat watching.

Victoria directed him to sit at a wooden table which along with four roughhewn chairs constituted the main furniture in the small room. Sheriff slid the box cautiously onto the table with his good arm.

"Thank you for helping."

"I haven't yet," the woman answered, her back to her patient as she worked at a small narrow table by the wall.

Sheriff smiled.

"Lucius Walthrope," Victoria confirmed.

"Yes."

"How do you know him?"

Sheriff hesitated wondering how much he could trust her.

She stopped to look at him, making it clear she expected an honest answer.

"I have a long story I can tell you if you want, but it will take all morning."

"The condensed version."

She was so articulate and immediately in control of the conversation that Sheriff almost forgot her race. "The short version is he murdered several people—including one of you . . . a few days ago—and I came to take him to justice." He noticed her posture straighten as he alluded to John's murder. This was no ordinary woman. That was clear. Proud. Aloof. Educated. Impatient. He instinctively felt he could trust her discretion and competence in cleaning and treating the wound. "You're a teacher and nurse?"

When she finished preparing, Victoria turned around, ignoring his comment, and called, "William, can you get a couple lanterns going? I'll need as much light as I can get."

"You live with your father, mother and brother?" he asked, trying to recover her good will, sure he had offended her.

She put the items in her hand down hard on the table. Eying him sternly, she responded, "I live with my husband and son. My mother and father died years ago."

"I'm sorry. I . . ."

Her voice softened slightly, "You haven't finished your story."

William brought in two blazing lanterns and set them on either side of the table. "Will that do?"

"Perfect . . . as always. Please send Adam to the well to get more water."

William disappeared down the hall. Sheriff heard muffled, sometimes stuttering conversation.

Victoria didn't speak again until William returned but moved to Sheriff's side and looked closely at the tourniquet and arm. "Your story," she finally said. "Why bring him to justice?"

"I was in past years a sheriff in Staunton, Virginia."

"Not now?"

As they conversed, William leaned against the doorjamb watching while Victoria examined and treated Sheriff's arm.

"No."

"Why not?"

"It's a younger man's work."

"You're not so old."

"I feel it. When I was sheriff, this Lucius Walthrope killed a man in Staunton. A few nights ago, he killed a slave," adding the last fact hoping the woman would think more highly of his mission.

"A far-fetched story. William, don't you think?"

Sheriff protested, "Unusual, but true."

"I didn't say it wasn't true; just far-fetched. For example: Why did you—no longer the sheriff—come to Washington City, capital of the Union, to chase any man? Why not let him go? He's not likely to harm anyone else in Staunton."

"You never met Lucius Walthrope."

"No. I've only heard your far-fetched story about him."

"He came to Washington to kill a woman."

"Why would he come all that way to do that?"

"He hates her . . . and loves her."

"Which?"

"Both."

"Can that be? I think you're getting it wrong."

"Try this. He came to kill her because she knows he killed a man."

"Which man?"

"The one a while ago."

"Not the slave."

"No."

"What's this woman's name?"

"I have the feeling you're interrogating me."

"We doesn't hardly knows what dat big word mean."

He knowingly laughed, but it was cut short with a scream of pain as Victoria probed his arm.

"Looks like the bullet broke your arm. Not too bad though. Nothing close to the worst I've seen."

Deathly pale, Sheriff was sweating and woozy, his stomach rebelling.

"Tell me the woman's name. You've had enough time to make one up."

His voice was tired, and he mumbled, "Do I need a surgeon?"

Victoria stopped ministering to his arm and stared directly into his eyes. "Since my dear husband let you through the door, you've insulted my intelligence, my family and my competence."

She wrenched the arm, and he screamed.

"That's to teach you respect . . . and set the bone. The lady's name? You don't need to go to a surgeon if you take good care of the arm. Keep it clean. Don't let anything hit it. What was her name?"

Sweat poured down Sheriff's face. He was panting and nauseated but grateful for the conversation.

"Her name?" She laughed wryly. "Now you pretend you can't understand what I'm saying. I believe you don't know the virtuous Queen's English when you hear it."

He whispered hoarsely, "Betsy Henderson . . . I mean Betsy Gragg."

William leaped toward the table, but Victoria glanced at him sternly, visibly cautioning him as she challenged Sheriff, "Can't decide on her name? That's not convincing. I believe we should contact the city police. You've obviously been shot sneaking into someone's house. You're a common thief or maybe a Southern spy."

Still breathing heavily, he responded, ignoring her last comment, "I knew her as Betsy Henderson, but she got married to a Mr. Gragg."

"What's Mr. Gragg's first name?"

"Hank, I believe. Or Henry."

"Ah, there you are, Adam. Bring that water here so I can wash Mr. . . . . I don't believe you gave your name."

Exhausted, Sheriff whispered breathlessly, "Mr. Sheriff, Robert Sheriff."

Victoria dropped her hands to the table, looked at Sheriff incredulously. "Does that mean?"

"Yes, unfortunately."

"It's good you gave up the office."

"At this moment, I'm thinking I made a mistake taking it in the first place."

"Perhaps. How are you acquainted with this Mrs. Henderson?"

"Mrs. Gragg. She owns some businesses and property in Staunton, although a lot of it was destroyed by the Union army. Her first husband died at Second Manassas. She remarried—and you'll like this—she married a Union man, someone she knew before the war."

"The Gragg fellow. You probably watched Mrs. Henderson grow up. Knew her when she was a little girl?"

"No, she wasn't from Staunton. I think she was from up north. Winchester if I recall it right. Yes, Winchester." His breathing slowed, and he wiped his trembling free hand across his wet brow.

"My husband's from Winchester." She looked beyond Sheriff at her husband. "William, did you know anyone named Henderson in Winchester?"

"No, don't remember anyone by that name. Course, it's all changed. May be Hendersons now."

"That wasn't her name."

"Changing it again?"

"I think her maiden name was Richman." Sheriff turned his head to William, hoping for substantiation of his story. "Did you know or hear of Richmans . . . in Winchester?"

Victoria shot a warning glance at William.

"Richmans? Hum? Think I have. Not sure."

Victoria smiled subtly, "Mr. Richman, could you please move that lantern back a hair?"

Sheriff looked from one to the other as Victoria dressed his arm. He suspected they were getting the best of him. "Is Richman really your name?"

William laughed, "It is."

He hesitated, "You know Mrs. Gragg."

"Yes," William responded soberly.

Victoria interrupted, "This Lucius Walthrope came to Washington to harm Betsy. Did he know Hank was here?"

"He'd figured it out."

William interjected, "Where's Waldrop?"

Sheriff turned his head as cold sweat dripped into his eyes, stinging them. "I shot him. He's dead." Victoria and William looked curiously at him, and he added quickly, "He tried to shoot me."

"Looks like he did shoot you," Victoria volunteered.

"Someone else shot me, but it was an accident."

"Probably part of the longer version I won't be able to enjoy because you are as fixed up as I can make you, and I have to get ready to go to the hospital."

She stood up to clear bloodied rags from the table and noticed the box on the table. She tried to move it.

He saw her and tugged the box from her. A metallic clatter sounded as the coins shifted within.

"I won't ask," she said, as she redirected her activities back to cleaning up the mess made in dressing his arm.

"What will you do?" William queried.

"A lady's out there . . . the one who shot me. I've got to find her. I hope she hasn't been arrested. Once I find her and I rest a bit, we can slip through the lines and go home. We can both live happily ever after, as they say. If she's arrested, there's not much I can do but escape on my own."

"Happily ever after? That, sir, only happens in heaven where the will of God is the sole dictate. As long as you're here where his will is most often ignored, you'll have no endless joy."

He looked at her seriously, "Then I return to endure unhappiness in Staunton. I must find the lady first."

"Why are you worried about being arrested, if you killed him in self-defense?"

"I'm a Southerner, as is the lady I mentioned. Last I saw, she was covered in blood. I think they would arrest either of us because of our suspicious circumstances and hold us as spies. Unlikely that anything we claimed would be believed."

Anna had nervously counted eight ambulances pass in the dark. Her patience was frayed, and she let the horse lope as soon as the last conveyance had crossed the intersection, realizing too late the pace had loosened the rope binding Walthrope to her. His body swayed slightly, side to side and forward, gradually pulling from her. She slowed the horse. Her fortune, she thought bitterly, was as tied to Walthrope in death as it had been in life. He sagged far to the side and would soon pull himself—maybe both of them—from the saddle.

Shortening the reins, she stopped the horse and pulled the rope tighter, but Sheriff had cut the rope too short to retie it. She looked up and realized they were in front of the Smithsonian. The detour and Walthrope's swaying body had distracted her. She couldn't remember the way she'd come. Sweat wetted her chest where it pressed tight against the corpse, and her heart quickened in sickening panic. She gripped the loosened rope in the hand that held the reins and bolted. If he rocked much more—she planned in disgust—she would let him fall to the road.

In the dark, she rode to the road's end where she entered the expected field and halted the horse. She wrapped her arms tightly around the body, still awkwardly holding the reins, and slowly walked the horse toward what she hoped was the river. It seemed an unending journey before she could hear and smell it. Approaching the barely visible bank gingerly, she positioned the horse at its top, parallel to the river, loosened the rope completely and shoved Walthrope toward the water. He fell short, hitting the ground with an audible thud before rolling into the river with a soft splash. She quickly unwound the remaining rope and tossed it as far as she could into the water.

As she turned from her horrid deed, she heard commotion up the bank: jumbled voices and someone crying, "Who's there!"

She glanced at the river, fearing they'd find Walthrope faster than Sheriff intended. Would that make a difference? Only if they caught her nearby. She kicked the horse with both heels, and it responded galloping toward the Smithsonian. Walthrope was at last gone, and she suddenly and desperately wanted to escape. She could not be caught covered in blood, especially if they'd heard the body fall. Lowering her head toward the horse's mane, she hoped desperately there were no unseen holes, people or things in the dark ahead.

When she reached the Institution, she adjusted herself in the saddle to a posture more consistent with her attire, tried to compose herself in spite of the blood and walked the horse on.

Chapter 47

July 1864, Washington City, District of Columbia

Mrs. Brown roused Betsy gently, whispering to her as she softly touched her shoulder.

"Betsy, you need to get up. Something's happened."

Agitated from her encounter with Walthrope and Sheriff, Betsy had slept poorly early on, but finally had fallen into a deep sleep. It took several seconds for her to consciously perceive Mrs. Brown's silhouette against the gas light streaming from the hall.

Mrs. Brown repeated, "You've got to get up, dear."

"What is it?"

"I'm not sure, but someone's in the kitchen and wants to see you. She says she's a friend . . . in need."

"Mary?" Betsy asked drowsily.

"No. She kept rapping on the back door, and Sally finally opened it. She wouldn't come in the drawing room, and I certainly don't want her in there . . . not in that condition."

Betsy wondered about the woman's condition.

"Get up. Hurry."

Betsy pulled herself to a sitting position, slowly swung her legs out and climbed from the bed, tied on a robe that rested on a nearby chair and followed her landlady to the kitchen, where a stranger looked up at her with expectant, nervous eyes.

"Good morning, Mrs. Gragg. I'm sorry to bother you at such an early hour, but I have nowhere else to turn."

She knew the woman's eyes and the voice was familiar, but she couldn't place her. "I'm sorry," she said tentatively, "but are you sure we've met?"

"Yes. Under different circumstances—circumstances that might make it hard to remember me." Anna squirmed in her chair.

Betsy examined the woman carefully, her eyes opening wide as she realized the visitor was wearing her favorite jacket spotted with large dark splotches. "What circumstances were those?" she asked as indifferently as possible.

The woman drew a breath and transformed her posture, voice and expression, taking on the persona of Miss Morrow as she announced, "I visited you in Castle Thunder."

Betsy stared at Anna, at a loss for what to say. A long, uncomfortable silence followed as Betsy's mind raced through the circumstances: Walthrope captured by Sheriff; an early morning call; a woman—Walthrope's partner in treachery—wearing her clothes. Betsy spoke harshly, "I remember you."

"Before you throw me out, let me tell you my story."

"Have you come because your friend has been captured, come to plead for him?"

"Please listen to what I have to say."

"Explain first why you wear my clothes—my favorite jacket—and why it's stained."

"I will."

"Quickly. You've awakened my kind hostess, worried her, and stirred the house."

"I didn't know what Daniel was planning to do."

"Who's Daniel?"

"You knew him as Walthrope, I think. I knew him at the time I was visiting you as Oskar Dante."

"Daniel then is just one more name he uses to abuse me," Betsy bitterly retorted.

"You're not alone," Anna added in disgust. "I actually married him thinking him honorable . . . that he loved me. I have since seen he had no feelings for me . . . and I suspect no feelings for anyone but himself."

"What's your real name?"

"Anna. Anna Whitehead."

"Ah, it's familiar. The monster must have mentioned it."

With clenched fists and pleading eyes, Anna explained in detail Walthrope's deception, claiming she knew nothing of his abuse of Betsy. She outlined her trip to Staunton, Caleb's kindness, Robert Sheriff capturing and releasing her, and Walthrope's ominous presence in Washington.

With visible shame and bowed head, she recounted Walthrope's telling her that on an early trip to Washington, he had arranged for rooms and houses around the city to hide in should Yankees discover him spying for the Confederacy. He had given her each of the addresses, anticipating a trip to Washington and the need to correspond. Walthrope had lied to her, claiming Betsy was a poor, deluded woman who needed his help if she was to escape a conspiracy framed against her by a cunning sheriff in Staunton.

Anna detailed her last three days in Washington: She had visited three of the addresses Walthrope had given her but found them seemingly unoccupied or occupied by someone else. Yesterday she had visited the final address—a small house on the Island—which he had mentioned as his safest refuge, the one he would use only in dire circumstances. He had described it as part of the Island where no one noticed or questioned anyone or anything.

She'd seen him enter this last refuge about four o'clock the previous afternoon. Angry tears appeared as she admitted she'd wanted to rush him and scratch out his eyes, but she'd thought better of it. She would return in the evening with a gun she'd taken from Caleb. She planned to sneak in and kill him while he slept. If he was right about the character of the neighborhood, no one would report a single, midnight gunshot or a woman entering by the front door only to slink away after such a pistol report. After killing him, she would straightway escape back to Staunton. She began to say escape back to Caleb but corrected herself.

Betsy wondered at Anna's verbal slip. Why would she feel attached to Caleb who had surely already married Marie Ann? She also wanted to ask if the blood dried on her jacket was Walthrope's—a pleasant thought. Or was the blood Sheriff's? Had Anna arrived to help Walthrope escape and killed Sheriff? Betsy, instantly worn out by the thought that Walthrope was free, began to fret, nervously biting at her lip. She wanted to eject Anna from the house but held her peace.

Anna with an unsure voice described arriving at Walthrope's shanty after dark. "I approached the door, opened it quietly. The room was lit by a single lantern. I was frightened and hesitated. Maybe he was still awake. Perhaps I should abandon my plans. But I wanted so badly . . . needed to be Daniel's destruction, so I kept on. I couldn't stop myself with him so close, even if I died in the process. By that time, I imagined Daniel had seen me spying on the house and waited for me with a pistol at the ready. I crept slowly, quietly across the floor, expecting a bullet from the other side of the wall."

Betsy's cheek twitched involuntarily. The woman's story was inconsistent with her knowledge, for Sheriff had Walthrope. Lucius would never have been free in that house to attack her. Betsy wished she had a pistol to point at the woman's head but was immediately repulsed by the violence of her owns thoughts. What had she become? What had they all become?

Breathlessly, Anna continued, "I heard something move in the backroom and raised the gun in the direction of the noise. If I heard it again, I promised myself, I would shoot all five bullets. I waited. It was excruciating. I knew he was waiting for me to move, to make a noise. At the slightest creak, I was sure he would down me with one expert shot."

Although Anna was showing appropriate emotions and using the right words, Betsy reminded herself that they were inconsistent with the simple fact that Sheriff had already arrested Walthrope and would be taking him back to Virginia. This fiend was quite an actress. What was she trying to do this time? Was she luring her to Walthrope, not knowing Walthrope had been captured? Was she hiding the pistol she boasted of, reloaded in her bag, planning to use it on her? She still hadn't explained the stains.

Anna was still telling her tale, "After waiting an eternity, I heard a soft crunch in the other room. It wasn't what I expected, but it was a sound. I pulled the trigger again and again until the gun was empty. I hit someone. I heard a groan and a thump as he fell to the floor a few feet away. I crept to the doorway and peeked in. A heavy man—not trim like Daniel—was moaning on the floor. I was horrified. I had shot Robert Sheriff."

She paused long enough for Betsy's feelings to shift from mistrust to panic. If Sheriff had been shot, had Walthrope escaped before Anna arrived? The stain on the jacket worn by this woman was Sheriff's blood. Walthrope was loose and coming after her. She could feel her mind retreating into itself. This was more than she could bear. Had Anna really helped Walthrope escape from Sheriff? Had they together killed Sheriff and concocted this story to trap, humiliate and kill her? Had they already murdered Hank in his sleep?

Mrs. Brown ignoring Anna's presence, moved to touch Betsy's cheek, noticing her darkening demeanor.

Anna stopped her story, comprehending Betsy's distress. "I didn't mean to upset her." Anna began to cry. "I came to tell her Walthrope was dead, and that I lost my way. Robert Sheriff shot him and wanted me to throw the body in the Potomac, and I did it. In the dark I couldn't find my way back to Walthrope's shack. Everything was so confused; looked different in the dark." Anna's hands moved quickly, frantically tearing her hat from her head and letting the tattered hat fall to the floor. "In the light, I could have found it, but it was dark. I had to find my way back. Mr. Sheriff would bleed to death if I didn't. Caleb had told me where you lived. It was easier to find, so I came here." She stood, looking pleadingly at Mrs. Brown. "I didn't mean to frighten her."

Mrs. Brown spoke in a soft, comforting voice, but Anna couldn't hear her. The woman cradled Betsy's face in both her hands, forcing Betsy to look at her, talking to her gently. It was as if Anna weren't in the room.

Anna was witnessing the unspeakable harm Walthrope, with her help, had done. "Come with me," she implored, sobbing. "At daybreak, I'll take you to Sheriff, and he'll confirm everything I've said. I pray he's yet alive. Or if you know where the house is, we can go now. That's why I came—to tell you that you have nothing to fear. Walthrope's dead. You have no reason to believe me. I've harmed you, but I swear on God's holy writ, I didn't know what I was doing. I thought he . . . I was helping. At least believe that. I didn't think I was doing you harm." She sat and buried her face in her hands. "You have to believe me."

Mrs. Brown let Betsy's face go and turned to Anna. "I think you've said enough," she said tersely. "I don't know what you've done or been involved with or who you are, but I will call the city police."

Imploring her hostess, Anna said, "Come with me Mrs. Brown. You can see Robert Sheriff, and he will attest to my intent. We can get him help."

"The police can sort this out."

"Please don't call them." She raised her reddened eyes, her hair falling in a tangled mess around her face. "Mr. Sheriff and I will be arrested. Don't call them. Come with me. Talk to Mr. Sheriff."

"Dawn nears. Perhaps the best thing to do is to wait for William who will pick up Betsy later. He'll take us—and a policeman—down to this house you mention. Then we'll clear it up. I'm going to take Betsy back to bed. I don't have a place for you to sleep, so you'll have to wait here. I'm up for the day, so I'll keep an eye on you."

Mrs. Brown helped Betsy up and was leading her out of the kitchen, when Betsy stopped, turned abruptly and asked, "Why are you wearing my favorite jacket?"

Anna was unprepared for the question. In her trauma, it took her a moment to remember that she wore Betsy's clothes taken from her Staunton wardrobe to replace the dress soiled in Anna's long-night ride outdistancing Sheriff. "I took it from your house because my dress was ruined, and I couldn't wear it to warn you about Walthrope. I would have been too conspicuous. I doubt I would have gotten this far. Caleb let me sleep in your room one night, and I found it."

Betsy glowered at Anna, weighing the evidence in her mind. She finally blurted out, "Is it your habit?"

"I'm sorry. What do you mean?"

"Destroying dresses."

Anna couldn't tell if Betsy was teasing her and decided that with Betsy's frame of mind she should accept it without disagreement. "Yes, I suppose it is."

"Why would Caleb let you stay in my room?"

"He wanted to help me, and I needed a place to sleep."

"I want that back," she declared firmly, then softly and resignedly added under her breath to herself, "Though I'll never again fit into it."

"I'm sorry I've stained it. It's blood. I fear it's ruined." Anna began unbuttoning it.

"You need a dress. I'll loan you one, but I assure you it won't fit you as that one does. Maybe it can be pinned to fit you. Maybe we can get the stains out of this one. You have no bag?"

"You see before you all I possess," she answered mournfully.

Mrs. Brown looked doubtfully at Betsy. "Are you sure you want to give her one?"

"Miss Whitehead cannot go around Washington City in such blood-stained clothes." She hesitated. "Can she take a bath?"

Anna nodded her head meekly. "Thank you."

"You seem fond of Caleb, but he's married."

Anna looked at Betsy questioningly. "I thought so, too. They didn't marry in the end. I remembered he was engaged to your friend. You told me she came with him to the Castle, but that friend began to believe the lies told of you in Staunton. They never married. Mrs. Gragg, Caleb is grateful to you for what you did and is a faithful friend in caring for your interests. The Yankees destroyed your mills and factory, but Caleb saved your house and a large store of grain by a ruse."

"Ruse?"

"He stored grain from the mills in the house—barrels everywhere. When the Yankees came to ravage and destroy your house, he sent a servant to assure the soldiers your husband was a Union soldier and you a Southern traitor arrested and sent north."

"He saved the house," Betsy ruminated, smiling reflectively, a distant look in her eyes. "Did he send you to Washington City?"

"He didn't. He didn't want me to come."

Betsy didn't respond but turned and left the room on her own with resolution in her step.

Anna didn't see Betsy again until she heard the open carriage pull to the curb in front of the boarding house. Bathed and fed, Anna wore a simple day dress Betsy had sent her. As soon as the carriage parked in front of the house, Betsy descended the stairs. She paused in the front hall, awaiting Mrs. Brown and Anna. When they had gathered, she opened the front door and descended first, but stopped immediately, staring at the carriage. William and Adam had alighted from the driver's seat. Adam was approaching a horse tied nearby, and William walked toward the three ladies.

In the carriage sat a slumped, heavy man with a broad brim hat lowered over his eyes. He wore no jacket, the sleeve of his shirt had been cut off and bandaging wrapped his arm. His clothes were bloodied.

William spoke quietly, hesitantly, to Betsy as if uncomfortable with the subject, "Man says he knows you. Says he was helping you and got shot. Says that's his horse Adam's getting."

Betsy responded graciously, "Thank you, dear friend. I do believe he was trying to help." She put her mouth close to his ear and whispered mischievously, "The woman who shot him is behind me."

William leaned his head back, looking suspiciously at Anna. "That her?" he whispered back.

"I think it is, but we can ask him. Where'd you find him?"

William's face brightened, and he chuckled. "Victoria's a bit famous down on the Island 'cause she's a nurse at the hospital. So when he was wandering lost, someone told him to find Victoria and she could nurse him up."

"It's a complicated world, William—a complicated world. When I think I understand what's happening, everything shifts places. Yet our steps seem guided and in the end blessed."

"Suppose they are."

Betsy smiled compassionately at him, touched his arm gently and made her way to the carriage. She beamed as she watched Adam tying the horse to the back of the carriage and said, "Good morning, Adam. What's the weather going to be?"

"Hot as ever. Maybe it will rain," Adam responded, smiling back at her.

"Maybe it will." She raised her head to look at Robert Sheriff and said, "I understand you solved your biggest challenge."

He raised his head, revealing how tired and drained he was. His shirt collar was wet. "Mrs. Gragg," he said weakly, struggling to show enthusiasm, "we are both free of him. You don't have to worry about Lucius Walthrope, and I don't have to take him back. It was his choice. I see Miss Whitehead abandoned me for you. I hope she told you about her heroic effort to protect you. Did she get him to the river?"

"She said so, but I'm not sure what is real and what conspiracy anymore. I would have liked to have seen the man's dead body to make sure it was him; that he was really gone. She says she dumped him in the river."

"Take my word for it. He is dead, though you'll never see his body. The best we can hope for is that no one will except the fish that feed on his carcass."

"He keeps popping up, and to see him dead would have done me much good."

Sheriff studied her thoughtfully. "Here, here's something for you." He tried to scoop up from the seat beside him the metal box taken from Walthrope. "The contents of this box belong to you. He would, I assure you, part with it only in death." Unable to get a good grasp on the box, he dropped it with a clunk and clattering. The box landed on its side, and the fall and shifting coins pushed the top off far enough that a few coins slid out.

She gasped, staring at the coins. "What does that mean? Why are they mine?"

"He stole it from you. He dealt in gold when he managed the factory operations. It was back when you still could get gold, and he demanded it—not for you, but for himself."

"He stole that money from others. I can't take it."

"It's impossible to determine where it all came from. Regardless, you need it, and it's yours—stolen in the end from you. If nothing else, consider it recompense for damage he did to your reputation and for driving you from your home."

"And for driving me nearly mad." She looked at him incredulously. "What do I do with it?" Remembering his wound, she added, "You got shot."

"Accidently. Victoria—I think you've met her—dressed it and announced me alive."

William interjected, "Arm's broken. Ball hit his bone but didn't shatter it. Victoria set it, and he screamed."

"I'll live."

Betsy smiled compassionately at Sheriff, reaching across the carriage to touch his unwounded arm. Betsy turned to Anna for the first time since their nighttime conversation, emotions filling her voice. "I owe you an apology. Forgive me, but in all the confusion Walthrope created, I could never distinguish his machinations."

Anna, fighting her feelings, said, "Nor could I. Forgive me for putting you in his power in Richmond."

"You helped get me out of Castle Thunder."

"You would have been released at some point."

"Maybe, but you and I didn't know that. I'm still not sure of it. Every day in there was an eternity of misery to me. You offered me hope when I had none." She smiled brightly, her eyes shining as she smoothed her blouse over her bulging stomach. "Shall we go overwhelm Hank?"

Mrs. Brown, awed by all that was happening and frightened of losing Betsy, interrupted, "Betsy, I hope this doesn't mean you'll move out."

Betsy embraced her warmly. "Not while I'm in Washington City; and I can help with expenses now."

Betsy, Anna and Mrs. Brown climbed into the carriage, as Adam closed the door and scrambled up beside William.

Betsy turned to Mr. Sheriff and asked, "How did you solve your dilemma?"

"I really never did," he answered, his eyes twinkling. "It evaporated. He'd offered a bribe if I would free him, and I demanded immediate payment. Of course, his payment and the one I wanted differed substantially. He kept both his money and his pistol in the same place—the attic of that little house. He chose to try to pay his way first, but I knew he would; counted on it in fact. I shot him before he could do me the honor. I checked the attic and found your money. You inadvertently financed his life, his revenge and your own suffering. A bit comes home to you."

"Caleb never married Marie Ann?"

Sheriff responded, "No, she ran off. She wanted to get as far away from you as possible . . . and that meant abandoning Caleb . . . to a much better lady." He gazed toward the passing traffic, distracting everyone from noticing Anna blush.

"How can I repay all of you for what you've done . . . for saving me?"

William laughed, "We are all beggars at the feet of sweet Jesus."

Chapter 48

Betsy helped Hank from his bed as Victoria watched silently. Victoria was on duty in the other ward but had abandoned her routine to be with Hank and Betsy as he left the hospital. She held ready a simple crutch—a long shaft that ended in a rounded cross piece which would fit under Hank's arm. He'd been using it for a week to make his way around the ward, putting increasing amounts of weight on his hip each day. The infection was gone but the hip would require a long recovery. He expected to use the crutch for many months, if not forever.

As Hank balanced his weight on his good hip and leg, Betsy helped him slip on a new Union jacket. She smiled as she remembered her prayers the jacket would only be for show, and Hank would never return to the active army. The conflict was not yet decided, but she pleaded with God that it would be over for her family—that they would never have to think, talk or argue about cause and cost again.

As the bloody summer approached fall, she looked forward to leisurely walks, hand in hand, through brightly colored falling leaves with the faint earthy smell of leaf decay. She longed for quiet winter nights beside Hank at a warm home hearth, reaching out to touch his cheek as she played with their happy, gurgling infant. The idyllic life Betsy imagined was sweeter than anything she'd ever lived, and it all began in her mind when they stepped out of the ward.

For the South and for Betsy war news had been grim: The reelection of Lincoln looked likely with Atlanta in Union hands; swaths of the Shenandoah Valley—their valley—had been destroyed; and Richmond and Petersburg continued suffering under heavy Union siege. In Betsy's eyes, freedom was collapsing under a new, colossal Federal Government crafted by the unexpectedly bright man in the White House. Lincoln's final victory would subject the valiant men of the South to grubby Yankee merchants. The final blow, when it came, would most assuredly destroy the gallant cavaliers, the heroes, the beauty of the Southern man and his culture. J. E. B. Stuart's death earlier in the year had been an omen. This new mammoth beast in Washington would imbed in the South a Northern seediness. No longer would men and women be called to heights of freedom. They would be trapped in factories as functionaries, slaves to industry and commerce. They would become mechanics living for the spin of a wheel and the power of steam. Loftiness of thought and power of republican freedom pioneered by their fathers, Jefferson and Madison, would perish. The future men of Virginia would be emasculated, gray, nameless, lifeless creatures cranking the wheel of life only because the new government required it, but there would be . . . could be no joy without freedom.

Betsy shook her head in frustration that such thoughts tormented her on this day of celebration. In spite of her annoyance at the distractions, her mind wandered again. She remembered Lincoln was a hero to Hank, Victoria, William; but only because they couldn't see his vain ambition. They talked of him constantly, proud of what he was doing and had already accomplished. They could never see what was really happening. The American Republic was crumbling into an empire as the Roman Republic had collapsed under Caesar's despotic hand. She couldn't imagine what grotesque forms it would take in the future. It would ever suppress freedom, meddling in lives and whittling away every citizen's rights—in the end prescribing thought and action.

She'd underestimated Lincoln and his abolitionist friends. Hadn't she in her heart long ago felt sympathy for freeing the slaves? Didn't she treasure Victoria and William in their freedom? Yes, of course, she had and did. She felt divided, and as she cursed the country's executive officer for destroying her homeland, she was grateful he had freed William. Her mother would never have done it. It required Northern coercion to liberate him. So was the North right? Yet what could the country do with so many freedmen? She inadvertently shivered as she imagined a colored man embracing a white woman; something she'd heard described and warned of a thousand times.

Coercion. Slavery. Freedom. Casualties. Deaths. Suffering. Starvation. Humiliation. She'd seen them all and was left not knowing what to want, what to believe, what to hope for, except for Hank and her child.

For Hank, this was his day of liberty—the day for which the couple had long yearned: when the war would no longer keep them apart, when they could create a life utterly different from what they'd endured.

As Betsy slipped his jacket on his shoulders, he turned and smiled at her appreciatively. Victoria silently handed him the crutch.

Rivenshaw, shadowing Victoria as usual, waited to say goodbye. Betsy knew he would soon be released from the army and wondered where he would go and how he would live, if not by begging.

Hank had listened earlier to Rivenshaw talking about Shakespeare to Victoria, but he'd noticed she'd shushed him, ignored his comments, focusing her attention on Hank and Betsy. He hurt for his English friend.

"Rivenshaw, I'm sorry to abandon you," Hank said thoughtfully.

Tears welled instantly in Rivenshaw's sightless eyes, hidden behind dark glasses which didn't quite cover the bright scars on his forehead and cheeks. But he didn't respond.

"Thank you for your friendship. Where will you go?" Hank inquired kindly.

"Sir, I am in the dark . . . as to that, without vision of the future. Where can I go? I hope to be adopted by Victoria and her family."

Hank smiled. He hobbled to Rivenshaw, placed his hand on his, attempting to shake it. "Goodbye friend."

"We won't see each other again, I fear. Of course, I'll never see you. Will you not see me again? Will you never return?"

"Betsy tells me we move west, away from all of this soon. The army has released me. So, friend, I think I will not see you again in this life."

Rivenshaw pulled his hand from Hank's. "I salute you as friend and fellow sufferer in Christ." He saluted in Hank's general direction, and Hank returned the gesture unseen by Rivenshaw, although Victoria whispered to Rivenshaw what he had done. "If you should see your way to write me, I would be obliged. Mrs. Richman will read it to me."

"Then you will be well read," Hank responded smiling.

Rivenshaw grimaced.

Hank nodded to Victoria and began making his way from the pavilion.

Betsy whispered to Victoria, grasping her hand quickly, as she passed her. "We'll visit soon. We won't leave yet, not till he's stronger; but I haven't told him."

"We'll await you."

Victoria watched as the couple made their way from the hospital, tears flowing freely and unchecked down the faces of both Victoria and Rivenshaw.

"What will become of me?" she heard Rivenshaw ask as they waited. "I'm not sick, yet I'm blind. I won't die, yet I can't live. What will become of me, Hank? What will become of me?"

Hank was too far away to hear his question.

A week later, Victoria led Betsy to her roughhewn kitchen table and helped her into a chair. She sat beside her, her hands cradling Betsy's. William stood behind Victoria and motioned to Sheriff and Anna to take the two remaining chairs. Adam watched from the kitchen doorway. Hank had stayed behind at Mrs. Brown's boarding house to rest.

Sheriff gazed across the table at Betsy, remembering the first time he had met her—how she'd attracted him. This was not the same woman. She looked older. Shock, suffering, worry, incarceration had drained the naïve energy he'd felt from her that day in her parlor. At that moment, she glanced at him, and he glimpsed a strong life force still within her. It was still there covered under layers of hard experience. He felt fatherly love toward her for the first time. He was proud of whom she'd become.

She spoke to him. "Mr. Sheriff, you said you could answer a few questions."

"Do you have questions? Or shall I tell you the story as much as I've discovered?"

"Why did he do it? Hank told me he thought it was pride. He said to me, 'Betsy, it's always the same thing. The reason you rejected my proposal all those years ago; the reason this bloodthirsty rebellion took place; the reason I ran; the reason poor Victoria and William were born as property and not free: It's always pride.'"

Victoria responded gently, "I never considered myself poor . . . not in any sense. Hank doesn't have to think that or say it to make us feel good. I am not poor. I can never be poor for I am free, difficult though it may be. More than that, I have friends and William and Adam. How could anyone look at me . . . at us and think us poor?"

"He didn't mean anything by it, just that the two of you and Adam had to go through a lot because of slavery."

"Please don't pity us."

Betsy smiled at Victoria, turned and asked Sheriff, "Do you agree with Hank? Was it pride that made Walthrope what he was?"

"I suppose. Pride is a funny thing. It didn't come from his great—and they were great—gifts, but from the shame that shaped him. There was always more to it though. He wanted to dominate everyone as he had been dominated and humiliated by his parents. But he used different tools to control. With women, he used his charm. With men, he used physical coercion with offers of power and money, though he never had any power or money to give. If none of that worked, he physically conquered the man . . . or woman."

"Sheriff, what will you do?"

"My arm's healing. Shortly Miss Whitehead and I will scoot across the lines and return to Staunton."

Anna winced. "You are kind to call me that, but regretfully I can't really claim that name anymore."

Sheriff huffed and responded, "You married a name that didn't exist. Miss Whitehead, you cannot marry someone who doesn't exist. Daniel Jefferson never existed beyond a carte de visite. You are and always have been Miss Whitehead. You are not a widow. You never married."

Betsy peered severely at Sheriff. "You will look after Miss Whitehead."

He laughed. "I hope she'll look after me. I think she can manage on her own. She is remarkably resourceful."

Anna blushed.

"I believe you're right." Betsy hesitated, glancing at Anna. "At the risk of being too personal and embarrassing her, Sheriff, is Caleb fond of Miss Whitehead?"

He thought for a moment, glanced at Anna, who was watching him intently, and pronounced somberly, "I am sure he is."

Betsy leaned back in the chair. "I will write him to demand it."

Anna said nothing, bowing her head to hide a slight smile she couldn't restrain.

Epilogue: Part One

August 1876,
Washington City, District of Columbia

"**P**ardon, Mr. Richman. A woman and lad are outside dressed in black. Her face is veiled. He asked if a William Richman still worked in the stable. I laughed. Told him you owned it. I heard her say real soft so I could barely hear that she was glad and that it was bigger than she remembered. I called out that it was one of the city's biggest—the best. She came toward me, and when she was real close, she asked real soft, fine-like, to see you."

William had been sitting at the desk in a small office with his back to the door, doing precisely what he liked least: pretending to review accounts. He was eager to get into the stable to be with the men and to touch the horses. He would take the accounts home that evening and Victoria could check and balance them. Adam could have done it for him, but he liked taking them to Victoria and chatting with her as she breezed through the numbers and totals. Every morning he would go through this exercise because he felt obligated to do so, but both he and Victoria knew the things he overlooked in a half hour of tense but distracted concentration, Victoria would find in seconds. Thus he was grateful for any disruption and turned to look at the young, slight and welcome intruder. Patient eyes rested casually on the youth.

William's graying hair was cropped, wrinkles creased his face, while his body still retained the appearance of broad strength. He was dressed in a business suit and sweat dripped from his face to the neck of his collar. He would change into his comfortable "stable" clothes as soon as he finished the accounts.

When William didn't offer a quick answer, the boy pressed, "What shall I tell her?"

William grinned at the boy's persistence. He was new to the stable, the son of a friend who could never quite make a success of whatever he tried. The family needed help. Even before meeting the boy, William had decided—without mentioning it to Victoria—to help the struggling family by bringing him into the establishment. The boy knew nothing about horses but was enthusiastic. William was convinced he could tutor and train him to contribute to the heavy and profitable work of the stable.

William wondered who wasn't aware he and Victoria owned the stable and several other businesses in the Federal City. His and Victoria's relationship had turned out to be a spectacular romantic success and a fulfilling business partnership fueled by William's hard work and Victoria's vivaciousness, fresh ideas and business acumen. Still passionately in love, they were ever sensitive to each other's needs, strengths and trials. Every day their most painful chore was parting to their respective endeavors.

William rose. "Enoch, I'll see what she wants."

The child grinned, "Good. I want to find out who she is." He stepped out of William's path.

In sure, strong steps, William passed the boy, ignoring his last comment and nosiness. Walking by a man driving a hack into the stable, William stopped to ask him in passing, "How'd he do?"

"A little nervous, skittish in traffic, but he'll be strong and useful once he's accustomed to it."

William smiled at the man. "Hoped he would be, but skittish? Don't need him bolting through town."

"I'll work with him," the man assured him.

William nodded as he walked toward the entrance. The morning was young, but the sun already blazed hot, and William inadvertently grimaced until his watering eyes adapted to the shock. Slowly his pupils shrank till he could see the woman on the sidewalk. Standing by her was a boy whose head moved quickly and constantly as he tried to take in the activity outside the stable and on the street. He didn't recognize them. The woman's veiled face turned in his direction, and he expected her to step forward; but she didn't move. William stepped from the stable's wide doors toward her.

When he neared her, she spoke softly—barely audible to him amid the noise of the busy stable behind him, "Dear William."

"You wanted to speak to me?" he responded in his most congenial business voice.

"Yes, I need to." She raised both her hands, pulling up her veil, draping it atop her hat.

"Miss Betsy . . . Mrs. Gragg," he stuttered, trying to control his excitement. He paused, not quite sure what to say after such a long time. Only slowly did he realize she was in full mourning.

She smiled warmly at him. "William, you own the livery stable. You've thrived."

William, uncomfortable with the attention, looked at the young boy. This was Betsy and Hank's son, the unborn child. What should he say? "You look well, Ma'am," he finally blurted out. He raised his eyes to see a jovial smile. His discomfort increased, but he didn't know why. He squinted in a partial look of pain recalling her deep mourning attire. He nervously glanced again at the boy. He had Hank's eyes; and in spite of his own embarrassment and Betsy's mourning attire, William smiled fondly. He spoke happily to the boy, "You young Henry?"

The boy, surprised the man knew his name, responded, "Yes, sir. How did you know? Mama said I never met you."

"I saw you before you were born and heard about your birth all those years ago in a letter."

William raised his eyes to Betsy, who watched him. "Mrs. Gragg . . ."

"Betsy, William; always Betsy to family."

Clearing his throat tentatively, he finally ventured, "Betsy, I'm confused and embarrassed. I'm pleased to see you . . . to finally meet young Henry, but . . ."

"William, Henry and I would like to take a ride to the battlefield at Manassas tomorrow."

"Bull Run. That's a ways. By horseback or carriage? Carriage would be long and slow; hard on the horses. You could always take the train. Much faster." He was relieved. He could easily talk about business and not acknowledge an unspoken death.

"By carriage. Do you have one we could . . . ?"

"Have one. Do you want a driver or will you drive . . . or young Henry?" He smiled, taking the opportunity to look at the boy and away from Betsy's gaze.

"William, will you take us? I hadn't heard you were the proprietor, with our letters tapering off as they did. I suppose I thought everything would be the same as when we left. But I'm sure you're probably too busy to take us."

"I'll take you. Things aren't the same. It's been really good for a long time . . . since the end of the war. I can vote. That's new. Things are changing. A lot of resentment though, and that's growing."

Betsy proposed, "If your dear wife would join us, too, I would be so pleased."

William couldn't answer for Victoria, but he spoke slowly, respectfully, "I'll ask. Hope she will. It's a long ride."

"How long?"

"Six, seven hours one way. Taxing the horses a tad more than we should. But I know just the horses."

With a long vacant look at William, Betsy considered the long expedition. "I'll arrange food for a picnic."

"What time would you leave?"

"Early, if we're to return before dark."

"Stays light towards eight or so. How long will you want to stay there?"

"A few hours."

"Leave at six? Five would be better, if it's not too early."

"Five would be fine. William, I don't want you to have to drive. I want you to come as a guest."

"Guest? In my own carriage? That's a funny notion, Betsy. I love to drive a team, even as old as I am. Don't get to do it nowadays."

"It is a funny notion. Could you have someone else drive? I can pay more . . . whatever it takes. I want you to come so we can hear all that's happened to you since . . . ." Her voice trailed off.

William picked up the thread, "Since you left for the west."

"Yes, and we'll tell you how we've fared."

"And Hank?" William asked tentatively, not wanting to hear the answer.

Betsy lowered her eyes. "He died last month. He never did get his full strength back. He practiced law, but he was never really strong. Like so many, he had the soldier's disease. He couldn't overcome it. He carried his little brown bag around his neck to the day he died. He kept that morphine with him . . . from the time he left the hospital. He never returned to the army, but he never could leave the war. Every summer evening when he was not traveling he'd go down to the center of town and sit with other veterans and talk about their experiences. We never did have more children. His hip mostly healed, but he always had pain, a little limp, so maybe the morphine helped with his suffering. But I don't think he would have stopped if he'd had no pain. He couldn't do without his little brown bag."

The boy at Betsy's side had wandered into the stable to explore, and Betsy alone with William confessed, "Toward the end, it became difficult . . . draining. The last four months, he lost interest in the law and began to believe Confederates . . . especially Virginians lurked everywhere. He spoke continually of Virginians creeping to the house to kill him." She shook her head sadly. "He never thought they were after Henry or me. He was convinced they plotted against him. He couldn't sleep towards the end. Some nights, he would slip into the woods to 'escape' them . . . so they wouldn't find him. His mind died before his body. Some veterans have—so far—held their lives together, and Hank did for a long time. We had many happy days, but at the end—the last months—it was as if his body weakened enough to wake the sorrow hiding in his mind. It quickly dominated him, twisted him into something unnatural, fearful."

Tears welled in William's eyes. "Best man I knew."

"He was a good man, and my love for him filled my world till it couldn't contain it. Young Henry didn't understand what was happening. Hank's parents and his sisters helped with Henry. They moved west to join us after the war. But it wasn't enough. It was hard for him at the end. Henry was devastated as Hank grew ever odder. I tried to hide as much of it as I could from the boy. On those nights when Hank disappeared into the woods, I'd tell him his father had gone to argue before some circuit judge; but it didn't fool him. He could see what was happening. I suppose we should be grateful it wasn't worse. Some have been locked up in hospitals for years for madness . . . all going back to the lunacy of the war. It's war that should be locked up, not men. Little Henry never understood what was happening."

"Too young to think about such things."

"He is. Nonetheless, I've come to pay tribute to Hank, for what he did and who he was . . . for Henry's benefit. I want my son to forget those final days and weeks. I want him to remember who his father was, what he did for him, for us, for the country."

"I want to tell him what he did for me."

"Thank you, William. If it comes from others, not just from me, it will mean more. Maybe if he knows, if war should return he will be able to resist its siren call . . . as we didn't in 1861."

"Henry doesn't know about living in slavery. I'll tell him about that. Hank was the first person who ever treated me human—no offense meant, Ma'am—like I was his friend."

Betsy's eyes watered as she responded, "I wish you could say that about me."

"You were better than most, too—you and your papa and mama. Why do you think I took your daddy's name? You may have thought I belonged to you, but you belonged to me, too."

She smiled bitterly as she began to cry. "It's not the same though is it. I'm sorry. You should have taken Hank's last name." She smiled through her tears at the thought. "We'd share the same last name."

"I like sharing your name and your father's. It was a big change. Many still treat me like a slave. Didn't realize how awful slavery was till I tasted freedom. Freedom is what gives us the strength to become what God wants us to be— least that's what Victoria always says."

Betsy blushed in embarrassment. "I should have helped you . . . should have freed you. I was blind."

"As blind as Rivenshaw, we like to say. It was like that old bible story of the blind leading the blind. Suppose money and wealth . . . and maybe most importantly a desire to con- trol others blinds us all a bit. Slave owners just got away with more than others."

She pulled a handkerchief from her handbag, cleared her tears and wiped her nose. "Hank would want me to tell you he spoke of you at the end and wanted to see you. The last few days, he kept talking about how you saved his life. He told Henry and me how much he loved us a few times, but scarce lucid moments surfaced at the end—most of the time it was as if he were in battle. Little Henry lost his father to the war as much as if he'd never made it off the field. He's not counted among the war dead, but he was killed by the war."

Interrupting them, Henry came running from the stable, his eyes wide and excited.

Betsy queried fondly, "What have you been up to?"

"Mother, another man in there says he knew about me before I was born."

William interjected, "Adam."

Henry looked up at William and, tempering his excitement, said respectfully, "Yes, sir. Adam."

Betsy asked, "Do you know his last name?"

"No, he didn't say."

"Ask him his last name."

Henry loped casually back to the stable, disappearing into its contrasting darkness.

Betsy turned to William, "Five tomorrow morning."

"Where you staying?"

"With Mrs. Brown. At her boarding house. She's moved." She held a card out to him.

"Should have known. I know where it is," he said, politely taking the card. "At five. Can I bring Adam?"

"That would be wonderful. I'll prepare us food for the day."

"Expect a long, hot day."

"Yes, judging from today. I'll make sure we have water."

"I'll have Adam drive. It'll keep him busy for the trip. Maybe young Henry can help."

"He'd like that. You of all people were—and I hope still are—our true friend."

"Family, if you'll let us."

"Family," she confirmed.

William could feel her discomfort and sadness as she turned and walked toward the stable doors. He stood still, observing her. She entered the shadows of the stable to retrieve Henry and shortly returned. Without glancing his way, mother and son walked away. He longed to stop them, hitch a carriage and give them a ride, but something held him back. He wondered about their welfare. Did they have money? They'd traveled from the west. They probably weren't starving. Or was this one last show that would exhaust their resources and leave them paupers? His eyes misted as the pair melted into the street's waxing morning crowd. He glanced at the stable where he discovered his son considering him closely.

Epilogue: Part Two

August 1876,
Washington City, District of Columbia

Several hours had passed since Betsy had been to see him, but he couldn't shake the anxiety as he remembered Hank, his friend, and worried about riding openly in a carriage with a white woman through portions of the Old Dominion. He'd heard stories of lynchings in the South. He feared that seeing a black couple sitting with a white woman would inflame the vilest Virginians along the way.

Yet he had to go with her for Hank's sake, for courage's sake, for young Henry's sake. Something—maybe his memory of Hank—pulled him to Virginia with the daughter of the man who had once believed he had owned him.

William would wage the battle he expected from Victoria and persuade her. He seldom pressed his desires on his wife, but this once, he would. She had to appreciate that he would go, even if she refused to join him. He had to settle and cure the pains of his past life and somehow forgive all his masters—those who thought they were good and those who had so completely debased him—and of all those who had slighted him because he had a darker skin color. It was the one last emotion he carried that kept him from total happiness. He wanted it flushed from his veins—replaced with an enduring flow of joy. Such ecstasy he knew came from Jesus, from forgiveness, from letting go of enmity that separated him from all of God's creations.

The hatred, resentment, jealousy: They had too long antagonized William. Flashes of rage still burned through him when he remembered some incident, large or small, which had declared him something less than man, something akin to an animal. Those moments tormented him. They needed to end forever. He'd learned that forgiveness did not lie with those who had harmed him, but within himself and in God.

How animal-like were all men. Didn't they get surly when hungry, like a wolf? Didn't they snarl when they didn't get enough sleep, like a bear? He was like that, but so was every other man. Victoria thought Jesus had felt those things, but he had responded differently. He'd overcome those feelings, and in overcoming them, he had raised man—all men and women—above the animals, above the physical world into something higher, something spiritual, where they could overcome the feelings, the hurt, the trauma. He had to convince Victoria to join them, to strengthen him, to help him put the past's pain and subjugation finally on the shoulders of the Savior. His thoughts were hopeful, but his confidence weak.

He frowned. The conversation would not be welcome. He foresaw a night of argument. Victoria would win. She would have a thousand reasons why she couldn't and shouldn't go, and why he would be in real peril and couldn't go either.

He imagined her logic: Hadn't this woman betrayed Hank in the first place? Hadn't she supported the Confederates to the end? She probably still did. Hadn't she momentarily rejected William in her anger that he had taken her father's name? "No," Victoria would say, "I will not let you endanger yourself by going with her. She asks too much. And you certainly won't risk our son by sending Adam. William, don't you pay attention to what's going on in the South . . . in Virginia? They're killing and destroying our people, our freedoms. And you want to cross the line into that iniquitous Old Dominion to satisfy some dyed-in-the-wool Confederate, daughter of the enslaving South. Shame be on you, William Adam Richman. Shame be on you."

He was already feeling shame just thinking of asking her. He didn't want the day to end, dreading his face-to-face encounter with his wife. He should have already started home to warn her of pending doom, but he was in no hurry.

He would have preferred being murdered on the way home to taking on this errand. A bullet would have been quicker than the torture and persecution Victoria would inflict.

Adam entered the office and asked, "Are you ready to come home?"

"A lot to do. You go without me."

Adam laughed. "Dad, you never do anything in this office but think. What has you so engrossed?"

"Can't guess?"

Adam smiled. "I already have. Go home. Don't worry. I'll stick around for a while, make sure we're ready for tonight and tomorrow."

"Would you drive tomorrow?"

"You couldn't keep me away. This is going to be fascinating. I want to hear what happened to the Graggs. I'm old enough to remember them."

"Thanks for helping today."

"I enjoyed it and got to meet Hank's son and see his wife. Tomorrow will be a day to mark." His tone rose to pure glee.

William scowled as Adam turned quickly and darted out of the office. He heard Adam laughing as he headed deeper into the stable.

William slipped quietly into the front hall and turned to soundlessly close the door. The house was silent as he fought to quell his anxiety. He half hoped some emergency had arisen to distract Victoria's immediate attention—maybe her brother had died, and she had already departed for the train station. A silent house was a good omen. He didn't even hear the servants. Maybe she had required they all take her to the train station. He made his way to the stairs knowing his hopes were nonsense—he wouldn't have thought them if he imagined them real—but they were better than the coming confrontation.

Victoria heard softly creaking floorboards from the hall. Nightly, William would call out to her as soon as he entered the house, so it couldn't be William. The servants never entered by the front door. Someone had broken in. She moved toward the hall warily. Her arms tingled with fear. For years Washington hadn't been a safe city, but of late, robberies had increased and several nearby homes had been burgled.

Where were the servants? They could overpower a thief. More likely, they would faint. The creaking footfalls climbed the stairs and across the landing as Victoria crept to the front hall. She was irritated by the audible swoosh of her skirts as she moved. She wondered how long it would be before the intruder would discover her. She wished she'd grabbed a pan from the kitchen for protection. Her heart raced, and she unconsciously held her breath. Her hands shook and sweated.

She reached the bottom of the stairs and climbed slowly. As she ascended, she remembered the loaded pistol William kept in the table drawer at the top of the stairs. If she could get the gun, she could stop him. She crept up, reached the landing and slowly slid open the drawer, pulling out the revolver. She'd never handled it before and was surprised by its daunting weight. She heard movement in the bedroom and moved to get closer. Her heart pounded louder than the noise coming from the bedroom. She stepped to the door. With half closed eyes, Victoria reached with her left hand for the handle, leaving the pistol dangling clumsily in her right hand. As she touched the knob, she felt it twist carefully from the other side. Her eyes grew big. She stepped back. Gripping the gun with two trembling hands, she tightened two fingers to the trigger. When the door opened, she fired.

The weight, pulling the trigger and the concussion pulled her hands backward and twisted them upward. Her eyes followed the trajectory of the bullet and saw plaster shatter on the wall above. She screamed, realizing someone had wrestled the gun from her grasp. It was William, and he stood with the gun resting downward in his hand, staring with horror at her.

His expression thawed to a wide smile, joined by loving laughter. "Should I call out the police? My wife just tried to murder me."

She was shaking, crying. William put his arm around her and held her.

"I thought you were . . ."

"Glad you weren't shooting at me . . . knowing it was me."

She returned his embrace with both of her arms. She had stopped crying, but her mind raced and her tone turned accusatory. "Why didn't you call me when you came in?"

"Ah."

"Ah is not an answer. You act suspiciously; and if I had shot you, I would have been justified."

William did his best to befuddle her. "Acting suspiciously? I wasn't the one with the gun . . . pointing at my husband."

"You don't have a husband . . . and you are the one with the gun."

Looking around, she realized several servants had gathered, watching in silence, while Rivenshaw shouted from below, "Has the war started anew?"

"Look, William Richman. I have witnesses." She turned to the servants. "Note this, every one of you: Who has the gun? Who obviously fired it in the house? What are you doing, William, shooting up my house? Have you been drinking? You better give that gun to me." She yanked the gun from William's limp hold. "There. We're all safer."

Laughing, William stepped forward to grab Victoria. She held up her hand to stop him long enough for her to put the revolver lightly on the floor before his embrace. She whispered in his ear, "You still owe me an explanation."

William nodded to the servants and called out to Rivenshaw, their ever-present houseguest, "War is over. We've triumphed again. Go back to bed, all of you." He lifted

Victoria off her feet, pulled her into the bedroom and with his foot closed the door. He took a deep breath and put her down.

She could sense an ominous mass on her husband's shoulders. "Is it Adam? Where's Adam? Is he hurt?"

The question pleased William. "He's fine. You don't need to worry."

"I'm glad he's fine, but worry I will till you tell me why you're creeping around the house like a common burglar."

"No common burglar, Mrs. Richman. If I were a burglar, I would be exceptional."

"I doubt that."

"I'll have to prove it to you sometime."

"You tried and almost got shot demonstrating your prowess. You're avoiding . . . ." She could see his worry. "What's happened? If it's not Adam . . ."

"It's you."

"Me?"

William, hoping for some intervention, divine or otherwise, began slowly, "I had a visitor to the stable today . . . a customer actually."

"An earlier wife? Are you worried about being a bigamist?"

"Not one of my wives."

"Can't be any of my husbands. I shot them all."

He laughed. "I'll tell you if you can be quiet long enough. It's actually hard for me to talk about it, and it may be harder for you to hear it."

"Speak up then, so I know if I have to get that gun and aim better." Shaking her hand, she reflected, "It kicks. I had no idea."

"Mrs. Gragg came to the stable."

"Mrs. Gragg. Betsy?"

"Yes."

"Extraordinary." She peered at him. "That's hardly difficult news for me. Why did you think I would be concerned? What are you not telling me?"

"She wants to see you."

"Did you invite her here? Was young Henry with her?"

"I met the boy."

"How's Hank?"

"He died."

"Dead?"

"Yes. That's what brought her to town."

"I'm so sorry to hear that. How painful that must be for her . . . and their son . . . and for you."

"Do you love me, Victoria?"

"Not if it means whatever it is that you're going to tell me."

His body stiffened. "She asked us to come, and I already told her you'd come . . . that all three of us would come."

"Come? Come where?"

"She's invited us to go on a picnic to Bull Run."

"Bull Run? We can more easily picnic in Washington."

"I believe she wants to visit Hank's first battlefield. Remember, he was a Yankee."

"Yankee. So was I. You were, too. So was Isaiah. That doesn't mean we have to picnic in Virginia. Let me remind you: She wasn't a Yankee. If they wanted to go to Gettysburg, that would be better. I'm not going into Virginia . . . and neither are you." She looked soberly at William who had moved from her. "I should hear you out. Please explain it, but don't forget Virginia is dangerous for you . . . riding in a carriage with a white lady."

"Hank went mad at the end because of the war. She wants to remind Henry of what his father did. Make him a hero to the boy. I also think she wants to visit with us."

"Why Virginia?"

"So Henry can see in his mind's eye, I suppose, what his daddy went through."

Shaking her head in exasperation, she charged, "You are the devil, Mr. Richman, for you always know how to tempt me. As long as you realize you might be lynched. I will go only on the off chance I can witness it. I would love to see

Betsy and meet Henry. It will be a long day, but I can't imagine a better way to spend it."

He was surprised she gave in without real objection, and
she noticed it.

"Why did you think it would be so hard to tell me?" She
raised her head and kissed him on the cheek. "Adam coming?"

"Yes, I told Betsy . . ."

"Did you call her that, or did you call her Mrs. Gragg?"

"I called her Betsy."

"Good."

"Adam will drive."

"Like a slave."

"No, I thought it would keep him entertained, and young
Henry could help him. They'll have a good time."

"Henry. He must be about twelve. What carriage will we
take? Why not take the railroad? It's so much quicker, easier
and much more comfortable."

"Not so personal. Not enough time to catch up or visit.
We couldn't ride in the same car. I thought we would use the
six-seat Rockaway. I like its privacy. With Adam and Henry
driving, it will give us time and place to talk. It will shade
Adam and Henry a bit as well, once the sun gets higher in
the sky. Unfortunately they'll start and end with the sun directly in their eyes."

"Whatever you decide will be fine."

Her coming morning trip to Manassas troubled Betsy:
Thaddeus Henderson, her first husband, had died there;
Hank had first seen the elephant on that farm field. Thoughts
of both men blew coldly through her mind.

When she heard a distant bell chime four, she silently
celebrated the end of a night-long frustration and sleepless-
ness. She sat up, slid to the edge of the bed and sought her
slippers with her feet. She slipped them on and walked toward the room's sole window. She picked up a light robe as

she approached the window, wrapped it around herself and pulled aside the curtains. The window was open, and she gazed across the warm, sticky, dark city. The street lamps had been extinguished, leaving only a few lights to break the early morning darkness.

She turned from the window and removed her robe. The room was sultry, and she was sweating. Her mind drifted to Hank in his last hours. He was in and out of consciousness, and when he was conscious, he wasn't with her, but on a battlefield. He kept talking about the button, the dying Confederate and his own bleeding arm. He would frequently reach across his body and grab his arm as if it hurt. He spoke to no one, but kept up a long, one-sided conversation. In the last minutes, his demeanor changed as his conversation became more animated.

Betsy had asked gently, "Who are you talking to, Hank?"

For one lucid moment, he turned, surprise on his face. He looked clearly into her eyes, smiled and said, "Your father, Love, your father and mine." As quickly as his eyes had gleamed, they dimmed. Again he spoke with unseen guests, and Betsy had grasped his hand, holding it tightly. She loved this man. It hadn't turned out as they'd planned. They had miscalculated, not anticipating their own mistakes and the nation's.

She leaned in to kiss his lips. She thought she felt him press his lips to hers, and the sensation sent electricity through her body. He was still in there, behind his reemerging fears and talking apparitions. He was still hers, and she would always be his. She kissed him again, but felt no response, no movement, no shallow breathing. She grabbed him, pulling him toward her in a frantic hug. She wailed in unrestrained sobs, barely hearing the button as it fell from his slackened grip to the floor.

He had left her with the staggering challenge of reclaiming their son for him. In the heat of the morning in Mrs. Brown's elegant boarding house, Betsy cried silently, quivering, watching her own pain reflected in the dressing table mirror. Could she do this? Could she go to the battlefield where Hank had fought, then found Thaddeus, his button and her letter; where it all ended and began anew; where what became her hope and life began in the darkness and ignorance of war; where all came together under an unseen divine hand?

She walked to the water closet and rinsed her face. As water dripped down her nightgown, she rested her hands on the edge of the basin and stared toward the wall. She missed Hank, craved holding him, talking to him about mundane things. Just to hear his voice would have been enough, even if it had been a voice of madness. Its tone would have healed her.

Five minutes before five, she and Henry entered Mrs. Brown's foyer. With her loving hostess' help, Betsy had prepared a picnic breakfast, dinner and supper, which sat by the front door. The boarding house was quiet. Mrs. Brown had already kissed her adieu and retired to the kitchen.

The horizon was visible, and Betsy could make out objects and muted colors outside the boarding house window. She was dressed in a long black jacket that matched her hip-fitting skirt. The jacket buttoned up the front and had straight, wrist-length sleeves. She held a simple black parasol in one hand and a black drawstring purse in the other. The same small black hat with a black veil she'd worn the previous day rested on her head and hid her face.

Henry, dressed in a black suit, couldn't hold his head still. With lively eyes, he glanced at the ornate ceiling or watched the street through a window. His mother had told him they were picnicking with his new friends, and he was keen to begin the adventure.

"When will they be here?" he asked for the fourth time since they'd arrived in the front hall.

"Soon. Sit down. I'll call you when they arrive."

"I don't want to."

"Stand by the door and watch for them. They'll come in a carriage."

"A carriage? What will it look like?"

"See if you can pick it out when it comes. Watch all the carriages that go by."

He ran to the door and pressed his face against the window to see more clearly. He looked back at his mother and petitioned, "Can I go outside and watch?"

She hesitated, remembering the rough town Washington had been, but acquiesced, and he pushed through the door.

She called after him, "Stay close."

He looked back, grinning ambiguously; reminding her of Hank.

She didn't know what his expression portended, but she was too frightened of her coming task to worry about his mischief.

Somewhere a bell chimed five. She could easily see out the window as the sun rose, and fear they wouldn't come darted through her mind.

Two of Mrs. Brown's servants joined her, standing silently behind, awaiting instructions to carry the baskets to the carriage.

The door burst open as Henry bolted toward his mother.

"Adam's coming! They're here. I saw him. The carriage has two horses. Can I ride in front . . . with Adam? I'll help drive."

She hushed him as overwhelming love for him surged. "I believe you may, but ask him."

"I'll ask."

He dashed out, and she followed slowly to the door, watching as the carriage slackened its pace at nearing the boarding house. She could see Henry already chatting animatedly with Adam, as Adam descended from the driver's seat. The young man was smiling, listening as he secured the reins. When he finished, he turned to give Henry his full attention as the boy kept chattering.

She smiled as Adam helped Henry climb to the driver's seat. He pointed out something on the carriage to Henry as William opened the carriage door and stepped onto the walkway. He glanced at Henry and Adam, reached back into the vehicle with one arm and helped a woman from the carriage. She was as lovely as Betsy remembered her. William and she spoke briefly.

It was time. Betsy looked back and signaled Mrs. Brown's servants. Then she stepped through the door into the dusty morning. She descended the stairs, approaching William and Victoria who were quietly conversing. She startled William, who in surprise exclaimed, "Ah, you're here."

Neither Victoria nor Betsy heard him. Betsy pulled back her veil, and they looked warmly into each other's eyes, without saying anything. Victoria stepped forward and reached out her arms to Betsy. Betsy, tears in her eyes, accepted the embrace. They said nothing, but held each other tightly, both crying openly.

The carriage and its hot, sweaty, happy passengers traveled the Warrenton Pike to the place William directed. When it stopped, each descended and looked over the farm fields and orchards around them. William announced that Adam, Henry and William would get the dinner and wine, and that the women should choose a place to picnic. The women strolled toward the field, each holding their parasols against the intense midday sun. They advanced toward the shade of a copse of trees and waited for the men, food and large blankets Victoria had brought.

When all was arranged and each had begun eating the meal, Betsy turned to Henry, and spoke quietly.

"These last few months have been heartbreaking, and you've wondered what was wrong with father. He loved you more than anything in this world. So much so he willingly sacrificed his life to maintain your freedom. He fought that William could be free, and that fight made him sad. I've brought you here to tell you about his war. He didn't like to speak about it, not with you; not much with me. You would ask questions, especially in the last several years, and he would always change the subject. I think he did that because he didn't want you to share his sad memories. He thought he could share them only with those who bore the same wounds. In the end, all his saddest memories came back . . . and he began to relive them."

She paused and reached inside her handbag. "I want to give you this button to keep and care for."

She handed Henry the button. He took it and examined it closely, turning it in his hand. "It's from Virginia. It's not father's. He was Union, Mother."

"No, it's not a Union button, and he was a Yankee." She smiled as the last word passed her lips. "Henry, I want you to know what he did for us, and if a merciful and just Heaven willed it, I'd stay right here forever to tell this same story of liberty and the sacrifice of body, mind and blood to your son, and your son's son, and his son."

Appendix A:

A Letter to Elizabeth Gragg

May 6, 1865

My dear Betsy,

I write in hopes that the mails are at last making their way by official means between Virginia and the North.

It is a somber time here. Soldiers are returning, and so many forlorn families are just now contemplating rebuilding their lives. Almost everyone has lost family members; thus, try as they will, nothing will ever be the same. Our mutual acquaintance, Anna Whitehead, informed me that she broke the sad news to you that Yankees destroyed your mills and woolen factory last year. I do not see much hope anytime soon that we'll be able to rebuild the factory, but I am making arrangements to rebuild the grain mills. The Valley needs them, and my hope is that with the grain we hid we will be able to raise enough money and crops to begin that work shortly. Your guidance on these matters would be greatly appreciated.

I write today to share my personal happiness for it is with great pleasure that I announce that Anna Whitehead and I were married before God this morning. It was a small wedding, and your absence was keenly felt. Anna plans to write with more details, but I wanted to tell you immediately in the hopes that you and Hank will share our joy at the news.

Our prayers are constantly with you, and we hope for the favor of a visit from you in the near future.

Your ever faithful friend,

Caleb Moore

Appendix B:

A Letter to Victoria Richman

December 31, 1864

My Precious Victoria,

Please excuse my lengthy delay in responding to your many missives, but heartbreak has kept me from writing. I still can't think of you and Adam leaving without tearing up. I've found the best way to deal with my grief is to avoid thinking about you at all. It sounds harsh and uncaring, but it is the opposite. In the end, it is impossible for me to not think of you. I miss you every hour of every day.

It has become clear to me that I will never marry and will have no heirs, so I have decided that after this war ends and things settle, I will divide the farm into small plots of land and give them to those slaves who have stayed on till the end of this bitter human conflagration. I have not told them of my decision and will not until war's end. I've thought about the trials you must be facing in Washington City, and it has brought to mind your people and the hardships they will face when they are freed. You have so many gifts that surpass those of the normal woman. Your people will need more support to adapt to freedom than you needed, and perhaps a little land might help. Most of them are accustomed to agriculture and will be able to take advantage of the offering. While you have no legal right to the farm, you do have a rich tie to the property, so I hope you approve. You will not benefit from my planned dispersion, yet I make it thinking of you.

You will be pleased that, although Kentucky as a state has taken no action to end slavery, the vile institution is careening toward extinction here faster than could have been imagined when you left for Washington. The price and market for slaves has collapsed. Everyone sees manumission on the horizon, and no one wants to be the last man to buy a slave. A few are still buying them in hopes of selling them to the deep south, but anyone with sense can see that with Union martial progress slaves will shortly be worthless everywhere, especially following Hood's recent defeat in Nashville and with Sherman rampaging through Georgia.

You have asked in your letters about the man with the horrific case of poison ivy. He died shortly after you left and was never able to tell anyone what happened. It is commonly believed that he rode through poison ivy in a drunken fit. The fellow suffered grievously before succumbing, and I admit to a guilty glee when I think of William's ingenuity.

Since your sudden disappearance, people have asked continually about you. Everyone expresses great concern for you and misses both you and Adam. I have felt it best to say that I didn't know what happened to you. They see my sorrow, so the town has concluded that you ran off with someone. No one remembers or really knew William, and since they haven't seen Isaiah since you left either, they always conclude it was "that Isaiah fellow." I do not respond, so the story becomes yet more deeply believed. It ever amazes me the power of gentle silence. It always leads people to see confirmation of man's worst imaginings.

They found the bodies you wrote of in your first letter. I cried to hear of your experience and Robert's death, and to think he gave himself so you could escape. I love him all the more for his sacrifice, though from what you wrote, I do not believe he expected to die. He did put himself in the power of those men, knowing it a possibility. As I read the account, I was left in awe of William's remarkable resourcefulness. His idea to use the remaining whiskey to kindle a fire saved us many accusing questions. The bodies and wagon were burned beyond recognition and have never been identified. Otherwise they would have tracked Robert and the wagon to me. I have no idea what happened to the horses that you didn't take with you.

I am glad you took William from all those you could have chosen. He's humble. From my few conversations with him, I am persuaded he would credit the idea to burn the wagon to someone else. I did confide to those who knew generally what was happening that Robert was killed in helping you flee, and no one beyond the farm has missed him.

I'll close this letter with a troubling report. Two soldiers from the 5th United States Colored Cavalry visited me recently to inform me of Isaiah who according to the two soldiers was also of that unit. I am still angry at Isaiah and will always be for what he did out of jealousy of your early friendship with William. Enticing the still-ailing William on an obviously futile attempt to enlist in the army was clearly unkind and wrong. He abused William, caused your near attack, and led patrollers to chase Adam through the countryside in the middle of the night. When I review all the circumstances, I uncharitably conclude that it was really Isaiah who drove you from your home, and I hold a grudge against him for that.

In spite of what he did, I hesitate to share the tragic news, but I cannot in good conscience keep it from you. The soldiers told me that Isaiah was murdered by a Confederate at Saltville, Virginia, several months ago. He was wounded and left on the field after a battle. The following morning a man with long hair, shabby beard, plug hat and butternut uniform without insignias shot him in cold blood. He, even with what he had done, did not deserve that. No man does.

Everyone on the farm is healthy, and we look forward to the end of the war and peace.

I will write again soon. In the meantime, please give my love to Adam and William. May each of you thrive and prosper in the coming year and throughout your lives.

Your loving and faithful brother,

George

I want to remember every minute, every word, every sigh, every tear, every silence of that night. But that I remember will never move me to hate, will never move me to violence, will never move me to deny the other person's right to dignity.

Elie Wiesel

About the Author

Michael J. Roueche grew up in Virginia and has an indelible affection for the Old Dominion. Always a romantic, only in recent years did he discover the Civil War that had always surrounded him, thanks to Bruce Catton books from his father's library and a good friend who gave him a copy of Michael Schaara's *Killer Angels*. He is ever inspired by the examples of those who maintain their integrity as they persevere and overcome obstacles.

With a deepening background in Civil War history and prompted by an "odd" experience at Manassas National Battlefield Park, *Beyond the Wood* was born.

He and his wife of 40 years now live in Colorado, where they enjoy hiking and exploring the High Plains and Rocky Mountains, with their alpine vistas, aspen groves and evergreen forests, and amazing wildlife. They have five children and several grandchildren.

You can visit him at www.michaeljroueche.com or follow him on *Facebook, Twitter* or *Google+*.

Beyond the Wood

Book One

*Winner of the 2012 John Esten Cooke Award
for Southern History*

A rejected marriage proposal propels young Hank Gragg into a turbulent and uncertain future. He abandons family, security and the South to enlist as a Union soldier, and later refuses retreat from his first bloodied action without proof he has been there. He takes it from a dying enemy.

Fed by the compassion he finds in the Confederate's last letter and his own unsettled dreams and troubling memories, Hank imagines a romance that drives him relentlessly toward an impossible rendezvous.

All the while, Elizabeth, the widow, struggles with burdens left by her husband, even as neighbors conspire against her. And what is she to make of this Union soldier — this enemy — so set on coming to her? Is there hope? Or is it merely a young man's futile fantasy?

A River Divides

Book Two

The Action and Romance Continue

It's winter 1864. While Eastern Theater soldiers languish in camp boredom; conspiracy, treachery and mystery envelop Confederate widow Betsy Henderson. Is there something sinister in a visit from the town sheriff? Did she tell him too much? Can she be true to all she's sworn?

In the meantime, William, a runaway slave, still craving his chance to fight for the Union, flees Virginia. Stumbling into the murky waters of Kentucky servitude and near death, he has nothing to offer but a worn body, exhausted spirit and troubled mind. Dare he imagine freedom, soldiering and even love? Or is he broken and fully spent?

In 1864, white and black, soldier and civilian, guilty and innocent are trapped in the tumultuous conflict, and nothing is as it seems.

Welcome to the river that divides them.